The Children

of

Midgard

By

Siobhan Clark

The Children of Midgard

Copyright © 2016 Siobhan Clark

Published in England
by
ABELA PUBLISHING, LONDON
[2016]

First Edition, 2016

ISBN-13: 978-1-910882-80-1

Email:
Siobhan@AbelaPublishing.com

Website:
www.AbelaPublishing.com

DEDICATION

In loving memory of my father,

Charles Maybin

Acknowledgements

With special thanks to my husband and family.

The Children

of

Midgard

To Lindsay

love,

Siobhan x

INTRODUCTION

ᚺᚾᛌᚱᛌᛞᚲᛁᚢᛌᛚᛁᛞᛁ

The year is 961 and King Harald Bluetooth of Denmark has his gaze firmly set on the Western Kingdoms of Norway where his nephew Harald Greycloak reigns. Bluetooth has declared Greycloak as his vassal King of Norway and will claim the establishment of the Jomsvikings. In doing so he will solidify the order, building a keep for the warriors he intends to use to create a fleet of men who will rule the seas under his command.

However, the order is older than one man's claim and consists of many who have their own destinies separate from the feuding monarchs. There are men of honour and worth and there are those who seek naught but power and privilege, searching only to prosper from the misery of others. There are tales of a legendary ring and a child who is said to be the progeny of the All-Father.

Chapter 1

ᚦᚢᚾᛏᛖᚱ ᛟᚦᛖ

The woman's heart was pounding in her chest, her legs ached from running but she knew she could not stop; the child was hidden and safe for now. Behind her she heard heavy boots crunching on the shore; the men were fast approaching and Liv realised she could not outrun them. It was like before when they had come for her husband and her guardian and now they were deceased.

"Stop!" One of the men bellowed.

Liv froze despite her mind telling her to move, her skin gooseflesh, the cool night air pricking her senses and snapping her back into movement. They would surely catch her now but she would give nothing away, she thought. Suddenly Liv was pushed to the ground, the gravel scraped her hands and face where she skidded along the uneven surface. Two men stood either side of her heaving body and each roughly grabbed an arm. Liv stifled a cry of pain as she was hauled to her feet and the men proceeded to drag her back the way they had come.

"You will pay now!" One of the men growled in her ear.

Liv swallowed hard, she knew what these men would do, they were Jomsvikings. Mercenaries, assassins and marauders, they had their own code and were fearless in battle. They selected their warriors through combat and were feared for their notoriety. The Jarl must have paid the men well to search for her; was he to stop at nothing, she thought. She did not recognise either of the men, but that meant little. The Jomsvikings that had been sent before to dispatch her husband and guardian would be looking elsewhere. They did not give up easily once set to task.

"She had a horse..." One of the men turned to her and in the dark she could make out strong features and a dark beard. "Where is it?"

Liv swallowed, "Grani is lame. I left him in the forest."

"Ha! Stupid woman calls her horse after the offspring of Odin's steed? See, I told you!" The other man snorted, removing his helmet she could see a mass of wild untamed hair and a nose that had been broken and poorly set. A mouth of crooked chipped teeth grinned at his comrade, "Women always think themselves so clever but you couldn't outrun us, could you?"

The man spat in the sand and gruffly shook Liv's arm. The dark-haired Viking guffawed and shrugged his shoulders, "We need no lame horse, Grani or not. Walk!" He barked.

Picking up the pace, the men strode towards the grassy field that ran alongside the shoreline. In the distance Liv saw a man on horseback with a lit torch in his hand. As they approached the rider jumped to the ground and walked towards them.

"Fetch me rope to bind her hands. I'll take her; the Jarl will want her brought swiftly. Get your horses." His deep voice snapped the orders at the two men who set about their leader's task without a word. Dropping Liv's arms they stalked off to their own horses, tied to posts hammered into the earth, leaving her looking at the third man.

The leader too wore a helmet which he did not remove. Liv could not make out his features as the light of the torch danced between them; the only clue to what lay behind the battered and scratched surface of the metal was long brownish hair. It was too dark to tell the colour of his eyes and she shuddered at the coldness of him.

"Where is the boy?" He growled.

"Dead..." Liv swallowed.

"You are unharmed?" The man lowered the torch to survey her. Her dress was ripped and covered in grit and mud. Her hair, though braided had come loose and hung over her shoulder, the colour of bronze and streaked with flashes of gold from many days spent in the sunlight. He saw that her face was bleeding slightly from the grazes on her chin and cheekbone.

"Why do you care?" Liv whispered looking away to the two men who were returning with rope and a cloth sack.

"I don't..." He spoke dryly, his eyes were fixed on the men approaching them. His hand wandered to the handle of the axe tucked into his belt, Liv saw his fingers grip the shaft and felt fear rise in her throat.

Suddenly the man swung the torch into the face of the dark bearded Viking, a howl of pain erupted from his mouth as he clutched his face and fell to the ground. The leader of the men then swung his axe, clipping the wild haired warrior on the shoulder who let out a low rasping grunt of pain. Both men staggered in the dark, groping for their own weapons and cursing their leader furiously.

Liv felt her hand being grabbed and pain shot through her fingers, roughly the Jomsviking lifted her by the waist and threw her over the back of the horse. Jumping astride the beast the man kicked it into a gallop and headed for the forest. As they rode he shouted to Liv, "Your horse?"

Righting herself into a seated position she pointed to a large fallen tree, where she had hidden Grani before attempting to flee on foot, the man pulled on the reins of his own horse and nudged it towards the tree. Behind the upturned blanket of root and earth Grani stood awaiting his master.

"Dismount!" the man barked at her. Obeying, Liv did as she was bade and landed awkwardly on the ground. Stumbling towards Grani she felt her shoulder jerked away before she could reach the reins. "We take your horse. They'll be looking for us, I'll leave mine here."

Once again, the man jumped astride but this time extended a calloused hand to her. Liv withdrew, taking a step away from the Jomsviking. "Take my hand or be dragged!" He said, flatly.

Liv took a breath and stared at the dark circles of the helmet where eyes should have been, she saw nothing and wondered if this man might be some demon trying to trick her or take her for his own. She had heard tell of such mischief and had seen much in her own life to attest to the will of that other than men. Reluctantly she took his hand and felt herself being half pulled onto Grani's back behind the body of the Jomsviking leader.

"Hold fast, we ride hard," the man pulled her arms about his waist and kicked Grani in the sides sharply. The horse grunted and proceeded on the path.

Quickly they made their way back to the settlement where Liv had first discovered the men had caught up with her. The owner of the tavern tried in vain to help her escape unseen and she wondered what had happened to him and his wife, she had been sure she heard screaming from within the tavern's walls. The first rays of sunlight were beginning to break through the clouds covering the dawn. In the distance Liv could see a large ship moored beyond the settlement's small harbour, littered with fishing vessels and the Chieftain's small but sturdy skute.

Gripping the man's waist, she felt revolted at having to hold him so closely and tightly, his rough cloak scratched at her face, aggravating the cuts from her fall. She could feel the cold hard steel of the axe, tucked into his belt, against her arm and an idea formed in her head. Quickly she slipped her hand underneath his cloak and grabbed the weapon, pulling it free she pushed with all her might on his back, shoving him forward on Grani, and jumped from the galloping horse.

The leap from Grani's back winded her slightly, Liv struggled for breath but fought to control herself and gradually she rose to her feet and frantically searched for a route in which to run. The man had pulled Grani to a halt, turning in the saddle he spotted Liv and yanked on the reins of the beast. Grani whinnied and stamped his feet, shaking his black mane, the horse reared and bucked at the commands of his rider. Liv thanked Odin for Grani's stubbornness and turned to run towards the grassy knoll to her right, from there she knew the forest grew thick before breaking out onto a rocky ravine. She could run there and hide, she would make her way, not stopping until she reached the most northerly point of the land and from there she would either swim or drown. She cared not; all that mattered was that the child was safe. Grasping the heavy axe in her right hand she made for the knoll.

A shout rang out from behind her and turning quickly Liv saw the man dismount Grani and start after her. He was terribly quick for being large and strong; he gained on her despite the weight of his leather armour and sword strapped to his side. Liv cursed her weary legs for not picking up the pace but she had worn them out from her earlier attempts at escape.

"Liv!" The man called.

Stopping short, Liv felt a cold shiver run down her spine. She knew that voice though how could it be, it was a voice from her past, but before her mind could recollect the man was upon her. Pushing her to the ground he loomed over her, grabbing her arm he twisted the axe from her grip and shoved her back onto the grass. The pain and harshness of his actions knocked the air from her lungs, in a moment of weakness; she raised her arm to her face to protect herself from the blow she thought was coming. Liv had taken many beatings, she refused to let this man deliver her the last but the man drew a breath and took a step back.

'Control yourself!' inwardly the man chastised himself. He was outraged at his roughness with the woman, he had called out her name and she had stopped, had she recognised his voice he wondered? Then the rage had taken over, 'Can she not see we must make haste?' his mind raced.

"Get up," he said, as softly as he could muster, "Please."

Liv dropped her arm and stared at the shadowy figure above her, again he offered her a hand, but refusing it she pushed herself to her feet. "Your Jarl will reward you well, twice I escaped and twice you caught me," she said, bitterly.

"We need to get aboard that ship before the other men catch up with us." He swung an arm and pointed to the long vessel in the bay.

Liv squinted at him, "You can reach the Jarl by foot."

The man growled, "Start moving. I won't ask again."

"You didn't ask," Liv said and placed one foot in front of the other, slowly heading back, to the waiting Grani. Stroking the horse's neck, she whispered softly to it before looking at the man.

The woman was causing him to feel, he did not enjoy what stirred in his chest and fighting with all his might against removing his helmet, he focused on the axe in his grip and breathed steadily.

"We can take the horse but move now," he spoke sharply and nudged both Liv and Grani towards the bay.

"Grani? Why? He does not belong to the Jarl!" her voice was low but shook.

The man shook his head and pushed them onwards. "Keep walking."

As they skirted the path and started along the shoreline to an outcrop of jagged rocks that stretched all the way to the ship, they steadily urged Grani finding their way with care. Liv saw the man stroke Grani's nose gently and felt a pang of anger that he was so patient with her beast yet so full of ire for her. She tore her gaze away from him and pulled her own dark woollen cloak about her shoulders. It had been gifted to her by a farmer's wife two seasons ago when her husband had been killed, her guardian had disappeared and Liv presumed he had been taken to the Jarl and either tortured or imprisoned somewhere. She felt sadness wash over her at the thought of the shrewd old man withering away or worse crying out in agony, until he met his end.

A group of seabirds cried out at the dawning of the amber sun rising in the sky, their calls sounded to her like the squawking of a small child, her thoughts betraying her into thinking of her charge. It had wounded her heart terribly to leave the child but she had no choice. She had to separate the child from the ring and had managed to do so but now it was her burden alone, the ring the Jarl sought was still concealed in the brooch her husband had made in the forge. So far it had remained uncovered, though it bothered Liv that the Jomsviking had not asked her for it nor had he inquired about the death of the boy.

Liv reasoned that the man was naught but a hunter, he had his prey, what need was there for questions, he had been taken on to find her and he had completed his task; there was no more to do than deliver her to the Jarl. Liv looked again at the man, the daylight gave her better sight to try and recognise him. He stood tall, broad shouldered and strong, his hair was the colour of soft brown leather from beneath his helmet. He wore no rings on his fingers but she saw a gold band around his wrist and wondered if he wore it as a sign of wealth or fealty. His clothes though worn were of good quality and she thought him to be proud of appearance, he was certainly stern, terse and hard. She saw nothing that revealed any more about the man except that his axe was indeed a fine weapon and the sword now slung across his back was heavy and inscribed with runes. She saw the rune for Odin and Thor, a bitter taste filled her mouth that he honoured the same Gods as she did, that was where their similarity ended.

They stopped a few feet from the side of the ship and the Jomsviking turned to her, "When we board look no one in the eye, speak to no one, I will tell the captain you are mute and deaf so no man seeks to bother you. Cause me issue and you will be sorry." His words were commanding and unapologetic, he barely looked her in the eye instead darting his glance from the shoreline to the ship, where a man was waving them to come forward.

"You won't bind my hands?" Liv whispered, facing away from the crewman. He appeared small upon the deck of the large vessel.

"No. Move."

Liv stood fast, "Why not?" Her eyes narrowed and tried to pull the eyes of the man towards her, "Is this your ship?"

"You are mute!" He snapped and pulled Grani forward, Liv followed, knowing there was little else she could do.

The crew member dropped a plank for them to climb aboard; the Jomsviking then led Grani to the hold, the crewman stood with his hands on his hips staring at Liv. Before the man could utter a word, the Jomsviking reappeared and roughly pulled Liv to a chest on the deck of the vessel and pointed at her to sit. He still wore his helmet and cloak and in the better light Liv thought she caught a glimpse of pale blue eyes. She frowned slightly.

"We are to set sail," he said, looking out over the horizon, gazing at the sky, he nodded at the favourable morning and unstrapped the belt from around his waist. Dropping his cloak, he motioned for Liv to shuffle off the chest and sit on the deck. Into the sea chest he placed the cloak and sword, rolling up the arms of his tunic he removed his helmet but turned away from Liv before she could see his face. Striding to the side of the ship he dipped the helmet into the water and poured the contents over his head. Leaning his forearms on the wood, he paused to collect his thoughts, before replacing the helmet and returning to the woman trying to peek at him beneath her lashes with curiosity. He realised he could not wear the armour for the entire voyage.

"You will avert your gaze at all times, I've told them you are a thrall, so look at the ground, never at me and never make eye contact with the others, understand?" As he spoke he untied the straps holding the leather armour to his chest, the cuffs about his

18

wrists remained, though he twisted them and flexed his fingers, "I don't like giving orders twice so obey, Liv."

He watched as the woman nodded and looked at her hands, carefully he removed his helmet and tossed it into the chest. Liv did not glance up at him or move at all, it struck him that she was being utterly compliant, he felt rotten inside to be so terse with her. It was not how it was meant to be, he thought, but at this time he could not reveal himself, though he doubted very much when at last she knew who he was, she would even care. She had betrayed their oath and it had meant everything to him, suddenly it irked him hugely that she had not known immediately who he was, how could it be she had forgotten him so swiftly?

Liv sighed, the man was intolerable, and she suspected, untrustworthy, he would not answer her questions. She knew full well that the Jarl's lands were easily reached by foot, there was no need to set sail and there was little need to bring Grani with them. She loved her horse but was prepared to abandon him to the settlement, it was the way of things in her life, she could not hold on to anything that attached her to places or people for the loss of her husband and guardian had taught her that well. Liv resigned herself to silence, she would do as the man asked, she would be mute and deaf and compliant for soon enough the only sound to fill her ears would be that of her own screaming, when at last the Jarl had her.

Chapter 2

ᚲᚺᚨᛈᛏᛖᚱ ᛏᚹᛟ

Sleep eluded Liv, as the ship made for open waters, though her mind and body ached dreadfully from exhaustion. Men had gathered on deck and taken their positions at the oars, the Jomsviking had instructed her to sit near the prow where his back faced her. She thought it odd he would do this as she might easily have escaped over the side of the ship but she also saw the man at the rudder was watching her, Liv suspected the Jomsviking had made this man aware she was his captive.

Massaging her temples, against the dull throb that had invaded her senses, Liv sighed heavily. Her task had taken its toll, the constant evasion of the Jarl's men and the danger she encountered being a woman on the run with a child had meant many sleepless nights, since her guardian had disappeared she was without counsel. For two years she had only her wits and guile to have gotten her and the boy this far and now she was captured. Her husband's cleverness in concealing the ring within the brooch on her cloak gave Liv hope but realising the men thought she was a thrall she tugged it from her shoulder and concealed it under her dress.

The touch of the jewel ignited a sensation of burning in her chest; she stifled a cough and watched as the Jomsviking turned his head slightly as she cleared her throat. She hated the weight of the ring, it had been draining her steadily over the last few months as the boy grew, Liv knew the time was coming when he would wear it and forever his fate would be sealed, she hoped it did not cause him as much anguish as it had her.

Liv looked at her hands and felt ashamed at the grime and muck under her fingernails, her dress was tattered and torn and she knew not what her scratched and dirt smeared face looked like in the light of the new day. Smoothing her hands over her hair she felt the sea air had already tangled it; Liv grimaced a small smile to think she was safe enough from any man on the ship given what she must look like. It occurred to her that this was the first time in a long time she had cared, always she had kept her dress simple and her hair tied back, it had to be that she faded into the crowds.

Her guardian had told her to be careful making eye contact and survey each gathering with a view that her and the boys' killer was there. Thinking back to the day when she had agreed to watch over her charge, sent a stabbing pain of regret through her. Liv had wished for a very different life but the boy's mother had to be protected and they had failed when she died; then the boy had to be watched over as he was the last of his line, that was six years ago.

Suddenly the wind picked up and the Viking manning the rudder shouted at the men to pull in the oars and raise the sail. They did as they were commanded and returning to their wooden chests they took the opportunity to rest. The Jomsviking ignored the men and walked over to Liv with a skin, averting her eyes she felt the skin drop into her lap.

"Drink," he ordered. Liv took a sip of the stale water and felt her chest loosen a little. "You are ill?" The man asked, startled Liv opened her mouth before clamping it shut and shook her head quickly.

"Good. My name is Gorm, look at my hands, should you need to ask for me use this hand signal." The man splayed his fingers in a wavering motion simulating the flight of a bird. "The men here all use this method when we fight... oft we cannot risk being heard. I will be watching... always."

Nodding her head, Liv darted her gaze back to the wooden planks of the deck, she heard the man sigh and rub his face with his rough hands. She felt the skin lifted from her lap as he took a drink himself, "You're not what I expected," Gorm said, almost sadly. "I thought there would be more fight in you, mayhap it's all but gone, no matter..."

Liv restrained herself from looking up at the man and instead turned away from him, angry that he made judgements about her, 'What right does he have?' her mind screamed, 'What I have had to do!' Instantly Liv chastised herself, anger and grief from the tiredness she felt was overriding her usually measured mind, she would not let her captor rile her, she focused on the boy's face the last time she held him. Tears pricked her eyes at the memory of their last words; she had promised to return to him after hiding the ring but now all he could do was wait.

Liv felt a dark ire surging within her, vowing silently that she would escape and return to the boy she channelled all her energy into forming a plan. She would not feel the Jarl's wrath yet; she would fight with every ounce of her being. The ring meant nothing to her; it was Liv's belief that the boy was powerful in his own right, it was naught but the greed of men that had forged the item to signify its wearers command.

Gorm looked at the woman he knew as Liv, his words had stung her and he berated himself for being so petty, it was true he had expected her to fight harder. She could have hit him with the axe whilst on the back of Grani but she did not, she submitted to his demands whilst on the ship and had uttered not one word. She looked tired and pale but still as beautiful as when they were young, as a Jomsviking he had seen what a hard life could do to a pretty face and was glad Liv had been saved from that but he wondered angrily how often she might have used that pretty smile to evade capture.

"You had a man?" he asked all too gruffly, he saw her nod hesitantly still turned away. "He is dead?" he pressed, and he saw her nod. "Then you are alone?"

Liv let out a breath and swallowed, wondering why he questioned her now and felt frustration tangle her thoughts. What was his interest and why had he not asked about the ring? Defiantly she raised her head and stood, stumbling slightly, as her legs were unprepared for the movement of the ship.

"Sit!" Gorm growled, clasping a hand on her forearm. "Eyes down."

Liv stood firm and turned her body to gaze out over the sea, "Take your hand off me," she whispered.

Gorm dropped her arm as if it was aflame and stiffened; a smile crept over his mouth as he leant in to whisper in her ear, "So you are not yet beaten? Good…but do not defy me again." With a heavy hand he pushed against her shoulder forcing Liv to be seated once again on the deck.

Watching the back of the Jomsviking Gorm walk away, Liv speared daggers into his flesh, with her mind's eye, she watched as he paused as though feeling her anger but shook it off and continued to his sea chest. Liv realised they were sailing away from the Jarl's territory heading north but where was still as of yet unclear. She thought of her homeland briefly but fought against recalling any memories, for what good could it possibly do her to look into the past again, and closing her eyes Liv allowed sleep to wash over her tired body.

When she awoke it was nightfall, the men were engaged in drinking from skins talking and playing dice games, the deck was lit by a few lamps and the sky was clear, with a round full moon shining down on the ship. The waters had stilled and there was no movement, the sail had been taken down and the anchor weighed, Liv stretched and peered over the side of the vessel seeing nothing but water on the horizon. Looking back to the men she saw Gorm standing with his back to her talking with the man who had been at the rudder, they appeared deep in conversation. Gorm nodded and Liv cast her gaze downwards quickly when he turned in her direction, and expecting him to walk over to her with more harsh words, Liv tensed and awaited his arrival but it did not come; instead Gorm sent another smaller man to her with a small bowl of dried fish and a cup of water.

Accepting the meal Liv nodded, fixing her eyes on the food. Chewing each mouthful slowly, she relished the salted fish and savoured the water even though it had taken on a staleness. She had not eaten since the tavern in the settlement and then it had been a weak broth interrupted by the arrival of the Jomsvikings. When she had finished the meal Liv rested her head against the cool wood behind her, pulling her cloak about her shoulders she felt night air fresh on her tired skin, sleep threatened her once more.

Her slumber was interrupted by the shouts of men, opening her eyes she saw two of the crew fighting surrounded by men who were slapping their thighs and laughing, the fight dispersed as quickly as it started and Liv saw it had been over a game of dice. Why men wasted their wealth on such things was a mystery to her.

She could not guess how long she had been sleeping but felt the weight of another blanket over her limbs, looking down, Liv saw that Gorm's cloak had been laid over her. Biting her lip she frowned at the gesture; why would he care to think of her comfort, Liv resigned herself to thinking that he wanted as good a reward as possible from the Jarl and should her health devalue her in any way it would cost the man. What good would she be to the Jarl if she were too sick or weak to interrogate, she thought.

For the rest of the night she fought to stay awake, when dawn broke through the clouds that had gathered in the sky she folded the cloak and placed it beside her. The crew rose at first light breaking their fast and waiting for their Captain's orders. Gorm did not approach her nor did any of the other men and Liv sat silently praying for an opportunity to present itself. She must escape she thought. Suddenly a rough hand yanked her to her knees, a scowl bore down on her and from the knotted fair hair and beard Liv knew it was not Gorm, her arm felt like it was in a vice and despite her efforts she could not pull away from the man.

"He says you're a slave? Don't look like any I've ever seen!" the man clenched his fingers around Liv's arm, watching with a grin as she winced in pain. "Speak!"

Liv shook her head and shakily pointed to her throat, if this was a test sent by Gorm she would not fail. She kept her eyes down daring only small sideward glances at the features belonging to the harsh voice. Puzzled the man furrowed his brow and looked at her before swinging a glance around the deck, Gorm was not in sight. Roughly he dragged Liv towards the hold, none of the crewmen looked up from their tasks, panic rose in Liv's throat as she realised Gorm's lie was the perfect opportunity for a man such as this, thrall status offered women no protection. Trying to steady her breathing, Liv thought of her small dagger in her boot that the Viking had not checked for and thanked the Gods. The man's pace quickened as he reached the plank leading down to the hold, Liv could smell the odour from the animals and prayed Grani was safe and that he might stamp his hoof into the man's head given half a chance. The grip on her arm loosened as she was swung around to meet face of her attacker.

"Since you can't speak, you can't shout for Gorm," the words slithered from his mouth as his lips pulled into a twisted grin.

The man raised a hand hitting Liv on the jaw, her head buzzed with the force from the blow and she staggered back, nausea overwhelmed her as she sank to her knees. Straining to keep upright, she fell onto the wooden decking, landing hard on her injured face and forcing her eyes open, she looked up at the figure before her, blurring into many shapes. As it loomed over her in a squatting position it pulled at her hair, then just as Liv prepared for another blow, a second figure appeared behind the man. The bearded figure turned, but it was too late the second man had raised his fist and smashed Liv's attacker repeatedly in the face. Rolling onto her side Liv felt the hold spinning, her eyes rolled into the back of her head, as strong hands lifted her shoulders and a voice whispered in her ear, "Liv? Speak!" Gorm's tone was hushed but filled with anguish; he was enraged that Freki had attempted to take Liv when Gorm had strictly forbidden the men to go near her.

The darkness of the hold prevented Gorm from seeing how injured Liv was, he cursed his earlier attitude towards her, lifting her over his shoulder he climbed back onto the deck and laid her in the spot he had ordered her to remain. Her jaw appeared unbroken though a dark purple bruise was beginning to work its way across her face; Freki must have caught her ear as a thin droplet of blood trickled from within. Looking about the deck, Gorm glared at the men who had done nothing to stop their comrade from his intentions. Cursing his plan to call her a thrall Gorm dragged his hand over his mouth, before swearing loudly, balling his fist and punching the wood of the deck.

28

Slowly Liv stirred and strained to open her eyes. She knew she was no longer in the hold but pain throbbed in her left ear, her jaw ached and there was a taste of blood in her mouth but using her tongue to trace her teeth she found none broken or missing. Swallowing she pushed back on her elbows and attempted to sit but the spinning sensation swept over her once more and she felt a hand gently pushing her down.

"Please rest. We'll depart the ship by evening, nod if you understand," Gorm spoke as softly as he could. He watched as she nodded, her eyes struggling to focus, he wished he had never told her to avert her gaze from him, he longed for nothing more than those green opal eyes to look at him with an assurance all would be well. "I'll seek out a healer if you have not yet recovered."

Liv shook her head and winced at the pain, she could not allow a healer to look at her, they would surely wish to inspect the rest of her body for injury and she could not allow that to happen. Groaning she raised her hand to the blurred figure before her and rested a palm on his forearm.

Gorm started at the touch of her hand; pulling back he reached for his cloak neatly folded into a square and tucked it behind her head, he waited for a moment until she appeared to have slipped into unconsciousness and stalked toward the hold.

Freki still lay in a bloody mess on the floor; the crewman had dragged his knees up to his chest both hands cupping the smashed nose on his face.

"You knocked out my teeth and broke my nose!" he spat.

"You were warned not to touch her!" Gorm roared.

"She's naught but a thrall! What difference would it make?" Freki whined, grimacing at the pain radiating his face, his eyes began to water as blood and drool dripped from his chin.

Gorm bent down and grabbed fistfuls of the man's tunic, dragging him to his feet, "You injured her, she's my property, you will pay one way or another," he growled into the man's face.

Freki squinted at the rage in Gorm's eyes, gulping he cursed himself for going against the wishes of the Jomsviking, this man was not to be trifled with. Though he had never heard of Gorm, he recognised the hardness of character and from the scarred face and hands Freki guessed this man had seen many a battle. This did not bode well for himself, he thought.

"I have coin in my chest," Freki stammered.

"Get it. If you so much as glance at her before we reach the township, I'll break the rest of your teeth and your jaw!" Gorm released his grip and watched the man stagger across the ramp and out into the morning light. "What am I doing?" he sighed. Dragging his fingers through his hair he felt weary, and angry at himself for not having kept both eyes on Liv. Taking a deep breath he followed Freki onto the deck.

Suddenly a shout for the men to man the oars arose and Gorm shook off the fury tightening his chest, taking his seat, he watched as Freki approached and tossed a bag of silver to him, before slinking back to his own chest. The captain at the rudder raised an eyebrow but Gorm was in no mood to explain and darkened his gaze with a frown until shrugging his shoulders, the captain roared for the men to drop their oars and pull.

It was still morning, the sky was grey, rain was on the horizon and not a breath of wind could be felt, Liv dreamt of her past as a youth, of a kindness she had known and the face of one she had loved. When next she awoke the day had turned to early evening and a misting of rain had dampened her clothes, swallowing back the pain, Liv felt tears well in her eyes as she relived the memory of her dream. Rolling onto her side, she struggled to regain her balance as she rose to her feet unsteadily, lurching towards the rail, she felt her knees buckle but a pair of strong arms caught her before she fell.

"Raise your hood," Gorm said, "We have reached the township. Let me lift you onto Grani and rest until I say." Liv nodded and covered her face with her hood, she felt Gorm lift her over his shoulder before he took the reins of Grani and led them over the side of the ship. Slowly Gorm placed one foot in the stirrup and patiently helped Liv into the saddle; satisfied that she would not fall, he nudged Grani to move forward.

"Gorm!" A voice rang out from the ship, turning Gorm saw the captain and stopped in his tracks.

"Ragnar?"

"Wait!" The captain bounded along the deck, leaping over the side of the ship now moored in the harbour, "The woman she is well?"

"I think she needs a healer," Gorm replied warily.

"Best be on your way and quick, you have a man here?" Ragnar asked.

"Yes why?" Gorm asked with growing concern.

"Freki is still smarting from your beating, one of the men told me he plans to get his coin back from you, now I know you can take care of yourself but your cargo says otherwise," Ragnar jerked his head of wiry red hair towards Liv. The captain had pale blue eyes that saw through many a guise and he figured this woman to be no thrall, no matter how convincing Gorm's story was. "With the Jarl's men on your back you don't need the likes of Freki doing the same."

Liv stiffened as her ears picked up on the conversation between the two men, could she have heard the captain correctly she wondered? Her heart started to beat rapidly in her chest; if this man had caught her for what purpose could it be if not to return her to the Jarl?

"Quiet, Ragnar," Gorm hissed, darting his gaze around the men loitering on and about the ship, "I thank you but we will be well. I am to meet with my man now and we depart the township in the morn…Freki is no threat and I doubt the Jarl has knowledge of what has happened yet. Can I trust you to say nothing if they should come looking?"

"What would I say?" Ragnar shrugged, "That some Viking came aboard with a battered wench? Happens all the time, mayhap you are some trader selling a thrall at market and my men change often, Freki does not sail with me again."

Gorm nodded and lifted Freki's coin sack from his belt tossing it over to the captain. Ragnar caught the sack with both hands and feeling the weight, nodded and winked at Gorm before turning and walking back onto the ship.

"Come Grani," Gorm pulled on the reins and started back along the path.

From beneath the heavy hood of her cloak Liv found the courage to sneak a look at the man guiding her horse, his own hood was down and he did not wear his helmet. As he pulled on the reins he turned his head this way and that, searching the crowd and Liv saw a strong square jaw bristled with short hair, his nose was straight, a series of small scars scattered over his jaw and neck as if some claw had attacked him and left its mark. Her vision blurred and she could not join the features into one image. She could see no more but as Liv fought against the pain in her head she saw Gorm raise his hand and heard a shout from someone in the distance.

Chapter 3

ᛞᚾᚪᚲᛏᛗᚱ ᛏᚢᚱᛖᛖ

The township of Gulafjord was bustling, the harbourside strained against the swell of bodies pulling their carts and wares strung over shoulders; Dag weaved in and out of the crowd, along the quayside littered with small vessels and larger ships. His humour was high this evening, he had secured them lodging on the outskirts of town where no one would think to look should Gorm have made any new enemies on the way and Dag reasoned that it was entirely possible given the task at hand.

King Harald Greycloak, grandson of Harald Fairhair, hailed from Sygnafylki and the region had prospered in his reign, in a few day's time Jarls would convene for the Thing debating over taxes and the concerns of their people. Harald Greycloak was the son of Eric Bloodaxe who had been next in line despite the many sons of Fairhair battling for rights to the throne.

Upon the death of his father Greycloak and his brothers allied their forces with that of his grandfather fighting many battles and being the eldest son Greycloak held most of the power he and his brothers gained after the defeat of King Haakon of Norway. Greycloak had been born into a dynasty at war with themselves, though now he had been proclaimed vassal King of western Norway by his uncle, Harald Bluetooth of Denmark.

Recently there had been talk within the ranks, grumblings that Bluetooth was offering land and ships if the Jomsvikings were to swear allegiance to him and though their code of conduct forbade dissent, there were many who bit back at the rumours that Bluetooth had proclaimed the order as being his creation but in truth, the Jomsvikings were older than this. The one thing that was agreed upon amongst the men, was the need for a larger citadel for the order of the Jomsvikings, currently they held residence in the great tower on the shores of a lake laden with crafts of many sizes and descriptions. To grow in number and power they had to lay claim to a larger more dominating fortress, which had been promised by Bluetooth.

Many ships had arrived during the course of the day, Dag watched as the cargos containing fine silks and cloths, spices and exotic foodstuffs were unloaded. Some ships carried fine looking steeds of the like the Arab men favoured, some carried slaves for the market which had stuck in Dag's throat, he neither appreciated nor respected the slave status. Who could allow themselves to be treated so unkindly, he often wondered, it was not a life and better the person sold into it ended it swiftly. Men shouted to one another preparing for trade in the township and organising meeting places to drink and eat, some were drawn to the women milling around the carts and storehouses looking for their own business. As dusk began to fall, Dag saw lamps being lit and the harbour took on a murkier tone, deals could be made with those who avoided the light of day, coin exchanging from hand to hand for passage onto ships leaving in the morning.

Dag had known Gorm since their enlistment in the Jomsvikings, the two men were similar in their skills and prowess but very different in demeanour, where Gorm was serious and reserved in temperament, Dag was loud and brash seeking the joke in every situation and enjoying the mischief he could inflict on his comrades. This had been the case at least until Gorm had approached him some weeks ago, after a messenger had sought him out and Dag hoped that the woman Gorm was after was worth the trouble that would soon be on their tails. In his mind, no woman ever was worth the trouble, he took maids, servants, whores; and whoever else smiled or batted an eyelash his way, no female had yet to convince him to settle down and in truth, why should he? So far with the Jomsvikings he had amassed his own wealth, which he had carefully divided before this expedition, none having to pay for a woman's upkeep. He fought many a battle and won his right to die well and enter the halls of Valhalla, what need did he have of a mortal wife when the riches of the afterlife would be much sweeter.

A roving eye drew Dag's attention to a comely woman struggling with a sack, he watched for a moment with an amused grin as she tried time and again to lift the load over her shoulder, puffing she swept a hand across her brow and caught his gaze. Tucking his thumbs into the leather of his belt about his tunic Dag swaggered towards the woman, "How come you find yourself here with such a load?" he smiled.

The woman tilted her head catching the glint in the man's eye, warily she looked him up and down and from his dark hair and rugged features she could tell he was no fisherman or farmer, she saw instantly he was a warrior and drew a breath, "My husband waits for me over there," she replied meekly.

Dag threw a look over his shoulder, as he turned he knew she would catch a glimpse of his heavy sword strung across his back, "Really? And he leaves you here to struggle?"

"Uh… ja, I'll be on my way," the woman blushed.

"Sure I can't offer you a hand?" Dag dazzled the woman with his straight even smile, she blushed further, he thought, this was again far too easy, he knew she had no husband here or anywhere. Catching her give him a sideways glance, he saw the bright blue of her eyes and the sharpness of her small features, lifting the sack he threw it over his shoulder with ease and offered the woman an arm, "Where to?" he smiled.

"You are a Viking?" She asked.

"Of a kind." Dag laughed.

"What kind?" She persisted nervously.

"The paid for and don't ask questions kind." He grinned.

"Thank you for your help but…"

Dag rolled his eyes and rubbed his chin. "No need to fear me woman, I offer help. Now where to?"

"The tavern." The woman pointed to a wooden feasting hall sitting amid a group of outbuildings some feet from where they stood, "I didn't have far to go really," she smiled and pulled her cloak tighter around her dress. "We don't see many such as yourself here."

"Am I so different?" he smirked.

"Ja, you look like you've seen many a fight, the raiders and traders have that look too but you're different, your weapons for a start. The sword is larger than any I've seen and you have daggers all along your belt."

"You see much and talk much too, tell me is there aught to keep the words falling from your mouth?" Dag laughed and winked at the young woman, enjoying the small smile spread over her lips.

Dag noted she wore the garb of a serving wench and wondered if she worked the rooms as well. Her face did not wear the look of a whore, but still, it made little difference to him. Gesturing for the woman to walk, he darted his eyes amongst the figures of the crowd, in the distance he saw a tall man in a dark cloak pulling a horse alongside, dropping the woman's sack he raised a hand and shouted at Gorm.

The woman sank to her knees by the sack and gathered the vegetables that rolled from its opening. "Nei, nei!" she cried.

"My apologies!" Dag laughed and helped her gather the roots and saw the sack also contained dried meat.

"Gods above he will tar my hide!" She shot a worried look towards the tavern and then to Dag.

"Who will?" Dag stood and looked about him for a sign of an angry man.

"My brother, he owns the tavern, I've already cost him and now the food is covered in muck. Pray I wash it off afore he sees." She raised her head briefly and stuffed the contents into the sack before struggling to lift the load once more.

"Your brother?" Dag took the sack and the arm of the woman before quickening his pace, standing outside the door of the tavern he glanced inside, "Is he there?"

"No. I best be gone, thank you and well... no thanks at all!"

"Hah!" Dag laughed out loud before catching the woman's arm as she disappeared over the doorway. "Your name?"

"Gytha. Why?" she asked crossly.

"Mayhap I return this evening and spend a coin or two?" said Dag.

"As you wish but... this place is trouble, it may be best you stay away." Nervously the woman looked away before wrestling her arm free, leaving Dag's sight.

Shrugging Dag turned about and set off towards the spot he had seen Gorm approaching from, absently he felt a little anger towards the brother of the young woman, the man obviously intimidated her, Dag was not fond of the ways men could do this to women but he knew her not and resolved to let the matter rest in his mind until he saw her next and if he saw her again. There was every chance Gorm would want them to remain completely hidden from sight until the morn.

Noticing Dag making his way towards them it had not escaped Gorm's attention he had been speaking with a woman, Gorm sighed and wondered if his friend ever kept his mind on anything else. He was pleased to see his friend though and knew Dag would have made the arrangements they had spoken of before he left. He had told Dag as much as he dared to, he knew his friend suspected there was much more to the tale, there had been little time to discuss the legend and the Jarl's obsession with the ring.

The legend he had known of ever since he was a child, sitting around the fire pit in the hall of his people listening to their Seer, had found its way to ears of men. All who heard tell about the ring or had glimpsed upon it craved it, apart from Gorm. It sickened him that greed could destroy a person and he could not understand why Liv had given up her life to protect it. He knew not where on her person she had concealed it and cared not, he had to deliver her to one man who could set the matter to rest, as far as Gorm was concerned the ring had to be destroyed.

"Gorm!" Dag laughed and slapped the man on the back, looking at the woman on the back of the horse, he raised an eyebrow, "She is ill?"

"Ja, some fool attacked her on the ship, we may have need of a healer."

"Mmm, mayhap. I have lodging for us, best we make haste, the owner of the house will be gone for days. When we arrive I'll look for a healing woman." Dag darted a look at the woman as she moaned quietly, slightly hunching her shoulders she sat weakly on the back of the horse.

"Best we move," said Gorm.

Liv struggled to keep herself upright; she heard a man talking with the Jomsviking and furrowed her brow painfully as she tried to remember the conversation he'd shared with the ship's captain. Where were they going, why had the man taken her and who was this new voice she could hear? The two men clearly knew one another and their tone was friendly but urgent. Peering from beneath her hood she saw the new figure walking with Gorm, he had long hair the colour of freshly upturned earth and she saw a strong face as he glanced over his shoulder at her, his beard was dark but short as if he had neglected to shave his whiskers for a few days. He smiled at her and she saw a spark in his eyes, she recognised the charm he exuded and sighed warily. He also wore a heavy sword on his back, his clothing was practical but well made, in the dusk and lamplight the blade glinted causing her to shiver.

"Your woman peeks from beneath her hood. All will be well..." Dag murmured leaning towards his friend.

"She was told to keep her gaze down!" Gorm growled but felt a little tension lift from his shoulders, that curiosity was awakening her.

"What woman can do as she's told?" Dag grinned, "and why down?"

Gorm scowled at his friend as they made their way from the harbour and started along a track skirting away from the township. The crowd thinned and became the odd group of men wearily carrying sacks and pulling carts or staggering fools who had spent or lost their coin heading back to their ship to rest their broken heads.

"She doesn't know, and keep your voice low. This way?" Gorm jerked his head to the path before them and Dag nodded.

"We are some paces from the house," Dag lowered his tone, "Why have you said naught?"

"There was no time to explain," Gorm muttered.

"What explanation would be needed when she saw your face?" his friend asked, frowning.

"She has not recognised my voice, mayhap she has forgotten me altogether, would be no bad thing now," he said.

Dag grunted and peered back at Liv, "Bothersome woman, you save her skin and say nothing? Mayhap your pride is wounded Gorm?"

"Nei."

"Humph, ja I think it so. How many years have passed since you saw her last?" Dag asked quietly.

Gorm tightened his grip on the reins, "Over six years."

"And you think she would know you by voice? In that time you have changed much, you are an older man now, even I would sound different to my mother's ears were she still living." Dag pointed to a small wooden structure nestled between a crop of stables and store houses. "Here, isn't much to look at but will suffice for now. Tis' warm and clean and dry, there is food. Do you want me to look for a healer?"

Gorm looked at the ramshackle buildings, they were in need of repair but would indeed do for the duration of their stay, straightening his back he shook his head, "Nei, you take her inside, I'll look for a healer." Gorm handed Grani's reins to Dag and walked towards one of the larger square buildings where a little smoke was drifting from the turf roof. The light misting of rain that had fallen during the day had dried and the path was firm beneath his feet. "Dag?" Gorm called back to his friend.

"Ja?" Dag raised his head slightly, his hand still stroking the horse's nose.

"Keep your hands to yourself!"

Dag roared with laughter, it was good that his friend saw fit to shed his grimness and jest with him, he would indeed keep his hands to himself, if the woman still meant anything at all to Gorm.

Reaching up he pulled Liv from Grani's back and carried her into the small house, once inside Dag laid her on the long table by the small fire pit and lit a lamp, pulling a bench aside he drew back her hood and saw she was staring at him wide eyed. The woman's face was scratched and bruised, Dag whistled at the markings, wincing as he realised the blow from the man Gorm had spoken of must indeed have been heavy and lifting a hand he gently tilted her chin to further expose the bruising.

"Are you still in pain?" he asked.

"Some," Liv rasped.

"Gorm has gone for a healer," Dag said, folding his arms across his chest.

"I don't need one," she stated firmly, "what does he plan for me?"

"Not for your concern right now," he smiled and looked at her green opal eyes, they were shaped like the sleek felines in the harems he had visited in the southlands, her lashes were dark and she looked something other than Norse. Her hair was of a bronze hue rather than the golden shades of his women; he enquired, "Where are you from?"

"Nowhere," Liv struggled to sit and shuffled from the table to the bench across from Dag, "why am I allowed to see your face?" Holding her head in her hands she balanced her elbows on the edge of the wooden table.

"Best you and Gorm speak about that. Besides is this not a fine face to look upon?" Dag chuckled slightly to himself, "I'll fetch you a drink."

Crossing the small room Dag lifted a clay pitcher and a wooden cup from a shelf, pouring the water, Liv licked her lips and drank greedily enjoying the crispness of the fresh liquid, filling the cup for a second time Dag watched as the woman looked up at him and thanked him with her eyes as she drank. 'Gods above,' he thought, 'what a fool Gorm is being!'

"Thank you," Liv said.

Dag nodded but suddenly the door swung open and a large figure filled the entrance, Liv immediately looked down, Dag stared first at his friend and then to the woman who had averted her eyes. "Give me strength!" he muttered.

"There is no healer nearby," Gorm grunted, walking over to the table, he lifted the pitcher and drank. With a jealous look, he glared at Dag and then to the woman, "I see she is much recovered anyway," he growled.

Dag shrugged his shoulders and rolled his eyes, "You two talk and swiftly, I'll return in an hour, we must rest well tonight."

"Where are you headed?" Gorm asked curiously.

"A tavern, I have an errand to run. There may be a healer there, she needs one," Dag smirked and stood, lifting the oil lamp to Gorm he whispered, "Mayhap this will shed a little light on the situation?"

Gorm grabbed the lamp and set it on the table, angrily swearing at his friend. Dag shook his head as he paused in the doorway. He was loyal to his friend but if they had any chance of succeeding further, the woman could not be forced to continuously look at the ground, swallowing he made a decision.

"One hour my friend… mistress?" Dag could tell the woman was listening keenly, "Would you not look upon the face of the man you know as Ari?" Dag slammed the door behind him and walked swiftly back along the path they had taken together some short time ago, he did not look back for he neither wished to see his friend pursue him or the fist he knew he had earned.

Chapter 4

ᛞᚾᚪᚳᛏᛗᚱ ᚠᛟᚾᚱ

Gorm's jaw hung slack, the room seemed to chill though the fire was lit, he stood rigidly staring at the door Dag had closed. His shoulders sagged as he turned to see Liv standing looking at him, her face was blank, her eyes wide and full, her hands clenched at her sides, she mouthed something he could not hear. Her lips formed his name.

"Sit," he said warily.

"No."

"Please," lifting his hands, he gently approached her and lowered his palms, "Liv…"

"Nei! Who are you? Gorm? You cannot be Ari," her voice was flat and dry; Liv heard herself speak but did not recognise her tone. Her chest ached and her heart tore in two, it could not be him she thought but as she looked closer at the man's face a cold realisation hit her, she had been lied to, this was Ari.

The man before her was tall and strong, his hair was longer than she remembered, his eyes sharp and blue like the pale winter skies and his face was as handsome as she had always known him to be but for the small trails of scars across his jaw and neck. Crossing the space between them she lifted her fingertips to his face before pulling away, "How is it you are here?" she whispered.

Ari sighed, misunderstanding her meaning, he had seen in her eyes she was amazed that he stood before her; why did she think she would never see him again? She appeared to be shaken by his very living, "I have to take you home."

Liv shook her head; she could not go back, there was nothing there for her, "no."

"We must…"

"No!" Balling her fists, she let her anger spew forth, "how could you treat me that way? Taking me your prisoner? The ship? Why would you do that?"

"You know!" he blazed.

"What?" Liv let her confusion spread across her face, Ari took a step back, his anger rose and he lifted the pitcher throwing it violently into the wall of the room, it smashed and water splashed on the earthen floor. Breathing heavily, Ari dragged his hands through his hair before tearing off his cloak and throwing it on the table.

"You have the ring?" he barked at her.

Raising her eyebrows Liv felt nothing but deep disappointment, it had come, the reason he wanted her, he wanted the ring.

"You cannot have it," she said firmly.

"Give it to me," he hissed. Facing her he leant into her face and looked her in the eye, "Where is it?"

"You… are not the Ari I once knew," Liv spat back venomously.

"You are right. You destroyed that man some years ago," he swiftly retorted, Liv took a sharp breath and narrowed her eyes. She had been lied to. She did not know from where his hatred sprang, did he not know she had been lied to by the one who had helped her all this time? Why had he come for her, to take her to their homeland but then asking for the ring made no sense?

"I did nothing to you…" her eyes watered and she fought the sting of the tears.

"Is that so? You made an oath and then ran! You took this foolish errand and for what? To escape me? Then I discover you took another man? You have no heart Liv," he scoffed in contempt.

"What?" Liv stammered, not quite believing what Ari was saying.

"I will take you home, you will hand over the ring and be done with this, from there go live whatever life you choose, I care not!" Ari sat angrily on the bench, covering his mouth with his hand. He was enraged at himself and could not believe the words that fell from his mouth.

Liv stood shaking, she wanted to run from the room, she wanted to jump upon Grani's back and ride hard out into the night. She fought the urge to scream; the child flickered into her mind and she thanked the Gods Ari had not mentioned him, she had lied about his death and Ari seemed to believe her. Fatigue and shock took over and Liv fell to her knees, a great sob broke through her chest and tears fell heavily from her eyes, "I did not know Ari... by the Gods I never knew!" she cried.

With a puzzled expression, Ari looked at the woman on the floor before him, her beautiful face covered by her hands, her sobbing tore at his heart and his anger faded. Kneeling beside her Ari wrapped his arms around Liv and breathed in her scent, she was exactly as he remembered her, how could he have been so vile to her he wondered, she was still his Liv - she had not changed.

"Why Liv? Why did you run?" Ari whispered sadly, breaking free from his embrace.

Liv looked into his eyes, "He told me you were dead."

"Who told you this?" he spluttered, outraged.

"Harvardr... but now he is gone... dead I think. The Jarl's men took him," Liv wiped her eyes and looked sadly at the floor. She could not understand why her guardian would have lied to her about Ari; what reason could he possibly have had to do so?

"Liv... please never look away from me again, I am sorry," Ari lifted her chin with his finger and gently stroked her hair from her face and offered a weak smile.

"Ari I swear if I'd known you were alive I never would have left, never agreed to carry this burden... I had no choice," she began.

"Liv we have so much to discuss, I am uncertain where to start, we must go home," Ari lifted her to her feet and gently guided her to sit on the bench, "but first tell me why you do not wish to return?"

Liv sighed and pulled her cloak from her shoulders, the room was beginning to spin around her and there was a buzzing in her ears as if the room were filled with dozens of gadflies, "I'm so tired Ari, please let me sleep, then we might talk awhile. I have so much I want to say... to explain... I don't want your hatred." Her voice trembled and as she spoke, a cold sweat broke across her brow and her hands shook.

Ari nodded, he could see she was in no state to continue, standing he walked to a pallet on the far side of the room and arranged the furs, returning to Liv he guided her to the makeshift bed and watched as she drifted off to sleep.

He wondered how far pushed into exhaustion she had become and how much was down to injury, his patience was thin and he struggled with the silence in the room. Resigning himself to waiting for Dag's return, he quietly picked up the broken fragments of the clay pitcher and left the room. Outside the dwelling the cold night air was crisp and fresh, Ari could hear Grani in the stable and wandered to the outbuilding to check on the horse, the evening was silent save for the snorting of Liv's beast.

"Shh Grani, your mistress rests, as should you," Ari stroked the horse's nose, removed the saddle and blankets from its back and lifted a bale of hay into the pen. The horse chewed on the dried grass, keeping one eye on Ari all the time. Finding a small stool, Ari took a seat and rested his head in his hands. 'Why would

Harvardr lie?' he wondered. Ari considered there was much that the old man had neglected to tell him; why would Liv spend the last six years on the run, protecting a jewel and a child that was not her own, she had been attacked by Jomsvikings, pursued by the Jarl and his men, had seen her husband killed and thought Harvardr captured or killed. Was a cursed ring worth protecting so fiercely he thought? He had asked her for it and she refused, but she did not wear it and so had not succumbed to the power it held. Ari began to wonder how much of the legend was true, when an agonising thought entered his mind, how had the child died and how had Liv taken the death? He desperately wanted her to awaken and tell him all that had happened, he wanted to explain his anger and hoped she would understand, he did not want her to think of him as a murdering violent warrior paid for and unquestioning, he did not want her to believe he was merely a Jomsviking.

Ari felt for the pouch tied to his leather belt and the necklace inside, he'd had it made for her when they were young, a simple amulet on a thin chain. He had discovered it next to her pallet with the other women thrall's after she had gone missing, it had wounded him terribly to think she had cast it aside so easily but if she believed him dead, it explained much. Had she nursed a broken heart all these years, he wondered, was there room for either of them to love one another again.

From the moment his captain had received the word to hunt her down, Ari had felt nothing but anger and sought an answer to the one question that had haunted him all these years; why? Now he knew, Ari was uncertain what any of it meant. It would take many nights before they reached their own settlement, Ari hoped that Dag would return with another horse, thus they stood a better chance of arriving earlier than expected.

Dag walked into the tavern with a sense of unease, there was something amiss here, the men drinking were all too quiet and the maids scurried from table to table instead of working the room for an extra coin or two. He saw the young woman called Gytha, carrying a large metal tray loaded with roasted meat, vegetables, breads and cheese. Watching her, he saw a worried frown on her face as she reached a table where two men sat with their backs to him and a third faced the doorway. The men were clothed in the same garb, matching cloaks slung about their shoulders, their swords still strapped to their backs and the third man facing him held a small dagger in his twitching fingers.

Recognising this tactic, he quickly looked away and spotting a passageway leading to the kitchens, Dag disappeared from the men's sight, standing in the shadows he awaited Gytha. She seemed to be taking longer than he liked and when at last she walked towards him he saw she was rubbing her right arm. Stretching a hand from the darkness of his corner, Gytha started and raised a hand to her mouth, "You!" she whispered, "What are you doing here?"

"Who are those men?" Dag jerked his head towards the taverns hallway.

"What is your name… you are a Jomsviking aren't you?" her voice trembled.

"Dag and yes I am," he replied. "Why ask?"

"They were asking about a Jomsviking but they did not give your name. Please, you must go, my brother is already seething! Their presence is causing the other men to drink more cautiously if he sees you here he'll be furious." Gytha swung her head back and forth along the passageway looking for signs of her brother.

"What name did they give you?" Dag asked cautiously.

"I think it was Garm or Gorm… I can't remember my mind was elsewhere, one of them grabbed my arm… another sorry bruise," she finished in a whisper and Dag stiffened.

"You're right, I must go…" Dag felt alarm rising at the Jarl's men looking for his friend. They might be strangers here and have hidden themselves in the small steading outside of the township but that meant nothing if these men asked the right person, at this moment that might be Gytha. "Your brother mistreats you?" he asked.

"He has a fear of healers… many do… but I have no choice," Gytha hushed her tone as a maid walked past them, scowling as she went, before seeing Dag and flashing a small flirtatious smile. Gytha rolled her eyes heavenward and Dag smirked before allowing the seriousness of the situation to take over again.

"A healer? Mayhap I have need of you, tell your brother a man came by and will pay good coin for your services, meet me in the stables behind the storehouses."

"No coin would be enough," Gytha's brother's hunger for prosperity was well known.

"Gold coin, for your time here tonight and the loss of any ale you might have served," he offered.

Gytha's eyes grew large, pursing her lips she stared at Dag, "I know you not, you think I'm foolish enough to wander off into the night with a Jomsviking who lurks in the shadows? The Jarl's men might notice I'm gone."

"Do this Gytha, I mean you no harm, meet me and quickly," Dag was not asking and strode away from the woman, exiting the feasting hall through the back door. Almost immediately the stench of an open sewer and rotten food assailed his senses, his boots squelched in the fetid mud, 'Disgusting oaf!' he thought and relished the opportunity to smack the woman's brother about the head. Dag knew well that where there was the rotten stench of decay, there was illness and disease.

The stables he sought out were but a stone's throw away, he could smell the manure of the beasts and the grass they ate, he would purchase one or two horses and make haste to the farmstead. A man stood outside the stables puffing on a large pipe, he was not much older than Dag but twice the weight and balding, he raised his eyebrows as the Jomsviking approached.

"I want two, strong and reliable, what have you got?" Dag grunted at the man.

"None for sale, some men came earlier and bought the last, they come to pick the nags up later," said the fat man, wisps of smoke leaking from his mouth. He had scraggly whiskers stained by the tobacco; his greasy skin glistened in the torch burning overhead.

"I can offer you more than they did... what's your price?" Dag jostled his coin pouch. The man stepped forward and ushered him into the stable, beckoning Dag the man waddled to the rear of the building where grains and tools were piled against a wooden panelled wall. "They were the Jarl's men, they paid as little as they could, you seem like a man of his word, so I'll take your coin. When they come back I'll feign stupidity... wait here I heard something!" the man picked up his pace and ran back to the entrance.

Dag peered over his shoulder and saw a small figure clutching a leather sack to her chest. "Wait, she's with me, Gytha, over here," Dag called the young woman and emptying a few gold pieces into his palm he offered them to the horse merchant who greedily swiped them into his grasp. His pipe still wedged between his teeth clicked as he counted his profit.

"Yes yes... take what you want but quickly I don't wish to explain myself with you here!" The sloth waddled away thrusting the gold into a purse hidden beneath his grubby tunic.

"He is dishonest Dag, best we move, often he's in the tavern," Gytha said as she watched Dag lift the bar and lead two strong beasts into the space between them. Placing the bits between their teeth and throwing a blanket over their backs, he handed Gytha the leather reins of one of the horses.

"Follow me," he whispered, "Did any see you come this way, other than the merchant? What said your brother?"

"None saw that I know of, my brother scolded me but thinks only of the money you offered, but the horse merchant may be headed to drink his fill at my brother's hall. He has a loose foolish tongue," Gytha worriedly stared into the blackness that had become the night.

Dag nodded and noticed her hair was hanging loosely from her braid on one side, "Did he mistreat you because of my request?"

"Ja but no matter, when you give me the coin for healing I have vowed never to return to him but head north. I can't even say at least I am protected in my brother's house, there's naught left for me here" Gytha's lips thinned and she looked Dag square in the eye.

"A woman travelling alone is a danger to herself, and the settlements to the north are smaller and fewer than here," Dag pointed out.

"Why say such a thing, what choice have I got?"

"None I suppose," Dag was perplexed with his feelings, he liked this woman despite himself but also had no need for a dependent female, he felt somewhat responsible for her most recent mistreatment. "Come… if your healing powers are worth the money, mayhap we will escort you as far north as we plan to travel ourselves."

"How many are you?" Gytha asked quietly, as she quickened her pace to keep up with Dag and the horses. They walked steadily to the path leading to the edges of the town, it was a walk she had taken few times, as the people there did not often call for a healer or visit the dockside taverns.

"Three," he lifted a finger to his lips and smiled, "Keep up!"

Gytha strained in the darkness to see where Dag was leading them, his pace was quick and she grew breathless, she wished he would light a torch but reasoned it was unwise to draw attention to themselves. More than once she cursed when stubbing a toe on an overturned rock and again when she heard the man in front of her snigger. He was handsome, she knew, with a bright smile that she guessed had won many a woman over, she had played coy and blushed when he looked at her but she would give nothing away, even if he was helping her escape. When they had met that afternoon she had felt that it would not be the last time they saw one another, it was her insightful qualities that drew her brother's ire and his wife's.

In childhood her mother had sent her often to the Volur women for potions and herbs to treat her ailing father, little worked and her brother became sour and distrustful, but the women took the time to teach Gytha their ways and encourage her sight. Gytha had prayed to the Gods every night that her father would recover and allow her to join the women in their encampment beyond the township but neither had happened.

Suddenly Gytha felt a shiver creep over her skin, her ears buzzed and flashes of light crossed her eyes, rubbing her fingers against her eyelids she stalled in her tracks.

"What is it?" Dag turned; sensing the horse behind him had stopped.

"I don't know," she replied unsteadily, "how far away are we?"

"Paces... here take my arm I'll lead the horses," Dag felt the woman's hand on his shoulder and he guided them into the small steading and tying the two beasts to the barn post, he turned Gytha to the door of the small longhouse and led her inside.

Drawing a sharp breath Gytha looked past the man who stood to meet them, to the form on the pallet behind him, dropping her hand from Dag's arm, she rushed to the woman laying covered in furs; her skin seemed unnaturally aglow, Gytha sucked in a breath and swung to face the men. "By the Gods, who are you?" Gytha almost shouted.

"What? Dag who is this?" Ari hissed at his friend.

"Be calm both of you! Ari, this is Gytha, a healer. Gytha, what causes you to act so, can you heal her?" Dag looked at Gytha in confusion.

Turning back to the woman Gytha placed a palm on her brow, she was in a fever, but as she removed her hand a stabbing vision exploded in her mind. She saw the woman with a child; a boy and they were walking across the rainbow bridge into Asgard. Around them the stars fell from Gimli and landed at the child's feet, the woman lifted the boy, who pointed to a man standing far away in the distance. The man held a long staff and slammed it into the ground, from the root of the staff the ground split in two and wondrous burning light erupted all about them. Gytha drew a breath and staggered back into the chest of Dag. The other man named Ari looked at her with concern, "What is it?" he asked.

"I must be sure, help me," Gytha lifted the woman's shoulders and wrestled her dress from her shoulders exposing the pale skin beneath.

"What are you doing?" Dag asked incredulously.

"By the Gods she is … what is her name? Tell me!" Gytha demanded, staring angrily at the two men.

"She is Liv…" Ari spoke quietly, "What is it?"

Gytha stood and folded her arms about her waist struggling to find the words, "She is a protector, her name means life, she's marked… there's a branding on her back. Who are you men… did you do this to her?"

Dag raised his hands, ushering Gytha to sit, Ari turned away, resting his fists on the table he slowly sank down onto the bench, Liv stirred slightly on the pallet and the room fell silent.

Chapter 5

ᛞᚾᚪᚲᛏᛗᚱ ᚠᛁᛈᛗ

Jarl Brynjar drummed his fingers on the wooden table impatiently, he had sent three men to Gulafjord in search of the Jomsviking Gorm who had failed to deliver the woman and the boy, two of the Jomsvikings had returned and been sent away unpaid for their dismal efforts.

"Tell me... how much must I pay?" Brynjar growled at his captain, "This woman evades capture again, how does she do it? Does the ring empower her with invisibility?"

"I cannot say Jarl," the captain replied.

"Must I ride out and fetch her myself?" he threw hateful looks at the man before him, "What are you doing about this?"

Holger bit his tongue, he hated the Jarl but could do little about it, he felt nothing but irritation for the quest Jarl Brynjar was set upon. It was ridiculous that a man of his standing should covet a legend to the detriment of his men. The Jarl also reneged on his word on many an occasion and Holger could not abide such a character but he was sworn to serve the man by his own foolish consent.

"The Jomsvikings were not our own men, there was no way of knowing their true allegiance, it appears the one called Gorm has taken an opportunity, mayhap we will receive word that he holds the woman and the boy hostage for more money? Perhaps he has killed them and taken the ring, then he is a thief and we will track him down, the three I sent are highly trained..."

"Your words are full of defeat! This Gorm will lose his head; nei he'll suffer a pit of vipers for betraying me so, further from my grasp this wench has become again! In my lands she trod and none could bring her to me!" Brynjar slammed his fist on the table and standing angrily, he shoved the heavy oak chair, his jaw clenched in fury. "So damned close, by the Gods I swear Loki is aiding her at every turn. Trickster, demon, witch!"

Holger watched as the man's eyes bulged, his thick hair tied back from his face showed the veins throbbing in his forehead, and with barely calloused fingers Jarl Brynjar massaged his temples. The Jarl wore the finest tunics and many jewels adorned his fingers but the shine wore away from all he touched, such was his greed and lust for wealth. Holger fought to think of a time when the Jarl had been honourable and just, he was harsh and uncompromising now, and he could not remember when it was the tale had been told of the ring and its rightful heir. It was the talk of old wives and worn out warriors who had seen too much life taken from them, their minds addled with grief and years of regret, his own mother had spoken in such ways before she died and he had hated the wistful look in her eyes when she spoke of seidr and myths.

The Jarl's hall was as richly furnished as its lord, it was adorned with wooden carvings on the posts and beams, large shields and swords hung from the walls and the platform, where the Jarl sat and feasted with his men, gave judgement and made plans, was swathed in rich tapestries woven by his wife and her women. To his shame the Jarl lacked one thing, the source of his ire and frustration; he had no children.

Though he had taken two wives and many mistresses, none were round with his offspring, his men said nothing but cast glances at one another when time and again the Jarl boasted of his prowess but had produced no evidence, Brynjar himself came from a large family with many a brother who sought to take the seat as Jarl and continue the line. Thus, Jarl Brynjar had cast out all his sisters who had proven fertile with strong sons and killed one of his own brothers in what many suspected was a dagger tainted with poison. Three brothers remained who had all vowed loyalty to Brynjar but they neither trusted him nor one another.

Holger himself had a son and a daughter; he knew the Jarl bitterly resented them as he considered his captain of lower ranking and therefore not an equal. It was only because he was sworn to the Jarl that he and his family remained in Srovberget. He had desperately hoped the Jomsvikings would find the woman and put the matter to rest but it seemed they had not been able to live up to their names. The Jarl's own men had been dispatched to Gulafjord, and the two who had accompanied Gorm revealed a ship had been seen in the settlement's harbour when they had been in pursuit of the woman. Gulafjord was a potential nightmare; from there Gorm might have taken any number of ships and escaped. Even if the man had taken the woman and child by foot, they would at least have horses by now and the roads to Gulafjord were heavy with those journeying to the Thing. The Thing was where Jarl

Brynjar should have been preparing to travel to but he shunned it, and that too would be noticed Holger thought.

"Thank Odin the Jomsviking was not informed of the boy's true identity," The Jarl regained his composure and sat facing Holger once more, "I want you to ride out to Gulafjord and find this Gorm…"

"If I am gone Jarl… there would be none to watch your back," Holger offered dryly.

"None would dare Holger, it is not your presence alone that stops the daggers plunging into my back, there are men aplenty to stand guard," Brynjar scoffed.

"Then you will not attend the Thing in Gulafjord?"

"No!" Brynjar slammed his open palm on the table, "What have you to say about it?"

Holger took a steadying breath, "Your absence will be noticed, we cannot appear weak in front of the other Jarls, and should word reach the King…"

"Once we have the ring and the boy none of that will matter," the words fell from Brynjar's mouth like pebbles, each one echoing around the dimly lit room as they hit the floor and with a nod Holger resigned himself to the knowledge that this was a pointless conversation, the Jarl was so deeply entrenched in his belief in the legend that he could see no sense, but another troubling point was emerging. Holger had noted over the last six years the frequency with which the Jarl's rages had increased, every time he was defeated or outwitted by the woman he appeared in physical pain often rubbing his temple or forehead. On these occasions he would slump into his seat as if the day had been spent training hard with the men, and drained of strength.

"Go now," Jarl Brynjar waved a hand in front of his captain and watched as the man turned and strode from the hall, it irked him greatly that Holger felt he had the right to challenge his decision on attending the Thing. If he himself saw it as no dereliction of duty or admission of loss of power, then what was it to Holger he mused? Brynjar stretched his legs from beneath the table and frowned when he noticed a tremor in his left foot.

For some time he had been ignoring the twitching of the limb, soon his hand would follow suit and he would call for the healer and have her prepare a brew. His demands upon her witchcraft were becoming more frequent; he detested the healing women with their secret knowledge and magic. If he had an interest he would have learned their art but he had no time for the darkness of women's souls; they were all alike to him. He had taken two empty vessels to wife and no potion, spell or prayer had provided him with a child from their wombs. He had taken many a mistress but all they were good for was sating his desire, in the end they all wanted one thing; to become the Jarl's wife, his only wife.

The tremor in his foot paused for a moment allowing Brynjar to raise himself from his seat and head towards the passageway concealed beneath the tapestries hanging behind his seat. The passage was dimly lit as he walked to his chamber; he noted the servants were conspicuously absent. More than likely they had heard his ranting at Holger and decided to make themselves scarce, 'Wise!' he thought with a grim smile. Reaching the chamber he found his wife was nowhere to be seen, thankful for this he lay down on the fur covered bed and allowed exhaustion to creep over him.

He began to think of the boy, it always started like this for him, the child was always first to enter his thoughts followed soon after by the prize: the ring. Brynjar thought of the day he learned of the legend and the man who had promised him his loyalty; where was that man now he thought? True he had sent messengers, his actions had been swift on the mere hint of a rumoured sighting, but it appeared that he was no closer to locating the woman for himself. Then came the suggestion of the Jomsvikings; the idea had not appealed to Brynjar as the mercenaries were costly, but that they might catch the woman more swiftly than he had been able to appealed. The man had the one named Gorm in mind for the task such was his skill at tracking; it would appear, Brynjar thought, he was as equally skilled at treachery.

Alarm tickled Byrnjar's pulse causing him to sit up quickly, could it be, he wondered, that this Gorm and the man were working with one another? For his contact had managed to find someone who had achieved what Brynjar had not; mayhap the old man no longer found him worthy of the prize?

A memory floated into the Jarl's mind; he saw his father with the old man who was much younger then, he saw them pointing to maps drawing plans together. They spoke of battle with other feudal Chiefs and the man correctly predicted Brynjar's father's victory in each case, he remembered the tears in the eyes of the man when Brynjar's father breathed his last and it was then that the man told him of the legend and swore his oath to Brynjar.

No, he shook his head; the man would never betray him although in the past he had indeed failed him, true it had been many a year since they had last set eyes upon one another, but through messengers they had maintained a level of contact.

At that moment the Jarl's wife swept into the room, catching sight of her husband's face she drew a heavily ringed hand to her chest and gasped, she was a fine woman to look upon but had lost her lustre somewhat over the past few years.

"Husband! What ails you?" she took a seat by Brynjar.

"My head aches, my limbs are weary... where have you been? Where are the servants?" he snapped at her. Meekly the woman looked at the floor and stood, turning she walked to the door and closed it. Brynjar only now noticed that her eyes were rimmed with redness and her cheeks stained with tears. "Your brother's wife... her labour was early, neither survived. The servants are preparing for her burial," she sighed heavily.

"No word reached my ears on this."

"You have been so busy Brynjar, I could not bother you with this news, and your brother does not know himself," she explained. A wry smile spread across Brynjar's lips, "You have done well wife, tis' my duty to tell him, ensure two of my men escort him here before he arrives home," he instructed.

"Brynjar… is that wise?" she asked nervously.

"You dare question me?" he snapped, wildly throwing a terse look in her direction he rose to his feet but stumbled instead of walking, "Woman, fetch the healer now!" he roared at her.

Brynjar's wife quickly walked to the doorway but as she passed him, resting his hands on the framework of the bed, the Jarl grasped her arm and squeezed tightly, "Do not think to question me again!" he growled in her ear, "No one speaks to Inge before I, understand Solveig?"

Shaking with pain, Solveig nodded, barely able to bring herself to look at her husband, warily she locked eyes with him and expected his free hand to deliver a blow, but it did not come. Breathing deeply she felt his grip weaken and pulling free, Solveig ran from the room in search of the healer.

Tears sprang in her eyes as she ran, her heart lurched from the pain of her brother-in-law's loss and the awful vengeance her husband had in mind, she wondered how much more she would have to take from the wrathful Brynjar. It was true that Inge was not in Srovberget, he was on an errand of mercy in her name for Solveig had asked Inge to aid her in escape from Brynjar. She had reasoned that of all the men to aid her Inge would have been the least suspected when the Jarl would have found her gone. Inge was the youngest of his brothers, and the least challenging to Brynjar by his own admission. On occasion when Inge was welcomed to the hall, Brynjar would often gloat that his younger sibling had never made an attempt on his life, nor was likely to. Brynjar did not hold Inge in esteem of any kind, for the man was a cripple and yet he still fathered children, much to Solvieg's joy and Brynjar's annoyance.

Solvieg had given Inge the last of her mother's jewellery to pay for passage to the far east of the kingdom, where her remaining family would hide her from the Jarl, in truth Solvieg suspected Brynjar would be enraged but not enough to send his men out into the world looking for her, at least not when he was so obsessed with the woman and the child. But now her plans were up in smoke, Inge would return to a house of death, Brynjar would deliver the terrible news with malice and such would be Inge's grief that Solvieg could no longer ask or rely upon his help to flee.

For a maddening fraction of a moment Solvieg stopped in her tracks and considered a terrible thought, the healer held no love for Jarl Brynjar, he often maligned her until he was in need of her craft, would she help Solvieg? Looking at the rings on her fingers she wondered which one might offer enough coin and not be missed by the Jarl if she were to offer it in payment to the healer for poison but as soon as Solvieg considered the possibility she shuddered and continued with her task, she could no more kill Brynjar than allow him to deliver the awful news to Inge.

On this she knew she would defy her husband, she would somehow get word to her husband's brother and prepare him as best she could, and mayhap if Brynjar's wrath was so great as to deliver her the beating that might end her life, so be it.

Chapter 6
ᚦᚢᚱᛕᛏᛘᚱ ᛊᛁᛒ

Though Gytha had argued against moving Liv, when she was so weak, the men would not consider the possibility of being caught by the Jarl's men. The three hunters were already in Gulafjord and them being only a short distance away was enough to set Ari's mind; they had to move and quickly.

"But to where?" Gytha panicked, they had still not fully explained who they were and what they were doing with the woman, however, Gytha felt sure that the one called Ari had not beaten her, such was the concern in his eyes when she examined her body.

"Giffni... the hot spring caves, our village is not far from there and we will be safe for a few days." Ari spoke quickly as he strapped his mantle across his shoulders and then the leather strap of his sword belt across his back. "Dag did you..."

Dag raised a hand and spoke swiftly, "A few hour's ride we will reach a fishing hamlet, there a small boat awaits but there will be no room for the horses aboard, mayhap we leave them in payment to the villagers?"

"It is not enough that you are Jomsvikings?" Gytha quizzed but took a breath as both men threw her fiery looks.

"People talk Gytha, buying silence is necessary. Gather your things," Dag spoke with military command. It shocked Gytha to see his easy going and humorous nature disappear to be replaced by a soldier, part of her admired his ability to switch between the different aspects of his personality but she also felt a fear, more so from the man called Ari whose dark stare and grim expression told her of the gravity of the situation.

"Who is the Jarl that seeks her... why?" Gytha lifted her leather bag throwing the strap over her shoulder, moving to Liv she pulled the worn clothing about the woman more tightly.

"Gytha if you come with us it will be a hard journey and dangerous, can you give us what Liv needs..." Ari spoke with no emotion.

"I'm coming! You can't leave me here, Dag! My brother... all I need is passage north and I will not leave her, she is watched over by the Gods!"

Both men stood, startled by the outburst from the woman, Dag's eyes flickered with interest that the small soft form of the woman had taken on a straight erect line, her shoulders squared and her jaw set, she was not what he had thought. "Come then, but no more questions until we have time to speak of it." Dag sighed.

Ari looked at Dag and shook his head; his friend shrugged his shoulders and guided Gytha to the horses tied outside. Lifting Liv from the pallet Ari carried her to Grani and set her gently upon his back. Climbing astride he took a rope and tied it about his waist and that of Liv's; he would not risk her falling from the horses back and injuring herself further. Throughout this Liv did not stir or flutter an eyelash, Ari swallowed dryly wondering how long it would take her to come round. The springs at Giffni were a refuge they had found when they were young and he hoped that she would not be too alarmed when she awoke to discover how close to their old settlement they would be.

It was a mystery to Ari why Liv did not want to return to their home, true she had lived there in thrall status but he had taken an oath with her, and his father had not argued the matter when Ari told him he was to wed her. She would have been freed from servitude and had his protection against all who would seek to harm her or command her, perhaps she was afraid of what the people might have to say at her hasty departure, they thought she was a runaway slave, and perhaps she feared punishment. It would not happen thought Ari, his father was the brother of the Chieftain and Ove was not a vengeful man, in fact all had been perturbed by her disappearance and when Harvardr had explained it was due to her wandering bloodline they accepted it, she had never been one of their own. Her people were nomadic; at least her father had been, Liv's mother had been pregnant with her when she had washed ashore near their settlement. The woman had been near death but held on long enough to birth her daughter, it was when they came to cleanse and prepare the body for burial, they discovered the thrall collar about her neck she had kept concealed under her cloak and upon the discovery Ove gave Liv to the thrall women to raise instead of casting her out to the elements.

Grani snorted as the fresh night air tickled his nostrils, Ari guided him to join Dag and Gytha where they sat on horseback with hunted stares and nodding to Dag, Ari dug his heels into Grani's side and the horse sprung into a gallop.

The three rode hard for hours stopping only once to allow Ari and Gytha a moment to check on Liv's condition, her eyes rolled back in her head and she groaned slightly when Gytha pushed her loose hair away from her ear to check for fresh blood and satisfied the bleeding had stopped, they pushed onwards.

The hamlet was little more than a few fishing huts adjacent to the beach, nets hung from trestles and racks for drying herring perched beside each household. The breeze held a briny odour, a faint smell of smoke hung in the air and Ari guessed that the inhabitants were sleeping, for not a soul stirred from a doorway as they approached. Dag jumped down from his horse, taking quick steps and rapped his knuckles against the door of a lean-to shack, a small figure appeared rubbing his face and gruffly swearing under his breath.

Gytha stared as the large Jomsviking prodded the bad tempered old man in the chest; the man raised his hands and disappeared back inside the shack before reappearing with his cloak and grunting at the group he beckoned them to follow. Gytha felt oddly aware that no one else had stuck their noses out of their dwellings and by now she was sure they would have known strangers had come into their hamlet. Could it be the houses were deserted and this man was the keeper of the land?

Ari, reading her thoughts turned and whispered reassuringly, "Most likely he remains while all else travel to the Thing in Gulafjord. These people are poor by the looks of it, there is coin to be made whilst so many are travelling." Gytha nodded and jumped down from her horse making to follow Dag and the old man. Ari led Grani by the reins with Liv's body slumped forward on the horses back, slowly they walked around a grassy mound on the shoreline and found a small boat dragged onto the shingle.

"It will do," said Dag clearly irritated.

"And the nags?" the old man grunted, Gytha could see he was missing many teeth as his sour breath reached her nose.

"Not a chance. Where is your son? This isn't the boat he showed me; does he hide from the beating that's due?" Dag bore down on the man grinning but without humour.

"He sleeps… some men from the township beat him senseless, he followed you to the docks talking about going Viking… what does a fisherman's son want with that?" The man stepped back and spat into the sand.

"Go and get him!" ordered Ari.

The fisherman hastily took the path along which they had come, moments later he dragged a youth behind him whose face was a myriad of cuts and bruises. Dag stood tall and crossed his arms over his chest; Ari placed a hand on the strap of his belt, the Jomsvikings glared down at the boy before looking at one another and nodding.

"I am not happy, my friend here less happy about this than I. What say you?" Dag spoke slowly. Gytha felt an anger rise in her chest, how could they be so unkind when the boy was clearly afraid, she saw the boy's eyes widen and his whole body began to tremble.

"Please! I made a mistake we did have a larger vessel, but I lost it in a game of dice," he scratched absently at the back of his head before casting his eyes downwards, "I will take a beating..."

"Gambling? Who with?"

"Viking traders."

"Which ship?" Dag cocked his head in query.

"One I tried to join but they laughed at me, cheated me in dice and beat me until I ran."

"You wanted to become a Viking?" Dag smiled, no wonder they had used the boy in jest he looked pathetic even now with his tufted hair sticking up and his clothes shapeless and hanging from his thin shoulders, but still to beat the lad was cruel.

"Like you," the boy shot a sideways glance at Dag before looking at Gytha and blushing. Dag looked at Ari and shook his head; the boy was too slight and had clearly never been in the training fields. He looked malnourished and the bruises didn't help to evoke any kind of masculinity about him. "Well boy mayhap you can still prove your worth? How well do you ride?" Ari asked.

"Uh... well..." the boy looked between the two men nervously.

"Your father can manage without you for a few days?" Dag quizzed.

The old man nodded quickly and placed a hand on the boy's shoulder. "Ja…"

"Then you will take our horses to Giffni, we will meet you on the edge of the great lake where the cliffs jut out into the fjord. Take the back roads, avoid anyone at all costs, you would be an easy target, one boy with three beasts. We need these horses and you need to prove yourself." Ari scrutinised the boy; his eyes hot with pride at the task that Jomsvikings had given him, he felt reluctant to let the boy become overly excited and stepped closer to him with a grave look in his eyes, "do not get caught."

The old man choked, erupting into a fit of coughing; his son turned and patted him on the back all the while feeling the eyes of the two large men watching him. Gulping, the boy nodded nervously, "I can do that… I'll disguise the horses, muddy them so they look old and worthless, I'll dress in rags and an old cloak so any I meet think me sick, they would be sure to avoid me."

"Cunning… I like it!" Dag grinned before gesturing to the old man and boy to set about their business.

In the dark before the breaking of the new morning sun, Ari and Dag dragged the boat down to the water's edge; they had two oars each and at first would row together. Gytha gathered her belongings and lingered by Grani until Ari returned to carry Liv and the packs from horses' saddles to the boat. Gytha noted a tinge of sadness about Ari when he handed over Grani's reins to the boy; she wondered about this sombre man, he appeared not at all like the Vikings that had frequented her brother's tavern, not that Dag was altogether what she expected either.

True, she had been a little flattered when first they met at the harbour, but much had changed since then. The thought of his interest had let form a foolhardy plot whereby Dag would beat her brother senseless allowing her to escape, but it had not come to fruition and for this she was glad. Violence was a natural fact of life but Gytha sought to heal and never inflict wounds upon any person herself.

She watched Dag silently, she guessed he was a rogue but something else told her there was more to the man, for did mercenaries and cutthroats have friends and did they try to bring healers to women who were secretly guardians? She thought not. And what of this man Ari? He obviously cared for the woman; this was an attribute that soldiers rarely indulged in, if the men of the drinking house were anything to go by. These men seemed to be a contradiction to their Jomsviking status, she mused.

Gytha held her leather bag to her chest, she reminded herself of one thing, what would happen when they reached their destination? They were Jomsvikings after all and she knew not what their mission was and furthermore it appeared they were not entirely informed about the unconscious woman.

Dag waved Gytha to come forward, stepping into the boat she slid into the spot beside Liv checking her temperature and the rapidity of the throbbing pulse in her neck, she desperately wanted Liv to awaken.

"I will have one last word with them," Dag said to Ari, who nodded and started to load their weapons, swords, axes and daggers, added to that he had two skins of drinking water and a cloth sack filled with flat bread dried fish and meat. All the while he darted his gaze here and there about the shore and the hamlet of small huts but the darkness was silent, no beating of hooves or the shouts of men betrayed themselves, and all was still.

"I can see the look of concern on your face Gytha… there is naught to fear from us," Ari said carefully.

"Thank you, for taking me with you, for as long as you will," she replied quietly.

"There may be danger ahead, we cannot guarantee your safety…should you have to run then do so," Ari narrowed his eyes as he watched the young woman stroke the side of Liv's face.

"How well do you know her?" Gytha whispered.

Ari straightened his back, climbing into the boat he sat on a small plank at the first set of oars from the prow, resting his elbow on his knees he sighed heavily, "Very well… once."

"Once?" Gytha cocked an eyebrow. "You were parted?"

"Ja many years ago, before I became a Jomsviking," he responded sadly.

"So you are not the boy's father?" Gytha instantly winced when she saw the man's face harden as he closed eyes; he seemed to be in pain she thought.

"How do you know about the boy?"

"I saw him when I touched her," Gytha explained slowly.

"Saw him?" Ari stared hard at the woman, she was smaller than Liv in height, her hair was thick and blonde, and her eyes were a pale hue. Her youthful frame was still soft and lithe, he realised what interest Dag had in her but this new idea that she had more knowledge than the workings of herbs and spells bothered him, "You are Volur?"

"Nei, though I spent much time with a settlement of Volur as a child, sometimes I see things but they are like dreams... until I touched her."

"Liv, you can use her name, she would like it, being on the run you don't use your real name often," he explained.

"Liv..." Gytha smiled at the sleeping form, "There are many men who distrust women like me."

"And women who feel the same about a Viking," Ari rubbed the back of his neck with a tired hand, "You have naught to fear from us."

"That's twice you have said that, I believe you, I'll do what I can to help. Her heart is heavy, it keeps her sleeping, and her mind needs time to set the present to right. I think she fears for the boy," Gytha sighed.

"Feared perhaps..."

"What?" Gytha shot a glance at Ari who was looking towards the dark figure approaching them; Dag was wading through the calf deep water and the boat rocked slightly in his wake.

Ari lifted the oars, staring at his friend, "The boy is dead," he stated.

Dag climbed into the boat and took the oars in front of Ari, together they pulled and the little boat pushed off into the open water. Steadily the men made a great distance before the sun began to rise and all the while Gytha's focus remained with the woman beside her. 'Why did you lie to him?' she wondered. Feeling drained and tired Gytha closed her eyes and listened to the men as they spoke of direction and how long it would take to reach Giffni, she knew not where that was, though the men had mentioned many days' travel. They muttered on and Gytha kept her eyes closed until Ari said Smols, in a flash she was wide eyed and staring at the two men whose brows were beaded with sweat, their tunics rolled at the sleeves, "Smols?" Gytha breathed.

Dag caught her eye and grinned widely baring his teeth, "Ja, Gytha, we sail to Smols! You will see Ari's mountain, Hornelen, where the Gods stand and watch over Midgard!"

"Hah, I've climbed Hornelen and I found no Gods!" Ari chuckled without breaking into a full smile behind his friend, all the while pulling on the oars.

"Your gloom scared them away!" Dag laughed heartily but suddenly stopped when Ari flicked water with the blade of his oar and soaked Dag's clothing. At once all three broke into a reverie of laughter, tears streaming from their eyes, struggling to regain breath, the men paused and pulled their oars into the boat.

"You have heard of my mountain?" Ari asked Gytha as he passed a skin of water to the dripping Dag, "Ja… I dreamt of it! I saw someone standing at the edge of its summit but never have I seen that person since. I thought mayhap it was a vision and I cannot deny that now!" Gytha smiled warmly.

"Visions?" Dag stretched his aching arms, "The woman keeps producing interesting talents."

"Indeed," Ari nodded at Gytha, he noticed her cheeks turning pink as she looked at Dag. Ari assumed his friend was winking or smiling at the young woman who appeared quite taken with him, 'Just what we need,' he thought, 'A healer, visions, and a fair face too. Dag is hopeless!' but Ari found himself pleased with the thought his friends roving eye had finally fallen on one so deserving. If only it had happened in a more peaceful time when they were not pursued or sheltering under the cloud of peril.

Chapter 7

ᛞᚨᚷᛏᛖᚱ ᛋᛖᚦᛖᚾ

The boy looked at the horses and attempted a quick calculation in his head on how long it would take him to reach Giffni, he reasoned the animals were strong and healthy, he knew he was light of weight and could ride the back of a different horse allowing the others to rest.

A week he thought, 'It will take a week, maybe less if I do not stop often?' The Jomsviking Dag had suggested mere days but the boy figured they would give him some lenience. After all he was delivering them their beasts and they could not travel far without them, even with his father's small boat they would be restricted to the seas and unable to cross land.

As he gathered his sack filled with dried fish, unleavened bread and a skin of water, he mused at what the men were up to. With two women, one being unconscious and the other a rumoured healer, with their need to leave the area of Gulen swiftly he paused to think that perhaps he was involving himself in something more than he could handle.

"Odin's eye Thorik! This was what you wanted, adventure!" he chastised himself in the smoky darkness of his father's hut, rummaging through the threadbare cloaks and hoods he would use for his disguise, "Finally a way out of this hovel!"

"Hovel!" Thorik's father cuffed him about the ear, he watched with disdain as the boy winced at the blow before throwing him a dirty look, "Ja, a hovel indeed! Go on your adventure, see the lands, but return the wiser for it!"

"Sorry father," Thorik grumbled, not meaning a word of it, "I won't be gone long and the others will be back from the Thing before you know it... there won't be time to miss me."

"Miss you?" the old man repeated much to Thorik's dismay, he hated that his father made a habit of this when they spoke. "I need help to fish, not sit and bemoan the loss of our talks at the fireside!"

"Well I won't miss you either." Thorik grumbled huffily.

The old man watched his son gather the cloaks under one arm with the sack in another and stride out of the hut, his small frame seemed overburdened by his load but it was nothing like what he was about to face. Taking a stool the man sat beside the smouldering fire and roughly rubbed his eyes with his sea-hardened hands, 'Why is he so wilful?' he thought. It was true that Thorik had always sought out trouble and more often than not it had not been a hard task, he fought with the other children, he swam too far in the sea, pushed the smaller vessels too hard, approached any stranger who happened to be passing by.

When they traded in Gulen, Thorik would always wander off and ultimately end up at the harbour, he appeared drawn to the wildest and roughest of men, where his appetite for excitement was always sated. Often the old man caught Thorik ogling the ships with keen interest or quizzing a grizzly crewman for tales of his conquests, the more gruesome the better.

Thorik was naught but mild amusement to these types of men and always the boy returned sullenly to his home. He dreamt of adventure and battle dressed in the garb of a Viking warrior, claiming treasure and the respect of those he would one day command, it was all nothing but foolish dreams he thought Thorik would never see, but now however, he had realised his ambition. Yes, it had taken a beating and a dent to his pride to achieve it but now Thorik was on his journey.

"Where will this lead?" the old man sighed wearily, he feared for the boy, perhaps if he had taken a stronger hand with him none of this would have occurred, mayhap the Norns had woven it this way with their threads of fate. The boy was thin and looked frail, his father knew he could haul in a net as well as any but what about fighting and defending himself? He never seemed to gain weight or look healthy; such was his waxen skin and dark circles around his eyes. He knew his son slept fitfully and this had contributed to his appearance since he had not recovered from his mother's death. The hamlet still mourned her loss but it was the way of the world, it was the way of men in Midgard to suffer so, not every death had meaning and not every death had dignity, it would be a lucky thing to pass into the afterlife in your sleep he mused.

Warily the old man stood and shuffled to the doorway, he saw his son jump astride the horse the second Jomsviking had ridden, the other two beasts were tethered with rope to one another forming a chain, with a nudge of his heel the horse broke into a trot and the party set off. Thorik did not look back upon his father's home and the old man prayed that the men were honourable and the Gods would favour his son on this task.

Thorik felt his heart beat in his chest, he imagined himself a strong man not to be trifled with, and he sat proudly on Grani's back feeling the strong muscles of the horse as it walked. He resisted the temptation to urge it into a gallop just yet; he would wait until his father's hut was far from view. The morning air was alive, with the breath of the sea wind upon his face and drawing in a deep breath, Thorik smiled to himself, he thought of the danger ahead and how he would defeat it, fingering the short sword he had pilfered from a trader on the docks some many months ago, he felt a surge of excitement that he might have to use it.

"I won't go looking for danger, Grani, fear not!" he stroked the horse's mane and it snorted at him. Sticking out his bottom lip Thorik wondered if even the animal thought him incapable, "You know Grani they trusted me with your delivery, so I'd be kinder to your master!" The horse shook its mane, without taking a command from Thorik it made its way from the main road to a less well used path leading to rolling fields littered with large boulders, the two beasts attached to them followed without question. "Do you know where we are headed, Grani?" Thorik questioned but the horse remained silent and shrugging Thorik loosened his grip on the reins and relaxed a little, the horse had taken the path he himself would have chosen so it was a wise beast he reasoned, he was in good company.

By the afternoon Thorik had ridden the horses hard and covered much ground, reaching a small stream he jumped from Grani's back and let them drink. The rest was welcome as he chewed slowly on the dried fish, watching the horses eat the wild grasses. The land surrounding them was entirely empty of life, neither wild deer nor boar was to be seen and he had hardly noticed a bird in the sky, it seemed an odd place and Thorik wondered if this was why no settlement had been laid. It was a windswept place littered with rocks and so would have been poor farmland; this was more likely the reason than ideas from his wild imagination.

Gathering the horses he tied Grani to the rear and jumped upon the one Dag had ridden, it was as sturdy as Grani but the boy favoured the other horse, not wanting to offend the animal he stroked its mane before swiftly kicking its sides into motion, it didn't seem to possess the character of the other beast. As they rode Thorik felt the hours pass in mere moments such was his joy at accomplishing a full day's ride without mishap. When at last he knew he had to stop and make camp he resisted the notion of a fire and instead huddled against the safety of a large boulder allowing tiredness to give him some sleep. Often he jerked awake throughout the night, each time rising to check the tethers on the horses, always they were secure, and when at last he could stand the restlessness no longer, he allowed the bright moonlight that shone down upon them to light their path. Once or twice he felt himself nodding off on horseback but finally as the new dawn arose he snapped awake and surveyed his route.

Still the land was strewn with rock and wild long grasses but in the distance Thorik could see the outline of the coast and the sea air filtered its way to his nose. He allowed Grani once again to take charge and they made their way to the shingle beach, as they approached Thorik saw that the beach stretched for miles, he took the chance and broke the horses into a gallop, there was no sign of boats or huts in fact no sign of human life at all. The sting of the morning air watered his eyes and the salt matted his short tousled tufts of hair and again the surging feeling of pride rose in his chest and he laughed into the wind, Grani was swift and graceful beneath him, "You are Odin's horse!" laughed Thorik.

When they had covered a few miles and the horses slowed to ease their limbs and lungs from the ride Thorik allowed them a moment's rest, pulling them to a stream trickling onto the stones of the shore he let the horses drink. A wild thought occurred to Thorik, throwing off his cloak he grabbed the short sword from his belt, lifting his right arm he swung the blade around his head, thrusting and jabbing at the invisible assailants surrounding him and cutting each one of his attackers down as they swung their axes and long swords at him. Deftly he leapt and ducked each blow, a war cry erupted from his lips and Thorik stood proudly.

Looking at the ground he frowned as his footsteps had done nothing but create a mess on the sand, he remembered the sparring of the Viking men from the ship when they practised and their steps had seemed so sure as if in a dance; his own markings in the sand were nothing like that. Those men had been twice his height and weight with larger heavier weapons; Thorik's light frame and meagre weapon betrayed his inexperience and fitness as his chest heaved and his brow slicked with sweat, his tufted hair ruffled in the breeze and grim determination set on his face.

Though his arms ached, Thorik lifted the blade once more, again and again he swung the blade slashing and slicing through the air, looking at the steps he took his gaze fell to his feet as he tried to make sure footings in the sand. All of a sudden the ground fell from beneath him and his body flew through the air, then the beach rose up to meet him and grit filled his nose and mouth, his chest heaved and his stomach lurched as the air was knocked from his body. Rolling onto his side Thorik spat the grit from his mouth and saw that he had tripped over an upturned stone. Grani looked at him with his large unimpressed eyes before turning back to the stream and feeling ashamed and ridiculous, Thorik pulled himself together and strode over to the horses.

Gathering their reins he tugged them into a slow walk back along the shore, he would advance upon his destination if he could not improve his sword skills. Thorik felt a dark mood descend over him and thought that at least there had been no one present to witness his foolishness. As he trudged along the wet sand littered with pebbles, smoothed by the continuous turmoil of the seas, he wondered if the men would reward him for completing his task. Thorik realised that he still had many days travel ahead of him and decided to take the opportunity each day, while the horses rested to practise his skills, there still might be some chance he would become a Viking.

It was not an unrealistic dream for a boy to have and Thorik felt sure that given the proper training he would grow into a strong warrior, it was not a possibility for him that he would remain this skinny wretch of a lad forever, for his father although a small man was broad enough and his uncles too were strong men. His mother had been a woman of slender build but Thorik shook the idea aside that he resembled a woman in any way, he would be strong, he would be fierce, but as he thought this a grumbling began in his stomach and he realised he had to eat.

Instead of stopping Thorik took a wedge of bread from his bag and chewed on it as he walked; if he came upon a river he might fish for fresh catch instead of the dried meat he carried with him. He would forage for wild roots and greenery to bulk up his meals and he knew he must sleep with more effort in the evening. All these things he would do and felt sure they would make a difference when next he would meet the Jomsviking men.

The beach took many hours to walk but the weather stayed on Thorik's side until the early evening, when the skies began to gather grey threatening clouds, the boy resigned himself to finding shelter and waiting out the rain that was promised on the air. Thorik thanked the Gods when at last he found a large crop of rocks nestled between the beach and grassy mounds; there he found a worn patch of ground where once a goat herder had taken refuge with his beasts. There were the remains of a long dead fire scorched on the flat earth, Thorik tied the horses together on a post protruding from the ground and took a few moments to survey the area. There were no signs of the previous occupants of the shelter, breathing a sigh of relief he started to gather dried wood thrown up from the shore and grass to start a fire, when he returned Grani looked at him with his large eyes.

Patting the horse on his nose, Thorik set about building his fire and humming a sea song he had once heard a man on the harbour sing, he remembered the words had something to do with the sea God Aegir, protecting them from a terrible storm that battered their vessel. Then Thor rippled a great thunder across the skies, before Odin slammed his staff into the high sea cliffs and bolts of lightning erupted from the earth. There were also words of sea-maidens as beautiful as Frigg and Freya tempting the sailors to their doom but Thorik thought nothing of women at his age nor found them remotely interesting, and never in all his days at sea with his father had he seen these temptresses from the deep.

Striking his flint, the bundle of grass smouldered as a small flame flickered into life, sitting back from his kneeling position Thorik slapped his thigh in triumph and began to build the burning mound, the sea air picked up a little pace but the breeze filtered past the little grotto of the boy and his charges. Dusk was beginning to approach and Thorik thought it best to eat and drink before resting his eyes, he would sleep for a few hours and see how the weather faired, if the night prevented them from travelling, he would not be silly enough to try and drag three horses through the wind and rain in the darkness; without a bright clear moon or stars to light the night sky he could easily become lost or walk in circles. Though he knew that keeping the sea to his left would prevent such a thing. Still one of the beasts might become lame and how would he explain that to the men?

Thorik pulled his cloak about his shoulders, feeling sleep beginning to burn his eyes and limbs with weariness. Untying his sword he propped it beside his leather bag, laying back on the ground he rested his head upon it waiting for a wonderful dream of fighting and adventure.

On the beach three men on foot pulled their horses alongside them as they read the tracks in the sand, the leader was tired and his brow furrowed, the other three were silent in his presence such had been his rage when discovering them eating and drinking in the tavern; he had been mightily angry. His ire was stoked even further when the fat squat horse merchant had arrived in the tavern apologising that since the Jarl's men had not come to claim the horses he had needed to let two of them go to the next purchaser.

Holger had sent one of the group back to the Jarl with a message informing him that a Jomsviking had been spotted in Gulafjord. Holger had a trail and meant to track the man along the coast, there had been no signs in the township itself and Holger reckoned the man would stand out so perhaps he had taken lodging on the outskirts to avoid detection. The township was bustling, it heaved with travellers and their wares, but somehow they had found the wattle and daub steading where they clearly could see fresh hoof prints in the earth.

The fisherman had been easy to press into talking, he revealed quickly that two Jomsvikings had been and taken a boat from him, he also hurriedly said that his son had been given the task of delivering their horses that he was intent on joining them and had already set off on the journey. Holger was but a day behind and intended to push his men as hard as it would take to catch up with the boy. It had not taken long and Holger had to admit the young lad was not slothful, many youths would have become distracted or taken the opportunity to lengthen their task by dalliance but it was not so with this lad.

The thought occurred to Holger that the Jomsviking men had either struck a cold fear into the boy or impressed the return of their horses with urgency either way it meant little to Holger, what really bothered him was that he could not persuade the fisherman to reveal who else travelled with the men, what their names were or their destination.

Holger also felt uneasy that now there were two of these men for him to contend with, he had not known this, thinking that the original group of three were all that had been deployed, however he had his own men and all he had to do was deliver the woman to the Jarl.

A gust of wind stirred about the men and a whiff of smoke filtered its way to Holger's nose, lifting his head he squinted along the line of grassy dunes and waved to the two men behind him. Steadily making their way to the dunes Holger halted and handed the reins of his horse to one of the men, slowly he found a beaten path in the growing darkness and the smell of fire and animals grew stronger.

Thorik started suddenly from his slumber, one of the horses was whinnying, Grani lifted a front hoof slamming it onto the ground and shaking his mane. The boy rose on his elbows and with a hand wiped the sleep from his eyes. The fire had burned to embers, a chill crept over Thorik's skin, fingering the blade at the head of his bag he tugged but the weapon could not be moved.

Thorik twisted and darted a look to the sword, upon it was a large leather boot, swiftly the boy sprang to his knees and shuffled backwards towards the stamping Grani.

"So boy... we have you at last," the man growled, the firelight cast a demonic look over his features causing Thorik to gasp. He saw a huge bulk of a man with thick fiery hair tied at the back of his head, his eyes were dark pools of anger, his short neat beard as red as his mane, almost seemed to snarl at him. He wore fine clothes that were travel weary but this man was rich or important the boy thought. In his right hand the man extended his long sword that too appeared to glint with evil intent in the glow of the embers, Thorik swallowed and felt fear but also ashamed that he had not come closer to completing his task before failure.

Chapter 8

ᚦᚾᚲᛏᛗᚱ ᛗᛁᚷᚾᛏ

The two men by the fireside held their sides as laughter exploded from their chests, the source of their amusement was the young boy, Thorik who sat bound with rope at the wrists and ankles. Holger was deeply unamused, the men had no place guffawing at the youth when he had successfully managed to get this far ahead of the Jarl's men. He resisted the urge to strike them with an open hand across their face's if for nothing else than to silence them.

"A Jomsviking!" the younger of the men pointed at the boy, "You!"

"Hah! My wife would make a better soldier than you!" the other wiped tears from his grimy face.

Thorik turned away from the men with a distant look in his eyes, Holger guessed that he had often been on the wrong side of a jest and knew well to hold his tongue.

Staring hard at the ground Thorik resisted the urge to cry with rage, he was dumbfounded by the turn of events; how could it be he was followed? He thought he had been careful, how would he ever explain his foolishness should he meet with the Jomsviking men?

Chastising his loose tongue he swallowed and tasted the copper of his own blood still salty in his mouth, it had only taken a few back handed blows before he submitted to these fierce looking men and mumbled a response admitting that these were their horses. The red-haired warrior had shouted at the men to cease and revealed his father had already told them of his desire to join the Jomsvikings and become one of them himself. The amusement it brought the other men grated on Thorik, he realised that their reactions confirmed the nagging doubts he had pushed far into the recesses of his mind. He would never become a Viking or a warrior and least of all a Jomsviking; he was too small, too slight and sickly of appearance, he would never grow into a strong sword wielding warrior.

If he carried any luck bestowed by Aegir, the God of the sea, fate would see him return to his father and fish until death saw fit to take him. 'My own father!' Thorik clenched his jaw in fury that his father could give him away so easily; what hope did he have when his own kin betrayed him, he wondered.

Suddenly the leader stood and ordered the men to survey the beach and the dunes surrounding them, the men grumbled before standing and shuffling off into the darkness. The man took a seat by the fire, Thorik felt his eyes boring holes into his skin, turning his head ever so slightly Thorik caught his gaze before looking away to Grani, "Tis' a fine animal... yours?" Holger nodded to the grey stallion.

"Nei."

"None of these are yours?"

"Nei."

"What do you own?"

"Nothing now," Thorik shrugged his shoulders and felt the tight rope bite into his skin.

Holger looked at the boy for a moment, aside from his small stature and wiry frame there was not so much to laugh about, his hair gave him an innocent but elfish look matched by his sharp eyes and he had made it this far on his own merit, "How old are you?" he asked.

"Twelve winters..." Thorik mumbled.

"What training have you had then that makes you worthy to join the Jomsvikings?"

"None... but..."

"...And you know to gain entry you have to fight a man, more often than not they are seasoned warriors," Holger continued.

"Nei. Ja, I mean, three more winters and I'd be stronger than now..." the boy muttered.

"Mayhap you thought these men would train you, turn you into a man? Why not go a Viking then? Surely you have sea legs?" Holger smirked at his own joke but felt appalled that his men had been so rough handed with the boy. He was just a foolish young child not yet ready for the world of men, and not too far removed from the fantasies of children, he thought of his own son and how angry he would have been if he discovered another had beaten him; he did not think this boy's father would care much.

"Tis' not wrong to wish for more of a life," Thorik spat the words and instantly regretted the venom he shot at the man when his face grew tight with anger.

Standing, Holger walked over to him looming above his face, "Boys like you have two choices. One; you accept your fate and hope to live well enough. Two; you become a trickster, filled with cunning and guile, a thief, a spinner of tales, at best mayhap a trader... the sharpness of your tongue lets me think the latter. What adventures would the Gods afford one with such limited abilities?" Holger's dark stare bore down on Thorik, threatening to crush him.

"I..." he swallowed, "I got this far..."

"Humph," Holger strode back to the meagre fire throwing a handful of driftwood upon it, "So even you have no idea what your future holds? All men must know this, all men must have a plan, for a man is nothing without a destiny." However, even as he spoke Holger heard Jarl Brynjar's voice and not his own. Turning back to the boy, Holger pulled a dagger from his boot, grabbing Thorik's wrists he cut through the rope binding his hands and then his feet, releasing him from his bonds he grabbed his shoulder and dragged him to the fire.

"Sit," Holger commanded.

Thorik stared at the large man with wide eyes; he stood as tall as the men he had failed, his shoulders broad and even beneath his tunic and cloak, the strength of his body showed. Holger was dangerous, Thorik thought; biting his lip he looked at the man's face and was surprised to see not a look of anger but weariness that fixed his features. He was a formidable sight with his long fiery hair, his eyes were a rich blue to match his cloak and his nose though sharp had at one point been broken, his square chin was covered with a thick beard. Thorik guessed he was a seasoned guard of his Jarl and his face bore the lines of an older man.

"Boy do you know aught of the Jomsviking way? Other than fighting? Tis' a harsh life, some men would think it harder than most, you would most likely die trying to enter their order," Holger lowered to the fire resting his elbow on one knee and prodded the flames with a dry stick.

"I know they are respected and feared," Thorik spoke with a dry throat, "I only want to be like them."

"Hmm, many do, many young like you and other men too but not all who seek the confines of their keep are honourable," he said seriously.

"Did you hurt my father?" Thorik asked suddenly.

"No." Holger looked directly into the boy's pale eyes.

"But he told you…"

"Pain is not always necessary to retrieve what you need," the older man explained.

"You threatened him?" Thorik stated.

"Ja."

"But he is well?" He pressed worriedly.

Holger lifted the stick and snapped it in his large hand tossing the remnants aside he sighed, "He is."

"The other men didn't threaten him," Thorik knew that wasn't strictly true.

"Well then, they must be honourable." A muscle began to twitch in Holger's jaw, Thorik saw it and swallowed nervously, realising his tongue had gotten him into deep water once more.

"Please let me go, I'll only take the grey, I'll return to my father," Thorik begged to little avail.

"Nei," Holger refused.

"Please..." began the boy, but Holger interrupted him, "If I let you go the last place you would go is to your father. Do you think me mad or foolish? A boy like you would set off for my quarry and warn them!" Holger laughed releasing one bronze brooch on his cloak and pulling it from his shoulders.

Seeing that he had little chance of release Thorik realised that escape was next to impossible and he stared again at Grani, whose large black eyes glittered hypnotically in the light from the fire and the torches the men had lit. A thought occurred to Thorik, "How come you know so much of the Jomsvikings?" he asked.

"I knew one," Holger thought painfully of his brother, he had enlisted upon the death of their father, the Jarl had chosen Holger to join the ranks of his men but refused entry to Holger's brother.

The man had little choice, with no land or coin to support him, at that time the whispers of the Jomsvikings were strong and though they numbered many they were yet to be unified, under one King.

The stirrings over the land were that the Danish King had plans and this bothered Holger, why Jarl Brynjar had started to forego his duties, as Jarl of the region was dumbfounding. Holger suspected that Brynjar not only lusted after the legend of the ring but failing he ever found it and harnessed it he would ally himself with a more powerful force than Greycloak. The petty Kingdoms were constantly at war with one another it had been so since Holger could remember.

"He is dead?" Thorik asked quietly.

"Ja, a long time dead. You should know many things about these men, Thorik."

Grani snorted urging Thorik on. "What?"

Holger looked at the boy and decided that the truth was all that would suffice; he was foolish to think that a strong spirit was all he required. The boy's ragged appearance raised a protective feeling in him that no doubt came from thoughts of his own son, and settling in a cross legged posture, Holger released the sword strapped to his back and rested it over his legs.

"Well," he began, "First you must be of age and then you must face the Holmgang. You know what this is?" The boy shook his head. "It is a fight, a battle between two men, he who wishes to enter and a man already a Jomsviking. Nothing will do but death for either party unless the leader halts the fight if both men are worthy."

The Jarl's guard smiled, Thorik saw that though the teeth were bright a few were chipped on one side and he wondered if a fist had caught him.

"There is a code all Jomsviking live by, tis' strict and violation comes with a price, break the code and punishment is expulsion... depending on the crime." Holger smiled again at the frightened look in the boy's eye, "Honour and oaths are all important. You are bound to your brother and sworn to protect them and defend them in battle. You will never speak ill of your fellow man or quarrel however... they are men after all and as such cannot be expected to turn away if provoked. So young Thorik, say a man, a Jomsviking brother, casts ill words on your character or accuses you of a crime, what then? Even the fastest of men will feud over something at one time. Should you feud with another, your commander will decide whether you fight out a resolution, for it is forbidden to raise your own hand in blood fury."

Thorik considered this for a moment and thought of the two men Ari and Dag, had they sworn such allegiance to each other? How was it they travelled alone, and what was their mission. He wished he knew all of these things and much more.

"So, Thorik, think you want still to be a Jomsviking?" Holger asked amused.

"Ja!" Thorik spluttered, awakening from his own thoughts. He glanced at Grani, whose eyes were now fixed on the man.

"Hah! Well more you should hear. Now you are a warrior?" Holger wagged a finger at the boy and winked, he was enjoying talking to Thorik much in the way he would his own son. "A Jomsviking may never show fear in the face of his enemy, whether he be of equal strength or weaker, but should he be outnumbered, only then is it acceptable to retreat and live to fight another day. You might become a rich man, if you live long enough Thorik, for the spoils of war are shared between all men. Gold, horses, land, but would you enjoy them knowing where your wealth came from?" A shadowy memory crept into the forefront of Holger's mind of how gravely his brother had changed from his travels. It was a sad thought.

"Know this lastly..." Holger's voice became grave and pained, "No wife may you ever take as your own, no woman or child may you protect within the safety of the keep, so long as you are Jomsviking. Should you wish to travel alone only a few days you will be given and no more, so best you use it to make your farewells from the life you knew."

The boy shuddered; it was a sad ending to the tale, and he felt the heavy weight of something more than the man spoke of filling the space between them, "Is it forever?" he asked.

"Is what forever?" Holger looked at Thorik, puzzled by his question.

"When you give them your word? You can never leave?" the boy quizzed.

"Ah." Again another memory surfaced forcing Holger to stifle a grimace threatening to wash over his face, "Tis' not known to any other than the Jomsvikings. Though let me tell you this…such men do not often live long enough Thorik to regret their chosen path. These men are hired to fight and as such life is forfeit… nothing is forever."

"I think mayhap, I prefer to have the choice," Thorik spoke holding the gaze of the grey stallion locked in its black pools of obsidian.

"Choice…" Holger grumbled, rubbing his hand across his chin as he considered it. The boy made a real and unsettling point, there was a choice to be made and Holger was fast approaching the impasse of his own life. His wife and children were living deep in the confines of Srovberget and their movements would be noticed at once, as Jarl Brynjar trusted no one. Even being his closest guard Holger knew the deep jealousy Brynjar felt towards him, since Holger, a lesser man of impoverished birth had sired children while Brynjar's women lay barren. It irked Holger that the Jarl was unlike many men he had met, who valued the work and sweat it had taken to have come as far as he had. There were many who valued their progression and the taking of a wife and creation of a line were all that truly mattered, it made him wonder if children would only become another possession of the man devoid of love.

For what use did Brynjar have for love? Holger felt himself grow desperately unhappy with his situation; he knew what he wanted to do but not how to achieve it without causing possible harm to his family. Then there was Solvieg to consider, he had silently sworn to aid her in any way he could, short of helping her and Inge conspire he had done little to keep her from the harsh uncompromising ways of her husband. Solvieg was a kind soul who had been dealt a weak hand, she was the sole child of deceased parents and her own surviving kin lived far from Srovberget. Holger watched her often and wondered how alone and miserable she really felt. Many women married to a man such as Brynjar at least had the comfort of children to raise.

Holger set his mind to the facts; he had sent a man to the Jarl apprising him of the situation, he had two men with him, who though already proved little better than tavern hounds were still men with iron and capable of putting up a fight if need be. He had caught the boy and the horses; the advantage was his except for the location of the men. He had to change the course of the game to his advantage once more, but first he had a decision to make, what would his next move be?

"Thorik… what does your heart tell you to do?" Holger asked the boy with a blank expression.

Thorik swallowed and could not tell what the right answer was to give the man. Eventually he spoke giving him all he could trust himself to be true, "It tells me the men need their horses, it tells me they are more than Jomsvikings." Then sharing a look with the horse he said, "It tells me to be honourable to myself."

The man looked at the boy astounded, he had often heard that children could say what men feared to, that they possessed the innocence to know what was right and wrong and question all.

But his own children had never been placed in a position to answer such a question and so the boy's honesty shook him.

"Come with me!" Holger stood and grabbed a line of rope lying in the sand, without a word he pulled Thorik to his feet and quickly bound his wrists, then he shouted to his men before fastening his cloak about his shoulders and the leather strap of his sword belt. The two men raced to the scene with relieved faces to see there was nothing amiss.

"Change of plan," Holger strode over to Grani and released his reins from the post wedged in the dirt, "the boy has spoken, I have the location of the men. I'll continue ahead while you return to Srovberget, by way of Gulafjord and make contact with the Jarl."

"Gulafjord? That lies in the opposite direction of Srovberget. It will add day's travel… should we not…" one man queried.

"Nei! We must ensure there are no others seeking to join them, keep your eyes open, suspect any who look out of place," Holger barked. "Once Brynjar receives word we have located the men he will understand my thinking, he has come close to capturing the woman before, a few days will make no difference, we must be careful. Should you discover more of their kind then you split and one remains in the fjord at the Thing and the other to the Jarl. Tell him I will return with the woman or the heads of the men. Either way I will return."

"He won't like this, Holger, I am sure of it, and you are one man! We've seen such men as these," the younger man spoke.

"My strength and fighting are in question, Agar?" Holger raised a heavy eyebrow before lifting Thorik onto Grani's back.

"Nei... nei," the man raised his hands.

"At least take one of us. And why take the boy?" the other man offered.

"Bait... and he knows the way," with a swift jump, Holger sat upon Grani's back and hauled Thorik from his feet to join him, "Do as I say!"

The men nodded and took the reins of the remaining horses, walking them over to their own steeds, the men each took a torch and turned to make their way back to Gulafjord.

Thorik gulped as Holger reached forward and handed him a small blade, "Cut your bonds, I trust you will tell me where they are, I mean to aid them, do not think to lie to me, Thorik. I am a man of my word and my family's lives depend on your honesty and mine. Now, where are they?"

Rubbing his raw wrists, Thorik saw the flash of steel but felt his heart still as he recognised it as his own, the man had given him back his sword. "They are in Giffni," he said.

Holger brought Grani to a slow walk and they made their way along the beach in the moonlight, "Where is Giffni?" he asked.

"Tis' along the coast, only fishermen and the settlements near there use that name anymore, there are many caves and cliffs it can be treacherous or a safe harbour if you know it well."

"Then lead the way, Thorik," Holger said.

"Do you really think more Jomsvikings are following them?"

"Nei, I said that to buy us time."

The boy twisted to look at the man sitting astride Grani behind him, his gaze was fixed ahead. Gingerly Thorik raised a finger to point and the horse broke into a gallop.

Chapter 9

ᛞᚾᚫᚳᛏᛗᚱ ᚻᛁᛗ

Liv strained to hear the muffled voices, her eyes opened to a dimly lit cavern, around a fire, three shapes sat. Lifting her head wearily she groaned as her stiff muscles cried out in agony. Succumbing to the need for rest she slumped back down on the fur bedding beneath her. One of the figures quickly appeared by her side soothing her brow with a damp rag and muttering soft words.

"Rest... you must rest," Gytha whispered.

Feeling nothing but confusion Liv struggled and rolled onto her side, propping her body up with an elbow, "Who are you? Where..."

"Liv, sleep, you are in Giffni," Ari's voice came from behind the woman and Liv saw the man Dag hovering in the background.

Gytha shooed the men back to the fire with her hand, turning back to her ward. "You have been ill, the blow to your head was worse than it seemed but you are mending, we travelled here by boat. I'm Gytha, Dag brought me to heal you, wait I'll fetch some water."

Liv watched the young woman return to the men nodding at Ari, who had a worried look on his face. Seeing the young woman relate something to him, his eyes rested upon Liv allowing a faint smile to cross over his mouth. Dag darted his stare between the

111

two eventually nodding to Liv and slapping Ari on the shoulder. At length the two men returned to their conversation with Ari glancing over his shoulder as Gytha returned to Liv's side.

"He feared for you. He has been by your side, sometimes he spoke as I told him it helps to soothe those in a deep sleep." Gytha smiled, "Do you remember aught?"

"I wish I did," Liv smiled sadly, she wished to know what Ari had said while she was unconscious, "How long have we been here?"

"In Giffni, two nights, you much improved with the heat of the caves, truly it is a remarkable place," Gytha marvelled.

"Ja… a sanctuary, the caves are a warren, we will be safe here awhile," Liv nodded.

"As Ari said," Gytha lifted the skin to Liv's lips and nodded with a set stare as Liv thanked her, "You are a guardian?"

Sucking in a breath, Liv narrowed her eyes and furrowing her brow pushed the skin back to the woman, "I know not what you speak of…"

"You are branded," she stated.

"Many former slaves are."

"Not with Yggrasil!" Gytha whispered harshly, "Your name too, it means protector of life."

"We all bear the namesakes of the Gods," Liv dismissed her with a wave of her hand.

"The markings on your body," Gytha scrutinized Liv, as she saw the woman realise for the first time her garments had been removed and she lay in a tunic covered with blankets.

"Who removed my clothing?" she hissed.

"I did... you were in dire need of a bath... I saw the markings. Who made them?" Gytha persisted.

"I don't know you..." Liv began.

"You can trust me Liv, I'm a healer, I came with these men to ensure you survived. You've been through much and your body was near to giving up. Please allow yourself to trust me." The young woman smiled warmly at Liv who felt too tired to argue.

"Tis' a long story."

"We have time, the horses won't be here for a few days, time for all to talk I think," Gytha cast a look over her shoulder to the men. She had not had much of a chance to speak with Dag, when the moments had arisen, he was his usual humour laden self even managing to raise a laugh now and again from Ari. "And... I also had a vision of you when we were at the farmstead... who is the boy?"

Closing her eyes Liv felt a pang of hurt stab at her heart, "That I cannot tell you, Gytha."

"Then say what you can," Gytha folded her legs beneath her and edged a little closer to Liv. The cave was warm and her patient appeared comfortable on the makeshift bed of furs.

"Many a year now I've had to run. The markings were made by the Volur women, under the instruction of the Yggdrasil Kynslod; they are spells. The branding; a mark from the Kynslod given to me by my own guardian, but he is gone now." Liv paused, "has Ari seen?"

"Yes, he helped me remove your clothing," Gytha explained softly.

"Ah..." Liv turned her head away and felt ashamed. He must have wondered who administered the tattoos and she knew he had an understanding of the runes. Her fingers trailed the line of small fine markings etched into her skin on her right arm, there were bands of runes on her wrists and down her right leg and on her back a script ran down her spine. The night the marks had been made she suffered much pain, the ink was tainted with viper venom and she had slipped into a delirium that caused terrible visions. Her guardian had helped to hold her down as she wept, the Volur tapping the needle over and over into her flesh, the women whispered their incantations evoking the will of the Gods.

"He was not repelled. There is not much that would keep him from you," Gytha ventured, realising with a wide smile that this was just what the woman needed to hear.

"Markings are one thing..." She sighed, "his ire towards me is gone?"

"Ja, was more hurt than anger. His life continued too while you were parted... you should talk... mayhap, the chance will arrive in the morn?"

Liv sighed and stretched her body beneath the blankets. "Gytha, thank you for your work, you are gifted. You mentioned visions...are you Volur?"

"Nei," Gytha said.

"What did your vision tell you?"

"I'll speak of it when you are ready to speak of the boy. Liv, Ari thinks him dead why do you not set that to right?"

"Trust, Gytha... I did not know he was Ari when we met. There wasn't an opportunity to tell him anything. I think perhaps you all know one another better than I do right now," she grimaced.

"Not Ari!" Gytha chuckled knowingly, "In the morn I will gather herbs and roots for my remedies... mayhap Dag will help... he looks the foraging sort!"

Liv looked at the woman and burst into laughter that filled the cave, the two men looked up from the fire, then to one another not understanding the joke. Gytha was a fair face to look upon, Liv thought and she could see why Dag would have taken an interest. It was not such a great leap to assume the woman felt the same, she had long, thick, flaxen hair, large round eyes of the brightest blue and a short sharp nose.

Suddenly the pounding in Liv's head returned and nausea roiled in her stomach, groaning, she raised a hand to her damp brow.

"Where are you from?" Gytha asked, looking over Liv's features.

"My mother was a thrall, who died at my birth. My father came from a nomad tribe but I do not know him," struggling to speak the words Liv's voice trembled, licking her lips, she closed her eyes.

"You sought him out?" Gytha saw the waxen expression on the woman's face and guessed she was not completely out of the woods. She probed her to keep talking while she dropped a few herbs from her pouch into a small cup. From the water skin, she mixed the contents and lifted the vessel to Liv's lips watching her drink without question.

"Nei..." It was a lie, but Liv would not reveal too much of herself to the perceptive woman, no matter how well at ease she was starting to become in her company. She knew her features often raised an eyebrow, she was fair of skin but dark of hair, her eyes were almond shaped and a curious mixture of colours they were neither blue nor green or brown. She was unlike the northern women, but shared many of their qualities, strong and brave and if pushed to fight would give her best, especially with what she had to protect. Given the chance she might have made a good wife with a prosperous home and borne strong sons but that would never be now.

"Your mother, you say she was thrall?" Gytha continued. "Ja but not by Ari's Chieftain. She still wore her collar when she died, but spoke a few words that were later told to me. She had a foreign tongue… she spoke of my father but never gave a name, only a place." Liv snapped her mouth shut and gritted her teeth, she felt stupid and cursed herself thinking only that the weariness in her body and mind had caused her to say too much. A slow burning had begun in her stomach, it's quelling ceased, and the ache in her head began to die a little. Her eyes began to droop and her breathing slowed to a steady peaceful slumber.

Gytha raised a hand and stroked the woman's shoulder, "My parents died some time ago and I was left in the care of my brother, a stupid, foolish man, I hope never to return and in truth I cannot, for he would see fit to beat me. Until you three I was close to despair, our lives take strange paths sometimes." With that Gytha stood and rejoined the men momentarily before taking her place on her own set of furs, a few feet from where Liv lay. Liv dragged her eyes open watching as Dag let his gaze linger a while on the healer before turning back to Ari.

Considering Gytha's words, Liv closed her eyes and let her ears drink in the soft noises of the cavern, the men spoke at length, but she could not hear definition in the sounds and gave up straining her ears. It had been a trying time, and against her better judgement she would let the safety provided by the group rest her soul for a few hours at least. The darkness that had come over her in her unconscious state had seemed like mere seconds fractured only by vague memories of being on horseback and rocking motion of being aboard a small vessel. Gingerly Liv stroked her jaw and ear, she wanted to know how bruised and cut her face was but did not know if the healer would carry a polished metal disk so often used to observe one's features.

Hours later, though feeling like mere moments Liv awoke to see the room slightly dimmed from the light provided by the fire and small oil lamps, the men appeared to have sought the comfort and rest of their own furs, for a moment Liv imagined herself alone. The muscles in her chest loosened a little and she pushed herself onto her elbows, looking around the floor space she saw three separate forms apparently sleeping, silently Liv stood with a slight wobble. A feeling of light-headedness lingered before she tentatively took a few steps. Her hair fell forward as she bent slightly, resting her hands on her knees before taking a deep breath and stepping closer to the waning fire. The thin tunic she wore and her skin smelled of lavender and something that reminded her of a spice called frankincense she had once encountered in a market. It felt good to be clean and free from her ragged clothes, though she wondered where they might be.

Stooping by the fire she sat and pulled her knees up to her chest. Stretching her hands, she rotated her wrists and flexed her fingers above the heat of the embers, not far from her position she spied her clothes drying on a large rock and a smile crossed her lips as she thought of a distant memory from a time when she and Ari had come to Giffni in the past.

"Liv?" Ari approached and stood a moment, waiting for the woman to acknowledge him; blinking wearily he saw her smile and took a seat. "Gytha says you are healing?"

"Ja… though I do not feel myself," rubbing her temples, she feared the throbbing would make an unwanted return, "Thank you Ari."

"For what?" Ari glanced at her with a puzzled expression.

"Bringing me here, for Gytha's help, you didn't have to."

"Nei…" He sighed, dragging a hand across his forehead, "I had to."

Liv looked at Ari and felt a terrible pang of sadness strike her heart, he seemed so unlike the man she had once known, she fought the urge to hold him and instead sat feeling the pull to him stretch to snapping, his eyes were full of a history she knew nothing about.

"Ari I don't know what to say or do," she said sadly.

"Nor I," he replied. They sat in silence, looking at one another. Ari observed the woman and started to recognise the traits he had once known; she was quiet and oblivious to her beauty even now covered in scratches and bruises. Liv sat chewing on her lip, which he knew was in frustration and nervousness, as a younger woman she had done this when deep in thought or when she worried over something. Her brow slightly creased and he guessed she was wrestling with the same questions he had. He felt terribly guilty about his behaviour when finding her but what could he have done? He had sought to know whom she had become without her knowing it was he who had found her.

Ari had needed to see the raw honesty of her life now, not clouded by what they had once shared together. He had believed her heartless and selfish, he had blamed her for the choices he had made because of a broken heart and wounded pride, but now he knew differently and wondered why they had been lied to. It occurred to him that she was still being lied to but he could not reveal that mistruth until she was stronger.

"I would have come for you, always," he whispered sadly staring at his hands on his lap. They were hands that had done terrible things in the past six years, hands that had learned how to fight better and kill quicker, hands that had earned him the name of Gorm Swift-Axe and helped him to vent his fury. How could she understand?

"You must know I thought you dead, I don't know why he lied to me, but Ari it was worse than that…"

"How?" his eyes shot upwards to meet her opal gaze.

"The reason I can't return with you to our home," she sighed.

"There is none?"

"Ja, there is… Harvardr told me you died in the fire they all believed I started, I saw the flames, I heard the screaming, I swear it wasn't me," she spoke in low urgent tones.

Ari glared, a rage swelled in his chest, but subsided as quickly as it came, and she looked at him fear written over her delicate features, "No Liv, do not think my anger is for you." Crouching he laid a hand on her shoulder and felt an old feeling tingle in his fingertips, "Do you speak of the fire in the woman's workhouse?"

"Ja," she looked away,

"Nei Liv, such lies you have been told and I don't know why. I am here before you now, how could you think any would blame you for my death?"

"I heard the screaming, Harvardr said he heard the women say it was me that started the blaze and it had killed you in the process. They said I was evil and unworthy, that I had witnessed you with another and taken terrible vengeance," she relived every word, the horror marking her features.

Shocked Ari removed his hand and rubbed his jaw with the back of his hand, new whiskers had sprouted since last he shaved causing him to scratch his chin in thought. This was all new and strange information; he could not understand Harvardr's motives. The old man had always been a friend to his people, he could only surmise that he had needed Liv and guessed she would not be easily moved without coercion. The markings on her body and the branding were signs of seidr magic, something Liv had never shown an interest in that he knew of.

"There is much to talk about, but you must know that although you heard screaming there was not one life lost in the fire, trust me we were all confused when we discovered you gone. It was thought you had been lost in the fire until we discovered no bodies and I found the necklace on your pallet. It was then I realised you had run..."

"But not from you Ari," she whispered.

"No," he nodded.

"I am sorry you thought it so," Liv stared hard at his face before tearing her eyes away and closing them to stop the stinging. There was a part of her that felt anger he could so easily believe she would run, but what else could he have thought? What lies had been offered to him she wondered. Looking back at him she began to recognise the man before her, the same pale eyes of the coldest winter sky, his strong, straight nose and square jaw. His hair was still the colour of the fine leather saddles of their Chieftain's horses and his skin bore the hue from many days in the sun. She saw faint lines around his eyes and mouth and felt warm to know that he did at least smile now and again though she had yet to see it herself. However, there was a face behind the one before her where sadness and darkness lingered and she knew she too wore the same expression from time to time.

"I would see you smile?" she asked lifting a hand to cup his face. Taking her hand Ari kissed the palm, letting a small smile tug at his mouth, "And I you."

Liv knelt forward and kissed Ari before wrapping her arms around him in a tight embrace. Initially Ari's back stiffened in surprise, but feeling the familiar embrace of the woman he had loved so deeply, his resolve melted and hungrily he held onto her form. For some minutes they sat entwined in one another's arms, until regretfully Ari broke away, lifting Liv's chin with a finger, returning her soft kiss he rested his forehead against hers and breathed in the sweet floral scent of Gytha's soap on her skin. He was eternally grateful to the healer as more than once it occurred to him that Liv could have succumbed to her injuries, he might well have lost her once more after only finding her, which would have been too great a pain to bear.

"How long do we have here?" She whispered.

"A day or two more, mayhap a third, long enough to hear both our tales," he said quietly.

"So much to say… there are things you must know Ari… more you must know," she began raising her head.

"Ja… there is much I must tell you but first we have this moment just to sit by the fire the way we once did," Ari pulled an arm around Liv's shoulders and drew her into his chest and leaning back against the rolled blankets he used as a rest he and Liv lay for some time. They spoke of Giffni and the time they had once spent there each feeling the pull of one another and letting it pass. Each feeling it was too soon and hesitant to try a return to what they once had, slowly a dreamless sleep washed over them both.

Chapter 10

ᛞᚾᚨᚲᛏᛖᚱ ᛏᛖᛁ

Dag listened to the voices until they became softer and then altogether quiet. He was on watch and allowed Ari to rest with Liv in his arms for many hours. His friend was in need of proper sleep and it appeared his soul was at peace for now. As the time silently passed he kept his mind alert by practising moves he would later use when next he and Ari played Tafl.

Of late the men had had little opportunity to play for any length of time and it was a game that required patience and tact. Dag carried the latticed board Ari had made for him in thanks, and over time he had exchanged the wooden pieces for soapstone and carved intricate details on each marker. The board was a treasured gift that replaced the one Dag's father had given him as a young boy, that board had been destroyed by another man whom Dag had crossed paths with and lost a fist fight to. It had surprised him that Ari would do such a thing since the gesture was greater than he required, he would have happily accepted the friendship in kind and in the years that followed they had formed a strong kinship.

To join the Jomsvikings was no easy task, entry required a battle with an established soldier. Young men often died trying to become one, and the older men who perhaps fled their previous lives or were seeking to hide fared no better. The first months were tougher yet, training was all that filled their days, small groups formed within the ranks, but trust was an earned privilege that Dag found hard to find. He had met Ari when the young man was sprawled on the ground after being set upon by a group of men; one of them, Hasti was no more than a drunkard and a lout. Hasti had accused Ari of theft and dishonour but Dag knew the man to be a liar and that most likely whatever he had said was taken from him had been lost in an ill-advised dice game sodden with ale and wine. It was against the code to attack one of your own but like everything in life it was subject to interpretation.

Dag had weighed into the fray and pulled the battered Ari to his feet, the pair threw blows to the other men, slamming their fists into faces and ribs, using their feet to kick knees from their joints and winding the guts of the men. They walked away with pride and the blood of the attackers on their knuckles, the rest of the men nodded in approval, the older Jomsvikings would accept no less a reaction to an attempt on their names. Men had to fight and these new recruits had proved a measure of their worth.

Each player had a number of pieces on the Tafl board, one player however had fewer but possessed the king who started in the centre of the board. The objective of the king was to escape to a corner of the board while the opposite player tried to capture him. Some men used dice to increase the risk and potential of winning coin, other men usually the older men used their wits and threw riddles at one another. That was how Dag's father and uncle had played when he was a boy and to Dag it was a method he would show Ari when they were old with wives and children. Then there would be time to enjoy the game better or so Dag thought. He had realised very quickly the life of a Jomsviking was short and swift but he had saved enough coin to pay his way out of the ranks and purchase land. Dag was not sure where this dwelling of the future might be but he had come to appreciate Ari's tales of his homeland and he had not come across any other place that suited him more.

Gytha stirred on her furs and stretched, opening her eyes she looked around the cave and then to Dag, smiling she raised a finger to her lips and pointed to the two figures together by the fire. Nodding his head, Dag signalled for her to sleep for another hour or two, Gytha smiled in response letting her eyes take in the dark hair and gaze of the warrior she had grown to trust. Turning on her side, she breathed in the earthy scent of the fur feeling at ease.

Returning to the game play in his mind, Dag absently let his eyes drift over the sleeping body of the woman, he knew he had let her under his skin but not quite as much as Liv had done with Ari. All the same it was a new experience, he was not entirely sure he enjoyed his appreciation of her for more than her form, he was used to having women appreciate him and revelled in it, but required nothing further and when he thought of a wife it was for the line he might create rather than love. But this young woman had shown him talents he did not possess himself and an understanding of the world, her world, that did not demonstrate treachery or scheming. True, she wanted to be free of her brother but she had hurt no one in the process nor abused trust and this was quite different from the women he was used to dealing with for they all had something to gain, and this woman had much to lose.

By the fire Dag heard Ari stir, the man rose and stretched before turning to see if his friend was awake, with a quick look the two men stood and made their way to the mouth of the cave and silently they walked along a series of tunnels before reaching the air of the crisp morning.

"How you never became lost is a mystery," Dag cocked his head back the way they had come.

"It took some time, but Liv marked the way with chalk, after a while we knew it without even a torch or lamp. Though I swear she can see in the dark like a cat," Ari laughed.

"Her eyes say as much!" Dag grinned, "You spoke?"

"Ja and nei, we will speak today, I need to think it through before I start," Ari looked at his friend whose tanned complexion did not hide the rings of tiredness beneath his eyes, "Go sleep, I will take watch."

Dag nodded, "Ja, an hour or two is all I need and then I will take Gytha to the wood for herbs and roots, and perhaps to explore the caves or a swim in the hot springs?"

Ari chuckled to himself and muttered a curse under his breath before slapping Dag on his shoulder, "You know well your herbs and roots?"

"Ha! A clever man knows a little about a lot!" flashing his wide grin he turned and headed back to his furs, he knew Ari would stand watch outside for as long as Dag needed to rest, but in truth he was eager to embark on his day with Gytha and forcing himself to rest, he slowed his breathing and willed each muscle to ease.

When at last he awoke it was to a wide-eyed Gytha shaking his shoulder roughly, swatting her hand away, he wiped the sleep from his eyes and looked about the room, laying a hand to his side, he felt his axe, "What?" he grunted.

"Gods above Dag! Tis' Liv, she will not awaken!" the woman cried. Dag came to his senses all at once staring with confusion at the healer, "What?"

"I cannot rouse her, her skin is almost cold to the touch, where is Ari?" the woman spoke quickly.

"Wait, I'll fetch him," Dag stood and disappeared into the tunnel. Gytha quickly scrambled back to the fire where Liv lay slumped against one of the men's packs, her face wore the mask of the dead but her breathing betrayed signs of life yet. Dark circles had formed beneath her eyes, her skin grey, and the pulse in her neck slow and weak.

The men returned to the chamber and under Gytha's instruction, Ari lifted Liv back to her furs before turning to the young woman, "What has happened? We spoke last night, she seemed well," his eyes bore no accusations, but were full of questions. Swallowing against the dryness forming in her throat Gytha grasped her leather bag and emptied its contents searching furiously through the pile of herbs, roots and small linen bouquets of medicine.

"I think... Mayhap..." still scrabbling through her belongings she felt Ari grasp her wrist, jerking her gaze to his she said, "The daudr svefn!"

"Nei!" Ari dropped Gytha's hand, swinging his gaze from Liv to Dag; he had heard tell of the daudr svefn among his men, but never witnessed it for himself. Many a man had fallen by his sword and axe, many a man he had seen slain in battle, these men died where they lay, breathing their last before his eyes.

"I've tried to waken her but she barely breathes and the pupils of her eyes are almost grey," Gytha's voice trembled. "The death sleep?" Dag breathed, "but how?"

"Injuries we cannot see?" Gytha's whispered, "Ari, I cannot heal her here, I don't have what I need, how far are we from your home?"

"Too far," his voice was cold and flat.

"There is a healer there? Mayhap they have what Gytha needs?" Dag offered.

"Too far," Ari dropped to his knees beside Liv, she did truly look like she was dying and he knew who could possibly help but he had no trust for this person now and knew Liv might resent him terribly for not having told her sooner. A firm hand grasped his shoulder, pulling his gaze away; Dag glared down at him, "Odin's eye man! Wake up! What choice is there? Are we hours or days away?"

Shaking his head Ari stood and faced his friend, "A day but that's after we get across the causeway, it's at least half a day from here. There may be one who can do something, but I cannot be certain…"

"Is there time?" Dag questioned Gytha, still kneeling at his feet surrounded by her supplies. "It is the daudr svefn," she explained, "it can take her at any time or… she might lay like this for days or more. She is weak Dag."

Dag turned away roughly pulling a hand through his hair, Ari sighed heavily throwing his axe to the ground. The rock that bore Liv's dress and her belongings sat undisturbed, though tattered and torn, he wished she would rise from the bed and don her clothing ready for the new day. Gytha trembled, her hands shaking she began to gather her supplies tossing them back into her leather bag; her fingers strayed over the items searching for something to help.

A small root poked from beneath a bundle of linen squares, she had not remembered gathering it but recognised it all the same. Gasping she lifted it carefully bringing it to her eyeline, "Ari…" She whispered, "Belladonna!"

"Madness!" Dag barked. "It will kill her!"

"Nei Dag, it will keep her heart beating long enough for us to reach Smols, the root is the most potent part of it and I can brew an elixir." She turned to Ari as she stood, "It is not without risk, I cannot promise…"

"Do it!" lifting his axe from the ground, he tucked it into the loose leather belt about his blue tunic and turned to face Dag, "let's gather our things." Nodding Dag swiftly moved to roll up and tie the bedding furs, Ari filled the small kettle on the smouldering fire with water from a skin for Gytha, who had set about grinding her root in a small soapstone pestle, from her bag.

Silently the men cleared the chamber, and carried their belongings to the mouth of the tunnel. As Ari threw down his pack, Dag grabbed his forearm, "By the Gods Ari..."

"I know," Ari nodded and slapped his friend's shoulder, but before he could rejoin Gytha and ask about her progress, a sound from the tunnels strayed to his ear, Dag too stiffened and caught the scent of something on the cool breeze filtering from the morning air outside.

Ari reached the cave mouth, and exiting the tunnels he saw a mist had fallen over Giffni. A light fog gathered at their feet and the damp smell of rain hung heavy in the air, he had expected their visitors to have concealed themselves in the wood watching and waiting, when no attack had presented itself in the warren of the tunnels. The scent that had floated on the air betrayed the presence of horses, but age and experience told Ari to be wary in thinking the boy had arrived so swiftly. The sight that greeted him pleased him initially, hope sprung in his chest until he realised that though Thorik had indeed arrived, he was not alone.

Dag appeared behind Ari almost walking into him as he had stopped abruptly, when he saw what his friend was looking at, anger flared causing him to bare his teeth at the man standing beside the fisherman's boy.

"The Jarl's man?" Dag growled, moving around the solid pillar of Ari to stand at his side, this was not what they needed now, his mind raged. "Ja… Holger, is it?" Ari barked at the man.

Thorik stood darting a scared expression between the man and the two Jomsvikings, like predatory animals they started to separate and move around them in opposite directions, each gripped an axe in their sword arms, their frames poised to attack, still dressed in their dark blue tunics, leather trousers and boots they looked fearsome, even without their leather armour. Feeling scared Thorik shrank back from the men he had so admired, sensing they might set upon Holger without realising he had helped him.

"Stop!" The boy cried out, Dag looked at Thorik, but Ari stayed focused on Holger. The Jarl's man lowered his own sword to the ground slowly and stood, raising his hands in front of him.

"He is the Jarl's man!" Dag shouted at the boy then, "How many have you brought with you?" he directed his question towards Holger.

"None!" Thorik shouted back, before Holger could open his mouth. Dag shot a wrathful glance at the boy and strode towards him. Shaking Thorik by the scruff of his shirt he glared at the boy. Wide-eyed Thorik feared the man was going to shake his limbs from his body.

"Leave him be!" Holger growled, eyeing the two men he saw their training, their fierceness, but also something else. He and the boy had happened upon them without a chance to alert them, surprising them, however their furrowed brows looked etched with worry. Hearing the man, Dag narrowed his eyes and shot a look at Ari, who now stood mere feet from Holger.

"Explain!" Ari growled, keeping his eyes locked on the man.

"He is the Jarl's man no longer! He wants to help, he brought me here with Grani, he sent the other men back to the Jarl," Thorik raced through his words, stopping for a breath, he saw Dag kick Holger's sword away, standing squarely before them with his arms folded across his chest. Ari had rested the axe in the crook of his folded arms and stood looking intently at Holger.

"We have met," Ari stated.

"Ja, briefly, when my Jarl hired your captain. You were given the task to find the woman and the boy." Holger replied.

Ari nodded, but Dag grunted, "So he speaks? I thought Thorik spoke for you!" throwing a dirty look at the young boy Dag saw the heat of shame flush in his cheeks and ground his teeth in annoyance, "How did you come by our Thorik?"

"Wasn't easy, the boy near outran us, we found him on the beach," Holger replied carefully.

"It was only when I let the horses rest!" Thorik cried, feeling suddenly like he must defend himself.

"Why should we believe what he says?" Ari jerked his chin in the direction of the boy, "You now decide to leave Brynjar's side? Why?"

"Many reasons... but for the one that concerns you I can no longer follow a madman who seeks out legends and hunts down women and children," Holger said.

"Honourable," Dag hissed, his voice heavy with sarcasm.

"Tis' the truth. I have a wife and children; they deserve better than Jarl Brynjar. I made haste with the boy here and ask of your services."

"Hah!" Dag grinned at Ari, "He wants us to work for him!" shaking his head, he fired an angry look to Holger, "You don't have the coin!"

Holger shrugged, lowering his hands, he stood looking at Thorik, "My family are all to me and if you kill me they will suffer in Srovberget, release me and I will employ others of your kind to free them from the Jarl's grip, if I fail in that, again they will suffer. There is only one chance for a life with them; I must find a way to bring them to me. There can never be a life for us while I work for the Jarl and when he discovers my treachery he will be wrathful," Holger's throat grew tight at his own words. He had hoped the men would listen, but something told him that they were ready to bind rope around his wrists and throw him over the side of the cliff.

"And if we do decide to kill you?" Ari spoke at last, reading the man's thoughts, "It appears you have risked much to come here, but why not return with your men to the Jarl instead of aiding the boy? What proof is there of your change of heart?"

Holger drew a breath and studied the face of the warrior in front of him; he seemed less angry and dark than when they first met. He had made an impression on Holger then, he was proud and strong, this man was still young but his vocation had taught him much and Ari was right of course, what proof did Holger have other than his word?

"The boy brought me to my senses," he said, "I had to help him… to find you and warn you of the Jarl's intentions."

"What?" Thorik gasped, pride washed over him for a moment before the dark looks of the men continued against one another.

"Intentions of the Jarl?" Ari spoke through gritted teeth, "His intentions were clear when he employed us."

"Nei… he is more determined than ever, you think he will not follow you? That he does not have his ways to find you? No man can disappear entirely, no woman either." Holger rasped and pulled a heavy hand through his beard. "Look at the lad, he is a waif, but his heart is strong, he reminded me that we are more than what we appear to be," Holger held Ari's gaze, it was unyielding and betrayed no emotion. The other man, Dag looked interested now instead of angry, but this did not necessarily mean anything positive for Holger. "Kill me or do not. Free me or do not. All I care about is my family, I will find a way to help them whether it be breathing in this life or the next."

"You seem eager to die?" Dag said dryly.

"You give up so easily?" Ari asked, nodding in agreement with his friend.

"I am tired. The bitterness and hatred, the lusting after legends of wealth, the warring of the Kingdoms, Brynjar will bring disaster to us all, even now he flaunts his disregard for our King by avoiding the Thing in Gulafjord, he lacks respect and I can find none any longer for him," Holger replied sadly.

"And you leave your family to this man in Srovberget?" Dag asked.

"I took my chance to act now," Holger eyed the man sadly, before turning away to stare at the woods beyond.

Ari took a step back, gathering Thorik by the shoulders, he instructed him to take Grani by the reins and stand closer to the cave entrance and walking to Dag, he questioned him with his eyes. Dag shrugged and grinding his teeth he looked at the Jarl's man, clearing his throat, he lowered his tone, "I cannot say, you?"

"Nei. But either we take him or kill him, he believes the Jarl's men will follow, even if we can trust him who is to say their trail is not already being tracked? I would not say he is a broken man, but there is regret, I believe he loves his family, mayhap we buy his trust."

"Buy it?" Dag raised an eyebrow.

"Ja, we agree to help him, take him to the settlement, then decide what to do. We can't risk staying here any longer."

"And if Brynjar sends an army?" Dag sighed heavily.

"The village would never stand up to that kind of battle, they are farmers and fishermen, traders, the Chieftain rarely orders a raid unless need be. The men can wield an axe as good as any but soldiers they are not," Ari stated.

"Then mayhap we have a use for Holger after all? We must move, let us take him, we can talk on it later, we don't have the time right now," Dag threw a look at the boy, who stood sheepishly stroking the muzzle of the fine grey horse.

"Nei... Liv," Ari kicked the earth and walked back to Holger with Dag, "Come," he said.

Holger glanced warily at the men, but when they turned their backs to him and entered the mouth of the cave, the darker haired one guiding Thorik with him, he felt a little tension ease from his shoulders. The one he recognised as Gorm had lifted his sword from the earth taking it with him, it mattered not, thought Holger, he still had his axe and daggers. The men appeared to be neither intimidated nor overly concerned with him, making him pause, had something happened, he wondered?

The darkness of the tunnel took him by surprise, stumbling over loose rocks on the cave floor Holger felt for the tunnel walls to steady his pace. Ahead he could hear the dark haired Jomsviking whispering to the boy while the other warrior strode in front and just as Holger's eyes were adjusting to the diminished light an amber glow began to seep into his vision and suddenly he found himself in a chamber. A small fire burned brightly and a smell of smoke gently scented the air, the room was warm and there was a feeling of moisture, Holger guessed there was a hot spring nearby.

The darker haired Jomsviking gruffly took Holger by the shoulder and led him to the fire, indicating he should sit then crouched beside him, "We need no trouble."

"None." Holger nodded.

"Thorik, come sit here," Dag flicked a finger to the boy who stood at the chamber entrance chewing his lip and pulling at a stray thread on his cloak, "My name is Dag, he is Ari, though you know him as Gorm," his words directed to Holger, "Thorik... watch him."

"Ja," Thorik frowned regretfully, but before Holger could ask a question, Dag crossed the chamber where Ari stood talking to a young woman. The woman knelt on the ground and as she turned to meet Dag, Holger saw with surprise there was another woman lying on a bed of furs, even with the warm orange glow of the embers filling the room Holger saw by her waxen appearance that she was gravely ill.

"Her heart is strong but her breathing concerns me," Gytha worriedly darted a look at each man before staring at the new member of their group, "He's one of the Jarl's men?" she hissed in alarm.

"Ja," Ari nodded grimly, "If I take Grani and ride hard, Liv will be at the village in a day."

"Do it," Dag grunted, "The man Holger will give me no problems, be sure of that. We will continue on foot."

Feeling weariness threatening to rob him of all his resolve, Ari roughly drew a hand across his whiskered jaw, "Damn us to Hel! Prepare her Gytha, Dag, the way is not complicated, the causeway can be walked twice a day at sunrise and sunset. Make haste for the tide brings in the waters all too quickly. Once you reach the shoreline of Smols follow it until you reach pastureland, keep in the shadow of Hornelen. Walk towards it until you reach the lake, it is large and will take you at least half a day to pass around it, I will return for you there where the forest meets the water's edge."

"If you are not there?" Dag asked.

"Blow your horn... I will hear it, but be careful, the woods are home to wolves and I'll not take the chance of losing you all to the hunger of a beast. Not now."

"If I didn't know you better I'd say that was good humour threatening," Dag suppressed a wry grin.

"Tis' not the time my friend, but know this, I'll be a sad man to find an old toothless wolf chewing on your leathery hide!" His thinly set grimace said nothing as Ari walked to their packs and disappeared to ready Grani for the task.

"Yours is a good friendship," Gytha lifted her hand up to take Dag's from her seated position by Liv.

140

"Ja," Dag nodded at her before walking back over to the fire where Holger and Thorik sat pensively.

Chapter 11

ᚲᚺᚨᛈᛏᛖᚱ ᛖᛚᛖᚹᛖᚾ

Grani moved swiftly for a horse that had already covered many a mile with two on his back. Now his long, graceful strong limbs set to work again riding out into the mist covering Giffni. Ari guided the horse by memory along a narrow path that stretched from the caverns on the cliff top to the rough shoreline leading to the causeway.

It took Ari all his strength to hold Liv against his chest without her drooping, Dag had helped to lash a rope about her waist and his so she would stay atop Grani without coming to harm. The weight of her unconscious body caused him to draw breath, 'how can she feel so heavy?' he wondered. The lapping of waves on the shingle as they cantered by, caused Ari to nudge Grani into a gallop; the tide was coming in and the way to Smols would be lost till the next morning if he did not make haste.

Above him in the foggy sky a bird cawed, it was the first Ari had heard in some days since they had sought refuge in the caves. Giffni had always been a haven for them and now he raced with Liv back to Smols, back to the settlement, back to the one he now knew could not be trusted but what choice did he have? Gytha for all her abilities was at a loss as to how to heal Liv and Ari would be damned to an eternity in Hel before he lost her again. Part of him did not welcome this new feeling, he had spent so long hating her, wanting her to return, resenting what he thought was true but he knew he had to let go of the past, it would serve him unjustly, he knew he must focus for there were new dangers. If this man Holger was to be trusted then Brynjar would make every effort find them, it would not be so hard Ari realised, he had his Jomsviking training to rely on but he and Dag were only two men.

He knew the group behind him would move as swiftly as Dag could urge them to, on his own, his friend had tireless energy running for days before he succumbed to weariness, and Holger appeared to be a fit man too though older than Dag. Gytha and the boy Thorik would slow them, but it could not be helped. Ari surmised they would be safe enough at present from the pursuit of the Jarl's men should they be advancing to Giffni, it was Holger he was unsure of, the man professed a hatred for Brynjar and a desire to flee with his family, his words had been reasonable but what judgement could Ari make. In Brynjar's hall he had observed Holger from the corner of his eye, the man had stood behind his Jarl, in the shadows, watching and listening. Ari had felt Holger's eyes upon him, as his Jomsviking leader accepted coin for Brynjar's task, but no words had been exchanged until now.

Feeling the weight of Liv's pack on his back, Ari shifted carefully in the saddle, Grani was picking his way across the causeway with care, should he slip or stumble it could mean a lame leg. The mists surrounding them hampered their progress and curses threatened to spill from Ari's mouth. When at last he could smell the pine from the trees on the shore of Smols he released a breath and kicked Grani into a quicker trot, darkness was fast approaching and Ari knew that he would make little progress this evening. The best he could hope for was to reach the lake, there he would let Liv rest and administer more of Gytha's elixir. At first light he would make the journey around the lake, through the forest, and onto the settlement. By the next evening he would have her seen to and return for Dag and the others. He hoped he would reach them before Dag felt he needed to use his horn for although it would lead Ari to them it may also alert others.

The straps of the pack dug into Ari's shoulders pinching the skin beneath his woollen tunic and he grimaced at the tightness, it was a strong leather bag, but made for smaller shoulders than his. For the first time, he realised that somewhere concealed inside was the ring Liv was protecting and he felt the weight of it; he would not search through her things for it, the ring was not what he wanted, though he knew it was part of a conversation they should have had by now. If only he had not been so full of ire towards her on the ship and missed the lackwit who sought to attack her, if only he had noticed the injury was more grievous than a smack to the head, 'What was I thinking?' he thought to himself. This was part of the problem he realised, his years in the Jomsvikings had allowed him to fight and think only with a warrior's mind; little else had been of interest to him, it had been stupidity on his part, he knew now.

The mist parted for a moment like the heavy curtains that hung in his Chieftain's longhouse, he saw a trail leading to the lake and pulled the reins to show Grani the way. They walked for some time before Ari recognised a ramshackle hut in a small clearing by the edge of the great lake of Smols and if the air had not been so filled with fog he would have seen Hornelen, his mountain.

It was said, amongst his people that Odin the All-Father himself had stood atop it, striking his staff into the highest peak and causing the skies to fill with lightning. As he had done so the heavens of Gimli showered down their praise of his honour, turning the night sky into a wave of rainbows. Any warrior who had witnessed the rainbow sky at night knew he would meet an honourable end and be granted entry into Valhalla, Ari had seen such auras in the blackness of the night, but had never felt certain about his future.

Untying the rope about their waists Ari gently slid from Grani's back and carried Liv in his arms. Resting her on the soft grass of late summer he threw down their packs and guided Grani to water. Leaving the horse to drink his fill and eat the sweet green grass, Ari inspected the hut. It was in a sorry state; clearly no one had thought to maintain it in years, the wooden panels were blackened with mildew and rotten, the roof for the most part was intact, but one strong wind or whisper of a storm and he reckoned it would flatten instantly. Pushing against the timber of the small square structure he heard it ache and groan with pressure, but it stood fast enough for him to think it safe enough for a night.

The beaten earth floor inside betrayed evidence of goats recently taking shelter. Looking outside Ari saw water rushes along the lake's edge, taking his dagger he cut through a handful and used them as a makeshift broom to sweep away the dried droppings. Satisfied the hut was clean enough, he unrolled a blanket on the floor and laid Liv upon it, she stirred for a moment and tried to open her eyes, but swiftly returned to her unconscious state.

Gathering wood for a small fire did not take Ari long, the first few sparks from his flint caught on the moss and smoke began to rise. From his pack he withdrew some dried meat and now stale flatbread, chewing slowly, he emptied the lukewarm water in his skin and refilled it in the freshwater stream flowing into the lake. Drinking the sweet cool water of Smols allowed him to feel at home for a moment, in some ways it was as if he had never left, but the reality was very different, he was a changed man now and had not seen his people in many years. He did not feel apprehension or fear meeting with his family once more; his thoughts were clouded by the one he must ask to treat Liv.

Turning to face the hut where Liv lay he knew the shock of discovering the rude, foul tempered Jomsviking Gorm, who had really been Ari had been too much, how would she react when she saw another familiar face and in the weakened state she was now in? Regret and anger raised blood to his cheeks and Ari tossed the skin on the ground beside the hut, sinking down, he sat and looked out into the stillness of the night.

"Ari?" Liv whispered, her voice hoarse. Spinning around Ari peered into the hut, "Liv? You're awake?"

"Where are we?" she rasped.

"The lake of Smols," Ari said.

"I feel weak, but my heart it rattles in my chest," she glanced at him placing her hand on her chest.

"Tis' the daudr svefn Liv, Gytha made a potion to keep it at bay but I must get you home, rest now for we have no choice but to wait for morning."

"The forest... wolves," frowning slightly Liv stared at the shoddy wooden roof of the hut, she remembered old Gunliek and his ragged herd of goats, they would use for milk and cheese, she wondered if he still lived. Slowly her eyes fell upon Ari, "Come here," she said.

Standing, Ari stooped into the hut and drew to his haunches beside Liv. "Ja?"

"How came you by these scars?" Liv drew her eyes across jagged trail of silver lines running from Ari's jaw down onto his neck. The amber flame from the fire illuminated the flecks in her opal eyes.

"Ah," Ari's eyes narrowed and the muscle in his jaw ticked, he hated the scars almost as much as the telling of how they came to be, he thought it ugly, for many a drunken tavern wench thought so, not that he cared aught what they thought truly. Scars were the way for a Jomsviking man, what did he care if those women scolded him with cold unfeeling eyes? He would never marry them nor see them again.

It was a fair question for Liv to ask, her own body was marred in the years they had spent apart, a branding and tattoos, he knew the same women who had scolded his appearance would have had much to say about Liv's. Women were not meant to be guardians or warriors, they were not meant to fight or incur the wrath of men. Viking women were to raise the children, run the house in the absence of their men, prepare the food for feasting and long winters ahead. At least this was the thinking of their people in the settlement, but though Ari had always known it would not have been a future such as this that he and Liv would share, he could not have guessed how different it would be.

"It was a raven, it belonged to the fiercest warrior I have ever met… but do not let Dag know I said so, he would be aggrieved to think he is not the fiercest," Ari smiled and sat cross legged on the ground facing the doorway of the hut looking out at Grani. "When I left our home I wandered for a time, working on farmsteads, fishing, then I joined a ship… working for the captain of the ship that took us to Gulafjord. One night when we were docked a man came aboard looking for men who could fight and keep their mouths shut, I had nothing to lose and went with him. His name was Raki Gormsson."

Sighing Ari tossed a handful of dry leaves and bark onto the small fire, seeing Liv's eyes watching him he sighed and continued. "Raki was a strong man, as tall as he was broad, but he was ageing too, had he lived, he was older than my own father is now. When I met Raki he had wild white hair and a beard he braided, white as the winter snow it was, his skin was tanned and leathery like an old hide but his eyes I remember being brighter than a child's. The most remarkable thing about him was the raven that perched on his shoulder. It was called Muninn after Odin's bird and had feathers blacker than coal. Its eyes were pools of tar, often I would dream about the bird's dark stare dreaming that I was drowning in their depths. Never had I seen such a man before, nor since.

Two men left the ship with me to do Raki's bidding, it turned out that he had been searching for a man for a long, long time. The man and Raki were bonded by a blood feud, it had raged on between their families for many a lifetime, the man had killed Raki's wife and children in hatred. Raki sought him out to kill him only, there was no other task greater than this, and he paid us to trap the man so he would not lose him to escape again. Raki knew the man was hiding out on a nearby farm with his wife's people; no harm was to come to the family, only the man.

We prepared ourselves one night in an empty barn next to the township's feasting hall; the other two men had gone to drink ale to slake their thirst after a long day's ride. When they returned, their faces were pale and they told Raki they would no longer work for him, they had discovered who the man was, they wished no part of the feud and refused coin for their troubles thus far. They tried to persuade me to leave but I would not hear of it."

"Muninn…" Liv murmured.

Lost in his thoughts Ari barely heard Liv but glanced at her face only to see her skin growing paler and the dark circles around her eyes increasing. He thought that it was perhaps a trick of the lack of light and the soft shadows thrown up from the glow of the fire, but he decided to continue his tale if only to distract them both for a little longer. It occurred to Ari he had not thought of Raki for a very long time and he had sworn to himself never to let the memory of the man fade from his thoughts; he had taught Ari much.

"We made haste to the farm, but alas the man had disappeared, Raki raged and swore curses upon the Gods. He screamed at the women of the house, but they cried and threw their hands up in despair and told him two men had approached and warned them of Raki's plans. We left them and rode out onto the hillside, from atop we could see the township's lights and ships moored in the harbour, the moon was a brilliant silver beacon in the sky as it glowed down upon us and at any other time it would have been a beautiful night.

Raki turned to me, sitting on his horse with the raven on his shoulder, his wild white hair and beard illuminated by the great disk in the sky, he looked like a God, I thought!" Ari chuckled softly and scratching his whiskered chin, he shook his head. "Not a God though, just a man, a man with vengeance in his heart. He told me never to relent, that when all has been taken from you and your heart is as cold as stone there is naught else left but revenge for the one who caused your pain. He told me that though there would be many to try and dissuade you from your path you must stay true, for what vengeance could his wife and children take when they were dead and cold in the earth?

I understood a little of his pain, but not enough of it to tell him so, I would have dishonoured him if I had, I was a foolish boy with a broken heart not a warrior with blood on my hands... not yet."

"I'm sorry," Liv whispered but Ari did not hear her.

"We rode on for weeks, we practised our sword play and I learned more about Raki, he told me of his past, a Viking raider and then a trader when he took his wife and she bore him sons, he told me of the Jomsvikings and urged me to take the path of a warrior, rather than a family. I was swept up in the idea of blood fury and warring, of battling men, and releasing my rage, I had walked away from our home and left the boy Ari there. Now I was a man who had seen and done much, I was changed, it was easier to become like Raki.

My skills grew, he was pleased with me, and though he was a hard taskmaster, he knew too how to laugh and often goaded me with his humour. He was a friend and a father, but he needed no son, only a man who could kill as well as he. It was as if the bird Muninn knew it, it was as if it reflected all the darkness in Raki's heart, always perched on his shoulder watching me and waiting. Raki could feed it and had trained it to hunt quarry when we needed meat, but for me it did nothing. Once I held Muninn on my forearm, its claws digging into my flesh, Raki laughed at my discomfort and I wanted nothing but to shake it from gripping me.

It happened by chance that we were riding along a beach, at a slow pace for the morning was calm and we had lost the trail of the man, I'd learned his name was Ulfur. Suddenly Raki pulled his horse's reins and sat staring ahead, in the distance I saw men on horseback. One man was wearing a cloak concealing his features but Raki recognised him at once, it was Ulfur, screaming a war cry from his throat Raki was seized by blood fury and sped his horse to the group. I chased after him readying my axe, I saw it happen too quickly, Raki sliced with his long sword through two of the men, their blood spraying onto the sands, they stumbled clutching the gaping wounds about their chest and neck; lurching and screaming they fell into the seawater turning it red.

Ulfur jumped from his horse and readied himself for Raki's attack, but it was a trap, more men appeared from the dunes and surrounded Raki. I stopped and jumped down from my horse calling Raki, but he did not respond, he stood there poised to leap at Ulfur who had retreated beyond the circle of men. Raki swore and thundered foul curses at the men who were all heavily armoured; I ran and burst through the circle of men to join him. Muninn flew above our heads cawing and screeching when one of the men shot an arrow at him and he fell to the ground. Raki seemed to snap from his ire and his face grew slack when he saw the bird land on the sand, it did not move. I shouted at Raki to move, to raise his sword arm, screamed and shouted for him to waken from his dream. Ulfur took his chance and swung a deathly blow with his axe from behind, Raki stumbled forward into my arms and dropped onto the sand, his blood flowed around my feet, he looked confused and shocked then understood he was dying. He pulled my ear to his mouth and whispered his final words. I understood.

Ulfur had begun to laugh, he grumbled with a dry crackled voice that he had ended the feud, the men around him stood sheathing their weaponry and sharing dark glances with one another. They were all dressed alike and wore hardened grim expressions, Ulfur sneered at Raki's dead body and from within his cloak retrieved a coin purse and threw it at one of the men and I realised then what they were, mercenaries, paid to protect Ulfur and dispatch Raki; hired men.

I stood gripping my axe, I pointed it at Ulfur, and I told the snake he was vile, I told him he had no honour, for what kind of man killed from behind? I challenged him to Holmgang there and then, Ulfur tried to back away but the men would not allow it. With no more than two blows from my axe I killed him, severed his head from his shoulders, watched him fall beside Raki's dead body, one of the men shouted 'Swift-Axe!' and thus I became Gorm Swift-Axe."

"Muninn…"

"Ja, Muninn. It appeared my slaying of his master's killer had not been enough, the men told me to join them and I did for what else was there for me to do? First I buried poor Raki in the dunes, and then I went to Muninn's body, the arrow still sticking out of his breast. He did not flinch when I pulled the arrow from him but as I lifted his body he let out a final screech and clawed my jaw and neck, his fury at Raki's killing at last appeased. Then he was dead and I was bleeding, the raven had only ever been loyal to Raki. I buried Muninn beside Raki and cursed the feathered demon's name as I dug into the sand with my bare hands.

By this time the men had gathered their horses and grown impatient with my delaying them, I took my own horse and we left. One night before we reached their compound a man approached me, he had ointment to soothe and disinfect the wounds that should have been stitched but none were competent and I wouldn't allow them near my bare neck. The man told me of the nature of birds, he said 'they are unlike other animals, they have no loyalty to man, their spirits are free never to be tamed'. I told him that Muninn had been faithful enough to Raki, but the man shook his head and said, 'it is not its nature it would have left him eventually'."

The small fire had all but nearly died out and though there was a coolness to the evening air, Ari decided to let it dwindle to ash. Liv was covered in his sleeping fur and warm enough and he did not want to alert any that might be nearby they had arrived yet. Knowing he should rest before setting off at first light Ari lowered onto his back, closing his eyes for a moment.

"A good story, Ari... Raki will know peace with his wife and children... mayhap Muninn sits on his shoulder yet?" Liv said quietly.

"Hah!" Ari smiled wryly in the darkness of the hut, "Mayhap, when next I see that bird I will pluck every feather from his carcass!"

"Odin would be displeased..." Liv sighed, gradually her breathing became heavier and realising she was sleeping Ari released a tight breath from his chest. He was glad she had come to for a time and spoken with him, Gytha had warned him to watch for signs that her mind was becoming muddled or if nonsense should fall from her lips, that the elixir should be administered. She had also told him that the daudr svefn might prevent Liv from stirring at all and Ari wondered if he had dreamt it. Sleep eluded him for the rest of the night, fearing she might pass in her slumber, he listened to every wavering breath or laboured sigh.

In the morning he was startled to find her skin had taken on a greyer hue and her lips were blue. As he lifted her onto Grani's back her body was limp and somehow weighed less than the previous day, a sweat glistened on her brow, but try as he might to moisten her lips with water, she would not drink from the skin. With his jaw firmly set Ari pulled Grani into a march towards the settlement and leading the way to the forest, he picked his way along the woodland paths ever watchful and vigilantly aware of the danger of wolves.

Pushing the horse to his limits, Ari reached the settlement before noon, hours before he had hoped to and looking down onto the collection of longhouses, cattle sheds and outhouses he saw the bodies of his people turn towards him. They were going about their duties preparing for the day when all at once the door of the hall flew open and the form of a man appeared, it was his uncle the Chieftain. Raising his sword arm, he shouted a welcome and beckoned Ari, recognising at once the young man who had left six long years ago.

Ari felt a surge of hope within, he had returned and his family was still here but as he walked down from the edge of the forest, to the clearing before the settlement nestled in a narrow valley, he saw another figure emerge from the hall and follow his uncle to greet him. Ari swallowed the rage that threatened to erupt, he must remain calm, for it was the man he knew had betrayed Liv and whom Ari now found himself delivering her to.

Chapter 12

ᚦᚾᚨᚲᛏᛗᚱ ᛏᚹᛗᚦᛗ

Ove recognised his nephew at first sight, he had been aware of his imminent arrival, the old Seer had seen to that, he did not like the turn of events that had brought the man back into their midst, but was powerless to do anything about it. The sight of Ari quelled his thoughts for a moment until he saw the body of a woman across the back of the horse he led.

Waving to Ari he welcomed him into the settlement, but he could feel the Seer behind him, hovering like a gadfly around a cow in the summer sun. A chill crept across Ove's skin; turning to the old man he glared at him furiously. "So he has returned." Ove growled.

"Ja, as I told you he would, when I gave him the task I knew he would find her."

"And as I have told you, should harm befall them or my people here it will be your head in the earth. We once welcomed you but those days are gone, your trickery and deceit saw to that."

The old man narrowed his dark steel blue eyes, his lips split in a snarl and he glared back with venom at the Chieftain, "for years you have prospered, I've done nothing to change that, don't be so foolish to think there isn't more in the world than your little island. Have I not been good to you? Healed your people, foreseen storms and disease, asked naught…"

"Tis' true... you asked for naught but took anyway. Here comes my brother's son, mayhap we leave our discussion until you have spoken?" Ove shrugged off the man's cold look and strode towards Ari.

The old man turned on his heel and made for his chamber in the longhouse attached to the hall, he had seen the body across the back of the beast. His heart thudded at the thought she might be dead, but he had felt no such passing and could almost hear her breathing. Surmising she was injured, he swore under his breath, gathering his medicines and the scroll he had used once before the Seer took a breath. He knew this was going to be difficult; the bear, Ove, had proven himself to be no fool, his secrets were being exposed one by one and reuniting with Liv would cause further problems. He knew not what had happened to her in the last six years, more importantly; he had to know about the ring and the boy, he sat on his pallet for a moment, thinking dark thoughts.

Ove was a large strong man; the elder of three brothers, though only he and Ari's father still lived, his long hair was still as full and bright as a young man's but his face bore the brunt of wear and tear in the hot summers and long cold winters. His nose had been broken once too often and sat crookedly on his square face, clean shaven, he smiled with a full set of teeth, his eyes clear and sharp, though oddly coloured, one being blue and the other brown. When he was a child his mother and father feared it was an omen their son was not meant for the world of Midgard, but Ove had shown them he was as strong and wise as any Chieftain's son should be.

The departure of Ari had been like a swift kick to the ribs from a mule, he had often thought his brother's son would take up the mantle of the settlement's leader one day, Ove had no sons of his own, though he loved his wife and their daughter dearly.

The flat worn earth of the yard crunched beneath his boots as he reached his nephew and wrapped his bear-like arms around him, he saw the changes in Ari, he saw the strain on his face and the scars on his neck. He felt the strength of a full-grown man in his arms and not the sinewy limbs of the boy he had known, this man had fought and killed, his nature was changed but still it was his Ari. "The Seer is not trusted here but be wary of how you react," Ove whispered into Ari's ear. "Ho! Come and see, Ari has returned to us! Fetch my brother, fetch his wife, we will feast tonight!" Ove then shouted to the gathering group of villagers.

The women clasped their hands in delight before running into the hall and setting to work in the kitchen, children jumped and whooped at the display of their Chieftain, chasing their dogs and running here and there in the yard. Men who had known Ari looked surprised and then shouted for joy before nodding respectfully and returning to their work. Everyone had seen the body slung over the back of Grani, but none pursued an answer, assuming only Ari had brought a slave or prisoner with him.

"Ove, tis' Liv, I need the Seer!" Ari jerked his head to the horse.

"Ja, ja, but Ari none must know she is here yet," Ove hushed Ari with a wave of a large hand, taking Grani's reins, he led the horse to the barn near the great hall. "My boy, my boy!" Ove slapped Ari on the shoulder before turning to Liv and lifting her down.

Taking a breath Ove stared hard at the woman, "What sickness is this?"

"The daudr svefn," Ari frowned. "She needs help... now."

"What! Nei, it cannot be so!" Ove laid Liv on a loose mound of hay and stared up at his nephew, "You are well?"

"Ja, my parents?" Ari asked, having noted their absence.

"Well... they will be here soon, they were at the farm and knowing your mother she will be flying down the hillside with your father on her heels," Ove stood folding his arms across his chest, "Liv is much changed, how came you by her?"

"I was sent by the Jarl, but before that word came to my captain in the compound, the Seer..."

"He is a snake," Ove snarled.

"Ja, but Liv knows naught... there was no time to tell her. How come you distrust the man now?" Ari asked.

"Six years is time enough to learn such things, think me a fool not to wonder about her going missing and he at the same time? I have heard stories about our Seer, I sent a man on their trail, this you would have known if you had stayed," Ove tried unsuccessfully to disguise the bitterness in his voice, but seeing Ari wince at the remark he sighed, "I sent the same man to find you." He paused, "There is much we will speak of but first we must take her to him, he will be in the longhouse, conceal her face when you carry her. I have no plan to explain this to anyone yet."

Just as Ari lifted Liv over his shoulder a man burst into the barn and stood in the doorway, he stood as tall as Ari and as broad and square faced as Ove, his tunic was rolled up at the sleeves and his hands muddied from working the earth that morning.

"Ari!" Slowly a broad smile crept over Ari's face; his father stood before him. "Ja," he replied.

"My son!" Ari's father, Ebbe stepped towards him, joy threatening to explode from his chest, but halted, seeing the body slung over his son's shoulder, nodding, he looked to Ove and glanced outside the barn door. Beckoning the men, they left the barn and walked towards the longhouse; Ebbe would welcome his son home later.

The dream overtaking Liv caused her breathing to increase rapidly, she stood on the rainbow bridge, staring across the divide to Asgard. It was the most beautiful structure she had ever laid sight upon, hewn from the wood of great oak trees, the bridge was a myriad of carvings, great beasts wrestled with dragons, splinters of wooden fire erupting from their snouts. Intricate runes were carved over the boards of the walkway causing Liv to think of the markings on her skin. The bridge was covered in a layer of ice that gave it the appearance of glowing in the blackness surrounding her.

A figure was standing next to her wearing a thick grey cloak made of wool and a mantle of grey wolf skin across his shoulders, he was pointing the way signalling her to take the long walk but she could not move, her heart told her it was not yet time, she had to return for Ei and for Ari.

The figure beside her took her forearm and brushed a hand across her forehead, he was tall and had the strangest eyes she had ever seen, they appeared to be made of molten lava, the irises a deep red, swirling and moving as they bored into her opal gaze, "You know me?" he enquired.

"Ja, you are Heimdallr, the watcher of Bifrost, the rainbow bridge, you can see into the nine realms and hear all that is said and unsaid; you are a son of Odin the All-Father," Liv said.

"You are the guardian of my father's line in Midgard, he awaits the day the boy will return, why have you come alone?" his voice was low and hard.

"I became sick, I must return for Eileifr…" she whispered unsteadily.

"You have hidden the child, he is safe for now," the man looked away across the Bifrost as if listening to something in the distance, "Ja, there is naught to fear at present."

Taking a step away from the god with the frightening stare, Liv drew a breath only to realise she no longer felt tired or ill, Heimdallr circled her, staring all the while. "Fear does not suit you, why are you afraid now?" he asked her, whispering into her ear. Shrinking away from the god, Liv turned to face him taking another step to increase the space between them, "I have never met a god, have I angered you?"

"Are you so sure you have never met one?" Heimdallr frowned, "none are angry with you here."

For a moment Liv tried to understand what he meant but could not tear her gaze from his face, it was proud and stern, "Am I free to return home?" she asked.

"Ja, you must for the boy." Suddenly the dark night sky that had surrounded them broke into millions of twinkling stars, each one fell from the sky and landed at their feet, creating a blanket of tiny sparkling lights, "Gimli has awoken," Heimdallr explained.

"The heavens?" Liv asked confused.

"You will go there Liv, but not today, my father struck his staff into the ground to shake the stars from the sky, see he stands at the end of the bridge," Heimdallr continued to stare into her eyes, but pointed to a figure in the distance, "'tis' time for you to go, but first…" Taking Liv's hand, Heimdallr took her to the edge of the rock they stood upon where Bifrost started, peering over the edge the god pointed down to a swirling mass of mist and water that stretched as far and as deep as Liv could fathom.

Suddenly Heimdallr turned her wrist over, tracing the line of runes encircling her skin, "You have been marked? These runes are spells, but this… what is this on your shoulder?" the god laid his palm flat on her shoulder blade, before jerking his touch away as if his skin was burned. "That is a mark made by men who do not understand Yggdrasil, no god would allow the life-giving tree to be burned upon the flesh."

"It was made by my guardian, but he is gone now, I will have no answers from him," Liv shrugged her shoulder away and followed the frowning gaze of the man before her.

"There," said Heimdallr, looking intently at her once more and pointing to a formation in the mist, "there is Hornelen, and Smols, and there is the hall in which you lay barely alive. There is the one who will betray you at all costs, but for now he is saving you. He is the danger, he wishes not for the safety of the boy, he wants only what he thinks he can gain."

"The ring," Liv whispered, her eyes strained as she looked down upon the rising images of the places and people she knew, tears of rage burned her eyes and set her throat on fire, she could not believe what she saw and feared her mind was as broken as her body had become, she could not understand the images in the mist and turned away from the edge of the bridge.

"Ja, the ring, you know it is cursed? Made from the ashes and tears of the gods when one of their own was killed. The strong and good of heart can carry it for a time, but it is worthless Liv," Heimdallr explained.

"Nei..." she breathed in disbelief, "It cannot be..." Heimdallr reached out and grasped her shoulder, Liv's head shot up and she straightened her back, her will was still strong she would not be afraid. Leaning to whisper in her ear, he spoke, "I have a secret for you..."

As Heimdallr spoke Liv felt every muscle in her body tense, her hands felt as heavy as a lead weight, but she clenched her fingers tightly, digging her nails into the skin of her palms. Even here in the world of the gods, she felt her blood surge and boil in her veins with fury and when at last Heimdallr finished, he turned her to face him.

"Ja, you are afraid no longer, for it is not in your making Liv, you are a protector and fear will betray you. Know that I am always watching and listening, when it appears all others have turned away or cannot come to you, I will. Now go and do what my father knows you must," the god instructed.

"My thanks," she nodded. "There is something I must ask you."

"Then ask," Heimdallr said.

"Why did the All-Father ever need me? Surely he can save his child without me?" she asked carefully.

Heimdallr closed his eyes and took a heavy breath; looking back across the Bifrost he drew his heavy grey cloak about his shoulders. "There are nine realms, Midgard is the world of men and so you must be allowed to live as such, the Gods cannot upset the balance, sometimes we walk among you as men and women, sometimes we take the form of birds or beasts. Mortals have short lives Liv; you must be allowed to live it, the fates work differently for us all and there is a purpose and a reason in all things."

"Is there peace at all in the future?" she asked sadly.

"Nei Liv, not for Gods and not for men but know that the life you live is precious and the one you protect more so. The boy is born from the love we lost when one of our own died, it was another son of Odin, who gave us hope again but this you already know. Call my name when you need me most and you will hear my horn thunder across the heavens. Go now, they are waiting for you," Heimdallr lifted the hood of his cloak over his head, concealing his deep garnet eyes and slowly made his way across the bridge, his arms folded across his chest, his feet leaving a trail through the fallen star dust.

Warmth spread over Liv's body; opening her eyes to the soft amber glow of the wooden panelled chamber she saw a figure leaning over her. Her eyes were weak and her vision blurred, a smell of burning incense filtered its way to her nose and then a sharper unpleasant smell replaced it. Sitting up suddenly she coughed and a hand that had been wavering a vial under her nostrils retreated swiftly, her vision cleared and shock struck all noise from her throat.

It could not be, her mind raced, the dream had warned her but her mind was muddled, the face before her was grim and set, his long beard trailing down his chest, his nimble fingers clenched in a fist before him. The surprise knocked her momentarily and her arms slipped back onto the furs, slumping she raised her head once more to make certain of the man now coming closer leaning over her once more.

"My girl… my girl." He whispered.

"Don't get too close… step away," the voice of another came from the shadows across the room, Liv sensed the owner rise and stand behind the man, she realised it was Ari who spoke. "I'm warning you Seer!" Ari growled at the man's back.

Liv massaged her temple and shook her head slightly, trying to make sense of what her eyes told her, but how it could be? She did not know but now the dream made sense, what Heimdallr had whispered in her ear, she remembered, and her deep anger replaced the fear that had threatened to creep in. She was strong, she must remember, she had survived and protected her charge even lying to Ari about Ei's death. "How is it you stand before me after all this time?" her voice rasped and then she spoke his name, "Harvardr?"

Chapter 13

ᚦᚢᚪᚳᛏᛖᚱ ᛏᚻᛁᚱᛏᛖᛖᚾ

The silence in the room was deafening, Ari looked upon Liv as she rose unsteadily from the pallet, her hair was loose and hanging over her shoulders, her grey dress was crumpled and the traditional brooches and apron were missing. She looked bedraggled and almost like a thrall woman, anger rose in Ari's throat over this man who, meeting Liv after all these years, saw only a slave and not the survivor.

Liv squared her shoulders, taking a deep breath; she straightened her back and looked defiantly at Harvardr. At full height she was nose to nose with the old man, the bruising on her face had subsided to mere shadows, her skin had returned to a healthy glow and her eyes burned fiercely. As she clenched her jaw, Ari saw the muscles twitch beneath the skin, she was enraged and trying hard to bury it he thought, 'Good!' Ari silently praised her, for she had to be strong, to show weakness in front of the man who had betrayed her would serve to hurt her further.

Harvardr looked at the woman and saw more than the girl he had trained, more than the being he had manipulated, he saw too she had gained wisdom; she was no longer the naive daughter of a slave who had believed his words so easily. 'Damn her!' his mind raged, for how was he to deal with her now, he had not been prepared for this, he had assumed that the world would have treated her harshly without the protection of a man for the last six years. He had reasoned a meeker woman would be standing before him, mayhap she would have hardened her emotions having to do what she must to survive but this woman had strength.

"Speak!" she directed her command to Harvardr through clenched teeth; she glared at the man, her hands trembling in balled fists at her sides, it was indeed her guardian, he was older and somewhat frailer looking but that was all on the surface, she now knew what lay beneath his leathery skin, the heart of a viper.

"Save your anger for another!" Harvardr stepped away and placed his vial of rancid potion back within his pouch on the chest by the pallet. A small oil lamp burned on the chest top causing wisps of black smoke to filter up toward the thatched roof, "You are alive now because I healed you."

"How did you survive?" she asked coldly.

"Survive? Ah, you mean the attack from the Jarl's men?" Harvardr pulled a small wooden stool from a corner of the room and lowered himself stiffly onto it; his tunic was a dark brown, dyed by the women in the settlement. Its rich wool was soft and felt good against his skin, but his feet ached in the rough boots he wore that were in need of repair and as the rains had not yet fallen he had neglected to do so. He had been so very busy with travelling to Smols and preparing for the return of Liv and Ari, now his bones ached and his joints were swollen, the skin on his back felt soothed by the garment.

"Brodr died, he was a good man, he didn't have to die, why didn't you?" Liv whispered the words watching the old man rub his aching fingers together. She saw the discomfort of age, but didn't care, she was standing, a bedraggled mess before her enemy while he sat well clothed and his cheeks were not hollow with hunger. Turning to face him and draw his attention fully she leaned in slightly, "They slaughtered him, the Jarl's men, but he didn't say a word. I hid with Ei, my hand over his mouth to stop him from screaming, and when at last they had hacked every limb from Brodr's body we ran but where were you? There were bodies littered everywhere, women, children, men but not yours. Do you know the guilt I carried thinking your corpse had been left to perish? Then after a time I feared the Jarl had you locked away in some pit, rotting with your heart still beating."

Harvardr tensed at the imagery Liv cast with her story, of course he knew what had happened to Brodr; he had arranged it all but he would not admit it to her, especially not with the looming presence of the Jomsviking in the room. "We were separated Liv, I searched for you but never found you. Then after many years there was a thread, just a whisper at first, you had been seen... but you were alone. A trader on a ship talking of a woman who had hired him to sail for her, it was his son who had loose lips, he had seen strange markings on your skin and thought you a witch. I knew then you were alive, I knew then I was only weeks behind you," Harvardr stroked his long beard with his talon like fingers.

"There is some truth in that part," Ari said, standing next to Liv, his hands tucked into his leather belt, across his back his heavy sword was still strung in its strap. "It was then he sent a messenger to the compound, to make sure word of you found its way to me, he knew I would come. After speaking with my captain, I discovered that Jarl Brynjar had also been made aware. Brynjar hired us, I made sure I was sent to find you." Ari glanced at Liv before directing his stare at Harvardr, "but for all your scheming Harvardr you forgot to weigh the measure of a man, you did not think that there would be forgiveness rather than wrath. Had you imagined me delivering her to you bound with rope and shackled with chains?"

"You were not to reveal yourself!" Harvardr spat.

"Why? To deceive me further?" Liv shouted.

"To protect Ei! To hide the ring, these are your tasks Liv! What good would it have done to realise the man before you was Ari? Better it would have been that you discovered all here and felt warmth in your heart, rather than the rage I see in you now! You accuse with your stares, believing I have lied, vent your fury towards me if you wish, but make sure it is justified!" Harvardr jabbed a pointed gnarled finger towards Liv and sneered, "You have come here without the boy, where is he? And the ring? I know you cannot have lost both, for the Gods would have smote you, by Odin I will do it myself! Nothing matters more than the child and the ring."

Slowly Liv lowered herself to her knees, staring directly at Harvardr eye to eye, "No more lies, I know full well the truth, you have never cared for Ei. All you ever wanted was the ring and you thought you had it, did you not? The night of the attack Brodr presented me with two brooches, one concealing the ring and the

172

other an empty copy. When the men attacked, I was knocked out by a blow to the head, I thought it one of the men mistaken in my identity... nei it was you. I awoke and found Ei crying in the corner of the blacksmith's forge, we hid as I said until it was safe and when next I had my wits and we had run far enough, I discovered one brooch was missing. Tell me Harvardr, how enraged were you and Brynjar to discover you had the wrong one? No ring, no child and no trail for you to follow!"

Ari felt as if his mind were about to explode, what kind of treachery was this? The old Seer had been at work for some time, but his deeds were of the worst kind, a terrible violation of trust and honour.

"Why would I have done such things Liv?" the Seer asked, cocking his head a vacant expression in his eyes.

"Because you grew to hate what you had been tasked with, you were severed from your own kind, lumbered with a legend and a child, you had tried to barter your way out of the task before, I realise that now. With Brodr and his Chieftain father, you wanted rid of us but craved the wealth of the ring, you betrayed us to Brynjar to gain wealth, and that man who has chased me relentlessly for the last six years was insane enough to be swept away by your words. Did he torture you when you failed? Is this your chance at retribution or did you run and hide from him, waiting and listening for my whereabouts, to try and strike again?" Liv said, every word fell like an axe.

"You have become a vile woman," he snapped.

"If I have then it is praise to you!" Liv stood, breathing evenly and calmly.

"Tell me of the ring, tell me of the boy!" Harvardr's voice crackled under the torment of frustration caused by the woman. He felt defeated and it did not suit him to feel much of anything he did not like.

"The ring? Thrown into the ocean before I was captured, and Ei? For that is his name... not boy. Never... never will I tell you," with those final words, Liv walked to the small chamber door, sliding the wooden latch, she left the room and paused in the hall. She saw two men standing opposite the doorway, their arms folded, grim expressions on their faces, and moving past them she paused a little farther along the passageway. Moments later, Ari joined her.

"Did you know any of it?" He asked Liv, she shook her head and took a deep breath. "He will be set under guard in a room out of sight. You did well," he said.

"I need air, we are in Ove's longhouse?" she asked and resting her head against the rough wooden panels of the wall, she wondered if it would be best to hide herself away from the sight of the villagers, her energy expended, she felt weak once more.

"Would be best you get rest but come with me, I have little time before I must fetch the others from the lake. They left behind us... you know you were close to death?" Ari asked.

"Ja, I dreamt as much," Liv nodded and turned to face him, "Ari you must go, I will rest in another room, mayhap speak with Ove? Your parents are well?"

"Ja. Come you must see something new and it is safe," taking her elbow Ari led her out of the hallway running between the longhouse and the great hall of Chieftain Ove. Taking a side step, they passed through the back of the hall and out into a small grassy yard. A small bench was secluded in a corner with a low overhanging roof to provide shelter; wattle and daub fencing enclosed the yard. Seeing Liv's confusion Ari gestured to the bench and sat beside her.

"Three winters or so ago Ove's daughter gave birth to twins, she was much sickened afterwards and had little strength to walk, Ove had this small yard made so that she might play with the boys as they grew. She is well now, but for a time not even the other women could approach her without her contracting some illness. Ove says she is now so strong she takes the boys with her and her husband everywhere, sailing, climbing, she will not be confined again," Ari chuckled, "but mayhap that is just a tale? I see a drinking horn resting near your foot, mayhap my uncle hides here to drown his sorrows when he has angered my aunt!"

"So there is!" Liv nudged the horn with the soft leather of her boot.

"The child is alive then?" Ari asked.

"Ja, he is," Liv closed her eyes, letting Ei's small laughing face fill her mind.

"We must talk of it," he said gently.

"Ja." She sighed.

The sun began to set on the last of the warm summer days, gnats darted here and there in the long grass and birds flew overhead, Liv felt a sense of return to her old home. Relaxing she let her back lean against the wall of the house and breathed in the sweet air, her skin began to cool and the aching that had been ever present in her head was almost completely gone.

"He read from a scroll, runic inscriptions, in our old tongue, the tongue of the Gods but you did not make it easy for him, what did you dream of?" Ari asked.

"Damn him and his magic! I dreamt I was talking with…" Just at that moment the sound of a horn in the distance reverberated through the trees and across the fields. Jumping to his feet Ari cursed, "Dag!" Turning quickly to Liv he motioned for her to stay there. "I must go, he would only blow the horn if need be, stay here I'll send Ove for you."

Nodding in agreement Liv watched Ari disappear with haste into the longhouse, she wanted to tell him to ride safely, that she hoped the others had not come to harm, she had wanted to thank him. Feeling weak once more she wrung her hands, a memory from her dream broke her thoughts and the sound of the horn rang in her ears.

"I remember Heimdallr," she whispered, for the moment she was safe, she had no need to call his name and it was not his horn that had rung from the skies.

Thorik at once realised his mistake, dropping Dag's horn he backed away from the Jomsvikings pack. The men had separated and headed in opposite directions, securing their position. They had arrived at the lake of Smols and found the beaten and ramshackle goat herder's hut, Dag found little evidence that anyone had occupied the hut recently save for the hoof prints left in the soft earth by Grani. On hearing the horn sound his head shot up from his crouching position, he had been sweeping a gaze back and forth along the line of the trees, now and then he glanced to Holger who was doing the same on the other side of the body of water. Then he saw the Jarl's man stand and run in the direction of Gytha and the boy, Dag sprang onto his feet and broke into a sprint reaching them moments before Holger.

Gytha was waving her hands at the men calming them before they approached but it did little to soothe Dag's temper, "By the Gods!" Dag glared at Thorik who stood behind Gytha.

"There is no harm Dag, please he was curious, I should have kept an eye on him better!" Gytha spoke quickly.

"Get from behind her skirts boy!" Holger shouted.

Feeling ashamed and embarrassed Thorik stepped forward puffing out his chest but all at once his bravado expired and he resorted to pulling at his tufted hair, "I only wanted to see if I could," he lamely explained.

"You blew the Jomsviking's horn? Madness!" Holger was exasperated, throwing his hands up into the air he let them fall and slap his side, "You have alerted all to our location, why, even the goats at the top of the mountain will know where we are!"

"Nei! It wasn't that loud!" Thorik took a breath, feeling hurt by Holger's anger, 'Why is he not proud I have shown I could make it sing?' he wondered 'Tis' not an easy task!'

Reading Thorik's thoughts Dag rolled his eyes and strode over to the boy, grabbing his arm, he shook him roughly, "You have shown your lungs are strong, but your curiosity has endangered us all, who is to say who or what is lurking on our trail? If we are attacked am I to protect you or let you fight?"

"Fight!" Thorik whispered.

"Nei, Gytha here would have to take you and hide. You're foolish Thorik, you were when first we met and you have continued to be so!" Dag said hotly.

"But… Holger I brought him to you, he is here to help, and Grani I brought him to you also! I'm not foolish Dag I want to fight, to be a man to…" Thorik stumbled over his words, feeling the shame of his foolishness colour his cheeks.

"Blow a Jomsviking's horn?" Gytha smiled at the boy feeling sorry for him, since he was only a boy, albeit one that had led a sheltered existence. He was not at all what she imagined Dag, Ari and Holger had been like as children, but the men were right, they might be watched at this moment and she feared the danger of the possibility. However, something told her with Ari's settlement close by there was only the smallest chance that some of the Jarl's men had been able to follow their trail and even if they had, they were a few days behind them.

Holger stepped forward crouching before the waif-like child, "You were lucky I saw sense and accompanied you here, but just as easily I could have been a threat Thorik. Remember when we spoke by the fire? I saw something in you that made me take a chance, please think with your head and make me not regret what I've done," he spoke as calmly as he could manage realising any further anger would wound the boy's pride terribly.

Releasing Thorik's arm Dag nodded at Holger, walking over to his pack he lifted the horn and attached a long thin strip of leather around the mouthpiece, satisfied the loop was fastened, he glanced at Thorik and beckoned him over. "Here, I give you the horn, but do not feel tempted to blow it again... unless by my command, understand?"

Enthusiastically Thorik nodded, but waited until Dag presented the horn to him before grabbing it with both hands marvelling at the prize.

"Besides, you make it sing better than I can!" Dag shrugged, he watched as the boy traced his small thin fingers over the wavering lines and circles of the bone. It wasn't a large horn, especially precious to him or as intricately decorated as some he had seen, but the boy had been drawn to it and he was happy it had been that rather than his axe, sword or daggers.

Standing, Holger walked over to Thorik and pulled him away, telling him to gather moss, leaves and kindling to start a small fire. He caught Dag's eye and squinted in appreciation of the gesture, and satisfied that the boy was busying himself, Holger joined Dag and Gytha by the water's edge, "Do you think we are being watched?"

"Nei, not by men, just the woods," Dag grunted, kicking small pebbles into the lake.

"The woods?" Gytha shivered at the thought.

"Creatures Gytha, no more than that, a fire will keep them at bay," Dag reassured her and watched as she walked over to Thorik. The boy had managed to light a small fire and was feeding it twigs while crouching on his haunches. The horn still strapped around his back.

"He dreams of becoming a Jomsviking," Holger said smiling sadly.

"He would not if he knew what that meant," Dag replied dryly.

"Thank you for giving him the horn. It will make him feel brave, worthy."

Dag stared at the man, he was very tall and strong, a good ten years older than himself, perhaps more, he thought. He had a crooked smile that revealed teeth still strong and not blackened with age; his hair was thick, untamed and the colour of a setting sun, the redness streaked with lines of white. Heavy deep lines ran along the man's forehead and around the creases of his eyes.

180

"He is stronger than he looks," Dag shrugged, looking across the lake once more to the treeline.

"Please do not encourage him to join your kind," Holger asked, "Once I knew a man who became a mercenary, he had a sad life and did not live long."

"My joining was necessity... the boy has choices, mayhap I encourage you to tell him it unwise to serve under the rule of vengeful Jarl?" Smirking, he saw the anger and then softening of Holger's features as he realised Dag was jesting with him.

Raising his thick eyebrows Holger turned and spat on the soft dark earth, "Hah! Done Dag, done!"

"You have left your family in Srovberget, did you not want to return to them first and take them to safety?" Dag enquired, looking out at the ripples on the lake and glancing at the tall man beside him.

"Nei it could not be done that way," Holger sighed scuffing more pebbles into the water, "I was days from them already and the moment I set foot in Srovberget that damned bastard Brynjar would know and send for me. His wrath at my failure would have been great, but I doubt he would have killed me; mayhap he would have punished me in other ways involving my family. I do not want them to suffer."

Dag nodded at the explanation and believed what the man had told him, "This Brynjar has a reputation. Think he will follow us here, to this island? It is small and far enough away from his lands, he would need a ship for I believe the causeway is not known to all."

"He is well informed, there is a man he knows that has aided him in the past, some kind of Seer I think but they are not friends and I cannot be sure what the Jarl knows," Holger mused rubbing his chin and considering carefully.

"Does Ari know of this?" Dag said in alarm.

"I don't know; there was no time to say much other than warn you that Brynjar will find a way to locate you."

Wearily Dag rubbed his forehead, "Then we must let fate decide what will happen."

Holger looked blankly at the man before him, "I will help you however I can, and then ask you once more to help me. I'll pay the coin, I have enough."

Dag slapped Holger on the shoulder and directed him to walk towards Thorik, Gytha, and the fire, "What say we talk of your family when the worst of this is over? I don't relish the idea of the Jarl and his men on this island, truth be told I don't know what will become of you when he realises you have severed ties with him. Make it through that and we will talk more then."

Nodding Holger let the matter drop like a pebble thrown into a calm body of water, his hopes were not dashed completely, but now he felt the coiling of dread within his stomach. He was not sure whether to wish for the hastening of the Jarl's inevitable approach, or pray for one more night's rest.

Chapter 14

ᛑᚾᚷᛏᛗᚱ ᚠᛟᚱᛏᛗᛗᛁ

It had been early in the day when King Harald Greycloak's man had arrived in the hall of Jarl Brynjar. There had been no warning that the man would come, so his arrival had taken Brynjar by surprise which Solvieg instantly realised was the plan all along. It had only been a matter of time before Brynjar's negligence of his duties to attend the Thing at Gulafjord was noticed as Srovberget was tightly controlled and earned the King much coin, it was foolish of Brynjar to have behaved in such a fashion.

Solvieg stood beside her husband listening to the obligatory courtesies spoken between the men. She felt wary and afraid of the man's intentions, he was of breeding she suspected, tall, powerful and strong, he stood taller than her husband and his presence was more dominating. His eyes were sharp and bright, his face equally so, his clothing expensive and adorned with a mantle of rich animal fur over his shoulders. Only his boots betrayed the evidence of a journey made swiftly, the first of the rains had arrived turning the dry earth into a sodden mire of mud and the man had tracked it into her husband's hall. She eyed the trail of muck from the heavy wooden doors across the rush strewn floor to her husband's chair, Solvieg sighed at the thought of her servant women having to sweep the floors and start over again, she was fastidious in the hall's appearance whether Brynjar noticed it or not.

"Jarl Brynjar, my arrival seems to have unsteadied you, are you ill?" the man spoke without concern in a cool calm manner, a chill crept over Solvieg's skin.

"Nei I am well," Brynjar grunted, sitting with his thick, heavy hands placed upon his knees, leaning slightly forward in the great chair. Indeed, he appeared unwell; his skin was pale and his hair damp with sweat.

"Then you have another reason for not attending in Gulafjord?" the man queried before turning to his own men, gesturing for them to take a seat on the benches around the long rectangular tables. Two men stayed at the side of the King's man while the others all sat facing and staring at Brynjar, none had removed their weapons and none had taken up on the offer of ale and porridge served by the hall servants.

"My remaining in Srovberget is not intended as a slight to Greycloak…" the Jarl began.

"Then what?" the man queried.

"What?" Brynjar snapped his head up looking the man full in the face he took a breath realising this was no mere guard; it was the son of Greycloak's oathbrother.

"You are not ill, you say no offence is intended, so I ask you again, why you are here?" the man furrowed his brow as slowly he unfastened a heavily decorated brooch from his mantle and swung the fur onto the table behind him. He quickly glanced at Solvieg as he did so, although the summer was waning and the mornings noticeably cooler, the fur was a statement more than a necessity. "Does it offend your wife that my men have trampled into her hall?"

"Tis' my husband's hall, and no it does not offend me. My women will aide me in its repair later in the day," Solvieg tried her best to sound uncaring but her voice trembled. She wished to appear as no more than a vain woman of Brynjar's, she wanted no attention brought to herself for her husband's nature could be cruel.

"Ja they will. Tell me... Solvieg how long have you been the wife of the Jarl?" the man asked.

"Damn you! Address me and not my wife!" Brynjar roared, spittle flew from his mouth; standing suddenly he clenched a fist in the man's face. "She's a mere woman, naught more, you seek to embarrass me in my own hall?"

"Ja!" the man roared back, then stepping forward, he prodded a finger in Brynjar's chest "I address the woman when I get no sense from her man! Answer me before I split you in two, why are you not at the Thing? Why is it I arrive in Srovberget when I should be with my men in Gulafjord!"

Brynjar staggered back a step, the backs of his legs touching the wooden frame of the great chair but before he could answer the door of the hall opened and a man with a staff made his way to the men. Solvieg gasped, catching sight of her husband's glare he fired at her as she did so. The figure with the staff walked awkwardly towards them, but his back was straight and his chin held high; it was Inge.

"Ah, finally we have one who might give me answers!" the King's man grunted, "Inge Agarsson! So, this is your brother, only once I have met Brynjar before now, he made no impression on me and continues to do so."

The insult made Brynjar grind his teeth, it had been over a week since Inge had learned of his wife's and child's death, he had remained absent from the evening meals even at his brother's request he join them. Inge knew it was only so Brynjar could rub salt in his fresh wounds. Solvieg had managed to get word to Inge about his family's deaths before the Jarl had the full opportunity to twist the knife into his heart.

"Why are you here Inge?" Brynjar growled.

"I was sent for," Inge spoke but looked only toward Solvieg, the fact was not missed.

"My name, since you did not ask is Rorik," the King's man interrupted, "Give me a reason before I continue, Brynjar, and make it good."

"Continue with what?" Brynjar spat, his dark glare darting between his brother and his wife. His brow was beaded with perspiration caused by rage and his strange sickness that had grown, the tingling in his arm and fingers had turned to sharp spiking throbs of pain and his leg continually ached. At night he could not sleep for the blinding headaches, no potions the healer woman could offer seemed to work.

Rorik turned to Inge and looked the man up and down, he was indeed crippled, but Rorik could see it had not affected the man's mind, his eyes were keen, bright and sharp like his brother's, and his face bore more honesty that Brynjar's had ever had. Glancing at the woman, Solvieg, he saw her worried eyes moving over the earthen floor, her lips were in a tight thin line on her oval face, her hair tightly braided, she looked like a woman who had heard the harsh edge of her husband's tongue once too often and perhaps more thought Rorik.

He felt some amusement in the torture he was bestowing on the Jarl, it pleased him this odious man was twisting and churning in his guts. He had met Brynjar before and like his father who was an oathbrother to King Harald Greycloak, he had no love for him. It had been said that Brynjar would break his word, had intolerable greed and lately had shown signs of madness, nothing Rorik had seen proved otherwise, the man was clearly not of his own mind, it was in the Jarl's eyes.

"Inge, how come you to be lame of leg?" Rorik queried solemnly.

"My horse was struck in battle, it fell and broke the bones in many places, it was not set properly and never returned to full strength," Inge narrowed his stare, holding his proud chin high; he hated his leg and the damned staff he was forced to use to right his body.

"Ah, then it is no malady from birth? Many a child is cast out for being a weakling, I myself gave my father cause for concern, but I grew strong and proved him wrong."

"I did not know that Rorik," Inge said.

"Nei, can you walk unaided?" Rorik nodded at the staff, his arms now folded across his chest. The men behind him watched silently as Inge considered his answer; they knew it would be key to what happened next.

"I can swing a sword, an axe, grapple with a man, but I will never run again and in the winter walking pains me. I have the leg, it would have been worse if I had lost it," Inge replied shortly. Solvieg took a deep breath and glanced furtively towards her husband's brother.

"He's a cripple!" Brynjar stood angrily slamming his fist on the engraved armrest of the chair, "He could never hope to be a whole man again, tis' by my good nature that he graces my hall to feast when he does naught to aide his Jarl. Nei, even his wife and child are dead such was his inability to care for them!" The hatred in Brynjar's voice was hot with rage. As Brynjar shouted his venom Rorik stood fast looking only at Inge, he saw the man listen to the vile words without flinching, taking only a moment to let a wry smile form on his mouth before it was gone.

Rorik licked his lips, preparing to speak, but it was Solvieg who spoke first, "Husband, know this, Inge is no more responsible for the deaths of his family than you are for the rising and setting of the sun and the moon. He is an honourable man, and this you cannot understand for honour has abandoned you completely. Be Inge a cripple or not he is still more a man worthy of a seat in Valhalla amongst his Gods and fellow warriors than you could ever be. He is your brother, your words should never have been said even if you think them to be true!" Her eyes were brimming with tears.

Before any of the men in the room could react to Solvieg's words a loud crack broke the silence as Jarl Brynjar's palm whacked against his wife's face. Like a woman who had felt the sting of such a slap before, she merely tilted her head away from her husband. Gently her fingertips touched the site of the blow and against the pain she smiled.

"Every word she said was true, you have dishonoured yourself," with care Inge laid a hand on Solvieg's shoulder, his eyes searching her face. He saw a lone tear trail down her cheek over the red welt forming on her skin.

"If she had been lying, she might have deserved the humiliation, Brynjar, but she was not," said Rorik, his arms now unfolded and one hand resting on the sword strapped to his thick leather belt.

"You... you will call me Jarl in my hall!" Brynjar jabbed a thick finger toward Rorik, "Your playfulness of tongue has come to an end, speak your mind like a man and not a woman hell bent on trickery and slyness of words... I am Jarl here!"

"Ah... but you see Brynjar..." Rorik paused stony faced, "You are not."

The King's men behind Rorik now stood forming a semi-circle behind their leader, each was well armed though all of Brynjar's own men in the room sat stunned and immobile, they neither reached for their weapons nor stood to defend their Jarl. Brynjar took in the betrayal and it stuck in his throat like a fish bone.

"You have come here to displace me?" he roared.

"You are stripped of your title, your lands and your wealth. You are banished from Srovberget, do not think to return, had the decision been my father's or mine, you would be dead. Did you think you could conceal the truth from Greycloak forever? You suffer from a weak mind and ill judgement on the company you keep, a messenger arrived confirming what we had long been suspected, your deception was revealed. King Harald Greycloak is your King, your word is bound to him only, and no other man not even his uncle," Rorik glared at Brynjar watching as defeat and then fury distorted the man's features.

"So you cast me out over some rumour? Your suspicions? I have had some spy in my midst that has fed you falsehoods..."

"You mean to say you have not sworn allegiance to Bluetooth should he replace our King of Norway?" Rorik asked in feigned surprise.

"Wherein lies the treachery in that? Would not Greycloak himself swear fealty to Bluetooth should this happen? Greycloak is his vassal!" Brynjar was grasping at straws.

"You plead ignorance to what I have said? You show stupidity by not hearing my words?" Rorik thundered, "We know that you have spoken of Greycloak's death... to make it clear to you Brynjar, that is treason."

"Nei... this spy cannot be trusted!"

"It is you that cannot be trusted. We have a King of our lands! Harald Greycloak has fought many battles; he is the son of Eric Bloodaxe and the grandson of Harald Fairhair! Bluetooth would desire wealthy provinces such as Srovberget, you are telling me, here in your hall that you have not given away your word in promise of wealth and power?"

"What!" Brynjar snapped viciously, had he been betrayed? It could not be, his mind furiously raced at the idea, but it sounded as clear as the light of a summer day that this man Rorik knew something of the secret quest he was on. Perhaps it was not so secret after all, had he been foolish and absent in his handling of the situation he wondered. "This King Greycloak, that the people seem too eager to call him with pride, is a man lustful for battle and extending his territories. He is watched carefully by Bluetooth, for such a man might start a conflict not even he could survive!"

"You have lost your mind!" Rorik's demeanour slipped and he spoke the words viciously.

"Such blind loyalty! I watch my back as well your Greycloak should watch his! You speak of his battles, what of King Haakon's death at Fitjar? Is Greycloak so arrogant he thinks Haakon's son will not avenge him?" Brynjar clamped his mouth shut suddenly, he was on the verge of saying too much and knew it, and he had already said enough to warrant death rather than banishment. It was not over for him yet, he had spilled his ire and now he would rein in his fury, for he was perilously close to confirming Rorik's thought that he was mad.

"Your other brothers have turned down the right to your chair, no doubt they fear your retribution and more likely they are aware of your dealings and those you are linked to," Rorik controlled his anger speaking as though he were talking to a simpleton rather than the conniving snake that stood before him, "But Inge here has proven to be an intelligent man, brave even considering what he takes on in your place. It is Inge who will now be Jarl and Solvieg's hand is also his. You will be escorted from the hall, take a pack and a horse, the blacksmith will provide you with a sword unlike one you have ever handled I suspect. No man will follow you, none would dare."

Rorik flung a filthy glance to the still seated men of the former Jarl, none nodded in agreement but neither did they protest. Rorik knew a few would follow Brynjar but he cared not, they would never attempt a return if they did so, the rat's nest must be cleared.

To Inge he spoke quietly as he took a few steps toward him, "This is your hall now, I hope Solvieg can heal what has been wounded, she is a brave woman to have spoken as she did. She could not have known what was to happen here and still she spoke for you. Treat her better than her former husband, I suspect you will."

Silently Inge nodded once, taking the proffered forearm of Rorik he grasped it and shook it without smiling or showing any signs that he felt anything at this moment when other men might have.

Solvieg stood staring at the two men, her gaze willing Inge's to meet her own, Inge said nothing, but took her elbow, leading her away from Brynjar and out of the hall into the passageway of the longhouse.

The King's men relaxed sheathing their swords once again, some still gripping their axes, Rorik jerked his head at two of them who, stepped forward at once, "See to it he is given rough clothing to wear and have him watched in the stable, he will have an able horse but not one of his own fine stock. I will be with you to escort him from the gates. Allow no one to speak with him."

The men approached Brynjar and roughly took him by each arm. At first he resisted, digging his heels into the floor and swearing under his breath. Then all at once he stopped jerking and twisting his shoulders, taking a breath Brynjar leaned towards Rorik with a mean snarl on his lips, "If I so offended the King why did he send such a thick-headed bastard to tell me? Is he afraid? Ja, that is it, he hides behind the men willing to do his bidding. Let him have this day for I will have many, many others, think you taking my title and my wealth is enough to stop me? Nei, I am a strong man and this is but a day I must end."

"It will end Bryjnar and tomorrow when another begins, I think even the Gods will hear your cries of anguish. Now get you from my sight before I defy my father and Greycloak and split you in half where you stand!" Rorik spat on the man's face watching the spittle trail over his nose and chin, he would very much like to have killed him, for though his father and Greycloak were hard taskmasters, he was loyal to them and would have no man speak ill of them.

The guards took Brynjar from the hall without resistance, Brynjar's men sat looking at one another unsure of whom they were duty bound to serve. Rorik saw their hesitation and swore under his breath and walking towards them, he again placed his hand on the hilt of his sword. "You will swear fealty to Jarl Inge, failure to do so will not be well received. Should any of you decide to follow the traitor expect no better treatment than he has seen. Your lack of voice when the punishment was being read out tells me there is no strong love for your former leader but know this, fail Inge in any way and I will return and set all your hides upon a pyre." With that, he turned and made his way to the passageway Inge and Solvieg had taken.

He knew they would be in the rear chamber that had belonged to Brynjar for he had told Inge to go there after the punishment had been dealt. Upon entering the room, he saw Solvieg's distressed face and Inge sitting on a heavily decorated chair carved with dragons and all manner of beasts sent from Hel.

"You planned this? Before Inge came you spoke? Why did no one tell me?" Solvieg cried turning towards him.

"I had to be sure you were trustworthy," Rorik spoke flatly to the woman, "When you said what you did about Inge I was satisfied. Worry not Solvieg, Inge vouched for you, but it was I who had to know, I am sorry Brynjar struck you."

"You let him live after all he said? He is a traitor and you let him go? I do not understand," Solvieg sat on the edge of the fur-lined bed, her head in her hands.

"Brynjar hides much Solvieg, we both know he would never give up the names of those he has conspired with, even under torture. He must think he has gotten away with his plans. He will be watched and we will learn more," and rising to his feet Inge stared at his new wife, feeling grief for those he had lost and the new turmoil entering their lives.

"Inge is right, Solvieg, now you must support your new husband and lead your people well. There is much strife in the land yet, Greycloak will push to secure his lands, and it is true that Bluetooth and the Dane will come. Why would he not when Greycloak has been so successful? We know this, but it will do naught to hamper the future of Norway, Haakon's son will present himself at some point on that there is little doubt," Rorik stated confidently.

"Nei, nei... you do not see it all!" Solvieg wept, wiping the tears from her face, she drew a breath, "he is mad, all you have said is true but Inge, I thought you would see it more, all Brynjar has in his heart is the damnable legend. What you men strive for he will turn from, for it is not his true course, he will lead you not to spies and conspirators, he will leave this place and chase down the one thing he desires; the ring and the child, he will take the jewel and expect immortality, endless glory and wealth, and he will kill the child he believes to be the mortal line of Odin in Midgard! Your

King, your politics, this land, they are nothing to him... in his lunacy he is focused on one thing only!"

Both the men looked stunned and gripping his staff tightly, Inge lowered his head and considered Solvieg's words. He did not believe in the legend, thinking it a peculiarity of his brother, not realising that it was in fact something altogether much different and stronger for Brynjar.

"Every man believes in the Gods... you cannot mean that Brynjar..." but Rorik was unsure what he really thought, 'could Brynjar be so twisted of mind?' he wondered.

"What we believe makes no difference," said Inge slowly, sweeping his gaze around the room.

"No matter, he will be watched, there is nowhere for him to go but to those he conspires with and eventually he will reveal what we need to know," Rorik made for the chamber door but as he lifted the wooden latch he heard Solvieg whisper under her breath.

"He will damn us all. He will lead you to nothing but the misery he wishes to inflict on those he seeks," she said.

"Solvieg he cannot harm us further, his quest will take him far from Srovberget, what is it you fear so much?" Inge's tone was firm but pained at his new wife's distress.

"He will lead you all to Hel! Death must be the only punishment he sees, there will be no peace. Where you think he cannot reach he will and his wrath will be most terrible. Ja, he is a traitor and now his men know, but there are those who will follow him and kill for him! There are those who believe as strongly as he! Rorik please spill his blood, for if you do not this hall will burn and all who reside in it, Brynjar will see to that!" her throat constricted and Solvieg crumpled onto the floor.

For a moment in the hall she had felt free of Brynjar, almost a sense of joy had entered her heart that now she was bound to Inge. There may now be some purpose to her life other than pain and sadness, but the realisation of her own words stung like nettles on her skin. She felt desolate and certain that Brynjar would yet have his day.

Chapter 15

ᚲᚺᚨᛈᛏᛖᚱ ᚠᛁᚠᛏᛖᛖᚾ

Sitting at the campfire with the horn in his hands, Thorik felt very happy inside, never had he been in such company, two strong warrior men and a young healer woman. He felt as though he was on a journey of great importance, he had not expected Dag to gift him the horn, he had never been given anything so wondrous before. He had thought the man would cuff him much as his father might have done.

The image of his father sitting alone, in his shack, in the hamlet, tugged at Thorik's heart for a moment. Though he had not been parted from him for very long, he found it curious he did not miss his father more. Thorik felt like a traitor, he was enjoying the company of Holger and Dag greatly, they were so much everything he wanted to be, his father reminded him of everything he was.

The men were playing a game of Tafl that Dag had brought with him, and the woman Gytha was watching them silently. Thorik noticed how her cheeks turned pink when Dag smiled at her and that he did it often, he did not think it was common behaviour for a warrior. Were they not always thinking about fighting and raiding? It confused Thorik and more so when Holger would often speak of his own family. Thorik vowed to himself never to fall in love with a woman and have a family, it would halt his plans for adventure and make him soft but instantly Thorik chastised himself for what did he know of such matters really, these men were still warriors not weaklings like himself.

The twigs and dry kindling on the fire crackled, the flames flickering in the darkness surrounding them, wisps of smoke rose into the windless air and the moon shone down through a cloudless sky. The men moved their board pieces back and forth, Holger was losing but Dag refrained from overly chiding him, Gytha closed her eyes and let the peace of the night fill her senses, as she relaxed she smiled, knowing the boy was watching them all intently as he fingered the horn Dag had given him.

All at once she felt the atmosphere change as Dag stiffened, Holger slowly reached for his blade and rose to a kneeling position and Thorik stared wide eyed at the sudden change in the men feeling apprehension at what had alerted them.

"You hear that?" Holger whispered.

"Ja, but I see nothing… wait, there it is again," Dag squinted into the blackness beyond them, but could identify no movement, "Gytha, slowly, move into the hut with Thorik."

Doing as he commanded Gytha shuffled over to the boy as quietly as she could, she saw the fear in his face but shook her head when he opened his mouth to speak, urging him forward she gently pushed his shoulders as he swung his head to stare at the two men.

Holger moved away from the fire as Dag crept sideways in the opposite direction, his axe firmly in his grasp. From between the rotten, mildewed boards Gytha peeked out at the now abandoned fire, watching for movement, she shuddered when a crunching came from behind the shack, feeling Thorik's small hand within her own she squeezed it tightly willing the boy to remain silent, he did and for that she was glad. Her ears detected the definitive sounds of footsteps approaching the men from behind. Gytha felt a cold sweat upon her brow as a large shadow filled the doorway of the hut.

"Gytha? Thorik?" a voice hoarsely whispered.

"Who…? No wait!" but before Gytha could say anymore she heard the flying pace of feet and another shadow flew through the air, but the first form ducked missing the attack. The shadow swiftly turned and pounced towards the assailant, grunting of two men wrestling in the darkness filled the space between them, suddenly a roaring laughter erupted, but one voice ordered a hushed silence.

"Thorik stay here!" Gytha moved toward the open entrance and felt the boy closely behind her, rolling her eyes, she silently cursed that he seemed unable to do as he was told at any point. In the moonlight she saw two large men, one slapping the back of the other, and then she heard more running approaching from the campsite.

"Ho! Holger stop!" Dag shouted, "tis' Ari!"

The running skidded to a halt and Holger looked to Gytha and Thorik, satisfied, he called out to the two men, "Show yourselves!"

Obeying, the shadows moved forward, a sigh of relief escaped Holger's lips as Ari and Dag came into sight.

"See! I should have known it was Ari with his clumsy feet!" Dag chuckled.

"And I you, when you missed your mark! Why did you sound your horn? I thought I'd find trouble here," Ari slid his axe into the leather belt about his waist, catching sight of the boy he walked toward him and turned him around, "Ah, you wear Dag's horn, did you blow it?"

Thorik felt heat rise to his face and thanked the Gods it was night, for he would hate them to see the embarrassment on his face, he nodded silently.

"You blow it better than Dag! Come, help me fetch my horse,"

Ari smirked and slapped the boy on the shoulder. The horse Ari had concealed in the tree line obeyed Thorik's tugging on its reins as he guided it to the campsite. The men walked together towards the campfire followed by Gytha, who was shaking her head but smiling with relief at the same time.

For some time Thorik listened to them speak of what had happened. The woman he had seen so ill was now awake and in Ari's village that lay beyond the forest. There was a man Ari was speaking of, a terrible man by the sounds of it, he thought, and something of a legend that had caused the events of their past and present to meet once more. Thorik tried to pay attention but weariness was making him drowsy, pulling the fur Dag had given him around his shoulders he felt snug against the chill that now filled the air.

Thorik was used to the sea air and the coolness that came with it at the end of the summer, he could smell the pine of the trees and the brown earth surrounding the lake. The low melodic tones of the men's voices pulled him into a deep sleep and he felt a hand stroke his cheek, if he had opened his eyes he would have seen Gytha with her warm, caring eyes ensuring he was well.

When the sun first started it ascendance into the sky Thorik awoke with a start, the men were already packed and ready to travel to the settlement, Gytha was bathing her face in the small stream near the hut and Thorik scampered over to her. "Slept too long!" Thorik gasped at the coldness of the fresh running water.

"Hah! You better hurry for they are eager to go," Gytha chuckled and walked back to the waiting group.

Giving up on the frigid water Thorik ran after them noticing Ari had his fur over one shoulder and there was nothing for Thorik to carry but himself and his horn. Within moments he was glad for this as the pace was swift and the terrain of the forest was tricky, great roots from ancient trees, thick thorny bushes and dead branches littered the woodland floor. The sun had begun to filter through the canopy of leaves trapping the heat and causing the temperature to rise but the men pushed on, paying little attention to Thorik as he scrabbled from one trail to another behind them.

When Thorik thought he could walk no further they broke into a clearing, the sight before him took his already panting breath away. Truly, it was the most beautiful settlement he had ever seen, it was nestled in a low valley covered with lush, long green grasses and surrounded by high granite cliffs. There was a scattering of small huts and longhouses around a wide earth beaten yard. One building stood out proudly, it was the Great Hall and attached to it the longhouse of the Chieftain.

As they walked towards the village Thorik saw people about their daily business, women were chattering in small groups, some were milking cattle and the others collecting eggs from the fowl in their pens. Men walked from the large cattle sheds, clearing out the muck and straw, some men were throwing fishing nets over large trestles much like he and his father would do. On the soft breeze Thorik detected the smell of a smoke house, he wondered if they were smoking meat for the winter too and his stomach growled at the thought.

He saw children running from a river nearby with wooden buckets strung with rope, he giggled absently as he saw them struggling and spilling more water than they collected. Some older women emerged from a round building with a thatch roof, their cheeks were pink and their arms laden with cloth and Thorik wondered if it was the bathing house or where they dyed the linen and wool.

A smell of food filtered its way to his nose, he could smell meat cooking, his mouth watered as he scratched his head, hoping upon hope that food would be present soon. Thorik kept pace with the group as they walked towards the settlement. The large oak doors of the hall were wide open as they entered the building.

It took a moment for their eyes to adjust to the dimly lit hall but when they did, they saw rows of tables and benches surrounding a large fire pit and the chair of the Chieftain at the far end of the long room. The smoke from the fire wafted up to the turf roof where it escaped through small rectangular holes. The walls were littered with old shields, swords that were highly polished, but rarely used, and woven tapestries depicting scenes from the sagas.

Women moved here and there, stirring the contents of large cooking kettles hanging over the fire pit, it was warm in the hall and they wiped their brows with cloth. Small children played on the rush strewn floor with a litter of young pups that yelped and barked in their excitement. The mother of the pups lay at the foot of the Chieftain's chair, Thorik cocked his head at the unusual look of the dog, he had seen many kinds, mainly hunting wolf-like breeds and large sniffing hounds.

"Ah, you see Vigi? Fear not she doesn't live up to her namesake!" Ari laid a heavy hand on Thorik's shoulder, feeling the boy jump, he grinned, "My uncle's dog, he isn't very good with naming creatures, Vigi is as soft as newly churned butter not a fighter or a killer of men and those are her pups, she is much too old to be breeding," Ari frowned and walked toward the animal ruffling his fingers through the thick hair on her coat.

"I've never seen such a dog!" Thorik edged up behind the crouched Ari whispering over his shoulder.

"She is used for catching seabirds," a voice whispered into Thorik's ear, "Lundehund come from very, very far to the north of our lands. See how she has six toes on each foot? And look at her stretch her legs, as she lets Ari scratch her belly, see how the legs bend? She is built to climb between the crevices of the sea cliffs and swim for her prey."

Thorik turned slowly to see a woman leaning over his shoulder, she was the woman from the cavern, but her health was much improved. She was very much unlike Gytha, whose blonde hair and blue eyes were like the women he knew of his land, this woman had strange eyes that were a myriad of colours and her hair was a rich brown flecked with red and gold. Her smile was warm and her skin smooth, Thorik felt at once intimidated and shy but the feeling subsided when her opal eyes connected with his and he attempted a lopsided smile.

Straightening her back Liv stood and looked at the boy, he was small and thin, his hair made her suppress a laugh, his face was however, defiant and his eyes keen and sharp. She noticed the leather strap across his chest and turned him gently to see a horn strapped to his back, cocking an eyebrow, she tapped the horn. "So it was you who blew the horn? I thought it was Heimdallr signalling to Odin!" Liv grinned at Ari, who now stood watching her with the boy.

Signalling with a finger he pointed to Dag, Holger and Gytha who all watched her with puzzlement and seeing Liv narrow her eyes at Holger's presence, Ari nodded assurance that all was well. Slowly she walked towards the group looking first at Gytha, "I thank you Gytha... you saved me," Liv took the woman's hands in her own and gently squeezed them.

"Dag, thank you," the Jomsviking nodded and dropped his pack to the floor before sitting and stretching his long legs out before him, gently pulling Gytha down to join him. Turning to Holger, Liv's face grew pale once more making Ari step forward and Dag's head to jerk up, "Do I know you?" she asked.

Holger looked at the woman and sighed, he had come across her path once before and had hoped sorely never to do so again, he had also hoped she would not remember him, "I'm Holger. We have crossed paths, once."

"Ja… a long time ago." Liv stared hard at Holger.

The woman made his blood run hot and cold at the same time, she had a proud face and her body though smaller than his and slight still showed she was strong for a woman. She was dressed in simpler garb than the other females of the settlement making her stand out more so.

Liv looked at the man in the eye, they were cloudy with weariness and rimmed red from the smoke in the hall, his beard was woven into a fine neat braid and his thick, unruly hair scraped back into a knot at the back of his head. He was large and squarely shaped, his face bore the brunt of a soldier's life, but there was a gentle quality to the rough exterior. He had been younger, but not much different when she had met him.

"You belong to the Jarl," she said, feeling Ari moving closer from behind her, Liv spoke quickly but softly, "You let me go… you let us go, why?"

"I couldn't let Brynjar take you or the child, you deserved a chance to run, my wife had not long given me my own son, I saw her face when you ran from the forge. Do not mistake that at any other time I would surely have given you to him had I found you, but at that moment I knew I could not," Holger explained meeting her gaze without any guile.

Liv nodded, "I ran across your path, you had a sword in your hand, it dripped with blood, I believe you when you say you would have taken me to him had you caught up with me again. But why are you here now? Ari and Dag would not have allowed it if they didn't trust you."

"We did not know this," Ari said, glaring at Holger, "Why did you not speak of it?"

"You would have not taken me with you, I needed to come. You must understand I worked well for my Jarl before I chose to betray him, there was no other choice! You men are Jomsvikings, you must have committed acts you'd rather not have or would rather forget."

"Ja, Holger, that is true." Dag looked to Ari, whose expression had changed.

"Holger came to Giffni with the boy, he has left the service of the Jarl and wants our help to remove his family from Srovberget. We have not agreed to do so yet. He has taken a great risk and this he knows," Ari spoke into Liv's ear.

"Does he?" Liv mused.

"I do. I am a man who can walk no further on the Jarl's path, I chose to leave everything for a chance to live in peace with my family if the Gods allow it, but that fate is uncertain. It pains me to know they are still in his grip while I'm here, far from them, unable to help them. I do not think the Jarl will realise my betrayal yet, but as I have told the men he'll stop at nothing to find you or the ring or the child," Holger drew a breath.

"He talks at length Liv, mayhap you decide his fate and give all our ears a rest?" Dag grunted pushing himself to his feet but seeing the humour flicker in Liv's eyes, he realised the situation was not about to become more strained and sat back down.

Gytha looked at all their faces, and once again settled beside Dag, confused that he seemed once more incredibly at ease. Liv had said little, Ari was looming behind her and Thorik had gone deathly pale.

"What say you Liv? Do we hang the man or give him a small measure of trust?" Ari asked.

"Holger, you brought the boy to Giffni? He trusts you?" she asked.

"Ja!" Thorik chirped suddenly, the group all looked at the boy who shrank back and scuffed the worn leather of his boots on the earth floor.

"A measure of trust it is then," Liv shrugged and walked over to the large kettle of broth steaming over the fire pit.

Holger remained where he stood, feeling like the wind had been knocked out of his sails, he felt confused and relieved at once. Slowly he slumped onto a bench and felt a tapping on his arm, Dag gave him with a sideways glance, "Time yet to beat me at Tafl… but no more secrets Holger, that was bad judgement. You see Ari only as calm and restrained, it would be a grave mistake to rile the warrior in him, many have done so to their great regret in this life and the next!"

"I had seen no fit time to reveal it, I didn't harm her or the child, it was a fleeting moment." Holger grumbled.

"So fleeting she still recalled you though," Gytha said, she felt a little for the man, he did appear to have sacrificed much and his past was one they could not agree with, "we all have a past Holger, none of us are innocent."

"Nei? Mayhap you and I speak later?" Dag chuckled at the young woman who blushed before jabbing her elbow into his side, "Stop woman! My bones rattle and my stomach aches from hunger."

"Here, eat," Liv had returned with wooden trenchers filled with stewed meat and vegetables. Ari sat astride the bench across from Dag and Gytha, next to Holger and Thorik. Liv watched as the hungry group ate, fetching large clay jugs of water and ale before filling each a horn. Then she slowly left the hall and took a seat on the wooden steps outside the oak doors.

Chapter 16

ᚦᚢᚾᚲᛏᛗᚱ ᛋᛁᚦᛏᛗᛗᛁ

From a distance she could see Ove talking with the men who guarded Harvardr in the longhouse, the Seer was now being kept from the villagers' presence, which was for the best Liv thought, though she ached to talk to him herself. She wanted clear answers not the lies that seemed to fall so easily from the old man's mouth. Folding her arms across her chest, she closed her eyes and breathed in the familiar scent of the village, it smelled of animals and grass, the warmth of bodies working in the sun, the smoking of meat and fish and the cooking in the hall's kitchen.

"Not all things in life change, when you were a girl you would sit much like you are now, I should've had my wife chase you back into the kitchen, but I was too easy with you, look where that has led!" Ove chuckled.

Liv opened her eyes to see the large bear of a man blocking the rays of sunlight from the sky, "I was a bad thrall," Liv smiled.

"Thrall? Hah! You wore no collar and Hel be damned if any could tame you! Nei, Liv, though you lived with the thrall women you had rights none of them could have dreamt of." Ove said.

"True Ove, but I lived in two worlds, some could tolerate me little more than the thrall women," she sighed sadly. "You have less of them I see."

Ove lowered his large frame sitting shoulder to shoulder with her, "People are glad you have returned. You will see it in their faces if you look around. Some still hold onto old ideas, but life is rarely one thing or another, and there are more than two worlds."

"A riddle?" Liv squinted her eyes at him.

"The truth! And ja, we have fewer thralls now, for no reason other than they cost coin and we are a small settlement. I treat those I have well, you will have seen the hardships other thralls endure no doubt... out in that vast land of ours," Ove waved a hand towards the coast and the large rock of Hornelen.

"Ja, I have, there was no slight Ove," Liv smiled, "I didn't want to return, it was under the belief of a lie, but now I am here I feel a little peace."

"For a time, my girl." Ove furrowed his heavy brows, "All things can last only for a time."

Liv nodded sadly, but felt his large hand slap her knee gaily. Glancing up, she looked at the ageing Chieftain's face; she saw the resemblance to Ebbe there and Ari too. "I think my nephew has plans to turn my village into a fort! He speaks of defences and training my farmers and fishermen, Gods above will he turn Gunliek the goat herder into a Jomsviking too? I'd like to see that!" Ove laughed heartily.

"And I!" Liv laughed along with him, wiping a tear from her eye. Gunleik was a wiry ancient man, he had been wizened since birth and Liv could never recall youth in him. His back was permanently bent and his fingers were gnarled and swollen with age. He had fewer teeth than his grizzled goat's and less hair on his head than a newborn babe. "He spoke of Brynjar?" She asked, this time all the joy had left her voice.

"A little, there wasn't time to learn everything. You needed healing. I see Ari has returned with his men, and a woman and boy?" Ove asked.

"Ja, the woman is a gifted healer, she would be of great use to you. As for the plans to defend the village I think it may be wise, but Ove, I would leave before the Jarl and his men descended upon you and destroyed your home. Something distresses me in Harvardr, I want to question him further, but fear nothing will come from it. I greatly mistrust the man, let me take him away from here."

Shrugging his shoulders, Ove leaned on the steps with one elbow and stroked his chin with a roughened hand, "When I was a young man I went raiding, bloody and foul, but it brought me some wealth. I've not always been a farmer, Liv; I can swing a sword and throw a dagger, mayhap just as well as Ari. I have a terrible fury in my heart for the deeds of the past, why should I not taste vengeance? Let this Jarl who would chase one of my own until her feet bled come here, let him taste the steel of my sword for it has hung upon the walls of my hall for far too long."

"You cannot mean to fight this man," Liv's eyes grew wide with disbelief, but she knew Ove was serious.

"This is our home, where our mountain sits proudly, didn't Odin strike his staff on it and let the wonder of Gimli promise Valhalla to the men who saw the fire of the night skies? I've seen such lights in the dark and I'll die with a sword in one hand and an axe in the other. I am a man Liv, beyond all else, and I will die like one. Ask any other here and they will agree," the Chieftain replied with pride.

"I'll not see you and your home destroyed because of me," Liv gritted her teeth.

"But it is not because of you though, is it? Are you forgetting Harvardr? Many years ago, he came, before I was Chieftain, and his presence never left. It was the Seer in whom we trusted and he has caused all of this... tis' our fate Liv, woven by the Norns, besides tell me you don't wish to see old Gunliek riding astride his goat and screeching his toothless war cry in the heat of battle!" Ove kept a straight serious face, causing Liv to chuckle softly.

"Tonight we feast and celebrate your return. You'll tell us more of this legend, I think it's time we knew," Ove stood and walked over to a group of men gathering tools before heading to work in the fields. He did not look back and for this Liv was grateful as she did not want him to see how his words had affected her. Taking a deep breath Liv bit her lip, frowning at the pain she caused herself.

"He's right, tis' time for Ove to take up his sword once more," Ari spoke from behind and slowly walked over to where Liv was seated on the wooden steps, lowering his hand, he pulled her up to face him.

"You heard all we said?" she asked looking into his eyes for the answer.

"Ja," his face was passive, but a spark of anger had hit him when he heard Liv mention taking the Seer away from Smols with her to protect the settlement, "If you took Harvardr where would you go? How far would you get?"

Liv looked away and felt sorry Ari had heard what she had proposed; it must have sounded terribly ungrateful. After all he had done to save her from the daudr svefn, she had not thought how he would react if she had left, she had not considered his feelings, only the preservation of his life.

"Harvardr worries me, he will bring harm to those I love," Liv said descending the steps walking into the yard until she felt Ari's hand on her arm causing her to stop, "Come," he said simply leading her to the barn.

Upon entering Liv felt the presence of her steed and saw Grani in a stall. The grey stallion blinked his large black eyes at her and whinnied shaking his mane furiously. "Grani!" Liv cried and turned to smile at Ari who watched as she stroked the muzzle of the fine beast.

"He has eaten his share and more, he's a fine horse, wherever did you find him?" he asked.

"Why, Grani found me. He was wild, untamed, covered in mud and matted. It took me the best part of a day trying to get close to him, but when I did he submitted… in a way. He carried Ei and I

215

many miles until we reached... until we separated," Liv grew quiet.

Ari shook his head wearily at the words she held back, he wanted very much to ask her what she had done with the boy but resisted.

"It is a hard thing to trust others, Ari, but I do trust you and I thank you more than you know for returning to my life," feeling the frustration of the man behind her, Liv sighed, "Am I a stranger to you now?"

"Nei, Liv, you are a mystery though," he smiled and reaching past her shoulder he stroked the horse's mane. "It was not so bad to return here was it? No one blames you for the fire, in fact the whisperings between the women in the hall all point the finger of blame squarely at Harvardr."

"Still, the women avoid talking with me, I've wandered around like a ghost until your return with the others, mayhap that is my own doing?" she mused.

"You are unlike the women here, they live sheltered lives and yours has been the opposite. What would you speak of?" Ari shrugged and leaning on the wooden posts of the stall he scratched his chin.

"Do you really think Brynjar will come here, can you see his finding our trail?" Liv asked him earnestly.

"Holger is sure of it, he knows him best, there's no way to say for certain but caution would be wise," Ari replied.

"Do you mean to fortify the settlement?"

"I do." Ari's look turned grim, his mouth set in a thin line.

"I could leave with Harvardr," Liv stared hard at Ari. She meant what she had said; it was tearing her apart that her presence posed such a threat. "I've done it before, leaving a false trail, he and his men are bound to question those they come across. I don't wish for any to suffer here, no matter what Ove says. He may be Chieftain but he cannot speak for all the men."

"But he does and he will," Ari grunted, he had no wish to see his father and uncle fighting, but it was the way of things, men had to do what was necessary, "You won't protect our home by running again."

"I can try," balling her fists at her sides Liv dug her nails into her palms. It was irritating her that Ari and Ove seemed intent on battle.

"Mayhap, you should stand and fight Liv? Have you none left in you?" Ari bit back, deliberately trying to rile her.

Turning away from him, Liv kicked a wooden bucket, dust flew up from the stable floor, hanging like a murky mist in the subdued light of the barn. He had angered her and she knew it had been to cause her to react; rubbing her forehead she wondered what it would take to make him understand. He was trained to stand and fight, she had lived her life for the past six years trying to outrun men like this.

"I've more to consider, if I die then Eileifr is at risk," she said.

217

"Is he not at risk now? Did you not hide him and leave him?" Ari asked pointedly. Furious at his words, Liv spun to meet his hardened eyes, "What!" she shouted.

"None of us can claim to be safe from harm, life is often a hardship. Say you leave with Harvardr what then? Jarl Brynjar will hunt you down, people will be hurt and lose their lives, better we try to end it here, where we have those we can trust close at hand," Ari shouted back, balling one fist he slammed into in the palm of his other hand.

"I have no wish to bury your family!" With the raised voices, Liv noticed heads turning in their direction from outside in the yard.

"Nor do I!" Ari lowered his voice, "What is it you think, that I have become so turned all I wish is to incite a battle that might destroy my home for nothing? I'd take the chance we can defeat Brynjar because it is a possibility! An end can be put to all of this, we have the advantage here, I know the land, the people and we have Dag and Holger. Brynjar would come into this blind."

"He has more men, trained men, and power at his disposal. I have seen what he is capable of! When Brodr died, when I first laid eyes on Holger, before he let me escape with a nod of his head, there was nothing left of that village; bodies hacked and split, puddles of blood that soaked into my feet, the deafening silence that comes only with death and because of me!" She said, the words flowing out of her like the blood on the ground in her mind's eye.

"Nei! Because of Harvardr and Brynjar, because of their lusting for what they must never have! Throw off this burden you carry Liv, if you don't it will kill you and Eileifr!" Ari responded gesturing at her in frustration at her obvious guilt.

Shaking her head Liv walked to the door of the barn, it was now late in the afternoon and the sun was tempting the sky into a soft golden hue of crimson. The yard of the village still hummed with life, the evening was hours away when the feasting would begin.

"I'm afraid," Liv sighed. "Look at these people, they are living and breathing, they are men and women with children. How can I see life taken from them? In the daudr svefn I dreamt my fear had been turned into anger, when I awoke it stayed with me until I walked amongst these people. My anger and my fear will not save them Ari, but my leaving might. Stay and protect them should Brynjar discover this island, but if it's trails he likes to follow I would lead him on a fine one."

"Fear is a good thing Liv, don't let it become anger, tis' a sign the heart is still alive. Trust me, letting anger consume you will destroy you, I know for it drove me many a season as a Jomsviking. Anger also makes you foolish, taking chances when the odds aren't in your favour to see what will happen. Don't let fear or anger rule you, use them in equal measure..." Ari's voice trailed off, he realised he was thinking of Raki, the man who had let anger drive him to seek vengeance for his family.

"You see running as a weakness, but compared to you I am weak, I'm a woman! I can never have the strength of a man," Liv, gestured between them.

"You are not honest with yourself," Ari grunted.

"You have the right of it, Ari Ebbesson you have gained much wisdom!" Liv smiled wryly, as gazing upon the hall she wandered out into the yard.

"I was always wise, you just wouldn't hear it!" He walked to her side, "I've been patient, but must now ask you what all of this means, the legend, Ei, the Jarl, Harvardr. Give me some understanding of it all."

Liv nodded, "Ja, come, can we talk elsewhere? Mayhap the enclosure Ove made for his daughter? There is much to say and we need to be free from interruption."

Finally, Ari felt the knot in his chest that had steadily been growing since he had taken Liv from the shore, ease ever so slightly. Taking her arm they walked to the longhouse, through the passageway and into the small enclosure.

"Before you begin, I will have your word," Ari sat on the bench under the wooden lean-to roof his elbows resting on his knees and his hands firmly clasped. "My word?" Liv sat beside him feeling her resolve sink a little; she knew there was little she could deny him.

"You will make no decision regarding Harvardr and the settlement without talking to me first. You will not leave without telling me, agreed?" Ari dug the toe of his leather boot into the soft earth.

"Agreed," and taking a deep breath Liv began. She spoke for some time pausing now and again to gather the threads of the tale, weaving the past into a coherent picture. She looked straight ahead all the while, refusing to read the expressions crossing Ari's face. At times she sensed his anger, though he remained silent allowing her to speak freely. Now and again he sighed. He had unstrapped his leather belt and laid his sword on the ground and when Liv stopped speaking, he thought at length about all she had revealed. It was a dark, sad story and part of him had no wish to dampen the mood of his comrades this evening with the telling of it but he knew they had only a matter of days or weeks before the reality of the Jarl's obsession might reach them.

Ari now realised why she was so keen to take Harvardr with her, but he remained firm with her, they would stand their ground and face this demon head on and the Jarl would fail because there was no other fate for men like Brynjar. Though in his heart Ari knew it might not be, however much he wished it to be true. He wrestled within himself over the fate he might have and the one he wished for.

"You'll not tell me where the boy is?" He asked quietly.

"Not because I mistrust you, should you come to harm because you knew…" Liv whispered, her voice full of anguish.

"That suggests you think I could be captured and tortured into telling?" Ari snorted.

"I couldn't live with the thought of harm coming to you again… I carried the blood of your death on my hands for six years Ari."

Taking her hand Ari gripped it firmly, "This is the way of it, I take you for mine, we once shared an oath we will share it again, it's our way to protect and honour one another. Ei is your charge and so he will be mine, tell me where he is and I will journey to protect him until my life runs out, I do this for you."

Liv took a deep breath; she wanted to argue with Ari, that it was madness to proclaim such a thing. How could he want to sacrifice his life after all she had told him? Her head spun so much she wondered if she was fully well but his face was serious and Ari's eyes told her he was certain of what he had said. It was their way to vow such things in marriage, but she never thought a time would come when she would hear the words.

Her hesitancy stiffened his back; she could feel his urgency for her to speak and Liv wrestled against the thought that should she agree to Ari. It would mean his death, it could mean losing what she had regained, but after the misery of the time during which they had been separated she realised one thing. They had been given a chance at a life together once more, this was something that could not be ignored, and thus fate had woven a new thread for them. Feeling his fingers tighten on her hand, she looked at him before opening her mouth to speak once more.

"I vow to honour you and protect you till the end of my days. I have no sword or knife, no tunic or cloak to give you, but I do give you my word," Liv felt a smile spread across her face. For a moment happiness replaced the apprehension she felt at their future, she had taken Ari's vow and given him her own. They were bound once more.

What she said softened his expression and lifting a hand to her face Ari gently pulled her forward and kissed her. It was done.

Chapter 17

ᚦᚾᚱᚲᛏᛖᚱ ᛋᛖᚦᛖᚾᛏᛖᛖᚾ

The hall was alive, villagers sat on benches at the long tables with laden trenchers of food, horns of ale brimmed and the sound of gentle laughter filled the room. The red embers of the fire pit glowed brightly, warm flushed cheeks and good humour graced the faces of the adults while the children sat on the floor playing with Vigi's pups. The women of the village who had prepared the meal weaved around the room carrying trays of roasted venison, small seafowl and fish, boiled vegetables and flat bread still warm from the clay oven. Freshly churned butter slathered the breads and dripped from the chins of the famished, who had been toiling hard in the fields all day.

Ove had instructed his men to start clearing a section of the forest; they had dragged fallen trees from the woodland floor and had started to fell large pines. They knew what their Chieftain had in mind and it was not the preparation of logs for the winter ahead.

Large earthen jugs of ale and mead sweetened with honey refilled the horns of the men and they swallowed eagerly to soothe their parched throats. The women smiled good-naturedly at their men who they knew would suffer greatly in the morning with dull heads and sore tempers but for now though, they talked amongst themselves of the summer's end and the preparation for the winter ahead. There were the same worries they expressed every season before the cold and the ice came but soon they were forgotten.

At a long table placed in front of the Chieftain's chair the group sat eating and enjoying one another's company, the men lifted their horns when shouts of joy at Ari's return came from the other side of the hall. The same voices welcomed Dag and Holger and frequently the women of the village would appear at Gytha's shoulder asking for advice or remedies for ailments. Gytha glowed in the appreciation of her art and smiled at Dag who nodded respectfully at her recognition.

Ebbe and Lena, his wife, sat at Ari's side, Lena looked worried, but thankfully she had her son home once more. Now and then they stared at Liv whose gaze flitted between the floor and the group of children playing in a circle on the ground. Ari had told his parents and uncle of his vow taking, they had not shown surprise and offered no words of concern. They knew he was a deeply thoughtful man and not one to take such matters lightly, therefore if Liv was still his choice after so long, they had no right to question it.

The dress Liv wore had been given to her by Lena before the feasting had begun, it was a simple gown made from finely woven wool, over a plain linen shift, it was of a deep crimson dyed by her own hand with madder root. A linen apron was fastened to each shoulder, but Lena noted only one bore a brooch while the other was fastened with a simple bronze pin.

It did little to detract from Liv's appearance, Lena could see what her son did in the woman, though she felt wary too. Ari's mother had always thought the woman strange, Liv's mother had been a curiosity and talk of her had lingered for a long time after her death. Lena remembered Liv had entered the world as silently as her mother had left it. They had buried the thrall woman under feet of snow and iron hard earth, she had stood holding the child in the frigid temperatures before giving her over to another of the women for a time.

It was how Liv was cared for and raised, she was fed and watched over by all the women, but never in the sense that she had a mother. It was their way to ensure the safety of orphans, but none needed another child and none wished to claim the girl for their own. Lena stared into her horn at the ale and thought sadly how lonely it must have been for Liv, she regretted not having given her more time, but Lena had a husband and her own son to care for, she had also buried many a child and her heart could not bear the pain of losing another. It was the way of things.

Ebbe leaned over to his wife nodding at the clay jug and let her fill his horn, he had spoken with his brother at length and discovered they were to erect a high fence around the settlement. Under Ari and Dag's instruction it would prove a useful defence and in all honesty Ebbe could not argue. They had needed protection for some time now, the world was changing and it was growing. He had been on a trading voyage with the younger men in the recent months and seen much to make him wonder, men with skins as dark as the midnight sky, women with raven hair, and then there were the men who proclaimed to honour one God only, and those who had scores of Gods with names he could not remember.

Watching his son, Ebbe felt a strong sense of pride in the man he had become, true, it was not a path he would have chosen, but he could not say that Ari was not a warrior. If anything he wondered more about the scars trailing from his jaw to his neck and resolved to ask Ari about it at some point, he thought there was a good tale to be told in the markings. The man, Dag, who had come with Ari, was interesting to Ebbe also. He was dark and his eyes glittered with the mischief of a child, but for all the humour he saw, he also realised a fearless fighter lay. The man Holger seemed troubled, though the mead had softened the frown lines, he seemed to have a permanent crease on his forehead.

Thorik looked at the men and women at the table and felt very proud he had been allowed to join them, his head was spinning a little due to the heat of the room and the ale he had sneaked into the wooden cup he drank from. His horn was still strapped to his back and he had spent most of the afternoon regaling the other young boys with tales of how he had come to own it but gradually the story had grown bigger and larger than Thorik could remember, and he gave up trying to impress them. He sat now with a bowl of blueberries stuffing them into his small thin lipped mouth, until suddenly a cloth landed in his lap and he looked up to see the woman Liv, laughing and pointing with her finger to her chin.

Blushing Thorik realised he had the juice of the fruit smeared on his face, and sheepishly, he smiled back at her and wiped the stains away. The woman kept smiling and nodded, he saw Ari wink at him from beside her. Before Dag could chide Thorik, Liv spoke, "Thorik, you did well to return Grani to me, you are a strong boy indeed. Grani can be full of temper!"

"He is fine, one day I wish to have my own horse much like him," Thorik gulped down a swallow of his pilfered ale.

"You don't have your own horse?" Liv asked, leaning her elbows on the table and rolling her horn in her open palms.

"Nei… my father is a fisherman but I don't want to be a fisherman, I want to be like Ari and Dag and Holger!" Thorik beamed a lazy smile and Liv smirked at the glassy look on the boy's face. She had guessed he was sneaking ale and thought his head and stomach would hurt very much tomorrow. "But I need to learn how to fight," he scowled.

"First you must be bigger, go fetch yourself some meat… and water while you are at it!" Dag grumbled before chuckling and lifting his foot to gently kick the boy's buttocks as he staggered to the other long tables laden with the trays of food.

Turning to face Ari, Liv whispered in his ear, "He's a good boy, such a strong mind, his body betrays him though."

"He wishes very much to become a warrior, mayhap he can," Ari shrugged and grinned at Liv, "I saw daggers in your pack, I can read your thoughts…"

Before Liv could answer Dag chortled loudly, "Hah! If I could read a woman's thoughts I'd be a very rich man, richer than I am now, what say you Gytha? Is there any herb or root that can do such a thing?"

"Tis' a rare mysterious root if it exists!" Gytha grinned and all seated at the table laughed.

Ove nodded to a group of three men who had pulled stools together in a semi-circle by the fire pit. Two men sat, one with a small wooden harp and the other with a leather skin drum, awkwardly and with difficulty an old man approached and took the last stool. It was Gunliek, in his hand he had his small panpipe made of bone and easing down onto the stool, he huffed and grunted until his body recovered from the movement. Everyone knew he was exaggerating the stiffness and pain in his limbs, as he climbed the hills and mountains as skilfully as his goats.

The men began to play in a soft rhythmic tone, many in the hall closed their eyes listening to the music while others continued talking.

"We have no skald, this is what we shall listen to tonight, that and of course Liv," Ove narrowed his brow and looked upon the woman.

"My thanks for the feast Ove, I wanted it to go on longer before talking to you all." Placing her palms on the table Liv stared at Thorik who sat at the feet of the musicians eating and drinking quite happily but feeling the eyes of the table upon her, Liv raised her gaze smiling quickly at Ari, "Begin," he nodded seriously.

"Ja," Liv cleared her throat and lowered her voice, she looked at Ari, Dag, Gytha, Holger, Ebbe and Lena and then lastly at Ove. "Harvardr came to me one night, a fire had been started in the women's workhouse, he told me I was being blamed and Ari had been killed. I heard the screaming and believed him, never had I been so terrified. He told me to come with him to safety and I did so... or so I thought, we walked for many days to the north and ended up at a Volur camp.

It was a strange place, I'd never seen the likes of it before, but the women knew Harvardr and welcomed us. They lived in small huts, fires were lit constantly to stave off the cold nights, smoke filled the air and stuck to my hair and clothing. One of the Volur instructed me to sleep in a shack, for nights I lay there thinking of Ari, the fire, the hatred felt towards me and Harvardr seemed like the only light in the fog.

At last he came to me again, he told me of a great task ahead and took me to the woman in charge of the Volur. She was a vile, twisted thing, her nails were yellowed and filthy, like talons from her fingers, her hair was matted and lank, her skin resembled dry onion skin and her mouth was all crooked and sly. I did not trust her, but had no choice but to stay and Harvardr was there so I reasoned I would be safe. The witch gave me a drink, soon I felt weary and light of head and I remember being laid on a pallet. Somewhere in the room another young woman was crying, her stomach was round with child and she wept with the pains of birth.

Harvardr explained to me that I was to become their protector, that the Gods had chosen me but what happened next could only have come from Hel for I felt no glory in it. The Volur witch stood over me, together they stripped me and she began mixing a paste in a bowl. Again she stood over me pointing to Harvardr to hold me down and with a needle and a small paddle she began inscribing my skin with runic script, she began to chant with Harvardr, I was in agony but could not move.

The woman in the corner cried out over and over until the child was born, when that happened Harvardr finally released me and I thought the pain was over but he reached into the fire pit of the hut and pulled a small iron from the flames. The witch cackled, clapping her hands, she shouted 'Yggdrasil!' again and again before he burnt my flesh with the branding iron."

Pausing for a moment, Liv willed herself to look at their faces, Gytha and Lena were pale and their eyes were watering. The men sat stony faced and rigid, arms either folded across their chests or hands gripping their ale horns. Thorik still sat with the musicians listening to the soft rhythmic tune of their song.

"When I awoke Harvardr was there, the young woman was sleeping, he held the child in his hands, such a small child Ei was, his face was lit with joy at the sight of Eileifr. He began to speak softly realising I had awakened, but his words were not soothing, there was only the legend and the real task.

He said, 'Liv you are bound to the child now by the seidr magic of the Gods, this boy is the progeny of Odin and he must be protected until his time comes. Long I have travelled searching for the mother who would bear such a gift; I found her and my kind cared for her. I am a Seer of the Yggdrasil Kynslod, the order in Midgard who protects the progeny of Odin, and this child will one day become the true king of Norway. He will banish all war, he will bring peace to Midgard and he will reign with all the power and strength of the Gods for he is Odin's son!'

There was too much pain in my body to react, the Volur witch fed me with potion after potion, vials of black liquid, my mind felt addled and my reason abandoned me. For days I listened to Harvardr in this state, believing all his words, becoming what he wanted me to be until finally, there was no more the witch could do and Harvardr let me step outside the hut. I saw winter in the sky, the air had turned cold, frost nipped my skin, but it was a relief all the same.

Harvardr sent me back to the shack to rest before we were due to leave the next day. The young woman's face was hidden from me all the while, she wore a heavy cloak and a veil hid her complexion, she rarely looked in my direction and seemed afraid to care for her child.

Harvardr told me I was to learn the art of fighting with daggers, he would teach me all he knew, but we needed to travel... we had to keep moving and keep Ei from the reach of men. That night he came to the hut, he had a lantern and I could see his face was uneasy, he told me the second part of Eileifr's fate.

'In my hand is the ring of a fallen God, he was killed by his own kind, it was said he could never be harmed as he was a son of Odin. His name was Baldr, and this ring was forged in his funeral pyre, it's made from the ash and bone of the dead and tears of the Gods for they loved him greatly. Hel took Baldr and Odin could not stop the sadness in his heart until a mortal son ventured to Hel to bring back the dead God.

He did not succeed, the fallen Baldr gave this ring in secret to the mortal as a gift, and for a time the act of Odin's mortal son healed the terrible grief of the Gods of Asgard. That man's name was Hermodr, Eileifr is his flesh and bloodline in Midgard, all that exists of a great man, and Eileifr will become a greater man, this ring I hold is his birthright for when he comes of age, it will empower him with the strength, knowledge and power of the Gods. With such wealth! Far greater than all the geld of the dwarf mines! Eileifr will become like Yggdrasil and reach into the nine realms beyond our dwelling of Midgard. He will have immortality, his battles won as he brings an end to the strife of men!

Tis' our task Liv, we protect the ring and the boy, we must prevent men from ever finding either of them until Ei has grown to manhood because they are precious beyond all measure.' He spoke with such intensity my eyes watered and tears fell down my face. How my life had changed, I had no will to resist what he was asking of me or telling me, I accepted everything he said for I had no choice. I was the protector of Ei and his mother, Harvardr was our guardian and this was our existence.

We set out at first light, in the centre of the compound there was funeral pyre, from a distance I could see the corpse of a man upon it but when I asked Harvardr who this man was, he shocked me. It was Ei's father, he told me his body could not be burned until Ei had been born. Harvardr told me the man had suffered greatly from sickness throughout his short life and when they tried to join him with the ring he lost all his senses. Ei's mother had been coupled with him to prevent the line from dying out, this bothered me greatly for there was no way to tell what possession of the ring would do to Ei when the time came.

Still I knew there was something wrong from the moment we climbed atop our horses, because the women of the camp huddled together, whispering and hissing at us. Ei's mother stumbled and she could not comfort her child, Harvardr appeared not to notice, although now I know better. We rode all day heading southeast, we never saw the coastline and for that I was glad as the memory of what had happened here was like a knife in my side. I thought constantly and it twisted and bled me of hope, little Ei was the one light in the darkness and I held him close as his mother limply followed us on horseback.

That night we made camp, and in the morning she was dead. Harvardr dug a hole in the earth and forbade me to watch the burial, I held Ei, expecting him to cry for his mother but he did not." A dark memory slid over Liv's gaze, one she had never spoken of, it was a lie of Harvardr's she had revealed for herself but she broke free from its grasp and continued.

"After some days ride we entered a small village, Harvardr knew the Chieftain and his son Brodr. I was kept from contact with anyone while the men spoke but often Brodr threw angry looks at his father and the Seer. When Harvardr approached me at the table in the long house he told me I was to wed Brodr, that this would provide safety as we travelled.

Now I know Brodr was tricked as I was, and indeed his father, Harvardr must have manipulated the situation to gain the protection from a sword arm, but also he had come to realise something else I think. Ja, I believe, though his heart was already twisted he had begun to feel the weight of the ring, he lusted after it though he knew full well, its damning power.

We moved here and there and Brodr worked in forges as a smith when we needed coin, it was at a forge he crafted the brooch to hide the ring; the one you see me wearing now. Somehow Harvardr betrayed us, as often he would disappear for a night or two, his explanations vague. After one such disappearance the Jarl's men attacked and killed Brodr, Holger you know of that night."

"Ja," the man nodded grim faced, "The Jarl had Harvardr as his Seer for many a season before your tale began. I had seen him often, tis' Harvardr that fed Brynjar with these tales of magic." Holger tasted the bitterness of bile in his throat and swallowed his ale before he lay the horn down, "Would be better to kill the bastard now, be done with him, flay him for the misery he has caused!"

"We must wait, our ire must not sway our decision," Ari said.

"Tis' quite a tale Liv, makes my own stories seem like children's adventures," Dag sighed.

"But it isn't all, is it?" Gytha looked directly at Liv, her warm gaze probing the woman's face, "It is not just a tale, for you have given everything to the boy."

"Nei… it is not just a tale. There is seidr, when I dream often I see a man in the distance he is always watching and waiting. I learned many a spell to blend into a crowd or disappear from sight and mind, it took a long time to do it but I hid Ei, I hope, where Brynjar cannot find him. What the Jarl wants is the ring, it's why he has pursued me so long," Liv paused and released the clasp holding the intricate bronze brooch to her clothing. Across the surface of the brooch was a myriad of lines, circles and small indentations. Gently she turned the small disk that sat proudly on its surface and tapping the brooch on her palm a small fine silver ring slid free from its hiding place, "this is what they will kill for."

The group stared at the item, it was not what they had expected. The ring was roughly made and instead of intricate knot work its surface was covered with a series of scratches, it held neither the wealth of the Gods nor the beauty of them.

"It could never be a wondrous item to those pure of heart, it could never be worth a life and in your eyes I can tell you see it as I do, worthless and poorly made. Something born of grief and death could never be beautiful but to Harvardr and Brynjar it appears quite differently altogether. This ring borne of great pain and misery will twist a heart, it was never meant for men without the strength of the blood of the Gods." Liv sighed. Her gaze drifted back to Thorik whom she suspected was listening to them and thought for a moment she saw his thin shoulders shudder.

"Brynjar believes it will bring him wealth, immortality and the name of King of Norway, he is resolute in this," Holger grumbled.

"He has been lied to." Liv brought her attention back to the table. "When Ari found me it was because I'd been foolish and not covered my trail well enough, still it cannot lead to Ei. At the time

I was seeking to hide the ring or destroy it, I failed in that. Finally, there is one more truth you must know, Harvardr has no idea and so it must remain, for if Brynjar does find us it may be our best weapon against him," Liv stated and as she finished telling her final secret the table remained in silence for a time.

Ebbe looked at his son, worry etched across his face, then to his brother who reflected the same feeling, but remained stoic. Thorik suddenly looked up from across the room catching Liv's eye, slowly the boy looked back to the men playing their music and she was at once struck by how small he looked.

Chapter 18

ᚦᚢᚨᚲᛏᛖᚱ ᛗᛁᚷᚾᛏᛖᛗᛖ

The room that now imprisoned Harvardr the Seer, was small and sparsely furnished, there was a pallet on the floor roughly constructed from wooden planks and laid with old furs. He wrinkled his nose at the musty odour and decided his body was not so weary as to lie there. There was a stool beside the bed, a small oil lamp sat atop it glowing meekly in the darkness. No fire had been lit in the room and the small square hole in the roof let in the chill of the evening.

He knew there were two men outside his door and he knew no matter what reason he could conjure, they would never allow him to leave, thick-skulled Ove had made certain he was trapped. Standing in the centre of the room, Harvardr craned his neck and stared up into the night sky, he could see no moon or traces of starlight. If he had been a younger man he might have attempted to break through the turf roof and escape, but he was old and even if he attempted such a task the guards would be dragging him back by his feet in mere moments. He was not strong enough to fight one of them let alone two.

He was angry and becoming more frustrated by the hour, he had thought Liv might have been tempted to question him further, it might have passed some time and given him an opportunity of escape. But she had not come and he wondered again how much she had changed in the time they had been apart, she had once been his willing servant but such days were gone and he knew her heart belonged too greatly to the child.

Mistakes had been made on his part, he knew this, and he was no longer a member of the Yggdrasil Kynslod, the faith he had held so strong had abandoned him, they no longer trusted him and had cast him out. No matter, he thought, his plan would reach a conclusion and soon, Brynjar would find him for Harvardr had left word in many an ear on his travels. It was but a matter of time and if he had to there was seidr magic he could use.

Knowing he should make an attempt to sleep Harvardr gingerly lowered his body onto the filthy pallet, dust puffed up into the room catching in his nose and throat. He was dreadfully tired of being an old man and he felt his fingers itching to have the ring again. Harvardr had regretted giving the ring over to Liv ever since he had done it but at the time he still believed and had faith, he had wanted to rid himself of its weight. It had been twisting his thoughts tempting him with visions of what could be. His life had always been that of a Seer, a giver to people, a receiver of the Gods but he had wanted more, he had grown angry and resentful, when he held the boy child at his birth he had not felt the love in his heart he had expected to.

In the distance Harvardr thought he could hear music, voices full of joy and laughter floated from the hall taunting him, "Laugh... laugh now, for soon it will be screams of terror ripping from your throats," he whispered menacingly into the emptiness of the room. "Soon I will be free, free from this prison, free from Brynjar's greed. I will have the ring and then I will kill her, but before she dies she will tell me where the child is and I will kill him too."

Closing his eyes Harvardr lay motionless, he listened to his own steady heartbeat as his chest rose and fell with every breath and feeling a sense of calm was over him again, he ordered his thoughts, he would have his reward and very soon.

The hall had grown quiet, the men had stopped playing their instruments and instead sat sipping ale and talked of retiring for the evening. On the far side of the hall, across from the fire pit and heavy oak doors, men who had no houses yet of their own had climbed into the rows of pallets that ran alongside the wall. Softly there were snores of the weary, the drunk and the young. Ove scanned the hall for his wife and saw her stroking Vigi's head. She had grown hard of hearing in the last few seasons and often sought solace with his hound. His daughter was with her husband's people and he noticed his wife retreated into herself at these times. He knew she missed their grandchildren greatly. Making his excuses he left the table, walking over to his wife he took her arm and gently guided her to the longhouse passageway.

Ebbe wrapped an arm around his wife's shoulders, "Come Lena, tis' late, we must make the walk home."

Lena nodded and rising from the bench, asked, "Ari, Liv, will you come with us?"

"Nei, but I will come tomorrow. Sleep well mother, father, it has done me good to see you so well," Ari said warmly. Gently Lena rested her hand on his shoulder, before gripping it slightly, "See you do come, your father could use another pair of hands even for a day and bring Liv for she is family now."

They had told the group of their vows and though all had wished to celebrate, Liv and Ari insisted against it. "It's for us only, we accept your love and wish only to live now, we have lost much time," Ari had said and all accepted it. He had wished he had spoken to his father before vowing with Liv, he had spent so little time with him and the man was beginning to age. Ari resolved to spend the next day with his father and leave the construction of the wooden wall to Dag and Holger.

Dag stretched his arms behind his back feeling the knots in his muscles ache, "It's been a long night." Watching Holger rise from the bench he saw the man walk over to Thorik and lift him over his shoulder, then finding an empty pallet he laid the boy down before removing his boots and tunic. Lifting a fur from the pallet and dragging one over the boy Holger lay on the floor to sleep. Dag smiled, the boy was making quite an impression and not one he had thought possible when first he met him in the hamlet.

"Gytha, you are welcome to sleep with Liv, it's a small room just beyond the passageway," Ari offered, but catching Dag's eye he realised at once his friend had other ideas.

"Your wife may not agree Ari!" Dag grinned, "besides, the night air is cool, Gytha will you walk with me?" With a sincere expression Dag stood and offered his hand to Gytha, blushing slightly, she rose and made her thanks to Ari and Liv before leaving the hall with Dag.

"I don't think there will be much walking," rubbing his temple with the heel of his hand, Ari jerked suddenly when Liv placed a warm hand on his arm. He had not meant to flinch at her touch and regretted his reaction when he saw the hurt in her eyes but in truth, he had not thought what would happen at the end of the night and he suddenly felt foolish and uneasy.

Liv removed her hand and stood, an elderly thrall man and woman were putting out the oil lamps, Liv thought she recognised the woman but their eyes made no contact. Without a word she walked into the passageway and to the chamber Ove had kindly given them. She felt weak and sick to her stomach; she had not expected to feel like this and wondered if Ari had changed his mind about their vow. Mayhap he had had time to consider her tale more thoroughly and disliked what he had heard for a second time in one day.

Before she could dwell upon those thoughts Ari entered carrying an earthen jug of cool spring water and a rolled-up fur under his arm. He was wearing a dark brown tunic made of tightly woven wool, gifted from his mother Lena, when she had given Liv her dress. Placing the fur and jug on the ground, he knelt in front of Liv as she sat on the edge of the pallet and took her hands in his own.

"Forgive me, it has been a long time Liv since we were us, I've been a Jomsviking too long," he explained his eyes searching her face.

"I thought perhaps…" Liv began.

"There is nothing else," Ari said firmly and as the lamplight lit up his face, she saw honesty there and accepted it.

"There has been no other since you and our time at Giffni," she whispered earnestly a light flush staining her cheeks.

"But you were wed?" Ari assumed she had been a wife to Brodr, he had not thought that it was for appearances only.

"Nei," she said as if reading his mind and looking away, she saw her leather pack on the floor, removed the brooch from her chest and feeling the burden of it lift, placed it inside.

Ari watched as she lifted the dress over her head and folded it neatly. As she stood, he pulled her to him, rested his head on her hip and felt the warmth of her skin beneath the linen shift. Gently Liv lifted his face to look up at her and pulled him to his feet. Ari took the palm of her hand and kissed it lightly, then turned her wrist over and traced the lines of runes on her skin with his fingertip.

"I wish I could remove them," she murmured, her opal eyes glittered in the lamplight.

"I would change nothing," Ari whispered in her ear and taking a deep breath he took her in his arms and kissed her with great need. He felt the years of torment and hurt fade, quashed by the fever of their want for one another. Laying her on the bed, he found her body with his hands, he felt her touch him, it was as if they were once again young and in the caves of Giffni.

That night they loved one another and when the morning came, they lay in each other's arms, laughing and smiling, sharing memories of their childhood. They shared their thoughts and healed the wounds in their hearts; both felt a sense of return to something they once had, they knew the past was done, and this chance they had been fated with was a gift. They would begin again, for it was a short hard life, they had what they both needed and wanted in one another.

Dag awoke in the barn; he stretched on his back and heard Gytha softly groaning beside him. The hay they had slept on had kept them warm through the night, though his skin was now itching. Rolling her into his arms, he lightly kissed her forehead, "Gytha?" he asked.

"Ja?" she replied smiling slowly.

"You are awake?"

"Ja."

"Good. You slept well?" He asked slightly awkwardly.

"I did… and you?" She looked up at him uncertainly.

Nodding, he pulled hay from her hair and smiled, "I have dishonoured you."

"Nei, I allowed you," she said firmly and sitting up she dragged a hand through her loose golden hair, "mayhap we should visit the bathing hut? I don't want to smell like cattle all day."

Rising onto his elbows Dag considered the woman for a moment, she had said it was consent, by the Gods it certainly had been, but with a clear head she might regret their coupling and he had not meant to ruin her. "You are not like other women I've known," he said it seriously enough to make her stiffen and hold her breath.

"Nei... but then you are not what I imagined a Jomsviking to be either," she reasoned.

"I've never wanted a woman, but you have my mind at work. Like a game of Tafl, I cannot reason my next move but know this Gytha, I don't want the game to end," he said seriously.

Smiling at him she rolled her eyes and snorted, "Game?"

"Hah! A poor choice of words!" Dag threw himself back down onto the hay, watching as she stood and donned her gown. From her pack she removed a comb and pulled it through her hair. He had never bothered to consider women in the morning after love play, he had simply returned to his life, he had not wanted anything else. He frowned at her and Gytha caught his eye and looked away, "but isn't it always the way with men and women..." an old unpleasant memory of his parents floated in his mind as he murmured.

"You don't owe me anything," she sighed, seeing the darkness in his eyes, and feeling a cruel knot of embarrassment tighten her chest.

"I know," Dag said absently as he rolled a blade of straw between his forefinger and thumb. Angrily Gytha stood, she glared at him feeling infuriated at the smile spreading across his face. How could she have gotten it so wrong, she wondered madly? She had thought of him too much, had she imagined the attraction between them more than a game, she felt foolish and used and grabbing her pack she rammed the comb inside and made to descend the ladder and storm out of the barn. Before she could do so Dag hooked a foot around her ankle felling her quickly, wriggling away, she swung her pack hitting him on the side of the head, but it made no difference and before she knew it he had her hands behind her back, gripping tightly. "Stop!" He growled at her, but now, looking closely, he saw the hurt in her eyes and regretted his boorish behaviour.

Gytha saw the dark-haired man's expression change quickly as he released her hands; she rubbed her wrists and resisted the urge to slap him. He had managed to anger her so quickly, she felt embarrassed and foolish at smiling at his jokes and thinking him trustworthy and honourable.

"Gytha…" Dag lifted her chin with his forefinger, "let me start again. My tongue leads me into more trouble than I can often handle. I meant to offer you different words."

"Ja?" She cocked an eyebrow.

Dag sat back, grabbing a handful of hay in his fist, "My father was a farmer, but when he died everything was lost. I became a Jomsviking, it's been a life of sorts, not a fine one, often hard and unyielding and I wish it no longer. I plan not to return to it… this place is as good as any to start once more. Ari has proven it to be all he spoke of, even the talk of his mountain was true."

For the first time since she had encountered the Jomsviking Gytha saw something new in Dag's face and it surprised her greatly. She let him continue, softening her face, waiting for him to talk without interruption.

"Ja, I think I will stay here and become old, I will have my own land and farm it and you... will stay here with me?" Dag watched shock cover the woman's face and for a moment he thought he had misread the possibility between them.

She was indeed surprised but decided rather than express giddy joy at the thought of his proposal she would remain calm and measured. Her feelings had been hurt, albeit unintentionally, but she would not allow herself to appear a foolish young maiden willing to throw herself at his feet. No, she was stronger than that, she was her own person and made her own choices, her brother had unwittingly seen to that. Would a man like Dag want a woman given to girlish bouts of giddiness, she thought not.

Slowly Gytha nodded, "Ja, I will stay with you," she stood and held out a hand to him, "but not with you smelling of cattle... come to the bathing hut." Dag laughed and felt bested with his own wit, 'Ja.' he thought to himself, 'She is a fine choice!' and with that, they left the barn and wandered across the yard.

A new day was dawning and bodies that had celebrated the night before were starting to rise; this day was to bring great change. Thorik yawned and rubbed his eyes, he did not remember going to sleep on the pallet but heard a man snoring, and peering over the side of the wooden box bed he saw Holger on the floor. Quietly he stepped over the man and made his way to the fire pit.

The room had been cleared of food and traces of the night before and here and there women and thralls swept and stoked the embers of the fire. Thorik's mouth began to water at the sight of porridge oats being dropped into a large kettle by the handful. His mouth had been very dry and tasted bitter when he had awoken but now it salivated at the thought of porridge with butter and honey. He could not see Dag or Gytha, nor could he see Ari and Liv but outside he heard a man barking orders and reasoned the Chieftain Ove to be readying his men for the day's work ahead. Holger stirred and dressing in his tunic he sniffed the garment before sitting next to Thorik.

"I smell of smoke and sweat and you smell worse! I'll find someone to fetch us clothing and mayhap a dunking in the river for you!" Holger laughed at his own joke exposing the chipped teeth of his mouth as he did so.

Sticking out his chin Thorik raised his arm and sniffing his armpit, he wrinkled his nose at the sweet musty odour. He smelled worse than when he had been fishing large hauls with his father, worse than when they had to gut and clean the catch. Scratching his head, he found his hair matted beyond anything he could recall and wondered what had happened to him in his sleep. Looking over the pallet he saw his horn strung on a hook above his head and breathed a sigh of relief.

Holger stood and entered the kitchen doorway next to the hall, a small woman nodded at him and disappeared before returning with clothing and drying cloths. Jerking his head in the boy's direction Holger ordered him to follow. Grudgingly Thorik obeyed despite the growling in his stomach and the promise of a hearty breakfast so within reach.

As they approached the bathing hut they saw Dag and Gytha leave, they walked toward the hall talking happily with one another. Nearing the couple Dag nodded to Holger, briefly they arranged to seek out Ari and eat dagmall together before setting about the construction of the defences.

Gytha laughed at the sight of Thorik and with the reaction of a scorned child he stomped off alone to the hut. Once inside, the heat from the hot stones hit him, the steam rising from the buckets of water clung to his skin. Kicking off his boots and pulling his soiled clothes from his body, he first tipped a bucket of warm water over his head before lathering a wedge of soap in his hand, and scrubbing at his face and head. He then reached for another bucket of hot water, but struggled to lift it until suddenly a large pair of hands pulled it from his grasp and poured it over his head.

Holger stood laughing as Thorik spluttered water and bubbles from his gaping mouth, "Hah! Well, now you are clean, but by the Gods boy you need to eat!" Handing him a drying cloth he then passed the boy a short stick of elm wood, "Clean your teeth," he ordered.

Thorik did as he was told watching as Holger disrobed and prepared for his own cleansing but as he pulled the tunic over his shoulders, Thorik gasped at the sight on Holger's back.

"You were whipped?" He cried in horror.

Holger froze, he had not thought of his scars for many a year, his wife no longer saw them and neither did his own children. "Thorik go and eat, I'll be with you shortly."

"Why? Were you punished?" Thorik asked, his teeth bearing down on the wood of the stick.

"I was disobedient," Holger sighed, "Now off with you, you'll need your strength. Go!" His last word was said too gruffly and impatiently, he regretted it when he heard the door of the hut slam, as he had not meant to bark at the boy.

Reaching over his shoulder, he fingered the welts and lines of the scars left by his Jarl. Indeed, he had been disobedient; he had let the woman escape but he also knew it was little in comparison to the revenge Brynjar would invoke when it was discovered Holger had abandoned him.

Chapter 19

ᛞᚾᚨᚲᛏᛗᚱ ᚻᛁᛗᛏᛗᛗᚻ

The men who had chosen to follow their former Jarl were not the best warriors Brynjar could have hoped for, as they mainly consisted of young hot blooded and inexperienced sword arms. None who had been trained directly by Holger had felt loyalty to Brynjar, choosing to remain in Srovberget with Inge.

Thinking about his cripple brother taking his seat in the hall, taking his wife Solvieg, taking everything he had worked for so easily stuck in Brynjar's throat. The rogue Rorik, sent by Greycloak had watched with a gleam in his eye, as Brynjar had ridden out of the gates of Srovberget on a pitiful nag of a horse, roughly woven clothes, poorly made weapons and moth eaten furs rolled up and strapped to his pack. Still at least some men had chosen to come with him and that had angered Rorik who had shouted abuse and words of disgust at their decision.

Indeed, they were a group of young, foolish men; if they had betrayed Brynjar he would have had them flayed, but he would see to it they became hardened and soon. At least, he reasoned, they were so unseasoned they would blindly follow his commands.

The two men Holger had sent back had arrived before Rorik, and Brynjar felt pleased at this small victory, he had a trail and the journey to the coast would take only a matter of days from

Srovberget. From there he would discover what had happened to his man for surely Holger must have apprehended the woman and Jomsviking by now, but equally it was possible the man Gorm had killed Holger and this boy he had taken with him. This particular fact struck Brynjar as odd, why would Holger have done that he wondered, what real use was the boy, surely Holger could have easily broken him?

Perhaps the child knew more than Holger had revealed to the men, certainly they had appeared unable to explain Holger's actions. Brynjar had pondered this, they had been unwilling to say, one way or another, what their feelings of their commander's motives were, 'Stupid men!' thought Brynjar scornfully, 'why did they not separate and one follow Holger?' but he realised the men had simply followed their orders without question. One of those men had chosen to come with him while the other remained with limp footed Inge.

When Brynjar and his twenty men rode towards the beach, where his man had said he last saw Holger and the boy, he felt nothing. The wind whipped about Brynjar's face, the salt air stinging his parched lips but his heart did not leap or quicken at the thought they were gaining on the trail. He wondered again and again why Holger had behaved as he had, the time that had passed meant they might have encountered Holger returning and yet there was no sign of him at all. They uncovered no hoof prints, no extinguished campfires, and no shelters. The vast empty moorland rolled and dipped as they rode, for miles they could see in every direction and saw nothing and now they had arrived at the shoreline, Brynjar sensed it would be more of the same.

"Agar!" he shouted to the group on horseback behind him, seeing the man dismount and walk towards him, Brynjar leaned down to speak with him, "This is the location? What lies north of here?"

"I don't know Jarl. I only know Holger set off in that direction," Agar pointed into the distance.

"North... fjords and cliffs... islands, too many to search them all," straightening on the back of his horse he stared at the rolling clouds forming above their heads, it would rain soon. Rubbing his chin with the back of his hand Brynjar felt the whiskers of many day's growth, his skin felt tacky with grime and the salt air, he felt dishevelled. He had always been proud of his appearance, but now he knew he looked no better than some wild-eyed berserker.

He thought of the old man and tried to remember the name of the island he had once spoken of, 'You told me once, but I did not care to listen!' he chastised himself silently. Turning to the men once more he shouted against the growing wind, "do any of you hail from these parts?"

Many shook their heads but one young man, no more than seventeen winters, raised his hand, "Ja, my Jarl, but inland, further north-east than here."

"Name the islands... if you can, no wait..." a memory speared itself in Brynjar's mind; a tale the Seer had once told him, of a mountain, "Come," he waved a hand to the youth who nudged his horse to edge closer to Brynjar's, "Ja my Jarl?"

"Have you heard tell of a great island mountain? One that Odin struck with his mighty staff?"

The boy's eyes drifted over the land and sea before them, chewing on his cheek he fell silent looking vacantly at his feet. Then he raised his eyes and squinted into the distance, "Hornelen, the mountain you speak of on the island of Smols. Tis' north, if we continue on this route we will eventually reach it, but the divide is great we would require a vessel to reach it."

"Fall back," Brynjar grunted; he did not feel it necessary to praise the lad or thank him for it had only been information enough to coax the memory into clearer vision. Seeing a darkening horizon Brynjar ordered Agar to make camp, he sent some of the men to hunt and fish but expected meagre rewards for their efforts.

That evening they sheltered from the wind in the dunes, but the rain fell and all slept fitfully in great discomfort, all except Brynjar who sat with his cloak pulled over his head. He stared into the flames of his small fire, listening as the sky emptied its tears upon him, watching it struggle against the downpour. His dull hair stuck to his wet face in lank tails, his brow was furrowed and his jaw set, his eyes were unmoving but his mind was greatly at work.

He thought of those who had betrayed him, Inge, Solvieg, his men, he thought of Rorik and wondered if he would fall with Greycloak when the time eventually came for Harald's uncle to seal his fate. He thought of the Seer and the nagging idea that the old man had been manipulating him, it angered him that Harvardr had the gall to deceive him after his past failures, the aged fool had stolen the wrong brooch, and Holger had let the woman slip

256

through his grasp; it had been witnessed by his men. 'Ah Holger!' Brynjar saw the man in his mind as clearly as if he were beside him.

Could it be that Holger had betrayed him, he wondered? If he had, why had this been? Was it a possibility the man lusted after the ring himself, did he seek to beat Brynjar to the reward? He thought this unlikely, as Holger had shown little interest in Brynjar's obsession, and in fact he had seen the man's distaste for it in his eyes on more than one occasion but it also struck Brynjar odd that Holger would abandon his family in Srovberget.

What had become of the man was a mystery so far but it would resolve itself, he thought. It was likely Holger had indeed been slain by the Jomsviking, he might be buried somewhere on the beach or perhaps animals had stripped his bones already thus no trace would be found. Brynjar did not believe Holger had any knowledge of the treacherous doings of Inge and Rorik, there had been no time for him to play a part, if he had surely he would have removed his family? 'Nei, he does not know I am no longer Jarl,' but rather than this thought calming his mind it angered Brynjar further, for if Holger had betrayed him it was when he was Jarl and not a banished man.

Could it be his sword arm had simply decided to leave the service? It was very unlike the nature of the man, Holger had taken a whipping for his past failures and continued in his duties thereafter. Brynjar seethed, though his mind was in turmoil he knew if Holger had indeed abandoned him, it was because he wanted the power he himself sought; Holger must have masked his true intent. Brynjar realised very quickly the number of men who would stand against him were growing in number.

Should they reach this island and find the woman, the Jomsviking, the Seer and lastly Holger, there would be a terrible penance to be paid. Firstly, he would have his small army rip this Gorm limb from limb and hack him into fish bait, he would have Holger lashed until the flesh fell from his back, then strung with rope around his neck and limbs before being pulled apart by horses. If Brynjar saw fit they would burn his wretched corpse and throw the ashes at Holger's wife's feet. The Seer would have much explaining to do and perhaps Brynjar would spare him, for his expertise might be needed but it was the idea that the old man had engineered the return of the ring and the woman to him by Gorm, which irked him much. How had the Seer managed it? The more he thought the murkier the plot became.

The woman, she would suffer, the wretched wench with her damnable ability to evade him would pay dearly, for it was she who had caused the recent events, she who had caused his downfall as short lived as it would be, it was she who would feel the most pain. Brynjar was uncertain exactly how he would kill her, but he knew he would firstly shame her until her eyes wept tears of blood, he would hack off her hair and rip out her fingernails, he would slice her skin and wring her scrawny neck over and over bringing her to the brink of death time and again. He might drown her or drag her to the top of this mountain called Hornelen and throw her off the side.

Her pain would be great, Brynjar smiled to himself, but before he killed her he would have the location of the boy. Then he would find the bastard child and destroy him, for there could be only one ruler of their fine country and it would be he, Brynjar, and no other. The Gods would realise he was as strong and powerful as they, Odin-All-Father would feel pride that a mortal man of Midgard had accomplished so much, and the ring that would adorn his finger would glitter as brightly as the stars of Gimli. 'Ja,' thought Brynjar 'I will be as they are… immortal… beyond defeat.'

His men were shifting from one side to another, pulling their rough cloaks around their shoulders, grumbling and grunting at the poor weather. They had eaten a small meal of fish caught by a long line and some of the men had used leather strips with small stones to fell seabirds. They whipped their hands into the air, freeing the pebbles to smash into the birds, but there had not been enough killed to fill their stomachs.

A pathetic river cut through the dunes crisscrossing the shore, finding its way to the sea, filling their skins they drank thirstily but it did little to kill the hunger that rumbled and twisted their insides. Some had knowledge of foraging and tried to boil sea plants and grasses, it made Brynjar feel sick that they were reduced to chewing on seaweed.

As the dawn approached the rain lessened, becoming a mist and smirr, Brynjar noticed the white pallor of the soldiers, their cloaks soaking from the downpour stuck to them like second skins. He knew they would become ill should the miserable weather continue, he knew that fever was a possibility when the body was weakened and malnourished.

A vision of Inge floated into his mind; he recalled the waxy look of his brother's skin that burned like coals to the touch. He remembered the grossly bruised and swollen limb that would never be set right enough for him to use it well again. He recalled how his brother swallowed the agony of his injuries; perhaps Inge was a brave man after all and not just a treacherous snake but Brynjar doubted this, he knew the old healer woman, who had been so inept in his treatment, had given Inge potions containing nightshade to kill the pain. His own pain had grown since leaving Srovberget, he was without the healers' medicinal tinctures and vials and he knew not how to replicate her sorcery.

Fisting his left hand into a ball, he fought the tingling pain shooting from his shoulder to his fingertips, he strained the muscles in his left leg to awaken the limb, but it felt sluggish and clumsy. He would not stand and make a fool of himself in front of the men; he would not let them see he suffered any weakness at all. His head throbbed mercilessly as the light of the dawn grew, his eyes watering under the strain.

Part of him wished to tear the hair from his scalp to relieve the agony. Grinding his teeth, he tasted the metallic salt of his own blood in his mouth, frustration began to build and he sorely wished to vent his rage. He waited for someone to goad him, he watched for one man to give him reason, but they all continued about their duties oblivious to his pain. Brynjar felt his cheeks flush as another wave of stabbing light ripped through his temples and a faint buzzing began in his ears and suddenly he began to feel light headed.

What was this he was suffering, was this death, he wondered, could it be a curse? But who would have dared such a thing, so many had a reason but none were brave enough to try. The jealousy that had been felt towards him was enough for any man, it could even have been his pitiful wife, or one of his mistresses, he knew there were many eager to remove him and yet it was the cripple Inge who had succeeded. Brynjar wondered if Inge slept next to Solvieg in his bed, had his brother forgotten his dead wife and child already? Did Solvieg go to Inge willingly for she never had to himself?

He heard a voice talking to him and opening his eyes, he saw Agar frowning and pointing northwards, and without bothering to ask what he spoke of Brynjar stood snatching the water skin from Agar's filthy hands.

"We leave now, ready the men! The boy who knows Hornelen, I want him up front with me."

"Ja. Will you eat? There is a lean broth," Agar swung his gaze to the smoking campfire, where a small kettle steamed in the air.

"Nei... dowse the fire, get the men on horseback now!" Brynjar gulped from the skin and shoved it back into the hands of young Agar. Walking to the horses he grabbed his beast's reins pulling sharply. Guiding the animal towards the beach he pulled himself onto its back, securing his pack and weapon to his shoulders. The icy breeze of the sea air cut him to the quick, the cold air catching in his chest, he inhaled through his nose and spat into the sand. Today he would push hard and by the evening he would find this island, there he would plan, then he would take what had been so long overdue.

Chapter 20

ᚦᚾᚨᚲᛏᚢᚱ ᛏᚹᛖᛁᛏᛃ

Gytha watched as groups of men pulled large trees, stripped bare of their branches from the woodland, with thick rope lashed to the trunks. A large pile had formed on the outskirts of the village where another group of men were digging a vast ditch stretching from left to right of the settlement. She did not think they had nearly enough logs to construct such a huge barrier and did not understand its design.

Dag was standing with Holger, exhausted from hauling the wood they were mopping their brows with the sleeves of their tunics when Gytha approached with a bucket of water and a large ladle. The men acknowledged her with a nod drinking greedily before shouting to the villagers to take a turn. Throwing down their axes and long double ended saws they enjoyed the brief respite. The morning had been fresh, but had now given way to a hot sun, despite the time of year and she thought the men might burn and blister for many had removed their tunics.

"How can you build it so quickly? Isn't it too large a task?" She asked.

"Nei, it's a simple but effective design, we Vikings are used to building with speed especially when need be," Holger said tugging thoughtfully at his beard.

"Holger is right, besides, we have an advantage as the rear of the settlement cannot be accessed due to the valley, do you see how it lies in the belly of it, but the entry to the yard comes from the woodland? We already have a wall of granite to provide security; the trees we've felled will be more a gateway than a wall. It need only stretch in a semicircle from one side of the valley to the other." Dag pointed to the high cliff faces that were covered in shrubbery, "Brynjar and his men would not waste time searching routes to attack from above, and the cliffs are too high at any rate."

"I hadn't noticed as the valley looks so wide and flat," said Gytha.

"The opening of the valley is narrow, notice now how there is a slight incline... a hump on which the hall sits? It gives a good view of any who approach," Dag now pointed back to the woodland. "That's our real problem, too many places to hide, but we can't destroy an entire forest."

"Nei..." she nodded thoughtfully, "Dag I must forage for herbs, plants, and roots in the forest before it becomes too dangerous," Gytha was not asking so much as stating a fact. If they were attacked, she would need all the medicinal supplies that she could gather.

"Take Liv and Thorik, don't stray too far," Dag nodded and with a look drew Holger's attention back to the task at hand. They left Gytha and walked towards a group of men who were tossing hay and water from the river in a large pit filled with sticky thick mud. With long wooden rakes they mixed the dried grass, Gytha could only guess that they planned to pack the spaces between the logs with the mixture and let it bake hard in the sun. She had a vague memory of her father doing this but on a far smaller scale when she was a child. As she turned and walked towards the longhouse Gytha spied Liv talking with Thorik on the steps before the heavy wooden doors, and as she neared Thorik beamed a large smile.

"Gytha! Liv is going to teach me to fight with daggers!" He said cheerfully.

"With daggers?" Gytha laughed, giving Liv a puzzled look.

"Ja… the men say I'm too small to help them work, Liv said she'd teach me something useful!" The boy grinned from ear to ear.

"Is that so? Ignore the men Thorik, being big and strong is not a man's only purpose, what say you protect Liv and me in the forest?" Turning Gytha smiled at the woman, "Liv, I must gather for my medicines will you come with me?"

"Ja… wait here, I'll get my things and leave word for Ove on where we are going," she replied.

"He is not with the other men?" Thorik asked, squinting in the brightness of the sun.

"Nei, he is the Chieftain and must attend to many things, wait here," Liv took Gytha by the elbow and whispered in her ear. "Wait here with the boy, Ove is questioning Harvardr, I'll not be long."

"Ja," Gytha walked into the longhouse gathering her leather bag from a table and returned to Thorik. The boy was wearing a clean tunic that was much too big for him, a long leather belt tied in a knot held the material around his skinny waist. His trousers too were fresh, the outfit a mixture of natural linen and brown wool, and his boots had been cleaned. Gytha thought he looked much better save for the wild hair on his head that refused to do anything but stand on end and she noted, for the first time his face held a healthier hue when free from smudges of dirt. He looked younger, but his voice told her he was his full twelve winters when he spoke. She smiled at his desperation to shake off youth and become a man.

"I could help Gytha, some of the other boys here are allowed to work and train with the men, Liv says she'll show me tricks. Then I'll show them!" He swung from the carved wooden post supporting the overhanging roof of the hall, the post was old and the dragons and sea serpents writhing upon its surface were ingrained with years of weathering.

"You have a horn Thorik, I'd say they were already impressed. Didn't you see how their eyes bulged at it? None of them have such a thing," she grinned and tossed him an apple from her bag. Taking one for herself, she savoured the tartness of the first bite. "Do you have any brothers or sisters Thorik?"

"Nei, my mother is dead, she lost many children before me. Tis' just me, and... my father," the image of his father tugged at his heart again, he did not enjoy the feeling at all. Sensing Thorik was struggling at the thought of his father Gytha changed the subject quickly, "If Liv teaches you how to use daggers, I could show you some healing ways? Every man should have a little knowledge... but what I teach you could be a little different."

"Different how?" Thorik's head shot up suddenly interested in what Gytha was saying.

"Well... there are plants used to increase strength, potions that sharpen the mind, spells for protection!" She lowered her voice and glanced around them, and with a conspiratorial tone she whispered, "Imagine having a strong mind and body, Thorik!"

The idea appealed very much to him and he remembered his conversation with Holger on the beach as they had sat by the fire. He recalled how the man had pointed out the future fates for a weakling boy such as himself. Thorik desperately wanted more for himself, he had never considered before there was more to a man than his brute strength but he saw it now. 'I'm a thick-headed troll!' he thought, for were not Ari, Dag and Holger intelligent men as well as strong?

"Ja, Gytha, thank you," he said.

"We'll start today, Liv will show you weapons and I'll show you plants but it's our secret," she smiled.

"Tis' a good secret too, besides I wouldn't feel safe being in the woods alone without a man present," Liv stood behind them with a small satchel strung across one shoulder and a skin tucked under the other arm. "There are wolves and boars out there, we need Thorik to frighten them off!" She smiled and started down the steps and out into the yard not waiting to see if Gytha and Thorik followed, "I know the best foraging spots," she called over her shoulder.

"She never makes a sound, twice now she has crept up on me!" Thorik whispered to Gytha as he stared after Liv.

He saw her hair glowing in the sunlight, her plain linen dress on her slight frame, her fingertips pressing against one another as her hands swung at her sides. He wrinkled his nose and rubbed a sneeze away roughly with his fist. The apple Gytha had given him was too tart, but he continued to eat it anyway, in his daydream he had not noticed Gytha was following Liv until he turned to speak to her again and saw her spot on the step was vacant.

He jerked awake and ran after the woman, his horn swinging on his back as he ran, catching up to Gytha he skipped alongside then, moved to the space between her and Liv. Reaching the site of the construction of the wall, he saw the men sweating in their labour, some of the wooden posts were being hauled into an upright position, with sharp pointed ends facing the sky, there were men with barrels of mud slapping the mixture into place.

Some sang songs Thorik had never heard before with language that made his ears turn pink. He looked at the women, but they showed no notice of the crudity, he saw Dag wave catching Liv's attention and she pointed behind her to the far end of the valley where Ari's father's small farmstead lay. Dag nodded and smiled to Gytha before returning to his work with Holger, none of the other men appeared to notice them and Thorik did not see any of the boys who had boasted to him earlier in the day.

It had hurt him when he heard they were to be employed to

help and none had thought to say to Thorik, however he now realised these boys were indeed jealous of his horn. They were most likely to be carrying out their fathers' tasks with the beasts, rather than working on the wall.

Suddenly Thorik sensed movement beside him and saw Vigi, Chieftain Ove's dog was walking alongside him, he ruffled the spot behind her ear grinning at the sight of her company.

"Vigi!" Liv whistled without turning to look around, the dog ran up to Liv who glanced over her shoulder and saw a look of disappointment in Thorik's face. Reaching into her satchel she took from it a wooden whistle on a loop of twine, tossing it behind her, she heard Thorik catch it and smiled. "Thorik, that is to call Vigi if she strays too far!"

Gytha shook her head and smiled inwardly, the boy was endearing himself to all of them because they had all known what it was like to be weak at some point and Thorik's small being reminded them of it. Liv had barely made a fuss of him, but Gytha saw how his chest was a little more puffed out than before, his chin held a little higher, his stride more purposeful, he strung the whistle on twine around his neck and walked proudly with Vigi by his side.

They walked along a winding trail heading into the depths of the forest, collecting and listening to Gytha's explanations of the finds as they went. "This purple flowering plant is Foxglove, nei Thorik, do not touch it with your bare hands, here I have a scrap of cloth in my bag," Gytha pointed to the bag on the ground beside the gathering pile of herbs and plants they had foraged and bound with twine. The boy's interest was waning and she knew he was eager to begin his teachings with Liv.

They had been in the forest for a few hours and Gytha had wanted to gather as much as she could, assured by Liv that there was a bountiful supply of honey in the longhouse's stores, they would use as an antiseptic for wounds and burns, and they were achieving her goal well. "Wild garlic, Thorik," she nodded to a bush a few feet away, the boy scrabbled over on his hands and feet pulling at the long-stemmed plant. "Make sure and get the root," she called after him.

The heat of the afternoon sun was suffocating in the dense brush. Stray hairs were plastered to Gytha's forehead, and her brow was damp with sweat. Standing for a moment she pressed against the small of her back, easing the ache from being hunched over.

"I have nettle and white willow bark, not much because the tree was already rotting, they are so beautiful but do not fare well, and this... elm shavings," Liv returned from a small nook of the wood.

"Ah, thank you Liv, we can make tea from these to ease pain," Gytha smiled at the other woman.

"We should think about returning soon. I see you've gathered much, tis' wise to have many medicines for wounds and such," Liv noted as she placed the bundles next to Gytha's bag.

"It worries me that we'll need it to treat the men at all."

"I share your worry," Liv absently bit her bottom lip and wiping her hands on a spare scrap of cloth she looked away from Gytha and Thorik. "What more do you need?" she asked, breaking free from her thoughts.

"Well, let me see…" Stooping down to inspect their haul she whispered aloud, "hemlock, foxglove, elm and willow bark, nettles, garlic… I have a large amount of chamomile and there is a medicine box in the hall that has the means to make ointment and salves. I think we are done."

"What is this?" Liv pointed to a crop of small flowering plants lying in a heap.

"It's for making soap paste! Gytha said, it can be mixed with lavender and spices…" Both the women laughed at the unexpected interruption of Thorik who tossed down his find of wild garlic into the pile. His hair, for once, was laying flat on his head sodden with sweat.

"Are we done?" He asked Gytha, seeing the woman nod and pack her bag he looked hopefully at Liv.

"Call Vigi," she said. Thorik did as he was told and moments later the dog returned carrying three wood pigeons in its mouth. "How on earth? Ah well done Vigi, should we have to camp tonight we will at least eat well! She must have startled them on the ground," proudly ruffling the soft fur on Vigi's coat, Liv stroked the dogs back.

Then stooping slightly Liv drew her own satchel from the ground and withdrew a long leather belt; fixing it loosely about her waist

Thorik saw the glittering of several small daggers tucked into small slots.

"What will you show me first?" Thorik breathed. The blades looked very sharp, so sharp he thought he might lose a finger if he was not very careful.

"I want you to try and get a knife from me, when you do it's yours," smiling Liv held her hands out, palms up. Gytha chuckled at the mock sincerity on the woman's face, this was going to be amusing she thought.

"Easy!" Though Thorik did not quite believe his own bravado, slowly from side to side, he paced around Liv, bending his knees and crouching low, she made no move only watching him pace. Suddenly Thorik leapt at her, but Liv simply took a side step and the boy crashed into the ground. Looking up at her, his face was covered in pine needles and earth.

"Try thinking about it this way Thorik, if I can see what you plan to do I can avoid it. If you trick me with something else, then I'm caught off guard, ja?" extending a hand, she pulled the boy to his feet. Swiftly she ducked as Thorik threw a handful of dirt and pine needles in her face. He missed, but showered Gytha with the muck.

"Thorik!" she shouted angrily at him, furiously brushing down her dress and picking the pines from her braid.

Liv smiled at him and winked, "Clever but a little clumsy, you learn quickly, but I still have all my knives!"

Thorik groaned and huffed before standing on his feet once more, "You're bigger than me!"

"And all men are bigger than me! Stop bleating and try again!" Liv feigned anger and disappointment, riling the young boy's temper. Turning her back to him she sensed him lowering to the ground once more. She saw Gytha staring open mouthed before her.

Suddenly there was a dull thud at her feet, Vigi who had been lying on the ground barked drawing Liv's attention, a large rock lay at her feet and then the sound of another thud followed by the shrill sharp blast of a whistle. 'Clever little sprite!' she thought. Thorik had picked up an armful of branches and rocks and he attempted to distract her not once, but twice using Vigi to do so. She would let him have this one, although she had realised his ploy she was more pleased he had not thrown himself upon her back when it was turned, and he was still trying tactics rather than brute force.

Thorik reached for Liv's belt as she glanced quickly at the dog and pulled free one small sharp dagger however marvelling at what he managed to do he became completely lost in his victory gazing upon the blade. He felt the sharp point of a dagger prod him between his shoulder blades.

"Distraction will kill you, keep focused Thorik! You didn't see me withdraw a dagger from my belt and come behind you," Liv pulled the blade back and slapped the boy on the shoulder. "That was well done of you," she smiled and then staring up at the sky through the canopy she sighed, "I'll show you how to throw the daggers, we have a little time left before we must return."

Thorik nodded eagerly and watched as Liv instructed him on how to hold the blade before throwing, to feel the balance, and the weight of the knife, how to pass it safely from hand to hand, and how to toss and catch it by the handle. They practised as Gytha dozed with Vigi nestled into her side, however as the light grew increasingly dim and they found themselves squinting for their target, Liv drew the lesson to a close.

"Well done Thorik, let us return, fetch Gytha and Vigi while I gather my things," Liv patted Thorik on the top of his head. She saw his bright blue eyes sparkle even though he was tired from the day's activities and for a moment she saw Ei in him, the simple innocence of a child, and she wondered if she might teach him the same skills, should she have the opportunity.

The walk back to the settlement brought surprise to them all as they approached the area of the men's work. A large wall of upright posts lined one half of the entrance to the settlement. On a raised platform they saw Dag and Holger hammering and tying ropes around a large opening, they were forming the gateway. Groups of workers were scattered around the fortification pointing and agreeing with one another that it was a fine construction.

Upon noticing the return of the women Dag shouted below and Ari stood to face Liv as she walked towards him, "by the Gods!" she exclaimed.

"Ja, tis' a fine job, the men have surprised even Ove, though he claims to have seen such things when he was a young man at sea. I think my uncle has been lost to the past!"

Liv grinned and grasped Ari by the forearm, "if the Chieftain heard that there would be trouble!"

"No more than he has dealt with thus far today," Ari's face grew serious, "he got nowhere with Harvardr, but you knew he wouldn't, the old man won't say a word to him about Brynjar."

"Ove wants to be prepared, to know what might be coming, Harvardr would only lie even if he did speak," she paused and watched Gytha and Thorik walk past them with Vigi, they stopped a moment to congratulate the men and continued to the hall.

"The boy now has a dagger?" he asked squinting at the glittering blade hanging below the horn on the boys back. "I knew you were thinking it, so tell me did he spar well?" Ari sniggered. Punching his shoulder, Liv glared at him, "Ja! He is clever!" she then let out a small laugh, "tomorrow you will practise sword play with the men?"

"At dawn, then we'll continue here, they won't be much good fighting with rakes and tarnished iron. Tonight after natmall we will clean and sharpen the sword blades and axe heads, take down the shields from the wall and repair the straps. Most can swing a blade, but attacking is very different from defending. Why do you ask?" Ari asked.

"Please let Thorik join you, let him feel the weight of the weapons, then I will instruct him for a while. It's important he spends time with you men, he cares greatly what the other boys think of him and they will be there with their fathers." Creasing his brow Ari placed a hand on Liv's shoulder, "Ja, I will do that. And what will you teach him tomorrow?"

"To run."

"Run?" Ari raised an eyebrow.

"Not as easy as it sounds husband!" Liv tossed him a look of mock disdain and wandered in the direction of the hall.

Chapter 21

ᚦᚾᚨᚲᛏᛗᚱ ᛏᛈᛗᛁᛏᛊ ᚬᛁᛗ

Ove sat in his heavy oak chair, he had spoken little throughout the meal and resting his temple against the large knuckles of his hand he leant an elbow on the carved armrest, he had been lost in his own thoughts for most of the evening. His meeting with Harvardr had bothered him, but he knew not where to start in speaking to his people.

He had been sure of his decision to fortify the settlement and sharpen the men's skills in preparation for battle but now as he looked upon the gathering of men, women and children feasting together in his hall, his resolve was beginning to waver and he wondered what his people could truly handle. They also looked to be feeling the tension, the men wore tired expressions, the women frowned or smiled thinly through the strain, the children grew impatient and raucous causing their parents to snap at them. He shook his head wearily and knew he must speak with them to ease the atmosphere.

Slamming a heavy hand on the table before him, he saw all the eyes of the room look up at once, "You have done well!" Ove raised his horn draining the contents dry. He darted a look to the three men who had overseen the construction and nodded, "we are safer than ever on our island, by Odin's blood we will have a long future here!" The room erupted into shouts of agreement, some of the men stood and shouted Ove's name before throwing the ale down their throats. The women looked at one another, their trays laden with cuts of meat and steamed vegetables, some stood with ewers of ale simply gazing at the floor.

Ove was not a foolish man, he realised the women must be in agreement with their men. He knew full well the strife that could be caused by a woman's tongue, though he also knew they often spoke sense in their arguments. Women, in Ove's view, held more power than they realised, it was they who ran the households when their men were trading or at sea, they who bore and raised the children. Their skills in weaving, mending and sewing, clothed their families' backs. It was the women of the settlement who milked the beasts and churned the butter, they made cheese and ground the grain for bread and they brewed the ale and the honeyed mead. Each morning they prepared the people for the new day and each evening they feasted. Ove knew well the purpose they served and their happiness would greatly affect the day to day running of the village.

"I can see the worry in your eyes but fear not, we have the Gods on our side, Odin watches us from the summit of our own Hornelen! Thor, his son, will smash all who seek to harm us with his mighty hammer Mjolnir and Freya, our goddess, will bless our harvest and our women. This winter we will eat well, we will grow fat and round, and in the summer we will begin anew! Tis' the way and will always be so," the Chieftain saw his wife nod at the women whose expressions eased slightly. A few of the men grumbled curses about their wives already growing fat and round, only to be cuffed about the ear by their spouses. Laughter rang out from the young men who had yet to marry causing them to proclaim they would never tie themselves down.

Sitting back Ove raised a hand, silencing the room, "my friends, our world is changing and we must prepare! I have swung a sword, every man must defend his home, and you too will do this. My wife has seen me gone for many a month trading and even raiding in my younger days. She ran my house; the women here will do the same. We are Northmen, do not forget this, we must honour our duty to the Gods and to each other! Eat, drink, and rest your weary bones. Laugh, sing and shout, I'll see all of you merry until such times danger befalls us and when that time comes we will destroy our enemy, tales will be told of our victory, none will think to challenge the people of Smol's again! We will raise fury and fire in our blood!"

Ari narrowed his eyes at his uncle, whose words were certainly inspiring the room and the atmosphere had lifted considerably. The young men and boys were jostling with one another proposing wrestling matches and talking about sport. The waning summer would see them competing in the fields as he had once done. The older men who had broken their backs for most the day nodded in agreement that a fight, whether it be now or in the future could not be avoided. They had known a relative peace from neighbouring clans raiding because of their location, they vowed it was unwise to become complacent and welcomed the opportunity to flex their sword arms. His uncle's face softened in the satisfaction gained from addressing the room and it pleased Ari to see Ove utter only a few words and his people were put at ease. He thought that until the impending attack from Brynjar occurred, there would be many an evening such as this.

Ove caught Ari's stare and beckoned him to his side, "sit, tell me of your father's farm," he said.

"You are there often," Ari laughed as he took his ease.

"Ja, but fresh eyes see what the old cannot." Ove gestured for Ari to begin.

"Ebbe is well, my mother is too, they have worked hard. The few cattle they have are producing, the foul laying, the small smokehouse is busy for many of the women use it. All is as it should be."

"And it worries you that if Brynjar succeeds all that may be lost?"

Ari sighed, he knew Ove too well and the years apart had not changed the man at all. "You are concerned? Liv has told me you were with Harvardr today."

"The scoundrel said naught! No intimidation could shake him. I've known that man for most of my life, his betrayal sickens me. A foolish old beggar, we are men and the Gods have better interests than us, this is the evil of men! No reward will bestow itself upon whoever wears the ring." Ove caught the attention of a serving woman who scuttled over with a jug of ale refilling their horns, "Nei, he is Hel bound."

"Do you wish to reconsider our plan?" Ari asked.

Ove scratched his jaw, his skin was lined and tanned from the sun; his eyes were sharp and flitted over the many bodies of the room finally resting on Liv. She sat with her back to the fire pit whispering with the young boy Thorik. "I gave it thought today… Liv had asked me to let her take the Seer. After speaking with him I wondered if it was for the best, I know you would go with her my boy, but nei, it cannot be so, we must face this foe together," he said his face grave but resolved.

"We could take him from here," Ari ground his teeth at the hint of urgency in his voice, "I could leave Dag and Holger, they would help to protect you."

"Nei Ari, for what I said is true. There will always be the likes of Brynjar, our world is changing, should you leave it only delays the inevitable. We are peaceful here, but I've had quarrels with many a Chieftain who seeks to expand his land and wealth. Each time I've seen them off with words or the back of my hand, but how long can that last? I'm ageing, I will die, but before either of those things happen I will protect my people."

Closing his eyes Ari took a breath and held it for a moment, he felt the muscles in his jaw tighten as he thought of his father's farm burning, the vision of people he knew laying face down on the earth, the smell of death in the air. He had seen it all before. "Never could I have believed any of this," he tightened a fist on the table, "and I'm used to dealing with deception, treachery, all manner of lies but none of them riled me as much as Harvardr. He's used me to inflict peril upon those I'd see no harm ever befall." Ari looked seriously at Ove, "you wish to stand and fight, but I don't agree. Damn it to Hel, I sat and convinced Liv she should stay when she spoke of removing Harvardr, now I'm as torn as her."

"Ari, you are only torn by the heart and mind of a young man!" Ove chuckled, "think of it this way, even if we kill Harvardr this very night it will not stop Brynjar. Nei, your words have only encouraged my bloodlust, I should like to sever this Jarl's head from his shoulders! Now go and sit with your wife, she is conspiring with that boy I can see it in her face, and Ari..."

Standing Ari smiled at the look of awe on Thorik's face, as whatever Liv was telling him was having an effect. "Ja, Ove?" he looked once more at his uncle.

"I meant what I said, I'm becoming an old man. My brother Ebbe too is ageing and one day we will need a new Chieftain." Before Ari could answer, Ove stood and walked over to his wife who sat with Vigi and gathering her about the shoulders, he guided her once more to the passageway leading to their longhouse.

Taking a seat on the bench with Liv, Ari chose to ignore what his uncle had said, he could not act with surprise, for he had always known how Ove felt, but neither could he accept or agree to the seat of Chieftain when his fate was so uncertain. "Did you eat well?" Ari called over to Dag who sat with Gytha. She had been informing him of her collection from the foraging in the woods and all the medicines she intended to prepare but Ari could see that Dag although listening to her, was thinking of other things.

"Ja, was a good meal," Dag nodded. Indeed, it had been, the women had laboured hard to reward the men, preparing haunches of venison rubbed with flowering onion heads and wild dill. Steamed onions, cabbages and peas in butter and now they ate freshly picked red currents and spiced baked apples and he felt very content and dreadfully tired.

For a moment Dag wondered if he was becoming an overly contented man, rubbing a hand over his stomach, he decided against ever becoming fat and round as Ove had suggested. A grin spread across his face as he thought of Brynjar's surprise as he approached an army of rotund waddling men screaming with axes in one hand and handfuls of meat in the other. He could hear Gytha chattering quietly beside him, it did not bother him to hear her talk as she did with great enthusiasm. He noted she had changed from the girl he had met at the harbour, but so had he it would seem and he realised he had not longed to return to the Jomsviking encampment or thought about it overmuch at all. He considered for a moment he was now about the same age as his father when he took a wife. Much had changed, Dag wondered if Ari had never been given the order to search for Liv, if Dag had never met Gytha in Gulafjord, would he have thought to drastically alter his life as he had?

A cold feeling of dread stabbed at his chest at the thought of the attack that was to come, and it would come, he knew. Looking at his friend Ari, he saw the same thoughts working through the man's mind. Scanning the room Dag saw Holger lying down on a pallet, with one arm behind his head, he rolled a small amulet in front of his face with the other. Dag guessed it was the small silver

Thor's hammer, which he had seen Holger wearing about his neck earlier in the day.

Dag realised Gytha had stopped talking and was staring up at him; there was worry in her eyes although she attempted to smile. "Come," said Dag, rising to his feet, "Ari has given us his room tonight, we must sleep." Dag nodded to Ari and Liv before taking Gytha's hand and disappearing into the passageway to the longhouse.

Liv turned to Ari and whispered in his ear, "everyone is weary. There will be no cleaning of weapons tonight."

"Nei," agreed Ari, "we will split the men between tasks tomorrow."

"Can I help?" Thorik asked, stifling a wide mouthed yawn with his hand.

"Ja, but to bed with you now," Ari commanded and watched the boy shuffle off without argument and hop over Holger's body, lying with his head at the man's feet. "What were you talking about?" Ari asked Liv.

"Defending himself if he is attacked; an elbow to the guts! A fist to the groin and a heel slamming on a foot!" She grinned.

"Really?" Ari raised an eyebrow.

"Oh ja, and a punch to the throat or gouging out a man's eye, biting and scratching. He seemed to enjoy it." Liv smiled, "I realise a woman shouldn't know these things or be filling a boy's head with it, but he has a right to know, considering…"

"I wasn't arguing! But it does make me wonder how often you had to practise such things," Ari replied.

Liv's gaze grew dark for a moment but then shrugging off the memories that threatened to throw a gloom upon her, she sighed, "too often, but I'm here now and so are you, tis' all that matters." She reached out a hand and took Ari's squeezing it gently, "do you think I might speak with Harvardr?" she asked.

"Why? Speaking with him will do no good," Ari said searching her face.

"I might succeed where Ove could not."

"And you might receive naught but lies. We don't need that. He's imprisoned, out of reach and unable to cause harm. Let it be for a little while longer," and hearing the commanding tone in his voice Ari cleared his throat, "consider it at least?"

"I hear you," Liv smiled and looked at the floor. "Where do we sleep tonight husband? I see Dag and Gytha have the comfort of a bed."

"The wall has sentry points, the men will learn to guard it as they have the hall, tonight we will take watch. Tis' a clear sky, the stars are bright and the moon aglow," Ari smiled back and standing Liv brushed down her dress, "let's go." They crossed the hall gathering a skin of water and a large bag made from hide. It contained blankets, their cloaks and a linen cloth in which Liv wrapped bread and dried meat.

As they walked to the wall, Ari saw the men were avidly on duty, keeping watch on the woods from the platform that stood high up from the ground. A man saw them approach and waved to signal that all was well. Suddenly Ari stopped Liv and took her hand pulling her towards the bathhouse. "Ari!" She laughed in half surprise.

"Ja?" He pretended to be distracted and ushered her to lower her voice.

"What are you doing?" Liv said in a hushed tone, she lowered her head and peered at him in the darkness.

"Come, I have need of you," he said simply and seeing the glint in his eye Liv felt the hot rush of her blood tingle beneath her skin. She smiled at his enduring effect on her.

Upon entering the hut the heat from the large stones warmed by the coals met their skin. Emptying a bucket of cold water on the stones, steam filled the room, causing a mist to swirl around them. Ari pushed the wooden latch over the door securing them from the inside. Liv dropped the bag in the corner beside the door, but before she could turn to face Ari he lifted her from behind and laughing, she grasped his hands as he swung her onto a bench before turning her to face him. She sat quietly looking up at him, "you are beautiful," he said, touching her face with his hands.

"You are fine also, Ari," Liv pushed back the stray hair that had fallen about his face. His hair was long, but he had tied it back in a knot at the nape of his neck. She liked to see his face like this, his tanned skin and square features, the slight darkness of whiskers on his chin, and the cool paleness of his eyes and reaching up, she lightly traced his jaw line and the scars that trailed down onto his throat. Clasping her hand Ari kissed her fingertips before drawing her up to meet him, kissing her passionately he held her close and Liv pressed against his body embracing the strength of his touch. Though they were both gentle there was a fever in their passion that night.

It was some time before they returned to the wall and relieved the men on watch. Climbing up the makeshift wooden ladder they walked along the platform. The structure impressed Liv, it was sturdy and well-made though it looked roughly hewn, she was glad Ove had seen the necessity of it. It was his arrogance as a Chieftain to have done without it for so long. They spoke of the days to come, the danger their loved ones faced, and they shared laughter at the banality of the commonplace events of the day. They talked of the future that lay before Dag and Gytha, they wondered about Holger's family in Srovberget questioning how they might help him retrieve them, however after a few hours had passed Ari urged his wife to rest a while.

As Liv drifted off to sleep Ari watched her breathing, he wondered what she dreamt of and if it soothed her. He thought of her closeness with Thorik and considered she must miss the boy Ei greatly. He knew he would return Ei to Liv one day, he wished to meet the child for himself, and he wondered what that would mean.

Chapter 22

ᚦᚢᚾᚲᛏᛗᚱ ᛚᛈᛗᛁᛏᛋ ᛚᛈᚾ

Brynjar wore a bloody smile that looked as though a knife had been slashed across his face. He had meant to kill the boy, he wanted an example to be made and it had succeeded, the men hung back, a look of shock and disgust on their faces. Stooping over the body of his fallen soldier, Brynjar swept a hand through his filthy mane and blood and dirt streaked over his forehead and hair. Wiping the sweat from his nose, he stood erect and walked back and forth glaring in his men's faces.

They had dismounted finding shelter in the tree line of a wood that stretched along the coast, however from the moment they had arrived Brynjar's mood had darkened as from their position he could see where he was striving to reach, but the impasse was immediately evident; they required a ship.

"Do not forget this!" He pointed the blade of his worthless sword at the body, "You chose to come with me for a reason, do not think me weak because I'm no longer Jarl!" He seethed spitting the words through clenched teeth. The men were young and too afraid to look at the ground, each one held the gaze of their leader as he ranted and glowered at them. Agar bit the inside of his cheek tasting his own blood, he was sickened to his very core. Brynjar had flown into one of his rages, worse than any he had ever seen or heard of before, the man he had killed had not incurred his wrath more so than any other present. It had been a bloody display of Brynjar's strength and fury, but it had also not escaped Agar that his former Jarl was struggling with the left side of his body and he wondered if the man was simply ageing or did he carry a sickness? Agar remembered the old blacksmith from his village who collapsed one morning, when he recovered he complained of a weakness on one side and had never worked the iron again.

"This sorry excuse for a Viking will disappoint me no longer, be warned if any of you think to dishonour me or your own miserable heads, then you will fall as he has!" Brynjar stopped in front of Agar, and taking the sword he wiped the dead man's blood on Agar's sleeve.

With his eyes he challenged Agar to stop him, but the young man simply stood grinding his teeth and holding Brynjar's gaze with steady stare. "If you kill any more of our men there'll be no hope of claiming what you seek," the words fell from Agar's mouth, but he did not reveal emotion, he simply stated the fact.

"You disagree with what I've done?" Brynjar snorted shoving the flat blade of the sword against Agar's chest and watched as the man looked down at the weapon pressed against his drab threadbare tunic. Brynjar's thick fingers turned white under the pressure of his grip on the hilt.

"We need men," Agar replied.

"Bury that one." Brynjar snarled.

"Dig with our hands? Expend what energy we have?" The younger man scoffed.

"Challenge me again Agar… I just killed your comrade, aren't you an honourable Viking? Don't you want to put him in the earth and send him to Valhalla?" Brynjar's anger was beginning rise again, how could this fool think of questioning him? Had he not seen what kind of example he was prepared to make?

"So we are Vikings now?" Agar asked, his focus burning upon Brynjar's face, imprinting every tortured feature, willing the man to betray any weakness.

"Agar… you are foolish to rile me," Brynjar hissed.

"Ja, Brynjar, I'm foolish but am I a Viking?" He shrugged, "I want to be a warrior, that's all." Agar saw the tautness in the man's face subside. 'Good' he thought, Brynjar had accepted the words as submission but Agar had not intended it to be so, he had been prepared at that moment to fight for his life if his former Jarl demanded it.

He wished bitterly he had gone with Holger, as at least that man had honour and a sense of duty and chastising himself, he realised with regret he had been arrogant and unwise to follow this man before him. Brynjar was mad, bedevilled by lust and greed, he was a heartless killer of innocent men, and women if the rumours held any truth, he was not a man undone by conspiracy and deceit and he was definitely not a man destined for an illustrious fate; Agar had chosen to follow the wrong man and his mouth grew bitter at the thought. 'Tell me how it is we have fallen so far, outcasts worse off than penniless beggars, killing one another. That man was sworn to you and all he did was complain of the cold, the rain, the emptiness of his stomach…' his mind swam with angry words.

"My father was called Agar… tis' a good name but not one he gave to his son's… nei. My brothers were named after Gods, but for me he chose a name meaning 'warrior' for I was the strongest and fiercest of his seed," Brynjar waved the other men off with a flick of his hand, but as they moved towards the body Brynjar shouted over his shoulder, "nei, let the birds and beasts pick his bones clean… unless Agar thinks you Viking men, for only Vikings would honour their dead!"

Nodding Agar took a breath before shouting over to the men, "Ja, bury the bastard!"

Laughing heartily Brynjar leaned forward, sneering at the young man, "you have a woman's tongue, lashes with one stroke and obedient with the other, was your mother a whore?"

"Perhaps, she was a concubine of yours, before you became Jarl. She is dead now and I've been in your service ever since," the words were cold and harsh and Agar watched the man's face contort and then fall slack with surprise. A few of the men listening in on the conversation glanced worriedly, they feared for their comrade's fate, Agar was one of the best of them and they thought he was throwing himself upon Brynjar's blade.

Taking a step back Brynjar looked the youth up and down. He was of average build, strongly made and as tall as himself; his hair was the colour of raw linen and his eyes as sharp and pale as a glacier. There was nothing remarkable about him, he was like any other Northman and he could have been sired by any of Brynjar's men and most likely had been. Shaking the possibility from his head Brynjar reminded himself he had no offspring, he had never been able to produce an heir, this man before him could not be his. Gruffly he shouldered past Agar and looked towards the horizon, they could see the island and the mountain, but had no way to cross the waters between. There was not a coin in any purse, they had found no fisherman or farmer who had holdings near the coastline and they had no tools to construct a vessel big enough for his men.

"Agar, you are not a foolish man are you? Skilful and mayhap a little deceitful... you have brought my mind back to the task and avoided being beheaded at the same time. You're like Holger... mayhap your mother knew him also?" Brynjar mused as he clenched his left fist feeling the familiar tingling of pain starting in his fingertips.

It did not go unnoticed by Agar. 'There!' he stared at the man's back willing him to move, even just a step to show the slight dragging of the left foot. Brynjar's shoulder sagged slightly as he grasped one hand within the other beginning to massage the aching limb.

"I must rest, split the men into parties, some will hunt and some with scout ahead. We must find a way. Build more fires, dry out your hides, rest and sharpen your weapons. I want the hunters to bring us meat, as we must eat, there must be a holding nearby somewhere and if so raid the pitiful shack and take everything of worth... like Vikings, and if they fail in providing we'll butcher the spare horse." Taking a breath Brynjar strode off towards his own mount and set about removing the saddle and reins from the animal. After doing so, he threw down his pack beside a small fire someone had thought to light before the commotion of the fight.

Walking towards the men Agar assigned them their tasks, keeping one eye on Brynjar all the time. He saw the man did not bother to wash the blood or sweat from his face, his hair hung about his head filthy and lank, a beard was sprouting on his face but it was patchy and sparse giving him a sickly look. Agar was looking for more; he wanted signs of ill health and he saw a slight twitching and ticking of muscle under the eye on the left side.

Suddenly Brynjar looked up and caught Agar's gaze, thinking quickly Agar nodded and signalled that the men were doing as ordered. With a small sigh of relief he relaxed for a moment when Brynjar lifted his chin in acknowledgement before returning to look at the smouldering pile of twigs. Agar moved off towards his own horse, lost in the myriad of possibilities before him. He had to think clearly and quickly, he had to think like Holger.

Harvardr sat on the edge of the pallet of furs gripping his hands upon his knees. He had been brought water and food, a weak broth of green vegetables and salted mutton, but his stomach refused to obey him and continued to churn endlessly, however he knew it was caused by his predicament rather than an attempted poisoning, though he would not put it past someone trying. Each day he festered in the room, he grew more restless and angry; Liv had not been to question him, how could she show such self-restraint he wondered. The Chieftain had been and gone, leaving with fewer answers than he had arrived with and that had amused Harvardr for a while, knowing he had irked the lumbering beast of a man, he would have had no chance in a physical altercation so he had used his mind and had won.

The guards outside his room changed regularly, but he rarely had a chance to identify who they were, this was a deliberate ploy on Ove's behalf, for if he had been able to guess who was watching him he might have been able to manipulate them. Harvardr made it his purpose to know people, he memorised faces and names, occupations and standing, appearing as a Seer impressing his willingness to help but admitting to himself now, Harvardr knew he had only ever had his own interests at heart.

He did not blame himself, he was only a man; men made mistakes and he had been negligent in his judgement. He now realised he had underestimated the intelligence and capabilities of those he had dealings with. He never imagined Liv could have carried on so long without him, and yet she was without the child, but she had brought the ring with her to Smols. He could feel its burning power like a throbbing blister from a hot coal and he would have it, one way or another.

It was clear he had also made a mistake sending Ari to locate and bring Liv to him. Harvardr had been so sure that the young man's heart had been twisted and blackened towards her. He had not foreseen their love was constant, he had been sure the Jomsviking was devoid of sentiment and he should have been, Harvardr cursed, the world was ruthless and harsh but it had not been cruel enough it would seem.

It was when he had been cast out by his own people that he completely lost his way and for a very long time he had grown embittered and increasingly resentful, he wondered if the ring had encouraged the slivers of these feelings to grow into sharp shards that cut through his soul.

The Yggdrasil Kynslod had abandoned him when they discovered his failings and his links to the Jarl. Harvardr thought often of the banishment from his sect, how they had welcomed him at first to the small dwelling nestled high up in the mountains. It had been a treacherous climb, his feet were bruised and his limbs ached, there had been no time to gather supplies and so his body was weak. He had escaped the Jarl's attack that had killed Liv's husband, but with the wrong brooch, the Jarl had been vicious in his wrath but also recognised that Harvardr was as driven as he and it would be but a matter of time before one of them came into possession of it again.

The Yggdrasil Kynslod was, however, uncompromising and unforgiving. They sat him down by the small fire in the wooden lodge, they offered him food and water, listened to his lies all the while knowing what one of their own had done. Then, when Harvardr thought he might rest, they pinned him down and burned the branding from his flesh with a blade taken from the fire. He screamed at them, they chanted and wailed, before he was tossed back out into the snow and ice. Curses rained down upon him from their lips as they stood in the darkness of the night draped in their cloaks.

Trying to focus he breathed steadily. His long silver beard trailing down his chest rose and fell with the movement of his bony ribcage. Closing his eyes, he brought the image of Brynjar into his mind, the burning insatiability of the man, even now shone like a beacon, Harvardr could feel his presence close by, a slow curving smile spread across his face. It was a twisted, malevolent smile; he would achieve a victory yet. With his mind, he reached out to Brynjar and saw he was sitting by a small fire, he looked awful, not at all like the man he once was, his clothing was poorly made and threadbare. Brynjar's hair hung about his face, his chin unshaven, his eyes were sunken and appeared almost blackened with soot.

Harvardr began to whisper, repeating the same words over and over, reaching a gnarled hand out before him, he envisioned resting it on the slumped man's shoulder.

"Hylda Brynjar... sja Brynjar!" He repeated the command for Brynjar to hear him and to see him over and over until slowly the man's head turned to gaze up towards the sky, his eyes were filled with confusion and darted to the men busying themselves nearby.

Harvardr tensed his fingers, he could feel a pain deep within the man, it radiated on the left side of his body, sharp and tingling and building. It appeared Brynjar was suffering an affliction; Harvardr smiled wickedly at this, for it would be used to his advantage.

"Brynjar!" He hissed at his vision. The man's head shot up and looked directly ahead, he imagined he could see the Seer before him, but shook the apparition away.

"Brynjar!" Harvardr hissed again and this time Brynjar saw him as clearly as if he was standing before him flesh and blood, "you must come, you are so close, there is a way across the divide... water cannot stop you."

Brynjar blinked and wondered if he had he truly lost his mind, how could the old man be here standing before him, none of the other men appeared to notice anything was amiss. Dragging a hand though his hair, he pulled on his ear and looked away.

"Nei... nei... I am here and I can deliver you from your pain. The ring is here on the island... you are so close," Harvardr reached out again with his hand this time beckoning the man to follow him.

Brynjar stood and wandered after the old Seer who was now pointing to a space in the distance, "That is the causeway. It was formed when Odin's staff struck the mount of Hornelen. The land shifted and we were granted passage twice a day for as long as the summer sun allows. The season is waning, you have a few days to make the crossing before winter claims the seas."

Brynjar followed the Seer's finger and line of sight burning the image into his mind. He was close indeed, he would gather his men immediately, push forward and the ring would soon be his.

"You must fight... you will have to suffer first to claim your reward, but it will be yours Brynjar, I will heal you but first you must fight."

"I'll fight... I'll kill to take what is mine," Brynjar said, his voice barely more than a hoarse whisper.

Somewhere in the distance Harvardr heard a gentle tapping which grew to a heavy pounding snapping him from his link with Brynjar, he was back in the room that imprisoned him and someone was banging relentlessly on the door.

"Harvardr!" A voice boomed from the passageway, sighing the Seer stood and removed the rope he had used to bind the latch to a loose nail he had worked into the doorframe. As he did so a guard threw the wooden panelled door open shoving Harvardr back onto the pallet. "You are the prisoner, don't attempt to keep us out!" The young man spat on the floor with a furious glare in his eye.

Before Harvardr could wrestle himself up from the pallet a slight form moved from behind the man and entered the room, shame and embarrassment flushed the old Seer's cheeks when he saw it was Liv. He grew angry that she had seen him in a moment of physical weakness. With a nod, she sent the guard from the room and stood looking down at him.

"I've come to speak with you," she said.

"You'll get no more than Ove did," Harvardr grunted, pulling himself into a seated position.

"They're feeding you well?" Liv crossed the small room and lifted the wooden bowl from the floor, "the room is small but you're lucky Ove saw fit to give you this one."

"Oh? A pit of vipers would suit me better," he sneered.

"I believe it would," she glared at him, "but the vipers wouldn't have you and so you are here."

"Here is where? I'm not in the longhouse, my belongings where are they?"

"The settlement has grown since we lived here, you must have seen that upon your return? This is another building… far from the reach of the village. Why do you ask for your things?" Liv cocked her head before turning away from him, "there's only one thing you desire."

"What are you here for?" Harvardr snarled, the venom in his voice was thick, seeing her back straighten and grow rigid he knew it had affected her.

"I'm trying to decide how to deal with you," Liv sighed.

"Deal with me?" he snorted with arrogance, he was the elder here and she would not belittle him. "I'm your guardian, you will come to see that you are powerless against me Liv. You were naught but a frightened little thrall when I chose you and you are nothing but a disappointment now!"

Liv turned to face her former mentor. Her eyes narrowed on the man before her and she barely recognised him. He was older, his face craggier, his hair thinner, lines etched across his weathered skin. His mouth only formed sneers and grimaces when he spoke, where she recalled gentler expressions had been in the past. She knew she was growing a deep hatred for the man who had lied to her but equally, she knew she must hide it and keep it from him since he would try to manipulate her no matter what it was she felt.

"Once you knew me, but no longer… I've been without my guardian for a long long time," she emphasised the word guardian, drawing his attention and she watched as his eyes gleamed with anger before he turned away in disgust. "I'm trying to decide on three things, mayhap you can tell me which choice is best? My first choice is to let the settlement wait for a possible attack from Brynjar, but would he want you or kill you?"

"Let the attack happen and many will die, mayhap I will be one of the dead, but then I might not be," Harvardr said leaning back on the pallet.

"Secondly, I could kill you now, here in this room, leave you on the floor with your blood and innards wet around your sorry corpse," Liv took a step towards the Seer letting the long blade of her knife slide from under the sleeve of her dress and into her hand.

"You favour death for a second time. Blood thirst! You are a wicked woman, but then your breed always is!" His strangled response sounded weak even to his own ears. Her face was blank and he could not sense her thoughts, she masked her emotions well and he wondered for a moment if she had mastered the spells he had taught her.

"Lastly… I could take you away. Take you far from our home before Brynjar ever had a chance to come close to the ring."

"This is less threatening a choice," he snarled.

"Mayhap it ends with me returning you to the Yggdrasil Kynslod, I know they would seek to punish you further, they would wish to destroy you after you continued on your path. I imagine they warned you when they spared your life?" Liv asked watching for a response.

"You are clever, how long did it take to reason it out?" Liv shrugged at him, giving nothing away, Harvardr sighed, he had misjudged her abilities greatly, "and what of Eileifr?" Harvardr raised a silver eyebrow.

"You say his name only to rile me Harvardr. You can keep trying, but you will never see the boy again, his location is a secret especially from you."

"But returning me to the Yggrasil Kynslod means danger for you. You've also failed them! Do you have the boy in your care and what of the ring? Returning only with it and they would assume you've been swayed by it. Nei, Liv it is another poor choice for me, after all," the Seer laughed thinking he'd won this bout of word play.

"Ah… so it is. Then we are left with only two choices," sheathing the knife under the sleeve of her dress again, she walked towards the door and turning her head slowly she waited for Harvardr to respond.

"Your first choice, mayhap it should be… wait Liv, for it is coming. I've told him how to find us!" Harvardr felt a moment of glory, a resurgence of his former power and authority over her and for a moment he had bested her.

"My thanks Harvardr… you've confirmed what I already thought," Liv sighed and edged her way to the threshold. Harvardr raged at himself, he was becoming a foolish stupid old man, the days and nights of being cooped up in the small room, with nothing to challenge or occupy his mind, had made him dull and as blunt as a spoon. He had nothing with which to rebuff her, he had no threat, no information to barter with, all he had was anger and the past; a past she knew nothing of yet, perhaps it was enough to sway her.

"Your mother died birthing two children… the night she came here the women presented you and your kin to Ove, he wanted neither of you, did you know that? Your sister was weak, barely able to breathe and in the Viking way Ove cast her aside, to let nature decide whether she lived or died. I snatched the child away, leaving you here with your precious village. Have they always been good to you Liv, I do not think so, you were no better than a thrall to them?" Harvardr paused, looking up at the face of the woman he had known since childhood. Still, her eyes were blank; he could not fathom why this was not wounding her more so. He continued, "I took the child to the Yggrasil Kynslod, twinned babes are very special and we had been waiting for so very long, and your father is from the nomads in the north, so you see you had magical blood but the child's mother was always weak, and her birthing of Eileifr was too much, it must pain you to know that the woman you shed no tears for was your sister and the boy you have carelessly abandoned is your kin. You're more than a failure!"

Liv took a deep breath and lowered herself onto the pallet sitting beside Harvardr and leaning very close to the Seer, she whispered into his ear, "you told me when I entered this room I'd have no more answers than you granted our Chieftain a day ago. You've failed, you've told me much! You should know this Harvardr, the night you buried Eileifr's mother, I waited until you slept, for you always slept heavily, and I dug her body from the earth and removed her hood. I saw her face was also my face and wept for her and for her son."

Liv drew back her face as Harvardr turned to meet her gaze, his mouth gaping, "if you knew..."

"I still trusted you, who was I to question? I had no choice but to stay with you. Count yourself with the luck of the Gods I saw fit to present you with three options," and with that, she rose and walked from the room.

Breathing heavily Harvardr rested his head against the rough-hewn panels of the wooden wall. The room seemed to grow smaller and darker; he had thrown his dice and again and it would appear they had not ruled in his favour but still he had one final hope, the knowledge that Brynjar was coming, he would be freed. Harvardr knew once he finally was released, he must recover Liv and the ring, he knew that before he killed her he would find out where the boy was and then he would kill him too.

Chapter 23

ᛞᚾᚨᚲᛏᛗᚱ ᛏᛩᛗᛁᛏᛋ ᛏᚢᚱᛗᛗ

Walking away from the small longhouse on the outskirts of the village, Liv breathed a deep sigh, the fresh morning air did little to clear her mind. It had drained her to confront Harvardr although she hoped she had maintained her temper. She felt the blade of the knife hidden under her sleeve was as hot as her skin; she knew she could have killed him, but she was not sure why she had not.

The Seer had tried to wound her with the tale of her past but she would not let it fester in her mind. She walked past centre of the village skirting behind the buildings, dropping her gaze to her feet to avoid catching anyone's attention. By the time she reached the great hall, she was feeling weak, her head ached and grabbing a wooden cup from one of the tables, she dunked it into a bucket and drank thirstily of the cool river water.

At the head of the room Ove stood with Ari, Dag and Holger. Gytha was by the fire pit with a small kettle bubbling away, the smell of her potions was earthy and rich. Thorik was nowhere to be seen and neither was Vigi. Liv could feel Ari's gaze on her, she tempered her feelings and slowly walked towards them.

"Did the snake have aught to say?" Ove grunted. On the table before them was a pile of swords and axes. They were preparing for the men to sharpen and oil the blades, some would be sent to the forge for the blacksmith to repair or strengthen.

Liv lifted the handle of a small single sided axe, which was lightweight and etched with a myriad of knot-work and dragon heads, she spoke. "Might I have a moment of your time Ove, I have a question?" Raising an eyebrow Ove brusquely nodded and jerked his head towards a seat beside his own. Catching Liv's eye Ari shouldered Dag and pulled Holger's attention from the table, "come, let them talk awhile."

"Is it wise to leave them be? She has an axe in her hand and a dark look on her face," Dag frowned.

"It's blunt, she'll bruise him and no more if that's her will," Ari shrugged and walked with the men out into the open air.

Ove watched them depart before turning to Liv, "What did he say?"

"Do you know anything of my father?" Liv asked.

"What did he say?" Ove sighed and sat back in the chair, clasping his large hands across his lap.

"My mother bore two children, I was kept the other was not."

"A decision I'm not proud of but there was little choice, it was a hard time for the village when your mother arrived, many had suffered…"

"I don't hold a grudge against you," she interrupted. "It's our way to send a child out when it is weak or none will care for it, you took me in. I learned to accept a long time ago."

"That surprises me, I can't say I would feel the same if it had been my brother," he said firmly.

"You have known Ebbe a lifetime, you would miss what you have known to be, I can't miss what I never had. I have Ei; I'll see him again. So I must know Ove what do you know of my father?" Realising she was still holding onto the axe she had decided to take for her own, Liv let it slip from her fingers onto the beaten earth of the floor where it rested at her feet. She looked earnestly into the eyes of the man before her, pleading silently.

"Your mother arrived here in a small vessel, it was made from animal hide. Her language was broken but we understood enough of what she said, Harvardr was feverish with the need to heal her. I know more of your mother than your father," he said and offering his hands he grasped Liv's gently. "She had been on a ship, taken as a slave, there was a storm and she was washed ashore somewhere to the north. Your father's people found her and took her in. These people became separated or attacked I can't say for her tongue did not have those words, her small boat found its way to our island. That is all."

Nodding Liv squeezed Ove's hand, "there's no more you can tell me? There is no other who knows?"

"Nei Liv, I can tell you no more, and neither could any man I know of. You are one of us; we will be your family until there are no more of us left. You have Ari once more, I thank the Norns you were fated to find one another again."

"That was all I needed to know Ove, it would not be safe for any to know of my past," Liv sighed with relief.

"You are not surprised with the knowledge?" He frowned at her, curious at her reaction.

"Over the years I pieced it together. You've not told me more than I already knew save for casting out Ei's mother."

The Chieftain shifted forward in his chair, leaning his elbows on his knees, "She became the child's mother? Harvardr has long been at work it would seem," and rubbing his chin roughly he shook his head. "Tis' a regret of mine you were separated from your kin, a very old one, but the past can't be changed. I know nothing more, know that no blade or axe could drag it from me," he said firmly, but as Ove looked at the young woman before him, he saw she was smiling.

"It's the answer I'd hoped for," Liv said, bending down to gather the axe from her feet, she stood and gently rested her hand on Ove's shoulder. Her smile faded, "Harvardr has made the causeway known to Brynjar, we have little time. I'll tell Ari."

"We must hasten our plans!" Ove clapped his hands, stood and shouted for his men. Heads shot up from their work and men began to gather in the hall. Liv nodded and made for the yard catching sight of Ari, he stood with Thorik, who was enthusiastically waving a wooden pole around as if it were a long sword or spear. Ari wore his blue tunic and had his sword strapped to his back, she had noticed Dag and Holger were wearing their weaponry also. She wondered if they sensed their enemy approaching, pulling her husband aside Liv spoke quickly, "Harvardr has told Brynjar of the causeway, we don't have long. Ove has called the men," she said quickly.

"He'll put them to work on the weapons and we will train the men swiftly, I would have liked more time," his eyes narrowed with annoyance at the lack of time to prepare, but he knew it would have always been so, "you left the old man alive?"

"For now." Liv answered, "it seems he thinks he has some hold over Brynjar, he trusts the man will free him, I'm not sure I share that thought."

"There's little any of us share in agreement with Harvardr," Ari murmured.

Liv grimaced and rubbed her face with her hands, it was still morning, but she felt the tiredness of long hard day's work, "are there eyes on the shore, the lake, and the woods?"

"Ja."

"I promised Thorik we would continue our lessons…" Liv began.

"Stay within the village," Ari said rather too sharply.

Unable to argue Liv gave Ari a look of annoyance, but cooled her temper seeing the concern in his face. His look was stern, his hair tied in a knot again at the back of his head, his proud features darkened, willing her to do his bidding. She could not help but smile, "I'm not running around the village, we'll look like fools and he will learn nothing."

"The boy can run already," this time Ari's tone was nearing exasperation. He folded his arms across his chest, "why is it you have grown attached to him?"

"He's young, he needs to learn and he is far from his home, we are responsible for him," she said.

"It's more than that," he frowned.

"Ja, he reminds me of my responsibility to Ei. Harvardr has succeeded in making me realise I am failing Ei by not being with him, I won't let that happen to this boy while I have a chance at least."

Ari frowned. He didn't like the tone of defeat and the mention of Harvardr on Liv's lips, she was stronger than this, "you delivered Ei to safety, you may not be with him now, but you will return to him. Sometimes the best protection we can offer is not being with those we love." Ari kicked the dirt beneath his feet, he wanted to feel the absence of emotion but his actions indicated he could not, sideways he looked at Liv, she appeared to be mulling over thoughts in her mind.

"I wanted to show him the path to Hornelen," she sighed.

Ari looked startled for a moment before he realised her true intentions, "you want to show him where to hide? The caves are as dangerous as any place out there right now. The village will be safe, I'll send him to help protect the women and children... with you when the time comes."

A cool breeze floated past them ruffling the loose hair around Liv's face and she shivered for a moment. Turning her gaze towards the rear of the settlement she looked to the valley where Ebbe's farmstead lay and up to the cliff face rising behind it. "I'm not foolhardy, I won't put ourselves at risk outside the settlement," she saw Ari's features soften as he guessed what she was thinking, "Thorik!" she called to the boy.

The child ran over to the couple with his long pole tucked under one arm his face flushed from his game play, his wild hair sticking up at odd angles. As he ran the horn from Dag swung on his back. "Did you see, Ari?" He squinted up at the Jomsviking, "am I getting better?"

"Ja!" Ari slapped the boy on the shoulder with a firm hand. Thorik stumbled to the side with the force of Ari's enthusiasm, "I want you to go with Liv and when you return this evening I'll have other tasks for you."

"What?" Thorik grinned widely.

"Go with Liv," Ari ruffled the boy's hair, swinging a glance over his shoulder, he nodded at his wife and walked towards the group of men preparing to practise their fighting skills, "keep her out of trouble!" he laughed over his shoulder.

Thorik looked up at Liv who stared after Ari. She watched as he joined Dag and Holger, exchanging a few words with them both they separated the men into two groups, ten men in each. Holger took one group and instructed the men on fighting with fists, where best to strike and how to avoid a blow themselves. Liv saw the man with a new appreciation, he was sombre at the best of times, but had made an attempt to integrate and appeared to desperately want to help against Brynjar.

Looking at her husband, she watched Ari throw Dag a wooden staff, before lifting one for himself. Ari laid down his weapons strapped to his body, as he ordered the men to form a circle around the pair. Without much warning the two Jomsvikings set about one another, they lifted and swung the poles against each other as if they were swords. They moved stealthily, their feet balancing their weight perfectly as the wooden poles smashed against one another in a series of attacks. They blocked, swung and thrust the weapons at one another.

After demonstrating for some time they walked to a gap in the circle and each lifted a shield. Again, they demonstrated attack and defence, the two friends raining blow after blow against each other's shields. When the poles were discarded, they showed the men how to swing the circular shield using it as a deathly tool, aiming for the head, shoulders and lower legs. Finally, they took axes from where they lay on the earth, the weapons were sharp dangerous and deadly, Liv took a breath and whispered to Thorik who was as engrossed as she, "watch this... watch this closely Thorik," she breathed.

Both Ari and Dag possessed a double-sided axe with a short handle on a leather strap. The handle was as long as each man's forearm and made from iron, they were engraved with runes spelling each man's Jomsviking name; Ari's said Swift-Axe and Dag's read as the Dark-Blood.

"Why do they use their real axes? What is one of them is hurt?" Thorik's voice wavered with fear.

"They will not harm one another, mayhap a scratch or a cut, but no harm will come to them. See... Holger has brought more men to watch," Liv crouched to Thorik's height and pointed to Holger who had gathered his training group forming a larger circle around the two men. His fiery hair was wild about his head and his brow glistened with the sport of fighting hand to hand with the men. He wore a smile and clapped his hands together to quieten the crowd that had gathered.

Without warning Dag roared and spun on his heel, extending his sword arm that held the axe he threw his weight into the blow, however Ari ducked and dropping to one knee, he kicked Dag's feet from beneath him, but the man simply tucked into a roll over his shoulder and landed in a crouching position on his feet. Ari came to full height and ran at Dag lifting his axe high above his head, he slammed the square end of the axe head against the handle of Dag's axe, which he had lifted into a defensive position in front of his face.

The two weapons locked for a moment before Ari lifted a foot to Dag's chest and pushed him onto his back, the man fell to the ground and rolled to the side before Ari could land another blow that resulted in his blade hitting the earth. Springing to his feet Dag moved with speed and agility about his attacker. Again with all his weight Dag swung the axe, aiming for Ari's left shoulder blade, but Ari saw the attack coming and swung full circle connecting his own axe head once more with Dag's.

The two men stood face to face locked in the heat of battle when a grin spread across Dag's face, for he enjoyed greatly the practice with his friend, squinting as Ari strained against the pressure of Dag's strength, for he knew Dag's methods and of the two men Ari was the stronger, but Dag sought to tire him out. Releasing the lock of their axe head's Ari jabbed his elbow into Dag's gut and kicked his feet from beneath him once more. Dag swung the butt of the weapon into Ari's thigh causing the muscle to contract and become numb with pain. Ari grabbed his right leg and stumbled to the side but before he could position himself better Dag was on his feet again and coming at Ari with a raised axe in hand.

Taking a deep breath Ari winced against the pain growing in his leg and letting the handle of the axe fall from his grip he took the leather strap and swung the axe around his head, creating the force that connected with Dag's left shoulder before he could gain more ground on him. Dag grunted and lurched as the flat side of the axe struck him, dropping his own weapon and grabbing the muscle of his upper arm he swore furiously under his breath. The fight was over.

The circle of men roared as a limping Ari stepped towards Dag and pulled the kneeling man to his feet. Holger shouted the loudest and ordered a man to run into the hall and fetch ale for the warriors. Thorik who had held his breath throughout the last final moments of the fight released a strangled sigh and watched the two men laugh and embrace one another, he heard Dag complain with a smile that his arm would be useless for days while Ari jested back that he would be dragging his leg behind him as he fought the Jarl.

"What did you learn Thorik?" Liv asked containing the smile she felt inside at the men's display of skill.

"They are fine warriors," he sighed with awe.

"Ja… they are fine. They used the best of themselves against one another. Ari has more strength, but Dag has speed, they both possess agility and each uses their abilities to out manoeuvre the other," Liv explained.

"I don't understand," he mumbled as his fingernails picked at the pole he had been practising with earlier. He suddenly felt very unsure in his ability in anything. Sensing his dismay Liv turned him from the men to follow her as they headed for the farmstead of Ebbe. "I wanted you to see something. In that case there was no weaker man, they are equal in their skill, but they are also different. I wanted you to see we all possess different abilities when it comes to fighting and we must use our skills where the opponent will feel it the most."

"You talk like a man, like Holger even, none of the other women talk like you. How did you learn all this?" Throwing the pole aside next to one of the cattle sheds they continued on the path, making for the rear of the settlement. The valley grew wider and Thorik noticed for the first time the long, thin stretches of field ready for harvest.

"I listened and learned as I travelled, I picked things up from people who thought it wise a woman on her own should be able to defend herself. Unfortunately, I learned a lot from a man who is now my enemy. I want you to learn something from me so you can defend yourself because while the men are big and strong, we on the other hand, are made a little differently," Liv explained as they walked on.

Shrugging away from her hand on his shoulder Thorik felt annoyed that she continued to think him small and feeble, "I can and will be just as good as them!" he huffed.

"Ja, you will Thorik, but for now you are small and slight, just as I am in comparison to them," she stooped to place her hands on her knees and ruffled his wild tawny hair. "If I can show you how to handle a knife or run faster than your feet can carry you over rocks and earth and sand then you can survive." She stood and pointed to the cliff face looming above their heads, "We will climb that today and run along the edge, you'll feel the rush of wind in your lungs and the burning fire of pain in your legs like never before."

"I wish I was stronger," he sighed. Grabbing the horn that swung at his back, he fingered its markings before wiping his nose roughly and feeling ashamed of his emotion he turned away from Liv trying to fight the frustration building inside.

"Thorik," Liv said softly but firmly, "If I didn't think you capable I wouldn't be training you, would I? So we might never be able to swing a long sword, so be it, we have our daggers and what if we never rush towards a man with our weight and pound him into the earth? We will make him chase us down until he drops from exhaustion! We already have skills that's what I want you to see. We are different, but we don't have to be weaker."

Dragging his sleeve across his face Thorik wiped away the moisture that dripped from his eyes and nose. He considered what she was saying for a moment and smiled, "like an assassin?"

Liv stepped back and laughed before slapping Thorik on the back, "You've spent far too much time on the docks, as Gytha told me! Have you been listening to tales from Viking marauders! Ja, Thorik you will become a fine assassin, a silent fearless warrior!"

Gently she pushed him into a steady pace along the path. As they passed Ebbe's farmstead Liv waved at Ari's father who beckoned them into the small yard, he had a long pipe hanging from the corner of his mouth, the smell of the smoke was fetid and Thorik wondered what on earth it was that brought more water to his eyes.

"Ebbe, how are you and Lena?" Liv asked as the older man embraced her for a moment.

"We are well, Lena's in the smokehouse, we've made our preparations."

"You will join us in the hall tonight?" She asked.

"Ja, my back aches from digging in the earth... Lena could do with some mead to soothe her voice from the endless nagging she sees fit to give my ears!" Ebbe winked at Liv. Laughing Liv nodded and winked at Ebbe, "her smokehouse is fine and its secrets better yet!"

"Ja, but our village has grown, we needed more space, Ari did well to help me the other day and I have finished with the concealment. Ove and his plans! I'd like to see that brother of mine lend a hand," Ebbe shrugged and sat on a bench outside the doorway of his longhouse. He looked as Thorik screwed up his face at the odd conversation, "where are you headed?"

"Up there," Thorik pointed to the cliff and the trail that was steadily growing in a steeper incline. Raising his eyebrows Ebbe shook his head and breathed out a plume of smoke, "So… you plan to lead this boy astray as you did my own!" Striking the butt of the pipe against the wooden panelled wall of the house Ebbe shook his head, "watch out young Thorik, this one will have you climbing Hornelen in search of Odin next!"

Stifling a hearty laugh with her fist Liv felt the joy of an old memory surface in her mind, she remembered climbing the cliff face with Ari as children, his parents had been half mad with worry and chastised them for hours upon their return but they had both known the adults were proud that they had succeeded in the climb and come back unscathed.

"Come Thorik, we shall see Ebbe and Lena tonight in the hall and he can tell you more of the mischief of his son!"

"Hah!" Ebbe let out an amused cry at Liv's words waving after them as they walked on and without understanding Thorik let out a chuckle running after Liv as she disappeared from the yard.

As they walked up the steep path Thorik bombarded her with a series of questions regarding her childhood in the village, her friendship with Ari and how they had found one another again and although her replies were short, they were friendly and encouraged the boy to continue. He frequently stopped, his mouth gaping open before shaking his head and running to catch up with her. He asked her what she would do when Brynjar attacked and was eventually killed by the men, with a small amount of fear he paused and scratched his head in confusion when she replied that they could only hope that Brynjar would be killed.

Thorik had not considered a defeat because he had seen how brave and strong the men were, even those of the quiet and sleepy village and all seemed to think victory was theirs. He wondered if this was a guise to protect the people from worry. Swallowing, Thorik winced at the pain in his dry throat and he thought of Gytha and her potions and herbs, 'surely there was a spell she knew to protect them,' he thought. Then a worrying nagging doubt crept into his mind, what if people did die when the enemy attacked. He remembered the death of his mother and the pain it had caused, he could not imagine one of their group no longer being with them. He knew this was a failing of his, for warriors accepted all dangers in life especially death.

When they reached the cliff face Thorik saw the climb was not as treacherous as he had been led to believe, as a series of roughly carved steps wound their way to the top of the rock. They pulled and heaved their bodies until at last they looked down onto the village. From this great height and distance, they could see past the forest to the lake of Smols and the shoreline beyond but more impressive than any of this was the great mountain of Hornelen.

"I've never seen anything like it!" Thorik gasped.

"From here we can see our part of the island well, what say you to being an eye that watches over us Thorik?" Liv wiped the palms of her hands on her dress before gathering bunches of the material and lifting the garment over her head.

Looking away Thorik felt a flush or red rise to his cheeks but hearing Liv sigh, he glanced back to see her wearing a strange outfit not usually meant for women. She wore a thin natural linen tunic cut to her shape with binding around the forearms and bodice. It reached below her waist, ending just above her thighs. She also wore thin leather trousers that met her boots which were strapped tightly around her calves.

"A dress is impractical for what we are doing today," she smiled.

"I've only ever seen women in dresses," Thorik admitted.

"This was a boring one!" Liv grinned. "When I travelled I found skirts often got in the way of running or riding Grani but when we reached a township I wore the garb of a woman to avoid attention, these clothes are lightweight."

"Ah."

"So will you be our eye?"

"What?" Thorik was confused by what she was speaking of.

Liv dropped to her knees and stuffed the dress into the small leather bag she had brought with them, upon standing, she tapped the horn attached to Thorik's back.

"Pay attention!" She scolded. "Each morning I want you to come here, make the climb and look out over the island. Watch for smoke, signs that men have arrived. Can you do that?"

"Ja, I can!" Pride caused Thorik's chest to puff out in his excitement swelling within him.

"If you see anything, sound the horn Dag gave you. Then run back to us as fast as you can, if it's too late you head for Ebbe's, understand?" Liv pointed to the small farmstead.

"Ja," Thorik answered, nodding, his intent gaze matched Liv's own. Seeing her satisfied that he understood, he listened as she explained what would happen when the attack came. Thorik swallowed at the idea he had now such a grave responsibility. Snapping his attention back to her Liv fastened her hair into a tighter braid before ordering him to turn and run along a narrow path at the edge of the cliff.

She told him to run as if his very life depended on it, for it would when he had to return to them or flee with the others. Her face, so calm and beautiful grew dark, her opal eyes glistening with pure energy. Thorik ran, as fast and as hard as his small body allowed, his lungs ached and he yearned to turn his head to see how far he had gained from her, but before he could turn, he heard her light step as she flew past him. Stopping feet away from him she shouted for him to start again and he did. Thorik ran until his body grew stiff and he could run no more and when at last they worked their way back to the village, Liv carried him on her back before laying him beside the fire pit where Vigi licked his sleeping face.

Chapter 24

ᚦᚾᚨᚲᛏᛗᚱ ᚠᛟᚾᚱ

The men worked as they ate at natmall that night, polishing and sharpening blades with oiled cloths and whetstone. As they did most evenings the women carried heavy trays laden with meat, vegetables and hot buttered bread. Ale was consumed sparingly for they were greatly tired and knew preparation time was short. They must be alert and ready even though it was widely thought they had a few days' grace left before Brynjar would make his presence known.

The Jomsviking men sat with Holger, Ove and Ebbe discussing how they planned to defend themselves against Brynjar. Holger provided them with everything he thought and knew of the man. Once they had concluded that Brynjar was intelligent but rash in his actions, and perhaps marred by his affliction, they agreed to err on the side of wariness. Brynjar's word could not be trusted no matter the circumstance, he would stop at nothing to gain the ring and exact his revenge. They could not agree, however, what that revenge might be if Brynjar got the one thing he truly wanted.

"He has never seen the ring, we could send the Seer out of the gates to him with some other trinket? There are women a plenty here with baubles on their fingers," Dag offered.

Liv arrived at the table with Gytha and the women sat, "nei, he knows the ring carries a weight that is instantly felt. Harvardr would know it was a deception too, and would tell him about it the first chance he got," she explained.

"Tis' true, I feel it," Gytha said, "Harvardr must feel its presence here if I can."

"Gytha is right," Liv replied.

Ari pushed his trencher of food away and rested an elbow on the table. Brushing the crumbs from the flat bread aside, he thought carefully, "anything involving the Seer would result in failure and I don't believe Brynjar would retreat simply because he thought he had the ring. I've met him and he's a man who must achieve all at any cost."

"We must assume he has his best men with him, I have trained them and they know how to fight. We've done well, but your people are still farmers and fishermen, with my respect Chief Ove," Holger raised his horn, but did not take a drink.

"Tis' a fair point, but farmers and fishermen know well the hardships of life, they are a hardened lot, the island has seen to that over the years," Ove drummed his fingers on the armrest of the chair, "Holger, how great is his desire for Liv's blood?"

Before Holger could answer Liv spoke, "Tis' great, he's hunted me for years, his thirst has never been quenched."

Gytha shot a worried glance at Dag who warned her gently with his eyes because he did not believe the Chieftain planned to put Liv in danger. He was satisfied when Ove spoke again.

"He doesn't know what Liv looks like, mayhap we use Dag's plan somewhat. One of us could go in disguise, when they get close enough, they kill the Jarl," the Chieftain raised his eyebrows at the group before him.

"If need be, it can be a plan," Ari said.

"Hah!" Dag snorted jovially. "It doesn't say much for Liv! We disguise one of our men? A fine woman you would look to Brynjar! What say we use old Gunliek or one of his goats!?" The joke broke the tension at the table and all smiled or laughed at the thought.

"I'm not afraid of Brynjar," Liv said slowly after silence fell over them once more. The room was warm and the oil lamps scattered here and there leant a soft glow to the hall. It smelled of smoke, food and delicate spices from the women's cooking. "If need be I'll face him."

"Nei, you will not," Ari said firmly.

"We must all face our demons," Liv spoke gently, looking at her husband, but he did not return her stare. She knew he would never agree to it and so she resolved to keep it as her own last measure.

"We are agreed the women and children will flee to Ebbe's farmstead and hide in the tunnels beneath the smokehouse. Liv has given the boy the task of watching from the cliff each morning for signs. We've men who will scout the forest and the lake for signs of Brynjar also. Gytha you will go with Liv and the other women when the time comes," Dag glanced towards the young woman who frowned at the suggestion, looking at one man then to the other.

"Nei! If any are wounded, they'll need my care," she pleaded with Dag.

"After the battle you will treat them, if the village is over-run I can't guarantee your safety," Dag cursed beneath his breath. He sensed this was not the end of the matter and longed for the night to drag on because he knew as soon as they retired to bed, Gytha would press him on the subject.

It was Ebbe, who interrupted the potential argument, "I will take my wife home now. We must all rest, tomorrow brings us closer to our fate," and resting a hand on his son's shoulder, Ebbe smiled, "we can prepare only so much, we must wait to see what the Gods decide. Enough talk, rest."

Turning, he walked towards the rear of the hall, and gathered Lena from Ove's wife's side. Thorik was stretched out beside Vigi stroking her soft, thick coat watching as the Chieftain stood and came for his wife as he did every night. Pulling himself from the comfort of Vigi, Thorik wandered over to the table and paused by the bench on which Liv sat.

"Why did Harvardr become your enemy?" He whispered in her ear.

"Some hearts become twisted over time and others were born black and rotten. I can't say what made Harvardr so, but he revealed himself and I can't forgive what he has done," Liv sighed. It was all she could offer the boy.

"If the ring is worthless, let him have it, let him run to the Jarl. Mayhap they will never return here and no one will need to fight?" he whispered again.

Hearing the conversation between the two, Holger leant closer and held Thorik's wide naive eyes with his own, "some men are wicked Thorik. Some men lie, break their oaths and dishonour themselves. We could never trust that Brynjar would promise to leave without retribution for those of us he feels ire for. He thinks he will become King when he has the ring, he would think himself invincible and be more encouraged to wipe us from the earth."

"How do they exist? If I got my smallest wish it would be enough," Thorik sighed and wandered back to Vigi.

Liv watched with a frown as the boy sat with his shoulders sagging, his face was etched with sadness and she resolved to lighten his spirits in the morning.

The concern Liv felt was akin to Holger's own, he had watched the boy and felt a pride at the cleverness and adaptability he showed. Thorik was learning quickly and he even looked healthier, this let Holger tell himself he had not made a mistake bringing him to the island, though he knew it had been the responsibility of the entire group.

Fingering Thor's amulet about his neck, he rose from the table, walking over to his pallet. He would let thoughts of his family selfishly consume him until he slept, then he would dream of them. He had fought hard enough and spoken long enough today. Silently, he nodded at the men as he passed them by.

Pushing the trenchers and cups aside on the table Dag lifted his Tafl board and pieces from a stool where he had set up the game before the meal. He had decided earlier in the day that his mind was aching for a match and Ari could do with the game-play also. Whilst the men engaged in a battle of wits, the women turned to face the fire in the centre of the room.

"I'm curious to meet this Harvardr, I've never come across one so strong, I can feel his presence... it is as dark as the ring," Gytha said to Liv.

"It would be dangerous for you to meet with him, he is much poisoned and would only try to hurt you. His mind has become strange, as though it's not as sharp as it once was. A lifetime of sorcery and lies have worn him out," Liv replied.

"And the ring... what will you do with it?"

"It belongs to Ei, I don't want to lumber a child with it but I am also weary of carrying it. It must be destroyed." Feeling the men engrossed in their game, Liv relaxed and tapped Gytha's knee, "You're happy with Dag?" she whispered with an earnest smile.

The young woman chuckled softly, her blue eyes twinkling before she winked, "I am. We plan to stay, Dag wishes to ask Ove's permission to build a dwelling."

"He will grant it just to rid his hall from the smell of your potions!" Dag growled, listening in on the conversation. Rolling her eyes, Gytha shook her head at Liv, "What will you do?" she asked.

"Return to Ei, from there fate will decide," she could not bring herself to look at Ari, who she knew must have heard her response. She was worried about the attack and knew that his life was in as much jeopardy as everyone else.

"If we defeat the Jarl what becomes of Harvardr then?" Gytha asked, pulling on a loose thread of her apron but before Liv could reply, Ari made a move with his draught causing Dag to groan as he looked at the chequered board in defeat.

Choosing to leave the question hanging in the air, Liv stood and walked over to the fire pit gazing into the hot coals. Thorik seemed not to notice her being close to him, lost as he was in his own thoughts.

"You don't want to meet with Harvardr, Gytha, nor should you take too much interest in him. He's dangerous and means only harm, that's why he's being kept from everyone here," Ari turned to look at the young woman. She was pink cheeked and had a guilty look in her eyes.

"What is it Gytha?" Dag asked, not liking the look on his woman's face.

"Nothing… not really. I'm curious about him, he is greatly gifted, I wish only to learn of his skills," biting her lip, she brushed blonde wisps of hair roughly from her forehead. Gytha sighed, feeling suddenly very tired, "I know what he's done, the danger he has brought to us all, I'm not foolish so won't disobey you all. It's that I've never met someone like him before, not even the Volur I knew as a child. He's different… very different."

The men exchanged glances before pushing the board aside. Dag filled both their horns pouring from a clay jug of ale on the table and swallowed slowly. Ari rubbed his eyes with his thumb and forefinger; he felt the strain of Harvardr's presence as much as the rest. He had managed to delay thinking about the Seer's situation but should the Jarl be swiftly defeated they would have to decide how best to deal with Harvardr.

"Be content with your own gifts Gytha, we will have need of them soon," Ari said heavily.

"Don't concern yourself with the Seer, his talents do not outweigh the damage he has caused, there is no way back for him. Don't pity him, and as for curiosity… save that for me," Dag smiled as the last words fell from his mouth and caught Gytha's smile. She blushed and shook her head. "Gather your things Gytha, I'll be with you in a moment."

Nodding the young woman stood, before heading for the passageway to the longhouse's rooms she first walked to Liv and placed a hand on her back. Offering a weak smile Liv acknowledged the woman and watched her disappear through the softly lit hallway.

"Ove gave us a room next to yours, it is not right to take your chamber and the barn has lost its appeal," Dag grinned with a glint in his eye, "tis' good of your Chieftain to open his house to us."

"You plan to stay here with Gytha? Once all this is over?" Waving his hand across the table Ari pulled the Tafl board between them again. Swiftly he set up the pieces this time taking the King.

"Ja. If the gods fate it, it will be a good life. Tis' a good settlement, the land is rich, my father taught me many farming skills. Gytha would be welcomed also, the women's healing abilities here are fewer and there aren't many who know the plants well enough to make proper use of them."

Cocking his head to the side Ari grinned at the thought of Dag becoming a farmer. It was not a surprising thought, but a pleasing one. He had often spoken of his father; it had pained him greatly when his home had been lost. To think of his friend turning from a fierce Jomsviking to a settled man cultivating the land made Ari feel at peace. It was a good plan, it was an enviable future.

Often he had thought of his own father Ebbe at work while he lay many miles away in the camp. He would try to shake off the feelings of guilt at leaving his father to continue without his son, but he always hoped Ebbe would understand. He had seen the look of curiosity given to his scars, but Ebbe was a quiet man, he would wait a long time before questioning his son.

His mother Lena, on the other hand was itching to talk with her son about his life, she had held him close and marvelled at how he had changed as a man. When he had gone to help his father dig deeper into the tunnels beneath the smoke house she had been working on her loom in the longhouse. Placing her spindle on the rack she had walked over to him with tears in her eyes, it had been a long time since Ari had stood in her doorway. With a light gentle touch she had cupped his face with her hands, her fingers had grown crooked with age.

"Look after Ebbe and Lena for me Dag," he asked, looking at his friend.

He saw Dag's gaze darken, his brow creased, "You will not ask me to follow you? We have been friends a long time Ari, I have always been there to guard your back, it would be wrong not to…"

"You have the chance of a life here with Gytha, you've said that's what you want," Ari sighed.

"Ja, but you are my oath brother, there is more to consider than a home and woman."

"I will not ask you to abandon what is important to you," Ari slid a polished stone draught with his finger across the board, "concentrate," he nodded to Dag indicating his move.

Glancing at Liv by the fire pit Dag felt his heart grow heavy, "where is it you will go? And will you return?"

"She has not yet said, but it would seem she has hidden the boy far to the north. If all goes well, we will return. I hope," shifting another piece of stone, Ari considered his next move.

"She is your wife now. Why has she not told you where the child Ei is? And the ring, where is it now? She doesn't wear the brooch it's concealed in," countering the move, Dag slid another stone closer to Ari's King.

Ari thought about it for a moment. He knew Liv, he understood her reasons, he was not sure Dag could however, "she fears knowledge of the child's whereabouts could be used against me… against us. I think she has carried secrets so long they are difficult to abandon. She will talk eventually." Lifting his horn Ari heard the men in the rear of the hall talking softly with their women. Children were sleeping on the floor near the fire and the younger men and women were drifting off to their pallets to share time away from the busy room. A gentle, lilting tune came from a corner of the hall where old Gunliek was softly blowing on his bone pipe.

"She's hidden the ring, it's a damned cursed thing."

"When Gytha asked what would become of Harvardr after the battle, what was your first thought?" Dag queried.

"Good question my friend. There's naught for him but death, he's like a venomous snake. Keep it imprisoned forever within a box and it will attack on first strike, set it free and it will attack at will, kill it and it can harm no person again," and looking his friend in the eye, Ari added, "Liv would do it now. She thinks about it often, she can see no other way and in truth, I think she burns to do it. There is a bond between them, an unseen cord that has become twisted and knotted, she wants rid of their connection."

"She's quite unlike women I've met. Gytha is different too, but her soul is not restless. Your wife, while calm and measured in appearance, hides turmoil as wild as the winter sea behind her eyes. She distracts herself with the tasks at hand, with the boy, with you." Turning his attention to the ale jug, he filled their horns once more, "but life is one distraction after another. She does not settle well, see how her mind is consumed at this moment, can a person survive like that forever?" Dag bit his tongue and silently scolded himself for talking so freely. He should have chosen his words more carefully and avoided looking at Ari's face to assess the damage.

"I prefer your humour to your gloom, it's affecting your game, mayhap you should get your dice out and claw back some hope of a win?" Smirking Ari reached over the table and slapped Dag where he had hit him with the axe earlier that day. Wincing against the dull ache Dag pretended to feel more pain than he really did, his face pained in a grimace, "you see the right of it, I know. But I know Liv, I trust her," Ari said confidently.

"Ja, trust is good. Now finish me off so I can join my woman and rest my head… and arm!" Nodding Dag watched Ari slide his King away from his last advancing stone and topple the piece with his index finger. Lifting their horns in victory and defeat the men celebrated the end of the game and moments later Dag disappeared into the hallway in search of his room and Gytha.

Feeling an arm wrap around her shoulder Liv felt Ari at her back and turning, she smiled and welcomed him, "is the game is over?"

"For tonight," placing his hand on her elbow Ari guided Liv towards their room. Looking back into the hall he saw Thorik was resting on his back on one of the benches, his eyes closed and his chest moving steadily, "The boy is asleep?"

"I think so, he has not stirred. Today tired him out but his mind is at work on many things," sliding back the wooden latch, they entered the small chamber and Liv closed the panel door and turned to Ari, "Can we speak?"

"Ja, but first lay down with me. It has been a long day and my leg is bruised, but Dag's arm is no better at least!" Ari smiled and rested his weary body on the pallet of furs. Raising an arm to prop up his head, Ari unbound the knot of hair at his nape scratching his scalp and massaging his temples. Liv knelt by his side and helped to pull his tunic from over his head, she saw a series of welts and bruises scattered over his arms and chest.

"Gytha might have something for the pain?" Liv asked, narrowing her eyes at the fresh scratches gained from a day of sparring and practising with the men and she wondered how the trainees had faired when the Jomsviking before her looked so battered.

"Nei, it's nothing, it's good to ache sometimes!" Ari winked at Liv and scratched the short whiskers on his chin and neck with his fingers dancing over the old scars.

Shuffling to the edge of the pallet Liv stood and removed her dress. Standing in her shift, she crossed to the wooden chest and filled a large wooden bowl with water from a jug, lifting a linen square from a pile she dipped the cloth cleaning her hands and face. Releasing her dark braid of copper and gold, she sighed.

"Speak," Ari said.

"I want to tell you where I've hidden Ei. It's too much to hold inside Ari, and if something should happen to me, Eileifr must be protected... by you," she said, quickly as the words poured out of her.

"No harm will come to you," Ari angrily shifted his full weight onto his back, rubbing again at his eyes with his rough calloused hand.

"No? I mean harm to the Jarl and Harvardr and it's only wise to assume they wish the same for me. We cannot say how tomorrow will end or the day after that. There's always been the chance..."

"Things have changed now, where once there was only yourself and Ei you now have me. Our home has welcomed us, they are fighting for us, and the odds are surely better than they have ever been for you?" Ari looked at Liv and saw her massaging her neck. Slowly she crossed to the bed and sat down beside him.

"Do you wish to know where Ei is?" she smiled.

"I do," he smiled in return.

"And the ring?"

"I wish you'd destroy it!" he grunted, but showed no ill humour in his face. He was greatly pleased Liv had decided to reveal a little more to him. Pointing to the heavy wooden chest Liv gestured to the beaten earth floor, "I've buried it beneath the chest." Turning back to Ari she closed her eyes for a moment before taking a deep breath, "What do you know of the Sami?"

Frowning for a moment Ari considered her question carefully. He knew she had been spotted after she had returned from the ship that had been far to the north. He had heard the name Sami said before, but farther to the south of their lands and to the east, the nomadic tribes of the far north were known as Lapps. It was at that moment he realised what she had done and why.

"Speak," he urged, as gently as he could.

Chapter 25

ᛞᚢᚾᚲᛏᛗᚱ ᚠᛁᛈᛗ

From his cell within the abandoned longhouse, on the outskirts of the village, Harvardr could hear the commotion outside. He knew it was late in the evening as the small square hole cut into the turf roof told him it was still night, though no stars shone in the sky. No moon cast its glow upon the floor of his room and despite the embers of the small fire he had lit earlier in the corner of the room a chill had filled the space, causing him to shiver. It felt as if Hel herself had reached up from her underworld causing gooseflesh to rise on his skin at her touch.

Craning his neck from the roughly woven material of the pillow, he turned his ear towards the door. He could hear nothing but knew that did not mean a great deal. The guards would not simply abandon their post due to a skirmish in the village. For a moment his heart skipped a beat; could Brynjar have arrived so swiftly? His chest fluttered alarmingly causing Harvardr to swallow and breathe slowly to calm himself. It could not be that the Jarl had arrived so soon, surely he was not so fortunate, he wondered.

Pushing himself up from his pallet Harvardr swung his legs onto the cold earthen floor. His feet were bare and instantly felt chilled. For a moment he thought he could hear voices from the other side of the door and stilled his movements. For long minutes he focused on the silence of the passageway, afraid to move again should he miss something. Then just as he was about to rest his body once more the sound of the wooden latch being pulled back filled the void.

Harvardr reached for the soapstone vessel holding the oil for his small lamp, with a reed he lit the liquid and peered towards the dimly lit doorway. The portal door edged open just enough for a small, delicate hand to slide between the space and push a little harder. Raising his eyebrows, he frowned at the person before him, "and who are you?" he whispered.

"You're Harvardr?"

"Who else would I be? I repeat my question... who are you?"

"You want the ring?" The voice trembled, but ignored the Seer's question again, "if you had it what would you do?"

Pursing his lips at the figure Harvardr began to feel a familiar sensation sweep over him, his mind sharpened at once, his body ceased to ache and he felt his vigour return, "You have it with you? You do, don't you?"

"What would you do?" the voice persisted.

"Where are the guards?" the Seer asked.

"A fire near the wall, everyone is fighting it."

A smile split across Harvardr's face. The sprite before him had used an old trick for distraction, one he had used himself. "I could easily take it from you, you couldn't stop me." He stood tall and broad before the figure. It had been a long time since he had felt so strong, now at his full height, he stood almost as tall as the Chieftain.

"I... I..." The voice backed away step by step until it stood on the threshold of the doorway.

"Nei!" Harvardr whispered, raising his palm to stall the figure, "What would I do you ask? I would leave, be gone this night never to return."

"Never? You would never return? You wouldn't harm anyone here?" The voice wavered slightly, it felt the power of the man before it and shuddered, this was a mistake, stupid curiosity and a foolish idea but it was now far too late. The guards were gone.

"That's right, I only came here to retrieve it, Liv doesn't understand its power. She can have the boy Ei, for he means nothing to me."

"And the Jarl? He comes to..."

"I know!" Harvardr bit too sharply at the figure. The ring was beginning to make his pulse throb erratically, it was calling to him. Trying to regain his calm he sucked in a breath of air, "if you give it to me, I will disappear! On my way I can stop the Jarl from coming here."

"I can trust you? Please?" The voice moved closer once more, its delicate hand outstretched. Slowly the fingers opened, causing Harvardr to sharply exhale, the ring was before him, its beauty and power surging and coursing with desire through his veins.

Unable to stop himself, he snatched out at the hand pulling the figure into the room and with a balled fist, he slammed it against the cheek of the voice, forcing the limp figure to the ground. With a dull thud he kicked the figure in the ribs and smiled at the small scream of pain that fell from its lips.

Reaching down Harvardr pulled the jewel from the hand of the fragile body holding it up before his eyes. Carefully, he slid it onto his index finger feeling the warm glow of triumph fill his core. The form lay on the ground muffling a small sob with the sleeve of its tunic.

"I know who you are. I see all, even if my eyes are locked within this room, staring at these four walls! I have seen what you will become and can't allow it, too much power, too much ability! So now you are my captive," jabbing a finger pointedly he leaned forward. "You will come with me to sea-cliffs of Hornelen and should any try to stop us I'll threaten to kill you and there is someone who would not wish that I'd wager." Harvardr stooped over the form before gathering his cloak tying it about his shoulders. He would abandon his satchel for there was little use for it now; he did not require the possessions of his former life, he had the ring, and one weapon he had managed to conceal upon his body. He had not been offered the chance or opportunity nor the strength to use it but now everything had changed. The tides were turning.

Stroking his long white beard with his gnarled fingers the Seer bent down and roughly grabbed his captive by the arm. "Stand up!" he snarled, baring his discoloured teeth, "we must make for the mountain."

Swiftly the Seer pulled the hood of his cloak over his head and that of his prisoner. The figure stumbled to keep pace with him as they moved through the passageway of the empty longhouse. Harvardr saw it had been devoid of life for the time of his imprisonment. Momentarily he wondered why it had been built since it showed no signs of occupation. Snorting, he strode through the house and made for the doorway.

Edging the oak door open he peered out at the village. He could see the light of a fire in the distance and smiled, it would be easy to skirt around the settlement unseen and disappear into the forest. From there they would head for the cliffs, taking the cave route within the sea cliff of Hornelen. He had stowed his small boat there when returning to the island, he knew the approach of winter would render the causeway useless as an escape route. Even with his gift of sight there had been no way of knowing how long Ari would take to find Liv, Harvardr might well have been trapped on the island for seasons.

They moved quickly, the smell of smoke was not thick enough in the air to let Harvardr think it was serious, certainly not a blaze the same as he had once ignited. The Jarl came into his thoughts once more as they neared the newly constructed wall at the opening of the valley, it would pose a very real problem to Brynjar and his attack could be thwarted. Harvardr was impressed for only a short moment at its construction and spying the guards had abandoned it completely, they made their way past the line of men and women passing buckets of water to one another, dousing the fire lit from dried grasses and a pile of unused logs.

Harvardr wondered how insanely wrathful the Jarl would become at this new treachery but it mattered not, by the time his disappearance was discovered he would be long gone. Then the village would have to contend with Brynjar, and in the ensuing calamity Harvardr guessed they would ultimately destroy one another. This pleased the Seer; his enemies would grow fewer without him having to raise a hand.

Pulling the weightless figure with him he found he barely had to expend any strength cajoling it along the trails of the forest. He was powerful once more and he shook his head that he had worried himself with thoughts of misjudgement, ageing and foolishness. Even in the blackness of the night he knew the path he took well, the same path he had spirited Liv away on, to the caves where they had once made their escape but the difference, however this time, was that Harvardr was not blighted by his oath to any other but himself. The ring was his, and only his.

The couple had only had a short time to talk when the shouts rang out. Swiftly they donned their clothing and weapons before running with the others to the source of the cries. From the hall they could see a fire ablaze near the newly constructed wall. Men leapt from their pallets in the hall, their huts and small dwellings in the settlement. They all knew the drill well; buckets and troughs filled with water were passed hand to hand and thrown onto the fire.

Ove paced back and forth in the yard shouting orders at the men as they set to work while the women cleared the outbuildings of people and beasts guiding them as far from the blaze as possible. Children were rounded up and sent to the safety of the hall.

Sensing Grani's anxiety Liv raced into the barn and freed him from his stall, slapping his rump she pointed him in the direction of the other cattle. It took seconds for her to catch up with the men and running with Ari and Dag, Liv grabbed a small bucket filling it with water from a trough. She drew a gasp when she saw how close the fire was to the wall, if the breeze were to turn the fire could easily catch and destroy their fortification.

Staring at the fire before her she saw it was the pile of unused logs and grass. Ari shouted to Dag and at a group of men to join them and tackle the fire from the other side. Liv saw the urgency in Ari's face; he also feared the turning of the wind. The heat from the burning timber caused Liv to draw back and shield her face. A cool breeze began to stir and the skies were flooded with dark grey clouds and as the air became heavy, thunder rumbled across the heavens in the distance.

"Where is Gytha?" Dag called over to her. Frantically Liv looked throughout the crowd, but did not see her, then as she started towards the hall the young woman sprung out of the doorway carrying her sack of medicines. Pointing to the hall Liv caught Dag's eye. Nodding, he grabbed a bucket from Ari throwing it against the wooden pyre.

Suddenly a hand pulled Liv aside and Holger stood before her, his face smeared with sweat and soot and etched with worry. His wild thick red hair whipped about his face in the growing wind, "The boy! Thorik, have you seen him?" he shouted to be heard above the worried cries of the villagers.

"Nei! He must be with the children in the hall," Liv felt a sickening wave of nausea wash over her, causing her to drop the wooden pail she had grabbed earlier and the water sloshed at her feet, "when did you see him last?"

"Natmall. I awoke to the screams of a fire and then ran here. Thorik would be here to help, to prove himself, something is wrong!" Holger gritted his teeth and turned to run back to the line, "find him!" he called over his shoulder.

She knew it was true, Thorik would have joined in had he been aware of what was happening, but where could he be? Running to Gytha she grabbed the woman's arm, pulling her with the crowd surging into the hall. Women and children along with the elderly crowded around the tables and benches. Vigi yelped as she cowered with her pups behind Ove's great chair.

"Is he here?" Liv shouted above the voices.

"Nei! I grabbed my bag to treat any injured when the alarm was raised, I don't know when I last saw him Liv!" Gytha laid out the contents of her bag on the nearest bench and she began administering ointments to grazes and cuts some had gained in the panic of the fire. Liv saw the fear of the villagers and she could also feel their eyes upon her, she saw how the older women wrung their hands in their aprons; another fire, would they blame her this time she wondered?

"There!" Gytha pointed to the bench where Thorik had last been seen, "his horn!"

Lifting the horn from the bench Liv questioned why the boy would have left his treasured item, then an idea began to form in her mind, she could feel something was dreadfully wrong and slowly she began the walk to her chamber. She could hear Gytha calling after her but before she entered the room, she knew what she would find. The sight before her made her groan with anger, the chest under which the ring had been hidden was upturned, the earth clawed at to reveal the small wooden box she had hidden it in cast aside.

It was obvious she sighed, the boy must have crept along the hallway and listened to her and Ari talking. Grabbing her pack Liv fished out her leather leggings and linen tunic and casting her dress aside, she pulled a leather vest over her head and swung her belt of knives about her waist. Tucking the small axe into the sling on her back she left the room.

Heading for the longhouse that held Harvardr she searched the rooms to no avail, cursing in the darkness, she ran for the yard of the settlement. As she ran she heard the shouts of people calling her name but did not stop until she saw Ari racing towards her, Dag followed with Holger, the looks on their faces told her something was terribly wrong.

"What?" Liv asked, catching her breath.

"Ebbe, he saw the glow of campfires by the lake, the rise on the farmstead gave him a good line of sight," Ari rolled up the sleeves of his tunic fastening the leather cuffs about his wrists, "Brynjar is here, he could attack at any time. Go with the women and hide the children under the smokehouse. We are gathering the men and our weapons, go now!"

"I can't! Thorik is missing!" Liv cried.

"Ja, Holger has said, but it changes nothing, Liv, the Jarl is on the island. Come! Ebbe and Lena need help to move the people," Ari turned with Dag heading for the hall before he stopped abruptly and looked back at his wife. "Harvardr? Have any checked on him?"

"He's gone! You see it don't you Ari? The fire, Harvardr missing, Thorik missing! I know where he has taken him you must let me go after them!" she cried.

"You know I can't..." Ari searched Liv's eyes, but met with a resistance he knew he could not fight.

"The ring is missing, he'll kill the boy Ari, I cannot let that happen," she stated firmly.

Holger bristled at the thought of Thorik held captive and also felt a burning anger to clout the lad for his misguided actions, "I'll go with her," he said, turning towards the men.

Shaking her head Liv shot him a defiant look, "Nei, you are needed here! If the Jarl and his men are by the lake they've made a mistake in alerting us to them. Do you think he's so foolish? He's looking for a fight not a raid on an unsuspecting village," and turning to Ari she pleaded with her eyes, "I'd be heading in the other direction, he has no knowledge of the island, I can run to the caves unseen."

The commotion in the settlement was reaching a fever pitch; children were being dragged from their homes and the hall by frantic women doing their best to keep some measure of calm. A single torch led a procession to the farmstead of Ebbe and Lena. Ari felt a rage building that made him want to tear the hair from his head, he knew he had to let Liv go and swore under his breath that Thorik would feel the back of his hand, but he knew his anger towards the boy was no more than fear. Ari did not enjoy the feeling and buried it away deep within and looking at his wife, he saw the burning in her eyes, as they glittered beneath the starless night sky and the glow from the dying fire and torches. A flash of lightning tore through the gloomy sky and thunder boomed above their heads. At any moment the skies would rain down upon them.

"Where has he taken the boy?" Ari asked through gritted teeth.

"The caves of Hornelen... I'm sure of it."

"You can do this? You can kill him?" he said, gripping her forearm.

"I can," she replied, looking deep into his eyes, willing him to believe her.

"What? Have you all gone mad! The Jarl and his wolves roam the island, what if he catches Liv and the boy?" Dag protested throwing his arms skyward and dragging his hands through his dark hair, "there is a storm upon us!"

The Jomsviking looked between the pair, Ari's eyes were fixed upon his wife; then he jerked his head towards the forest telling her to go. Liv stood holding his gaze, and raising her hand to his face, she cupped his chin and nodded, a slight frown creased her brow. Then she turned and ran towards the forest disappearing within the darkness.

Holger shrugged his shoulders and grabbed a fistful of his beard, raking his fingers through it, he gruffly shouted to a group of men to barricade the gate making sure no man could leave or enter. Then he strode to the hall swearing and cursing to himself as he went to gather his weapons.

"Come, we had better find Ove and ready the men," Ari spoke quickly.

"Ari!" Dag choked. "You let her go? After all this, Thor's teeth man, the bastard who seeks her is here!"

"He couldn't find her in six years... she has a chance, she knows the island, he doesn't!" Ari replied and breaking into a run the men made for the hall. Once inside, they gathered their axes and saw that the men of the village were doing the same, swords strapped across their backs and each carrying a heavy wooden shield.

Gytha emerged from the passageway and headed for the two men, "Liv?" she asked worriedly.

"Hel's blood what are you doing here? Have all the women turned into fearless Valkyries!" Dag barked barely able to contain his temper any longer, but before he could launch into a tirade he heard Ari reply.

"She's gone after Thorik," Ari cast a look at the men preparing themselves, he wondered how many men the Jarl had brought with him. Ebbe had only seen a handful of small fires, which was curious.

"Alone?" Gytha gasped raising a hand to her forehead as she searched the men's faces with her blue eyes.

"Why are you here?" Dag countered in frustration.

"I'm of more help here than hiding in a tunnel! Don't fight me on this Dag, you won't win," facing Ari, Gytha stared at him, willing him to speak, "you let her go?"

"Finally! See the madness in it? But you are no better woman! Get to Ebbe's now, I can't fight with you here, I need a clear mind and worry will only…"

"Enough!" Ari snapped, "she's gone, Liv can take care of herself and the boy. If I don't question it, neither will you!" He paused drawing a steadying breath, "Gytha if you are staying arm yourself and at the first sign we are being overrun make for the farmstead. Dag is right; he can't worry about your safety and fight. We don't know how these men will behave, you are a woman. Do not put yourself in jeopardy, no matter who is in need of care."

With a dark look Dag grunted his displeasure throwing silent curses at both Gytha and Ari with his eyes, he saw Gytha nod and return to her medicines, grabbing a dagger he strode over to her. Pulling her to face him, he knelt at her feet, lifted her dress, exposing her leather boots beneath. Sliding the dagger into the fur-lined calf he stood, turning her around by her shoulders, he drew a sigh and fixed a short sword to the back of her belt about her waist.

"It will have to do. Can you use these?" he growled angrily.

"Before I met you I was a maid in my brother's tavern and many a man thought to try his luck and failed. I know full well how to use a dagger, but I promise to run before testing how well I can use it," Gytha summoned all her strength to sound fearless, but she felt sure the beating of her heart was louder than the storm brewing above them.

"You'll not listen to me? Women can be hurt in ways…" sighing Dag dragged a hand across his chin.

"You are a Jomsviking, Dark-Blood, have you become soft over a woman?" Her pale azure eyes gleamed in the low light of the hall.

A smile split across Dag's mouth revealing the brightness of his teeth and he appeared at once pleased and wild with his wolfish grin, "you will see how a Jomsviking fights!" Shaking his head, he looked back to his friend before becoming serious once more, "you will run at the first sign of danger." It was a command rather than a question and satisfied when Gytha agreed, he returned to Ari's side before both men walked from the hall towards the gate.

Gytha let out a breath from her chest that threatened to explode. The tension in the room was like an over-stretched hide as men filtered out of the hall after the Jomsvikings until only Holger remained watching her from the doorway.

"Gytha, these men with the Jarl are dangerous, but none more so than Brynjar. Please obey your man and run, don't tarry waiting for him for he'll fight to the last," Holger heard the sadness in his own voice. He had trained many of Brynjar's men however he did not agree with the methods some had adopted and he resented the techniques Brynjar had used on those closest to him, including Solveig. Taking a step towards her he jerked his head to the blackness outside the hall, "do you wish to be like Liv? Even she must tire of the constant danger. It is not a life, to risk your own at every turn, Gytha."

"Nei Holger, but I admire her strength. I know I can do this, I can help, like you we have something to prove to ourselves," and seeing the frown grow upon Holger's brow, Gytha reached out and grasped the man's thick forearm.

It was true Holger thought; he was unsure what to make of the impending confrontation with Brynjar. The man would by now have guessed he had betrayed him, at best Brynjar might think him dead giving Holger the element of surprise. He thought of his wife, his children, without him and unprotected in Srovberget, a place where the Jarl had eyes and ears in every workshop, hall, and home. He had to return to them.

"You are strong and brave Gytha, and right! I must prove to myself I am worthy of my family," Holger's lips formed a thin line beneath his beard and turning to leave the hall, he fingered the amulet about his neck invoking the power of the god Thor, who it seemed was raging his fury of thunder upon them as they prepared for battle.

Chapter 26

ᛗᚢᚾᛏᛖᚱ ᛏᚹᛖᛁᛏᛋ ᛋᛁᚦ

The storm began to whip and whistle through the trees bordering the lake. Brynjar looked up into the sky, seeing nothing but thick grey clouds until a flash of lightning cracked in the air, he squinted at the shadows the flare created in the heavens. If he believed in omens, as muttered about by the group of men, he might have thought the Gods were proclaiming his arrival to Smols or trying to delay him.

He kept one eye on the forest, it was black within the thick woodland, no movement betrayed itself, but he had a feeling there was far more in there than he could see. The old Seer had been truthful about the causeway and it had been a blessing for Brynjar who had been beginning to lose his mind with frustration.

They had pressed on that very moment even though their stomachs were empty and their bodies exhausted. Brynjar knew he had lost weight and sagging folds of dark skin hung loosely around his eyes. He was leaner than the formidable Jarl he had once been, his appearance drew stares from the men. He cursed at that, they were becoming too free in their disapproval of him, eyeing his movements with beady furtive glances and chewing their cheeks in thought. Still, he would reprimand those who required it once he had what he had come for.

Agar's insolence still irked him; the man had said naught of any worth since they arrived at the lake, he had not questioned Brynjar when ordered to light fires for the men to rest at or even raised an eyebrow when Brynjar delayed them taking shelter against the weather. He would order his men to enter the forest, soon, but first he was waiting for the Seer to come to him again. He had to know the way, the path to the village, he was not so filled with lust for the ring that he would wander through a wood and risk his life without a route. He had heard the Skalds tales as a child in his father's hall and they told of fearless warriors who lost their senses in the depths of dark and murky lands, cursed to wander without purpose or end. It would not be him.

Tossing a sideways glance at the men who sat or squatted by their meagre fires he spotted Agar watching the skies. Each flash of lightning or rumble of thunder in the distance caused him to poke at the ashes of the campfire with a long stick and Brynjar wondered what he was thinking, he did not trust this young man with his father's name, but then he did not trust anyone. The men were a sorry state, their clothing was as ragged as sack cloth, their furs moth eaten and poorly patched, they all appeared grubby with grime stuck to their skin and underneath their fingernails.

Sighing Brynjar closed his eyes where he stood half turned between the lake and the forest. He could feel the old man was nearby, a residual throbbing in his mind from his vision of Harvardr lingered and the sensation had grown, the closer to the island they had become. A soft whisper floated on the swift breeze that began to whip his greasy mane about his head. The throbbing intensified, encouraging the tingling and needling pain in his limbs to increase; flexing the fingers of his left hand, he ground his teeth and strained to hear the words.

'Your desire will lead the way…' Brynjar's eyes snapped open. Could it be so simple? Was he to follow his instincts, his gut? The notion caused him to bite down hard on his lip, his teeth cut into the flesh.

"So be it!" he growled, spitting a globule of blood and phlegm onto the stony shore of the Smols lake. He jerked his head towards Agar who sat with his poking stick watching him, his gaze hard and dark, "douse the fires, gather the weapons, we head into the wood."

Agar stood, tossing his stick aside and kicking dirt upon the flames, "you know the way?"

"Ja," Brynjar strode towards him. Then to the rest of the men he growled, "you will shed blood, but these Jomsviking men are well trained and they are fearless and ruthless in battle. You are weakened now so hear me when I say you will invoke the blood fury, become the Berserker Vikings you are meant to be! Any who survive this will gain great rewards when I am King!"

Grinning Brynjar waved the men to follow them. Agar took the rear of the group watching his former Jarl briskly increasing the pace. The men grasped their axes, their swords strapped to their backs and waists, but their shoulders appeared weighed down by their leader's demands and they were unhappy about the course of their actions, and it read on their faces.

He might have been lacking in years, but Agar was not foolish, he knew well they would be outnumbered. Did Brynjar think the two Jomsviking men would be sitting in their Chieftain's hall swilling ale and growing fat on meat? If Holger had taught Agar anything it was never to underestimate the enemy. How could Brynjar expect these young men to achieve anything in the sorry state they were in, he wondered?

A thought pierced Agar's mind, perhaps Brynjar was using them as some sacrifice, perhaps they were a simple tool to let him sneak into the village and acquire his precious ring. Surely the village had men watching them, the blackness of the night and gathering storm might be concealing them from sight. He sorely wished Holger was alive and well, it would do the men good to see their captain for the former Jarl was no leader of men. Scolding himself once more for following the Jarl instead of swearing loyalty to Inge, Agar shook his head and swore to regain his honour. In this pursuit there was none to be had, it was folly, and he felt sure that if he did not try to rectify his mistake Hel would take his soul.

There was the possibility of attacking Brynjar but Agar could not be sure he would succeed in killing him. He had watched him closely; the man's vigour seemed renewed since they had crossed the causeway to the island. Still, his left hand trembled, but it was not the arm that wielded his sword. Agar was young and had strength on his side but the Jarl had age and experience.

He had heard tell of a young man who had fought an ageing warrior on horseback, a travelling Skald had visited Srovberget some time ago and left the memory lingering in his mind. The young man had fought for the right to win back his betrothed from the warrior who had stolen her for himself. A long fight on horseback wore on until every sword, axe and shield lay broken on the ground around them but still their beasts stood proudly. The young man spurred his horse into a gallop smashing into the warrior.

Both horses died from the impact, the young man wept for his fine animal, but those tears turned to joy when he saw the warrior dead on the ground. He had been crushed by the weight of his fallen steed, his eyes and mouth open facing the heavens in a silent scream. The young man retrieved his woman and made her his bride claiming all the lands and wealth of the fallen warrior. In his sorrow he vowed never to ride the back of a horse again earning himself the name Eric Longfeet.

Agar wondered what any of this meant, why should he remember such a tale now? What would happen to him should Brynjar succeed, and what if he did transform into a God? They all knew the legend; some of the men believed it and some of the men feared it. Feeling his body weary, and his stomach aching from hunger, Agar made a decision. He knew Brynjar would dispose of him at the first opportunity; Agar decided he would not provide one.

Harvardr the Seer stopped abruptly, causing Thorik to slam into his back. The old man grunted, his hood fell from his head as the wind increased. It was coming in brisk gusts even between the broken barrier of the tree trunks.

He could feel Brynjar's presence, he could sense the desire and malice, it prickled along his skin feverishly blistering his senses. The Jarl's lusting was increasing the weight of the ring Harvardr had strung upon a leather thong and tied about his neck. It was safer there for now, closer to his heart, unable to slip from his finger. Grasping at the jewel he felt a searing heat emanate from it. This had never happened previously, it had never felt so wondrous and terrifying at once. For a moment he considered why had it never caused him such feeling before? It had to be the malevolence and intent of the Jarl, Harvardr knew himself to be capable of holding it for he had done so many a year. The jewel vexed him, caused him to turn his back on all he had ever known, but he would wield it with the strength of a wise learned man, not a barbarian whose temptations and passions drove him more fiercely than his rational mind.

The child at his side drew back and shuddered. He was blinking at the strange look on Harvardr's face, was it awe or fear the Seer wondered. Grinning the old man smoothed the long thin braid of his snow-white beard, "we must reach the sea cliff, the man who has come for the ring is powerful and he would kill a skelf of a boy like you in a heartbeat!" Leaning forward, he sneered in the boy's face, "Can you feel his presence? Doesn't your feeble child's mind allow you to sense him yet?"

"I'm not feeble," Thorik hoarsely whispered. His shoulders were hunched, he felt as hollow as a rotten tree stump, his foolishness had jeopardised all he had cared for and he knew it, "why would I sense anything?"

"Don't you know you are gifted? Didn't your people tell you?" Harvardr distractedly snarled as he looked about their spot.

"My people are fishermen, Aegir the God of the sea..."

"Hah... Aegir! Tis' only the All-Father you should concern yourself with, even with one eye he sees all!" Dragging the boy by the scruff of his tunic Harvardr gained a few paces before stopping once more. Glancing around them, he turned on his heel, and saw nothing in the blackness of the woods but he could feel it, he could feel Brynjar waiting for him, he could hear the man's thoughts calling out to him. Closing his eyes, he whispered under his breath so quietly Thorik could not make out the words, but as if provoked by some unseen force he spoke before Harvardr could finish, "the caves..."

Sucking in a breath Harvardr opened his eyes and glared at the boy, "never speak when a Seer is casting spiall! You contradict the flow, interrupt the spell, you will remain silent!" Dragging his nails across his balding scalp Harvardr sneered between gritted teeth, "he could well have heard your words... that was not my intention!"

"You're afraid of him! You don't want him to know where we are going!" Thorik hissed the words at the old man and struggling against the grip on his shirt he clawed at the Seer's fist as feral as a wildcat. "You try and frighten me with threats of what he'll do to me but you're afraid for yourself!" Spitting the words past his teeth Thorik ripped himself from Harvardr's grasp stumbling back and falling onto his side. The knock bruised the tender spot on his ribs where he had earlier received the kick causing pain to thrust the air from his lungs.

Suddenly a blade flew past Harvardr's nose lodging itself in a

branch feet away. Turning on his heel the old man fled along the path against the force of the wind and the howling of the increasing storm. Thorik heard a pair of feet approach, soft swift breathing stopped by his side and a pair of hands roughly turned him over.

"Thorik! Are you harmed?" Liv breathed quickly, her eyes searching the boy's pain riddled features. Loosening her grip on his shoulders, she pushed aside wild tufts of hair from his face.

"Liv!" he choked, "forgive me, I never meant..."

"Wait here. I must go after Harvardr!" As Liv pushed Thorik back against the forest floor, he clawed at her forearms refusing to release her hold, "nei! The Jarl is here!"

"I know Thorik, the men will deal with him!"

"Please Liv, don't go, he's not a weak old man! The ring has changed him, made him stronger, please!" but even as Thorik pleaded he could feel Liv disentangling herself from him, "please don't leave me!"

Liv stalled and looked at the boy, his eyes were wide and afraid and in the darkness, she could clearly see the whites pale and stark against the night. Her heart lurched, he was so very much like Ei.

"Nei Thorik, I'll not leave you. We must return to the village and pray Brynjar has not arrived yet. Can you walk? Run?" she said softly.

Nodding Thorik scrambled to his feet and clutching his bruised ribs, he leaned on her arm for a moment, "I started the fire. I thought if I gave the old man the ring he'd take it far from here, he said he'd stop the Jarl from attacking if he met him on his journey. I wanted to believe him, I couldn't lose all of you."

Staring down at the boy Liv bit her lip before looking away. She was deeply angry with him, but finding him safe and relatively well had calmed her emotions. Her hatred towards Harvardr was greatly increased and more than anything she wanted to chase him to the caves and hurt him badly for the pain he continued to cause.

The wind was rising; the tree branches were groaning with the force of the gusts, dampness filled the air. The wood smelled of freshly upturned earth and fallen pine needles and rain would begin to fall at any moment, Liv knew they had to move fast in returning to the settlement.

"You're young Thorik, we've all done foolish things in our youth," she gently pulled him along the trail behind her showing him where best to place his light footsteps.

"I've dishonoured myself," he groaned, "the men will never understand, they might die because of me."

"It's not the men who have come after you," Liv glanced back at him with a sharp stare, "you think Ari and Dag have never made mistakes? You know Holger regrets much."

"I'm responsible..."

Stopping Liv swung around and leaned into Thorik's face. Grasping his shoulder, she fixed her eyes on his, "for yourself! As all men are. You must decide who you are, not what you want to be, we can all dream Thorik but to live is a far greater challenge!"

Wiping his eyes Thorik avoided Liv's stare for as long as he could, "but if any of you die..."

"You did not tie the threads of fate to any of us. This day was foreseen by the Gods a long time ago Thorik, tis' you who have been swept up in it. No action of yours past or present has caused this, we live and we die, tis' fate and no more! Hear me, Thorik, for a long time I thought as you did! We have one life, one chance, we must try to do the right thing and that's all you have done," she stared hard at Thorik before turning once more and pulling him at a quicker pace along the winding trail on the woodland floor.

"They'll have harsh words for me," he groaned again, stumbling slightly and tugging on Liv's hand.

"Ja, but words are better than silence. Your ears will be hot with their anger!" Despite their situation, she smiled slightly letting the boy sense her moment of humour, "why does it matter so much Thorik? We all think well of you."

"Before I had only dreams, now there's more and I don't want it to end," the din of the growing storm above forest muffled his voice, but Liv heard him despite it.

"When we reach the wall I want you inside quickly," raising a hand, she ushered them to a stop and dropped to her knees. For a moment she thought she had heard something up ahead, but her eyes could not make out any movement in the darkness. Pulling Thorik closer she wrapped an arm around his shoulder before raising a finger to her lips. In the blackness of the night they crouched, their breathing hardly audible. Liv drew a blade from her belt offering it to the boy before indicating they should move ahead once more. Before they reached the broken line of the forest, where the wall of the village proudly stood, she whispered in the boy's ear, "all things come to an end Thorik... good and bad."

From their position the land leading up to the wall was deserted, no lamp or torch shone from the platform behind the pitched wooden spikes and there was a silence in the air that betrayed no sign of life. Pressing her lips together Liv knew she had to alert Ari that they had returned, but she could not tell if there were others hiding in the tree line. Beside her Thorik took a sharp breath clutching at his side, she could tell he was in pain, Gytha would be able to help but first they had to get back inside the settlement.

Deciding there was no other option Liv cupped her hands around her mouth and let out a piercing shriek, which she knew Ari would recognise immediately as the eagle cry. She also knew any trained soldier would prick up their ears at the sound but for a long time there was no response. The heat of her own blood rose in her cheeks, her heart thudded so hard against her chest it caused a painful fluttering but then, as she rocked back on her crouched feet the call came, she knew it was time to move.

Pulling Thorik with her Liv ran down the slope making for the gate. As they approached, she saw it open a little allowing a tall figure to squeeze into the space but Thorik stumbled and fell landing hard on the ground. Stopping to pull the boy to his feet Liv felt the first few drops of rain hit her head. The figure reached them, locking his hands about their wrists and then lifting the boy over his shoulder, it was Ari.

As they ran a series of bird cries rang out from the trees causing Liv to stop and turn back to the broken tree-line. Lightning broke the darkness, illuminating the land surrounding them. It was then that she saw him; standing arms splayed widely apart, his hair sodden and plastered to his face, his furs stood on end around his shoulders increasing the sense of evil from the man.

"Woman!" Brynjar screamed at the slight form hovering in front of the gate. It was her, every fibre of his being told him so, finally she was revealed, but only to die. He seethed with rage that she did not fall to her knees before him. He had never been this close to her, and she was here staring at him.

Ari tossed Thorik to Holger who had squeezed an arm through the gate. "Get her now!" Holger snapped, his eyes aflame with ferocity and fear as Ari ran back to Liv placing a hand at her elbow.

"Jomsviking!" Brynjar screamed, pointing a finger at the man he knew as Gorm "give me the woman!"

"Nei... leave now or die!" Ari bellowed. His eyes narrowed at the curious sight of Brynjar, he was much changed, why did he stand alone and where were his men? Pulling on Liv's arm Ari whispered for her to move and quickly and silently Liv turned and broke into a run with Ari back to the gate. Holger dragged them into the settlement by the shoulders sparing only a moment to look upon Brynjar for himself once more. Then he and Dag drove the heavy door into its frame and pulling the weighty barrier across, they sealed themselves inside.

"He's changed!" Holger wiped the raindrops from his face with the sleeve of his arm, "This isn't what I expected."

"A disguise?" Dag asked, squinting against the drops of rain growing heavier by the second, "why not show his numbers? Does he not want us to fear the force of his army?"

"Something has changed," picking up the boy again Ari tossed him over his shoulder, "Holger?"

"Never have I witnessed the Jarl looking like that, he's too proud, even for a disguise. What would be the point? He favours a show of wealth, coin, and strength. Not a crazed man dressed like a raider!" Shaking his head, he turned to look at the platform, seeing the men on sentry he turned back to Ari, "the boy needs Gytha, I'll stand watch, go and inform Ove."

Nodding Ari beckoned Dag with his hand and both men marched towards the hall, Liv stood for a moment longer looking at the flame haired man before her. He was troubled, more so than usual.

"I don't think he saw you Holger," she shivered in the growing cold of the night.

The man looked at Liv with a warning stare, "but he will know eventually... thank you for finding the boy." Then he walked towards the ladder ascending the rungs and joined the men on the platform.

Hearing a whistle from behind Liv snapped back to her senses, turning to follow the men walking towards Ove's hall.

Chapter 27

ᚦᚾᚨᚲᛏᛘᚱ ᛏᚠᛘᛁᛏᛋ ᛋᛘᚦᛘᛁ

Wrapping Thorik in warm furs, and resting him on the pallet on the far side of the hall, Gytha sighed at the sorry sight of the boy. She had made a warming broth, but he drank it gingerly only screwing up his pinched nose once before falling into a slumber. He still shivered, but she was convinced all was well, his ribs were bruised and his wrists also, but for his misadventure there was little else to be concerned about.

Ove stood talking with Ari and Dag, the men all wore frowns grumbling at each other quietly. There were a few men in the hall standing guard and the fire pit was low, the room felt tense and lacking of all warmth from the feasts they had enjoyed there. Liv sat on a bench where Gytha moved to join her, "Thorik is well," Gytha sighed, "but this waiting is jarring my nerves. Why does he not attack, didn't Holger think he would be swift in his ire?"

"Brynjar… he's not what we prepared for. He looks like a madman; he stood alone with no other sight. Tis' the first time I've seen him, the men he sent after me all this time were nothing like him…" drawing a breath Liv grasped Gytha's hand, "will you not join the women and children?"

"The look in your eye worries me, you're the third, nei, fourth person to ask me to go. Just before you arrived Ove was giving me a piece of his mind, but I promised Dag I'd run if need be."

"Please do Gytha, no harm must come to you, there's a sickness in that man and it bothers me greatly," Liv jerked her head to the door of the hall.

As she looked for Ari the heavy wooden doors burst open and two men dragged a filthy stranger by his arms. Behind them Holger entered and slammed the doors of the hall shut. The Jomsvikings grabbed their weapons as they approached the group.

"This is Agar!" Holger spat and with a heavy hand, he pushed the young man's shoulder causing him to drop to his knees, "Speak now!"

"How did you catch him?" Interrupting the prisoner before he could answer Ari looked hard at the two men with Holger.

"He approached the far side of the wall, we heard scrabbling and then he appeared over the posts," one of the men answered. The other man smiled and wiped a bloody fist on his tunic, "he got a hiding before Holger ordered us to bring him here."

"Never beat a man until he gives you reason... this one poking his head over the wall alone was mayhap not reason enough," grunting at the two men Holger slammed his sword down on the table, shaking his head, he sighed as Dag told the men to return to their posts. He noticed that neither Ari, Dag nor Ove congratulated the men on the capture, and the guards sloped off, realising they should have taken more care with their prisoner.

Eyeing the young man's grazed face and bruised cheekbone Ari extended the blade of his axe resting it under Agar's chin, "you heard Holger. Speak."

"He's lost his mind, the men are afraid of him, we are barely twenty," Agar began.

"Liar!" Holger spat at the man, "this is trickery, why would the Jarl bring only twenty? And you Agar are not one of his best men to make that number!"

Fury rose in Agar's throat, he had been relieved at first to see Holger but the man's reaction to him was one of anger and distrust, "He is the Jarl, no longer! Inge has been given his title and lands, Brynjar was banished by Greycloak! He was found to be spying and selling his information to Bluetooth. We were all who would follow him, and damned for it!" He cursed glaring at Holger.

Silence fell upon the room; Liv's eyes grew wide and locked on her husband's form. Ari straightened his back fixing his stare on the young man. Dag looked to Holger who slumped on a bench and closed his eyes, "when did this happen?" he asked.

"Days after you sent me back from your capture of the boy," Agar looked at his captain. "I've been foolish, abandoned Inge to follow a man I thought wronged, I was sworn to him! I realise my error and wish to make amends. Holger, you must know the men think you dead or disappeared, even Brynjar, but they would swear fealty to you in a heartbeat if they saw your face. Kill him, we're not strong enough, but you are!"

"Nei, you men are not strong enough, only foolish and misguided boys, and you have not yet the skill or fury in your blood," sighing Holger stood, facing the two Jomsvikings, "I will do this because I must, I swore to help you, and like Agar I must make amends… alone."

"You will not," said Ari.

"Your family Holger!" exclaimed Dag.

Neither of the two men thought anything they might say would change the man's mind. They knew he suffered his own pain; his misery at his actions and separation from his loved ones. The torment that made him sombre and dry had to be destroyed, as for many a year Holger had carried out the wishes of a man he feared would wipe out all those he loved and now he had his chance to obliterate Brynjar's existence from the earth.

Understanding the silence between the men Ove glanced over to Liv and Gytha, both the women wore stricken expressions but it was Liv's eyes that caused him the most concern. Was she thinking of her own battle to come with Harvardr or was she thinking of the boy Ei, her charge whom like Holger and his family she was separated from?

"Holmgang," she said, nodding Holger returned her stare and whispered in agreement.

The Jomsviking men followed the red-haired warrior from the hall out into the rain. Stroking the short bristles on his chin Ove looked at the young man called Agar, "Gytha tend this man, I'll have guards watch him."

"Nei, please let me join Holger, when he kills Brynjar I will rouse the men in Holger's honour," rising from his knees Agar clenched his fists, pleading with the old Chieftain.

"Go," Ove flickered a glance at two of his men who each took an arm of Agar and marched him after the men, "Holmgang," he sighed and gathering his own sword, he too left the hall.

"What is this Holmgang?" Gytha asked, her voice trembling as she glanced at Liv.

"A fight between two men, to the death, no other may interfere. Often time is given to prepare but this fight will happen now."

"Should we go?"

"Nei Gytha, stay here," Liv stood and walked away from the young woman. Gytha sat mutely. She felt incredibly alone despite a few farmers who had now been given the position of guards and Thorik remaining in the hall. Swallowing, she forced back the tears that threatened her eyes and turned to her medicines. She hoped with her entire being she need not have to use her treatments on Holger.

Brynjar grinned at his men, he knew how to fire their blood and bring colour to their faces. He had heard the healer woman, who had treated him in the past speak of a plant the Berserkers would eat before a battle. The small red capped mushroom with white gills, it was a beautiful but dangerous item. The healer had boiled it and prepared it as a medicine for Brynjar's agues, but he knew well that to eat it fresh from the ground would induce the veil of ferocity his men now required.

Once as a boy he had ventured out into the woodlands of Srovberget with his treacherous brother Inge, Brynjar had eaten the fungus wanting to prove his bravery and fearlessness. He had awoken the next morning, his body battered and bruised, his fingernails broken and torn from his hands. Though he had been weakened and exhausted, it had not stopped his father from delivering a beating. It was some days later when he discovered that in his psychotic state he had tried to throttle Inge and had slain a number of the small caged birds his father's mistress adored.

None of that mattered now he thought, as he scanned the forest floor with the torch held low in his hand, he would ready his men, they would attack, and the woman would die but not before she gave up the location of the ring. He had seen the fear in her eyes, contented he still held power to dominate the weak, as she had stood rooted to the spot, the man Gorm had taken her away. He wondered what might have happened if the village had shut the gate upon her, would she have crumbled at his feet and begged for mercy? He thought not, something in her stance and the way she was dressed told him so. She had spent a long time eluding him, she had guile and was not to be trusted.

Waving the lit head of the torch Brynjar found what he was looking for. A small crop of red capped mushrooms with bright white stalks sprang from the mossy stump of a tree. Grasping with his thick grimy fingers he plucked them from the ground, and calling two of his men he instructed them to find more. When a small hoard had been gathered, he drew his men around him but did not see Agar amongst them.

"Where is Agar?" he asked, but received only blank faces in reply, "none of you have seen him?"

"Nei," a youth shook his matted head, "he was with us I'm sure, but I've not seen him since they closed the gate."

Brynjar seethed. He had been right to distrust the man, all the looks and stares, the questioning and defiance. Had the snake planned to defect all along? What did the turncoat hope to achieve by betraying him? "No matter! Eat this, you will feel strong and lust for the fight!" Thrusting the bag forward, he watched as the hands warily delved into the sack each pulling a small mushroom from within.

Some of the men watched as others sniffed the red caps, some were so hungry they stuffed the mushrooms into their mouths barely chewing. Brynjar nodded at them, jabbing a finger at the small group of men, he grinned viciously, "do you feel the power of the seidr magic coursing in your veins? Are you not stronger, are you not gnashing your teeth together with the smell of their flesh? Remember you are my men, you will heed my word, and no one will attack until I say. Now come, you are my Viking Berserkers and we are here for blood!"

Ove shouted for the men to open the gate, as Ari and Dag waved the men back and walked with Holger to face Brynjar. None believed Brynjar would honour the Holmgang and would be damned to Hel if Holger was slain unjustly. Ove commanded the gate closed, once the trio had passed, and sealed with the heavy wooden log locking it in place and climbing the rungs of the ladder, he made his way up onto the platform.

The rain pelted on the ground, creating large puddles of water. It sloshed about their feet as the three strode out into the clearing and though the wind had died, the thunder and lightning raged on in the heavens.

"Brynjar!" Holger bellowed loudly against the din of the skies. In the distance he could see the light from a single torch at the edge of the tree-line. The light moved forward, moving slowly down the hillside and towards him on the clearing.

The three men stood side by side as they watched the figure approach, a torch held above its head with one hand and his sword readied in the other but then as he drew nearer they saw a line of men appear from the gloom behind him, there were at least twenty but even from the distance Ari could see there was something wrong. Their faces were contorted and twisted, appearing as ghoulish monsters in the faint glow of the torchlight, some bared their teeth and shook their heads violently and all were armed with swords.

The line of men staggered and swayed behind Brynjar, some began to drop to their knees tearing at their hair and scratching their faces but the former Jarl seemed not to care, his own face was blank and pallid, his eyes were hollow and so dark that not even the lightning illuminated them. By the time the line of men

378

reached Brynjar's side there were perhaps only nine that still stood. The rest of them had fallen on the ground, writhing in agony, or lay unconscious in the mud and rain.

"Holger!" Brynjar screamed in disbelief, "so you have betrayed me? I thought you dead!"

"Nei, not dead!" Holger shouted back and extending his arm he pointed the blade of his sword at his enemy, "I'll have your head Brynjar, I challenge you!"

"Hah!" Brynjar tossed his head back and laughed, his chest heaved, his bearded chin quivered and his eyes wildly looked at his men. For a moment he was confused by the sight of some of them lying on the sodden earth but those who remained by his side were as transformed as he. They held their ground waiting for his command to attack despite their frenzied state, "You will taste my blade Holger, and then I'll take your woman before killing her! The blood of your line will seep from their throats! From Muspellsheimr you will smell their bodies burning!"

Ari felt Holger bristle with fury, allowing the man to step forward; he kept an eye on those with Brynjar. Glancing at Dag he saw his friend nod. Each man drew their swords from their backs and their axes from their belts. In each hand they held fast their weaponry.

Holger walked out into the clearing readying himself to attack Brynjar. Slowly his enemy moved forward, tossing his torch into a puddle on the ground.

From the platform on the wall Liv stared out at the fight about to commence. She saw her husband and his comrade create a wide space between themselves and Holger, side stepping with bended knees. They were positioned and poised should any of Brynjar's men try and interfere or attack Holger. Her nails dug into the wooden posts, her hair plastered to her head and her clothes sticking to her drenched skin. Ove tried to give her a cloak, but she shook her head and stared straight ahead, he then walked along the platform tensing his fingers around his wrists.

It was Brynjar, who made the first strike, aiming for Holger's sword arm, but Holger was too swift, and blocking the blow deftly with his own sword, he shoved Brynjar backwards. The man staggered for a moment before launching himself towards Holger again, swinging the blade, it connected with Holger's sword over and over. Being the larger man Holger used his fists and elbows to make contact with Brynjar's jaw, ribs and gut. The man lurched, he was winded and struggled to suck a breath into his lungs. Slipping on the mud Brynjar lost grip of his sword sinking onto his hands and knees.

Holger spat on the ground, the distaste of such a poor fight made him sick, he had wanted to wound the man, to make him plead for his life, but it was not to be. Standing over Brynjar, Holger raised his sword above his head, rain dripping from his wild red hair and beard. As he lowered his arms to deliver the blow, Brynjar pulled a dagger from his boot and drove it deep into Holger's thigh.

The blinding pain caught Holger by surprise and he dropped to one knee, clutching at the blade buried deep in his flesh. Standing

Brynjar stumbled to his sword and lifting it, swung blindly at Holger, slicing into the flesh of the man's left arm.

The Jomsviking men watched in horror as the blade connected with Holger. Their blood boiled when they heard the cry of pain erupt from Holger's lips but before they could react, Brynjar screamed at his men to attack and they had no choice now but to fight.

Liv held her breath and watched the scene, her blood ran cold, her heart stilled in her chest. Holger lay on the ground bleeding into the earth; Brynjar's men raced towards Ari and Dag like feverish animals screaming and waving their swords. Finding Agar standing at her side Liv grabbed his arm, "Come with me now!"

Pulling the young man with her, she climbed over the post heads of the gate and slid down the wall. Crouching, she pulled Agar closer and pointed to Holger, "we must get him to safety, Ari and Dag can take these men, help me!"

"You are her? The one he was after?" Agar drew a breath. He had not realised the woman he had heard of so often had stood beside him and was now dragging him into the fray. They crept towards the bleeding Holger, Liv held her breath as the sound of shouting and blades colliding filled her ears. Daring to look she watched transfixed at Ari and Dag fighting Brynjar's men. They had taken four men down already, the fallen laying on the ground broken and twisted, their bodies mangled from the wounds of the Jomsvikings axes and swords. She saw Ari covered in blood and praying it was not his own, she watched as he swung his axe and thrust with his sword, swinging his blade through the advancing men as if they were made of straw and cloth.

They reached Holger, and hooking an arm beneath each of his own, Liv and Agar hauled his limp body through the mud but as they neared the gate Agar heard a shout and saw Brynjar pointing one of his men in their direction. Agar watched as the former Jarl hung back, hunched over and gripping his sides, as his men were felled one by one.

"Agar, call Ove to open the gate!" Liv shouted as she fumbled for her own axe. As the attacker drew nearer Agar frantically pounded on the wood, shouting for Ove to open the portal at the top of his lungs he saw his hands were covered in Holger's blood.

Seeing his men struggle Ove leapt from the platform pulling at the gate as the man on the other side pushed. The mud slowed the process causing their feet to slip and slide in the mire. Cursing loudly, he heaved with all his might, his disbelief at Liv's appearance on the opposite side of the wall with the prisoner spurring on his actions. He would speak with her sternly after this, as he was sure Ari would.

Suddenly the man racing towards Liv and Holger stopped in his tracks, his body jerked violently and he fell face first onto the mud. Looking up Liv saw Dag turn back to the fray; he had launched his axe at the man breaking his spine in two.

"Come!" Agar shouted to Liv, but turning to face him she shook her head, "Nei, take him to Gytha!"

Agar squinted at the woman as she looked longingly at the Jomsvikings cutting down the last of the men he had travelled with. Brynjar was retreating, leaving those who had fallen where they lay. As he looked back to Liv, he saw her running into the woodland; with the confusion he took relief in the fact that she had not headed in the direction of Brynjar.

Feeling a hand on his shoulder Agar turned his head to see the great bear, Chieftain Ove, grasp Holger's good arm and proceeded to help pull them both through the gate and once on the opposite side, Ove heaved the warrior's body over his shoulder quickening his pace towards the hall.

Chapter 28

ᚦᚾᚨᚲᛏᛗᚱ ᛏᛈᛗᛉᛏᛋ ᛗᛁᚷᚾᛏ

Thorik awoke to the sound of great commotion in the hall, his body ached, but the pain disappeared when he saw the Chieftain carrying Holger and laying him upon a table. Gytha was covering her mouth with her hands and a young man, he recognised as one of Holger's from his capture on the beach, was standing shaking his head. He was covered in blood as was Holger. Suddenly Ari and Dag burst into the room, they too were covered in blood, but appeared uninjured. They shouted at men from the hall to man the gate and threw down their weapons on a table next to Holger's body. Thorik pushed himself from the pallet and staggered towards the scene.

"Gytha!" Dag pulled the woman's arm, "what can be done?" All the colour had drained from Gytha's face; her hands trembled as she took a step closer to the wounded man, "Dag…" she stammered, "place knives into the fire, they must be red before we can use them."

Gently she pulled at Holger's tunic on his arm, drawing a breath as fresh blood surged from the wound, "Gods above! Ari, place your hands here on the wound, help staunch the flow, now let me look at his leg…"

Gytha called to Ove who peered at the blade protruding from Holger's thigh, "could be in the bone, you want me to pull it from his leg?" Ove asked, grasping the blade with his thick fingers. Gytha nodded and Ove removed the blade with a quick jerk of his wrist, "the blade's whole, it came away clean. Only a flesh wound."

"Good, press your hands upon it, I must clean the wound then it must be sealed with one of the blades from the fire." Turning back to Ari, Gytha looked again at the arm; Holger's blood oozed between Ari's fingers as he applied pressure, "the bone is severed. His flesh is too greatly damaged, Holger will lose the arm."

At that moment Holger groaned and struggled to raise himself from his back. Thorik dashed forward, grasping Holger's shoulder easing him down again; brushing the tears from his eyes with his sleeve, he stared at the man who had been so strong, so formidable to him once.

"Thorik, good boy," Holger mumbled.

"Drink this, Holger," Gytha approached with a wooden beaker, she had mixed her herbs to form a concoction laced with a droplet of nightshade to dull the pain, "Holger the men will hold you down, I'm sorry, but to save you we must take your arm… do you understand?" Her eyes brimmed with tears, but she smiled at the wounded man refusing to let them fall.

Before Holger could reply, Gytha motioned for Ari to take Holger's shoulders, Ove his feet and Dag the man's chest. Taking a deep breath Holger reached out for Thorik's hand, "stay with me boy! Take my hand," he said in a hoarse whisper. Thorik stared wide eyed at Ari and Dag whose faces were set with grim expressions.

"Do as he says," Ari replied, trying his best to look kindly at the boy, encouraging him to grasp on to Holger's sword arm.

"Do it Thorik," Dag nodded, but did not look at him, instead he took the heavy handle of a sharp knife Gytha handed him.

"I may not be strong enough... to sever it completely," she whispered in Dag's ear. Seeing her man covered in blood and sodden from the storm she felt a surge of strength enter her core, she had to do this, to save the life of Holger she had to be strong.

As Gytha began to work Holger felt a warmth flood through his being, the pain disappeared, his body became weightless. A low humming filled his head, causing his eyelids to grow heavy; he had no recollection of time, but felt only the tight grip of someone holding his right hand.

Many hours passed in the hall before Gytha was satisfied the blood had been stemmed and the wound cauterised. Holger was breathing and was as well as could be expected, his face was pale and she feared the loss of blood would lead him to death, but each time he stirred she thanked the gods and set about brewing more potions for his treatment.

Agar sat by the fire, disturbed by all he had witnessed. He saw the wretched cruelty of the events etched on faces of all present in the hall and he listened as they spoke with one another, learning their names, hearing the concern in their voices. It was then that it struck him, the woman. Looking for Ari, the one Liv had been watching with intensity as he fought, he found him standing hunched over a table with the other Jomsviking and the Chieftain. Hovering at his back, he darted to the side when he saw the questioning look, the men gave him, "the woman… she ran into the woods," Agar paused. The rage washing over the Jomsviking man's face was frightening.

Grabbing Agar by the scruff of his filthy tunic Ari shook the man, "you tell me this now?" and thrusting the man back, he slammed his hands on the table.

Dragging a hand across his own face, Ove reddened at his foolishness, "by the gods my boy, I didn't think to look for her coming behind me. I grabbed Holger and made for the hall, thinking she was following!"

"Why was she outside the gate?" Ari roared at the men.

"I saw her too, but returned to the fight, I struck down one of the Jarl's men as he ran at them," Dag lowered his tone jerking his chin towards Agar and Holger laying on the table, "forgive us, there was much happening."

"She asked me to help her retrieve Holger…" looking at his captain on the table, Agar felt little regret for their actions, save for the fact that the Jomsviking's woman was now gone.

"Nei… she is my responsibility, none of you are at fault. Thor's teeth how did I not see she was missing?" Turning to Agar he spoke, "the woods? Was she followed?"

"Nei, and Brynjar entered at a different point," the younger man replied.

"We'll find her," Dag sighed, roughly rubbing his forehead darting a look at Gytha who looked up momentarily from Holger's side.

"You recall Liv said she knew how to disappear in a crowd, become invisible? This is her way, don't judge yourselves harshly. She must have had a reason for she wouldn't risk any of you," she said, before turning back to her patient.

Looking at his friend Ari swiped his axe and sword from the bench and strapped the weapons about his body, "stay with Ove, watch over Holger, Gytha and the boy. If any of Brynjar's men stir use our best men to subdue them. When all is secure find my father."

"I sent Ebbe and two men to guard the tunnels beneath his smokehouse, he will be well, Ari," Ove said assuredly.

"Thank you Ove," Ari nodded, and with a rough hand he smoothed back his hair, fastening it into a knot at the back of his head. It was still wet from the rain and flecked with the blood of his dead foes. His face was smeared with dirt and his chin bristling with dark whiskers that made him look angry and fierce.

"Don't thank me Ari," sinking into his great oak chair, Ove placed a rough hand over his mouth.

"Brynjar is still out there, where would she go?" Gritting his teeth, Dag could not help but feel angry at Liv's behaviour. She risked much, not only her own life, but that of his comrade.

"She's after Harvardr, before he can escape. I know where she's headed," Ari said firmly.

"And Brynjar?" Dag pressed.

Ari's eyes shot up, the pale iridescent blue gaze hardened, "We were planning to hunt him down, this changes nothing. He doesn't know the island and his mind is broken. Liv... is not so foolish as to place herself in his way."

"Ari, we all know she is capable, but if Brynjar finds her first..."

Leaning forward Ove pressed his heavy palms on the table top, "when all is secure here, Dag will follow you."

Shaking his head in disagreement, Ari lowered his tone and darted a look towards Gytha, "Dag has more to consider than running after a madman. The village needs you Dag, if I don't return I must know you are here for these people..."

"You insult me!" Dag hissed, roughly grabbing Ari's shoulder, "did I not slay as many men as you out there and did I not put an axe in the back of a man who ran for your wife? Ja, Ari we all missed Liv slipping away, but that is no reason to spurn my help!"

"You insult us both Ari Ebbesson! While you were a Jomsviking our settlement survived and prospered, do you accuse your Chieftain of no more than good luck? Pah! Mayhap I should beat sense into that thick head of yours!" Ove roared, causing the entire room to look at the three men.

With regret written all over his face, Ari raised his hands to silence the men, "Nei... don't misunderstand me. Tis' I who have failed, not you." Taking a deep breath, Ari sighed and shook his head in defeat, "Ja, I insult you both, forgive me it was not intended. I seek only to protect what I can, I can't worry for you all, when I go now to find Liv."

"Go... you have until sunrise. All will be well here," grudgingly grasping Ari's forearm, Dag held fast and looked hard into his friend's eyes, "much has changed for us it would seem."

"Ja, my friend, it has."

"Then make haste... mayhap I don't wish to run about the woodlands after all, when I have a woman to warm my bed," allowing himself a slight grin, Dag nodded and released Ari. Folding his arms across his chest Dag jerked his head to the doorway before glancing at Ove, who watched as his brother's son left the hall.

Thorik sat still clutching Holger's remaining hand within his own, he blinked at Gytha who was wiping her eyes with the back of her hand. Dag approached the table and whispered in her ear and Thorik saw a small smile pull at the corner of Gytha's mouth and felt glad she looked less worried than before. A lump began to well in the young boy's throat as he realised he might not see Liv or Ari again, the overwhelming realisation of his actions burned into his mind. Liv had gone to face Harvardr, and the man who had sought to kill her for so many a year was loose on the island.

"I only wanted to help," he breathed the words into Holger's fist and felt a slight pressure of the man's fingers around his own.

The Hornelen sea-cliff rose as a monstrous looming presence in the night sky above Liv, her heart thudded dangerously in her chest. She could not tell if it was fear or excitement, or her body screaming against the pace she had set herself. But now she had arrived at the foot of the mountain where the caves Harvardr had led her to so many years ago, held him again.

She required no torch, the memory of the network of tunnels was as fresh in her mind as the day she explored them as a child. She and Harvardr had required no light to guide their way the night he spirited her off on their journey, he knew the land as well as she, there was no advantage here.

Liv wiped her hands over her linen tunic beneath the leather vest she still wore; her knives hung from the leather belt about her waist, as was her small axe resting against her back. Realising her hands were shaking she suddenly felt weak and sick to her stomach, her legs threatened to collapse beneath her on the gravel pathway and lowering to her hands and knees, she allowed herself a few deep breaths. It was the ring, the damning presence of it was pressing down upon her.

A rustling in the grasses behind her snapped her senses back, squinting into the darkness she saw nothing. There was a clearing of rushes and grass roughened by the salt air. Gravel and pebbles scattered the ground all along the network of small paths made by the feet of men and animal alike. There was no place a man could stand and hide, but she knew a man laying on the ground might appear no more than a mound of earth in the darkness. Flashes of lightning lit her surroundings for a moment, but revealed nothing. The thunder that had filled her ears began to subside rolling away into the distance.

Taking a breath she stood and made her way into the cave, absolute darkness swallowed her sight. Closing her eyes, she recalled the number of footsteps to take before making a slight turn to the left, brushing her fingers against the tunnel walls she felt the grooves of erosion and time carved into the rock. She walked slowly, one foot in front of the other, crouching now and again when she heard sounds betraying themselves against the wind and waves crashing on the rocks below.

A breeze sifted into the tunnel, Liv licked her lips and tasted the salt air, she was close to the place Harvardr would be hiding, she was close to where he would have his small boat waiting to set sail. Opening her eyes, she saw the rough cavity of the cave she hoped to find him in. Stepping inside she let her eyes adjust, dawn was breaking through the night sky, slowly the space filled with the gentle touch of morning light framing the outline of a hooded figure. It stood looking over the edge of the cave floor, it was staring down at the rocks, listening to the crashing of the waves.

"The storm destroyed my boat..." Harvardr whispered hoarsely, as he turned he raised a hand to finger the ring tied about his neck and Liv felt the nausea wash over her again and shivered.

"Strange it affects you so… but no matter. Soon we will be gone and you will feel it no longer."

"You must give it up Harvardr, it will not serve you as you think, surely you know this?" Her voice rasped as she fingered the hilt of a knife on her belt.

"It is a blessed thing, made for men by the Gods," turning to face her fully Harvardr shoved his hood back revealing his balding scalp and long white beard trailing over his chest.

"Nei, it is cursed, it can only cause harm!" Liv cried.

"Liar!" Baring his teeth the Seer grasped at his throat, "you had your chance and you could not appreciate its gift!" he hissed.

Straightening, Liv took a breath, "it was born of grief and death, and it cannot offer you or any man wealth and power! For those with an impure heart, it hastens their destruction. You held watch over that ring for years, it wore you down Harvardr… do not damn yourself!"

For a moment the Seer looked hard at Liv, his mind turned her words over and over and he remembered a time when he had believed in his task from the Yggdrasil Kynslod. He had sought to protect the boy, he had hidden the ring, but it had become too much. His own desires as a man had pushed aside the feelings of his true heart, "never will I run for them again, never will I give my life for another, tis' time you realised that Liv," Harvardr took a step forward, his face creased and his mouth formed a cruel twisting snarl. "Mayhap you have already, where is the child, Liv?

Don't you hear him in your dreams? I do, I can hear it all, oh how that boy screams! He howls your name! You've forsaken him!"

"He is right... I've heard his cry!" The voice echoed in the small cave.

Cold fear trailed down Liv's spine and turning her head, she saw Brynjar leaning against the wall of the cave mouth. His hair hung over his waxy complexion; his eyes were full and glaring at her with burning hatred. In his sword arm he held the weapon with which he had wounded Holger, his tunic was caked with mud and dripping with rainwater but the man's body quivered with rage. "Harvardr... I found you!" His lips formed a twisted smile as he stretched out his hand to the Seer, "my prize, I'll have it now."

"Nei... I must know where the boy is hidden," Harvardr struggled to contain the apprehension in his voice. He knew he could not trust Brynjar, his skin held the scent of the Berserker plant and his look was wild. "We must kill the boy Brynjar. Hold her... I must reach into her mind... I must see what she hides!"

"Give it to me," Brynjar growled, "I will not be denied now, it was promised to me... and you promised to heal me! I have not forgotten!"

Narrowing his eyes Harvardr assessed the man; he could still be of use to him but not in his current state. He knew he must pacify him and buy himself time to glean what he could from Liv. "All will be yours, my Jarl," Harvardr opened his hands out to Brynjar as if offering him some invisible gift, "trust in me one more time... we must know what she conceals. *Hlita* Brynjar."

"He uses the old tongue to cast seidr upon you Brynjar, because you are weak!" Liv spat at the man, as feral as a cornered feline. "You will learn naught from me, but this... the ring is cursed and worthless to men. The tale of great wealth and power was planned only to entrap, a promise in order to protect the boy! The Gods knew that men would honour protection if they thought they would be rewarded! Heimdallr revealed this to me and more, Harvardr!" Staring hard at the Seer's face, she saw first the disbelief and then the anger.

"The bitch lies!" Brynjar roared at her.

Defiantly Liv glared at the man, "the ring is cursed with sadness. It was born of grief, should a mortal man unworthy possess the ring he shall know naught but destruction. His greed and lust for power will lead only to damnation. Only the blood of the Gods can bear its weight. A pure heart can bear the strain for as long as the body allows, but there is no reward like that which you seek! How many have held it and been rewarded with geld? None!"

Stepping forward, he grabbed her arms, shaking her body with all his might. Letting go of her for a moment, Brynjar shoved her to the ground before grabbing a fistful of hair and glaring up at the Seer, "do it now, then give it to me, as you promised!"

Nodding Harvardr grasped Liv's face, cupping her temples with his palms, at first she tried to struggle but the grip of Brynjar's fist threatened to pull the skin from her scalp. Quietly the old man began his seidr magic, casting his spell he closed his eyes, searching though her memories for the answer. He could hear her struggle to contain a cry in her throat, the pain of searching a mind was terrible Harvardr knew but he would risk nothing, the boy was a threat and had to be killed and for this he would manipulate Brynjar.

Liv's heart began to thud harder and harder, she struggled to bury the images of Ei in her mind. She hid the sleepless nights when she had watched over him, her fear when he had become sickly and her joy when he had first spoken her name. Trying to hide the last moments they shared, her holding his small body against hers in an embrace, his tears and confusion as she walked away from him, back to the boat, back to Grani and to Gulafjord where she had hoped to dispose of the ring, his small voice calling her name.

Struggling against the wave of emotions Liv desperately clung to one thought. Ari, she thought of his fight with Brynjar's men, she thought of his quiet strength and sense of honour that had never left him.

"She fights you!" Brynjar grunted twisting his hands in Liv's hair. Pain ripped through her body as the man pulled at her head, craning her neck and Harvardr dug his long sharp fingers into her skin. Liv's body began to sag with the torment of the attack before suddenly Brynjar's grip released. Harvardr gasped and took a step backwards towards the edge of the cliff face.

Slumping onto the rock floor of the cave Liv painfully lifted her head to see Harvardr backing away against the wall of the cave, as Ari fired blow upon blow upon the face of Brynjar with his fists. The stunned madman stumbled as the Jomsviking beat him, falling to his knees, he stared up at Ari for a moment seeing the man through his blood smeared gaze. Thrusting a hand forward Ari grabbed a fistful of Brynjar's hair twisting and pulling as the man had done moments before to Liv, "your time has come to die Brynjar!" Ari's voice, though laboured by his heavy breathing was low and calm. Jerking Brynjar's head up and stretching his neck, Ari brought down the blade of his axe, with a forceful swing, he hacked the man in two, severing his head from his shoulders.

With disgust Ari threw the head aside, stepping over the body to Liv and pulling her to her knees, Ari looked over her face for signs of deeper injury.

"Forgive me. He had to be stopped," she croaked.

"Ja..." nodding Ari smoothed the loose hair from her face satisfied she appeared unhurt.

Seeing the Jomsviking distracted with Liv, Harvardr reached within the sleeve of his cloak and removed a long thin steel needle. Raising his hand to drive it down into the back of Ari he stopped as Liv caught sight of his intent, and pushing herself in front of her husband, Liv summoned the last of her strength, screaming at the top of her lungs, "Heimdallr!" her voice echoing in the cave.

Confusion swept over Harvardr's craggy face; again he raised his hand to thrust the needle this time in the direction of Liv, but Ari seeing the attack pulled Liv against his chest and grabbed once more at the handle of his axe.

However, before Ari could lift his hand towards Harvardr, a low rumbling came from above them and then a crashing thunderous roar of rocks rolling down the side of the cliff and smashing into the sea.

A horn sounded in the distance, its aching mournful wail calling out to the mountain to shed its load upon the earth. The cave shook and trembled under the weight of the mountain's deluge. Harvardr stumbled on his feet, his renewed strength leaving his body, the old familiar aches returning and lurching backwards, he felt the edge of the cave mouth beneath his feet, struggling to maintain any balance he clawed at the air for stability, his eyes wildly dancing in his head, frantically looking for help.

Liv watched as the old man disappeared over the side of the cave mouth and down into the swirling sea. As he fell his last cry echoed through her mind before the blackness of unconsciousness consumed her.

"I see him! I see him!" Was all Harvardr could scream as he fell.

Chapter 29

ᚦᚾᚨᚲᛏᛗᚱ ᛏᚹᛗᛁᛏᛋ ᚺᛁᛗ

Sitting on the smooth well-trodden steps leading to the doors of the hall, Dag took a deep breath before looking out on the village he now thought of as home. Inside the hall Gytha tended to Holger and those who had suffered scrapes and bruises in the frenzy of the fire. Most of the people had returned to their homes; Thorik left Holger's side only once to gather Grani and return him to his stall. Dag watched the boy, with his horn slung over his shoulder, and the great grey steed as they walked silently.

Upon Thorik's return to the hall, he stopped at Dag's side, his small face pale and pained, he was guilt ridden and the Jomsviking knew it.

"All will be well Thorik," Dag slapped the boy on his shoulder as he sat down beside him.

"I never meant any of this. I didn't think the fire would become so big. That Holger would lose his arm... or Liv would go after Harvardr... I've ruined so much," he whispered the words looking at his small dirty hands resting in his lap.

"Mayhap you've become a man after all young Thorik? It takes a great deal of courage to admit one's mistakes and I've known many who could not," thoughtfully rubbing his dark chin with a rough hand, Dag looked at the boy, "the fire grew because the wind changed, but no one was hurt and nothing was damaged.

401

Holger lost his arm fighting a man he knew he must, he would do it again, and he still has his sword arm which is all that matters. Liv too had to face her foe, Harvardr must see a reckoning and by her hand, and though I wish she'd chosen another time it was her choice. You only quickened what would have happened."

"You think?"

"Ja, I do but you do deserve a beating for the fire!" Dag grinned and roughly jostled the boy with his shoulder, "what say you sound the horn and show Ari and Liv the way home?"

"I'm not sure I deserve it, Dag," sadly Thorik pulled the horn over his head and traced the runes before offering it back to Dag.

"Do you know what the markings say?" He asked.

"Nei," the boy whispered looking at again.

"It says only a burning heart can sound the horn of Heimdallr, tis' the horn's name. I can make it sound, but not like you, not like you did at the lake. Sound it Thorik, a Jomsviking is commanding you to," sternly Dag pushed Thorik to his feet and pointed out into the darkness of the night.

Taking a breath Thorik raised the horn to his lips blowing with all his might. The wail lasted moments but rang loudly, reverberating over the hills all the way to the mountain. When he finished Thorik turned to Dag, the sadness heavy in his eyes and slowly he made his way into the hall where he took up his vigil over Holger.

Dag had kept watch throughout the night and when the first rays of the new day's sun began to break the dark rolling clouds overhead, he heard a cry from the gates, Ari and Liv had returned. Springing from his seat he marched to the gate and embraced his friends warmly before leading them back to the hall.

Sleep crept over the village of Smols for a few brief hours. The Jomsvikings reprieved the men from the watch, as the guards of the gate, letting them return to their families and duties as men. Ove eventually ordered the two warriors to their own beds. In his own mind, he knew the gate secured the village well enough and his people were safe and taking up watch on the platform, he ordered the young man Agar, whom he had brought with him, to brief him on all that had happened in Srovberget.

Taking Gytha from the hall had not been an easy task, her protestations at leaving her patient had been long, eventually Dag had grabbed her satchel and lifted her weary body to the small lodging in the village, Ove had newly gifted them. When he laid her down on their bed, she drifted into a dreamless sleep. Looking around the small room containing a pallet of furs, a small fire pit, finely carved stools and two chests, Dag could not help but feel a sense of pride. This was his dwelling, his and Gytha's, in time it would grow but for now it was more than he or Gytha could have dreamed of not so long ago.

In their chamber in the longhouse Ari and Liv sat on the pallet without speaking. Taking his hand she lifted his palm to her lips and gently kissed his fingers and with the same hand Ari turned her chin gently moving her face to meet his, staring in her opal eyes, brushing the tip of her sharp nose with his finger, "how long?" He sighed, smiling.

"Ari, I'm so sorry."

"I'm tired of such words, it's all you've said since Harvardr fell from the cave mouth; our enemies are dead. What's left to be sorry for?" Pulling the knot of hair at his nape Ari freed his hair, and dragging his fingers through the tangled brown mass, he tugged his ruined tunic from his shoulders, before resting back on the pallet.

"When?" He sighed wearily.

"If you ask me to wait, I will, but the seasons are changing, and there isn't much time."

"We can leave in a day or two?" Ari offered. Stunned, Liv looked at him and slowly a wide smile spread over her face and her eyes glittered with joy, "So soon? I thought..."

"Smile like that for me more and I'll deny you nothing," he sleepily replied, "for now let us rest. You'll have Ei in your arms soon Liv, I swear it."

Leaning onto her side, Liv rested beside her husband and tracing the outline of his sharp, strong features in the lamp light with her gaze, she felt a sense of peace and calm, except from the one aching pain of her heart. Pushing the feeling aside she thought of how she had never dared to dream of such a future.

"There are no words, Ari," she whispered in his ear.

"They are not always needed," and pulling her atop his chest, he kissed her before rolling her back on her side and ordering her once more to rest.

It was many hours later when Liv finally awoke. From their room she could hear no sounds coming from the longhouse or adjoining hall. It had been the dream that had roused her from her slumber, the image of Harvardr, holding a small child's hand within his own, pointing up towards the heavens of Gimli, from where they stood on the rainbow bridge. She had tried to call out to Ei but no sound came from her mouth and in the distance a man with a staff stood, watching the Seer point out the constellations.

Suddenly Harvardr ripped the ring from the thong around his neck and threw it upwards. The child pulled his hand from the old man and ran in the direction of the figure with the staff but before he could reach him, Ei stumbled tripping over his short legs. Harvardr clapped his hands and the ring exploded into thousands of fragments. Each fragment became another ring showering down upon Harvardr who laughed with great pleasure.

The figure moved towards Ei gathering him within the heavy hooded cloak that trailed along the ground and slamming the foot of his staff on the wooden boards of the bridge, the rings burst into piles of ash as they touched the Seer's hands. Harvardr cried out in dismay and Liv called out again for Ei but the man with the staff led him away towards the great walls surrounding Asgard.

She had awoken with a broken heart. Wrestling herself from the furs and making sure Ari still slept, she donned her clothing and crept into the hall. All was silent, the fire now glowing embers,

405

and bodies filled the pallets against the walls. Stepping out of the doorway Liv walked across the yard to the stable. Inside Grani stood watching her as she approached, his onyx eyes followed her unblinking, as from a bucket of water, Liv plucked an apple and offered it to her horse.

"We've not had much time together my friend, still, I'm glad you've had time to rest," she whispered as the horse took the apple from her hand and chewed on the fruit. Looking into his inky oval eye Liv saw her reflection, reaching out she stroked the horse's nose and smiled as he nudged her hand for another treat.

"I must go for Ei, Grani. I'll return to you soon."

"Tis' not the end," the voice came from behind her shoulder, causing Liv to start. As she turned Liv saw Heimdallr staring at her with his ruby red gaze. "I'm still dreaming?" she asked him.

"Nei. You called my name, the horn was sounded," taking a step further into the stable Heimdallr lowered the hood of his cloak, revealing his face, with strong features set around his fiery gaze, he reached a hand out to Liv, "come, the All-Father has lit the skies, I want you to see."

Gently Heimdallr led Liv out into the yard and he pointed up at the twilight sky where the blackness was lit by an aura of green and red, waves of purple and gold weaved and misted their way across the heavens.

"Tonight the child sees what you see, he looks for you every night, and the All-Father stands atop your mountain watching and waiting."

"You know I mean to offer Ei a choice. He's a child… does he not deserve the chance to live a simple life? To grow into a man…" Liv asked plaintively.

"Ei is special, he was born of twin daughters, one the sun and the other the moon. Never before has his mortal line seen this. You offer Ei no more than his father seeks to." Circling her Heimdallr fixed his crimson stare on her with a sad tone in his voice. "Not even the Gods can fight fate. We all have a destiny. Be strong Liv, he requires it of you."

"Eileifr or Odin?" she whispered.

"Both."

"Odin could take Ei whenever he wants. Why does he not do so? Will he let me give the child a choice?"

"The All-Father waits, for Eileifr must face many battles. Odin loves those who dwell in Midgard, tis' why he wandered the land for many a year among you. We Gods can be bound by our wrists, as can men. There is much we are forbidden to do, rules we must obey, we observe threads of fate spun by the Norns," Heimdallr rested a hand on Liv's shoulder.

"I don't understand how your hands can be tied," Liv sighed.

Sternly Heimdallr caught Liv's gaze with his own, she saw anger, it burned with intensity and she felt it was an old deep burning pain. "Should the enemies of the All-Father learn of the boy, what do you think they would do? There are nine realms and Midgard is but one, and you are not as strong as we. You of all the children in Midgard understand Liv, that sometimes we hide what we must protect beneath secrets and omission?"

Tilting his head toward Hornelen, Heimdallr frowned slightly, "bring the boy to the island, his father waits atop the mountain, but make haste for winter is close and there is still peril on your journey."

Before Liv could question the God further, he disappeared before her eyes, "no… Heimdallr please, what do you mean?" she cried. Taking a deep breath, Liv massaged her temples with her fingers before looking back up into the skies and the beauty of the display. "They are gone, they are dead, what more danger awaits us?" For the first time in many, many months Liv let a tear roll down her face, before turning and slowly walking back into the hall.

When dawn broke Ari arose from his slumber finding his wife in the hall, she sat at a table, her daggers and axe laid out before her. Her leather pack was ready, with their Hudfat sleeping bag, made from hide and lined with furs, rolled and bound with rope. Liv wore her leather vest and leggings over her simple tunic and her cloak was hanging over the bench.

Ari approached warily and looked upon her, her face was still beautiful, but showed signs of restless sleep. Her eyes glittered in the low lamplight, but appeared bruised and dark where fatigue had made its mark upon her skin. Her mouth spread into a warm smile and his heart calmed for a moment, gently stroking her

408

cheek, he pushed her long bronze, braid over her shoulder. Without saying a word he retraced his footsteps back to their chamber gathering his pack and weapons, he had known they would depart swiftly and part of him had expected her to be waiting for him like this.

When he returned to the hall he saw Gytha and Dag had arrived, Gytha was holding Liv's hands and trying not to shed tears she would likely feel foolish for later. They would return, Ari was certain of that. He saw Gytha hand Liv small cloth bundles, she explained their purposes, medicine for pain and infection as a precautionary measure.

Dag shifted from one foot to the other before he darkly threw a glance at the door and retreated from the hall. Following, Ari found him leaning against one of Ove's great wooden posts.

"We'll be back before winter sets in, we've a few weeks before the northern shores are covered in ice," Ari spoke with a matter of fact tone.

"It'll give me time to perfect new Tafl strategies" Dag shrugged, "even with one arm Holger plays better than you, prepare to lose coin upon your return."

Raising an eyebrow Ari grinned, "Tafl may not be your game Dag… perhaps you should try another, dice? I'd wager you'd win against a few of the children here!"

Laughing Dag shoved his weight from the post and took a seat on the steps where Ari joined him. The village was starting to come to life, it appeared none the worse for its trials over the past few days. "There is much to do here, besides readying the stores and preparing the land before the frost sets in. Holger needs help to regain his strength, when he does there are Brynjar's men to deal with. They'll no doubt swear fealty to him, but what then? They are poor warriors, but I doubt somehow they wish to become fishermen or farmers," Dag mused.

"Unlike the Jomsviking beside me," Ari rubbed his jaw with a heavy hand, "when Holger recovers, he'll wish to rejoin his family in Srovberget. Perhaps Inge will take him as his sword arm and captain, he'd be foolish to cast him aside. Men like him are rare and that makes me wonder about our own captain of the order, he is no Holger but what will he make of our desertion?"

Frowning Dag took a deep breath, the smell of wood smoke hung in the air, it was the smell of his childhood, of a time long ago, when his father would beckon him to break his fast by the small fire in their longhouse. The taste of porridge stirred with butter and honey, the cool, crisp water collected that day at dawn. "You worry for our word as men? That we dishonour ourselves by not returning? We have broken our oath, I know that."

"I left enough coin and jewelled baubles in payment for us both, mayhap it will soften the blow?" Ari grunted digging the heel of his boot into the hard earth below the steps.

"Then we are poor men for so did I! I saw your face when first you heard of the task, and I had naught to lose myself. Do you think we would have returned if you had not found her?" Dag narrowed his eyes on Ari. Shaking his head, Ari blinked up at the morning sky, "there is little to be concerned over in that matter then," he replied without answering Dag's last question with words.

"No doubt our comrades will have heard of Brynjar's banishment, word travels swiftly where Greycloak is concerned. I don't think any will look for us; a mercenary's life is unpredictable and often short and for that I am grateful."

"I'll not miss that life either. We were taught to fight, and we did it well, but a man tires of such things. I want this to be my last fight... in bringing Ei here I hope to start again. There has to be more, the Gods wouldn't have given Liv back to me if it wasn't so," glancing at Dag he saw the man nod in agreement.

Narrowing his brows Dag frowned, "tis' too early in the day for such talk. I always thought I made my own fate, mayhap we agree on that, never have I seen the Gods take interest in the matters of men."

Standing, Ari extended a hand to his friend and grasped his forearm, "until now," he said with a wry smile.

Letting out a low chuckle Dag slapped Ari on the back and followed him inside the hall where the women had remained. Liv and Gytha had crossed to the pallet where Holger lay. With soothing words Gytha lifted a wooden beaker to the man's lips and watched as the pain creasing his brow began to subside. Kneeling on the flat rush strewn floor Liv whispered something in Holger's ear that brought a smile to his dry parched lips. Wringing a cloth in a bucket by his bedside Gytha wiped the man's skin with the fresh stream water. Checking his bandages she pursed her lips when he shifted in the bed, laying a hand on his chest Liv shook her head and smiled. At once Holger lay still, his wild red mane was still matted but washed clean of mud and blood, and he rested back onto the furs.

As the women moved away from the warrior they shared a brief glance, each reassuring the other Holger was strong enough to recover. Ari and Dag wanted to share their optimism, but furrowed their brows at the scene, too often they had witnessed their own men falling to such injuries. True Gytha was a skilled healer, but Holger was badly wounded and the loss of blood had been great, for now all they could do was hope.

Gathering their supplies Liv and Ari bid farewell to their friends, but before they could turn to leave the hall Ove entered from the passageway to the longhouse.

"I sent men before dawn to prepare the skute, it awaits you in the bay. You're both strong enough to sail it, return it to me for it is finely made and cost me much!" He slanted a look at Ari, "you were planning on taking one of the fishing vessels? They wouldn't see you far in the northern waters."

"My thanks Ove," Ari grasped the older man's shoulder and watched as the Chieftain nodded before guiding Liv to the yard by her elbow.

As they reached the gate Ari saw his father standing with Thorik. The boy was clasping his horn while Ebbe was pointing up to the cliff at the rear of the valley. As they got closer he could hear Ebbe was telling Thorik about the duties he was expected to perform on watch over the village until he and Liv returned.

"We will return Thorik," Liv smiled and ruffled the boy's hair.

"Heed my father's word, he'll let me know if you've upheld your duties," glancing at the boy sternly Ari nodded when Thorik stood a little straighter.

"Until you return my son… make sure this time you do not leave it so long," Ebbe grasped Ari's shoulders before turning and striding off on the path to his farmstead.

Chapter 30

ᛞᚾᚠᚳᛏᛘᚱ ᛏᚾᛁᚱᛏᛋ

Chieftain Ove's skute was swift and it cut through the water as if Aegir the God of the sea propelled it himself. It was a fine vessel, large enough to hold eight men with oars for six, a mast stood proudly with a dark blue sail dyed by the women of the island. At the prow of the boat was a finely carved dragon head complete with a long trailing tongue and teeth as sharp as if the wooden creature might have been alive itself.

The winds were favourable on the open water and their course sped them along the western coastline northwards. The lands to the north were sparsely populated, but the scenery was breathtaking; fjords broke the cliff faces and shorelines, islands of all shapes and sizes sat proudly in the frigid waters. Indeed, the winter was coming.

Manning the rudder Ari guided them into a small inlet when the breeze began to drop. Dusk was threatening and the air, though cool out on the open water was just as chilling when they reached land. Jumping from the ship Liv began to gather wood washed ashore and moss from the few trees that were scattered here and there. Striking her flint she blew gently on the bundle willing it to catch fire, at last she had a small pyre burning and left it smoking to join Ari to gather their supplies from the boat.

Ari drew the sail down and lowered the mast onto the deck of the skute. Fastening a heavy rope he secured the boat to a large rock on the shore and dropped a small anchor fashioned by Ove's blacksmith. As Liv approached, he lifted their packs from beneath the flat wooden benches at the oar holes. With the load he wearily wandered along the gravel strewn shore to join her. Taking her pack from under his arm Liv smiled, taking a deep breath of the fresh sea air, "do you think it's safe enough here?" she asked.

Surveying the shoreline and scattering of trees here and there Ari nodded, "we aren't near any settlements I know of... but I've not been much farther to the north than this. My travels with Dag took us to the Southlands and the east."

"I had a ship take me a little farther than this before the journey continued on foot," Liv mused gazing at the emptiness of the small bay, "at least we have the fire, it'll be a cold night... we won't attract attention will we?" she asked uneasily.

"Nei," Ari shook his head then shrugged, "there might be settlements of some kind, but the land betrays no sign of use here. No boats, nets or animal tracks," he observed.

Their meal was a simple affair, dried fish with flat bread. They drank from a skin of water before Ari pulled a wooden flask from the bottom of his pack.

"Wine made from berries, my mother still makes it," Ari moved from opposite the fire to Liv's side and offered her the flask.

"I remember its potency!" She wrinkled her nose as her fingers pulled the stopper.

"You need to sleep, you need rest. This will help," nodding at her to take a drink, Ari grinned as Liv lifted the flask to her lips and took a hearty mouthful.

"Was it your mother, or Loki, who brewed this?" She coughed and spluttered as the liquid burned her throat and warmed her chest from within.

"Hah!" Grinning Ari took the flask, taking a drink for himself. "Thor's teeth you aren't wrong!" He gasped.

Tossing the flask back into his pack Ari drew a weary hand across his eyes and wrapping an arm around Liv's shoulders, he pulled her closer, kissing her gently on her forehead, "tell me about your people and tell me about Ei."

"Ja, I will," but before Liv started Ari raised a hand and drew a small whittling blade from his boot and wedge of wood from the pile beside their small fire, "what are you carving?"

"I don't know yet, begin," he nodded to her then focused on the rough wood in his hands.

"They are the Sami, I first heard of them when Harvardr was talking with the Volur women of the camp. He often assumed I wasn't listening when he spoke with others, I always appeared busy with Ei or other tasks."

"Thank the Gods for his foolishness," glancing from beneath his lashes towards Liv, Ari sat crossed legged, his elbows resting on his knees, but his hands working with the blade on the wood.

"Ja," she smiled gazing into the small burning fire. The warm red glow found its way to her cheeks despite the coolness of the night air. "After the attack on the forge, when it was just Ei and myself, I grew braver in the settlements we passed through. I always tried to keep us from being seen, larger towns are good for that but villages are dangerous because people remember you when they see far fewer faces."

"How often would a lone woman and child come upon them? Most likely how you evaded Brynjar for so long," he mused.

"As I said before, Harvardr taught me how to disappear from sight in a crowded space, melt into the shadows or vanish from memory like a wisp of smoke but I was lonely and Ei only a child, I would watch and wait looking for those who I might talk to. Those, who could be trusted for a short time. I came across an old man who had been a trader most of his life. In time I learned his son had taken over from him, sailing his ship full of furs, cloth, everything you could imagine to markets along the coast of our lands.

He would walk in the woodland most days, always alone. One afternoon I hid Ei with Grani in the woods and tracked the man to his steading. It was a fine home; he had clearly done well in his time as a merchant. Days later I returned carrying Ei on my back, pulling Grani by his reins, he was shocked to see me at his door, but said he remembered my face from the inn where he had been

418

drinking and telling his tales of the travel. He thought I was a woman whose husband had died while travelling to claim land to the north and he felt for me, alone with a child. I let him think that was so, though I've often wondered who this woman was he spoke of, why correct him? It might have been a mistake to be so bold."

"Nei, I like to think you were led to him Liv," Ari looked up once more, pausing in his work, "would I be right in thinking it was his son's ship that aided you northwards? And it was upon your return that word of your sighting found its way to Harvardr and Brynjar?"

Liv stared at him with large shining eyes, as the glow of the small fire illuminated his strong proud features, again he had pulled his hair back into a knot, his chin bristled with the dark whiskers, the dark blue of his Jomsviking tunic appeared almost black against the pale azure of his eyes. She could sense his thoughts and pulling her brown woollen cloak tighter about her shoulders, she listened as he continued.

"If you had never sought the merchant out to question him we may not be sitting here now. You would never have hidden Ei in the Northlands, Harvardr would not have sent word to my Captain and Brynjar instructing me to find you... the rest you know," he shrugged, then flicked a chip of wood into the fire and raising an eyebrow, he urged her to continue.

"Who tells this tale Ari Ebbesson?" She flashed a smile at him. "He told me of the Sami, a nomadic tribe far to the north. They were hunters of the land and sea. He told me of those who lived in the fjords scattered along the coast, and those who hunted the reindeer. They followed the herds from the valleys to the mountains but they often retreated from sight, having no wish to deal with him.

Once he came upon a tribesman who was curious about his ship, they traded small items, he learned a few words, but most of all he was struck by the man's eyes. Eyes, he said, much my mine. I believe in the Gods, Ari, I know we are fated to certain paths, however much I was sworn to protect Ei, I know a part of me took a chance in taking him to the Sami. It was my curiosity that drove me to believe it was the right action to take."

Liv stopped for a moment. She had never spoken the words aloud to any, not that there had been anyone to listen. She had felt guilt about her decision, but ultimately she believed it had been the correct course to take.

"Who is to say why we think as we do, why we take chances and trust our instincts. You had to find your people," Ari murmured focusing on the shape forming in his hands.

Sighing Liv stretched her back, rolling her neck and shoulders, she took a drink from the water skin before continuing, "the man agreed, after much talk, to let me take Ei northwards on his son's next sailing. He promised to care for Grani while I was gone; he would accept no coin from me and asked little of what my intentions were. I wonder if he still lives, he deserves my thanks."

"He had Grani?" Ari looked up, "how did you take him back without the merchant's knowledge?"

"When I set foot back on land I had a feeling something was amiss. I watched and waited until nightfall before taking Grani from the man's farmstead, wherever the old man was he was not at home," she explained with a wave of her hand. "His son was another matter. He had watched me with sharp eyes, with his men he was a hard taskmaster, making room in his cargo for a woman and child had obviously angered him. Luckily I had brought my own provisions for the journey as he offered us nothing but stale water.

His father had told him to take us to a remote fjord, where a settlement he had traded with over the years for animal hides worked, before turning back and setting sail for the western isles. Upon his return he would wait only one day at the settlement. In all I had little time to find the Sami and ask them to care for Ei.

We are near that fjord now, we shouldn't stray too close; it was no more than an outpost for hunters. When we arrived, I could see the shore from the side of the ship. Rows of skins drying on racks in the sun, the large vats of urine used for tanning the hides stank along with the smell of animal carcasses. The men had used every bit of the beasts they had caught for selling to traders. The rankness of the air made me sick to my stomach. The men there were no better, they looked wild and untamed, their beards thick and unkempt hair. Their clothes were bloodstained and worn. If they made any coin at all it was not worn on their own backs."

"I've met such men, mayhap they were banished from their homes or running from our laws?" Ari said thoughtfully.

"Whoever they were or had been I do not wish to return to that place. Their eyes said dangerous things, it was with luck that I slipped away with Ei when they began to barter," she shuddered with the memory of the experience.

"And upon the trader's return?" Ari asked carefully, pausing in his whittling and looking at her intently.

"I stowed aboard at first light, till then I hid in the woodland by the shore, watching as they drank, laughed, quarrelled and fought with the hunters. When the trader went below deck and saw me sitting in the hold he simply shook his head. Most likely it was heavy with the ale he had drank the night before and he cared little at any rate. My passage had been set by his father, there was naught to question."

Resting his forearms on his knees, Ari let his hands hang limply, still holding the whittling blade and the carved object he frowned shaking his head slowly, "how great was your fear? For a man to attempt what you did there would still be risk, perhaps we must appreciate the talents Harvardr taught you... tis' the one good thing he gave you."

"There was always dread, but Ei needed me so I swallowed it; holding it inside until it festered and rooted within me. When there was only myself, it broke free and tormented my thoughts every day. Harvardr sensed it, he tried to use it, told me I had abandoned and failed Ei, and then there was Thorik..."

"Hah!" Ari suddenly flashed a smile, "the boy! He seeks adventure, and he found it, mayhap a little more than he bargained for."

Laughing, Liv agreed with her husband who looked upon her with warmth in his eyes, "he's special Ari, I think more than we know. Look at what happened when he blew the horn, his strength shook Hornelen! Mayhap he will become a Seer or a healer?" She wondered if Harvardr had felt anything in the boy.

"He wishes to fight... like a Jomsviking... or a woman who runs the lands with daggers strapped about her!" He pointed the blade of the whittling knife at her before tossing it in the air and catching it expertly with his fingers, "I want to hear more of the Sami, tell me so I'm prepared for when we meet."

Uncrossing her legs Liv stretched and lay down to rest her weary body on the Hudfat. Propping her head on a rolled fur she continued to watch Ari work by the fireside.

"After I had carried Ei many, many miles we stopped by a small clearing. In the distance I could still hear the sea lapping, but we were sheltered by long grasses. Ei slept soundly, but I tried to fight the weariness, eventually dreams took me. I saw the hooded figure with the staff, the bridge and the stars of Gimli. When I awoke Ei was not in my arms, but standing with his back to me. I grabbed him but he simply pointed ahead, when I followed his line of sight I saw an old woman in the distance. She was watching us.

She wore a simple dress made from animal hide, her feet were bare and her shoulders covered by a thick mane of grey hair. Her eyes were the most beautiful I have ever seen, they glittered with youth, though her skin was weathered and lined. She beckoned to us and without thinking I followed.

Slowly we came upon another clearing, but this time there were three dwellings the likes of I'd never seen before. The structures were tents made from animal skins stretched over a simple framework of poles, she called it a Lavvu. They sat low on the ground, but looked strong. There are few trees to the north and the winds are fierce, but the Lavvu stood well against it.

The woman disappeared into the largest Lavvu, when she reappeared a man was with her; he was bare-chested but wore loose trousers also made from hide. Some children and a young woman poked out their heads from a flap on the side of the Lavvu peering at us with large bright eyes. Ei smiled at them, but he was unsure, he had never spent any time with other children." Liv took a breath against the tight knot forming in her chest. "The man pointed at me to sit. I did so on the grass and he approached me staring hard, and muttering to the old woman. She was nodding and pointing at my face, and then he rushed at me and grabbed my head, forcing me to look at him in the eye. He repeated the same word over and over 'Aslak! Aslak!' but I didn't know what he meant.

The old woman pushed him aside and he disappeared inside the tent, then ran from it out towards the rise of a low hill. As I sat I saw packs and bundles of cloth and skins on the ground. There were long poles in a pile and long thin boards much like the skis we use. The young woman appeared by my side and offered us dried meat and a skin of water. The children hid inside the Lavvu; now and again they would poke their small brown heads from the flap before giggling and retreating. The young woman pulled at my clothing. She wore a simple dress like the older woman whom she looked to and pointed at me saying 'Gakti?' The older woman shrugged.

Suddenly they turned and looked towards the hillside. There a man stood staring down at us as we sat the in the clearing, the older man walked ahead of him waving him onwards. When he did, he was soon followed by two other men and women who had come to see the strangers. The old woman approached me and took Ei, at first I held him close to my chest, but she wrestled him free and took him to the other children in the Lavvu.

When the man who had been fetched reached me, I stood. In the clearing surrounded by the tribe I remained silent as they circled, the women frowned and looked at my clothing and hair, they touched me as if I was made of vapour, or a fetch, and might disappear before them. The men all wore blank expressions; they had high cheekbones sharp noses and small glittering eyes that glanced to the man who appeared to be their leader. Their hair was dark and their skin bore the warmth of the sun upon it but whether man or woman they all bore the same striking eyes, they were beautiful, like wildcat's eyes or crescent moons."

"Like your own," Ari whispered as his hands continue to work on the wood.

"Then he spoke. He said 'Aslak' and pointed a rough finger to his chest. I could see he was older than the men he had with him, but not quite as old as the man and woman I had first met. With his palms he told me to sit and without warning tugged at my braid. Lifting it into his hands, he smiled before looking at me with a sad gaze.

'Eadni... vuokta...' he said and then he cleared his throat and speaking in our tongue, he said, 'Mother... hair.' Dropping my braid he tilted my head and stroked my eyes with his thumbs. Nodding, he smiled, his teeth were bright and white against his skin, his own opal eyes shining with tears, 'Aslak... bearas... family,' he repeated the words until I understood."

Ari had stopped his carving and sat with a sad expression, his eyes searched her face not knowing what to say. Clearing his throat, he sat motionless, "this man was your father? Aslak?"

She nodded, "we had little time but shared the few words each of us could understand. I trusted Ei with him. There was nothing to gain from each other, only protection of the boy, Aslak had made it clear when he saw me he was a man who had a heart... a pure heart and that is all that matters where Ei or any other is concerned.

I learned his tribe was of the mountain Sami; they herded Reindeer and lived from their meat. They fashioned their clothing, tools and shelter from the beasts, their hides and sinew. I watched the women at the Doudji, their craftwork; they made clothing and boots as well as sacks from grass to hold provisions for the men while they worked. The men would sit in the evenings carving as

426

you are now, but with knives and tools made from antlers. We slept in the Lavvu, men, women and children together.

One morning Aslak woke me beckoning me to follow him to the hillside. When I did I saw the grandest of all reindeer, its short summer coat shining brightly in the dawning sunlight. He was built of muscle and bone, huge beside the other smaller beasts that foraged the grasses filling their bellies. Never have I marvelled at the face of such a beast since I first laid eyes on Grani. Aslak called him 'Silbasiidu' the silver reindeer.

Reaching out I stroked the muzzle of the beast, it was soft like the velvet they sell in the market towns near Gulafjord but worth so much more, it was living and breathing, its breath hot and alive. Aslak took my hand and told me he would protect Ei. That morning I took Ei aside and held him as he cried; I told him I loved him and would return. He didn't understand, he wailed and cried my name as Aslak picked him up and strode towards the hillside where Silbasiidu grazed.

The women wiped their eyes of tears as I bade them farewell, I did not look for Aslak or Ei on the hill… I couldn't have lived with it being my last vision of them."

Leaning onto his side Ari moved onto the Hudfat beside Liv and pushing a loose strand of hair from her face, he stroked her jaw and smiled. "Sleep." He said.

Throughout the night, Liv stirred often, each time she awoke, she found Ari whittling at his carving or laying back on the Hudfat gazing up at the stars. At dawn she awoke to find him sleeping and was thankful he had at last found some rest. With stealth she gathered their belongings, stowing their packs aboard the skute. She knew Ari would have been roused by now with the sounds of her feet upon the gravel and when she bent over his still body he suddenly caught hold of her hand, pulling her into an embrace on the Hudfat.

Laughing Liv squirmed within his arms as he held her fast, and before she could free herself, he placed a kiss on her neck stilling her instantly. Turning her head, she stared at the pale blue eyes smiling at her.

"What does this rune mean?" he asked, turning her head to the side and kissing the spot on the back of her neck once more.

"You should know..." she whispered. The memory of the pain she endured with the paddle and needle on her spine had been sharp, but it was just a memory now.

"Nei... I can't say... tis' old script," he replied.

Wrestling herself from his grip she pushed his chest and moved above him, her knees either side of his waist. Smiling wickedly he raised an eyebrow and she lowered her face to his.

"Remember on the ship, when I thought you Gorm? You told me to use a hand signal..." she began.

"I don't like those memories, I treated you unfairly..." his smile faded but before the moment was lost Liv pressed her lips to his ear, stroking his face and neck with her fingertips. "Nei Ari... the signal was of a bird... your signal. The rune is an eagle, for Ari

428

means eagle. When Harvardr told me what each rune meant, the spells they cast, this was the only one I grew to love," she whispered.

Seeing her husband's smile return, she let him pull her close to him again. He kissed her and, returning the kiss, she felt his hands move over her body. Their love was fierce and strong and when it was over they held each other tenderly for the short time they allowed themselves before making their way to the skute.

As Ari raised the mast and the sail, Liv rolled the Hudfat fastening it with twine. As she stood, she saw Ari's whittling knife and a small carving laid on the pile of blankets at her feet. The carving was small and delicately made, so fragile looking that she thought it might break if she touched it. At first it appeared to be a small horse, but when she lifted it into the palm of her hand she realised it was a reindeer. During the night Ari had carved Silbasiidu. Clutching the carving to her chest, she closed her eyes.

This man she had come to know and love once more was precious to her. The man who had once been as naive and as young as she, had transformed into a strong and feared warrior, but a man whose heart was simple and honest, and he was hers again. They had survived the lies, jealousies and greed of men who had used them to their own end.

If she and Ari roamed the realm of Midgard forever more, with no coin or honour to their names, they would still have one another. It was as simple as that, they had love and it had survived all they had endured.

Siobhan Clark

Chapter 31

ᚦᚾᚨᚲᛏᛗᚱ ᛏᚾᛁᚱᛏᛋ ᛦᛁᛗ

It was a fine morning to be at sea, Ari thought, as he manned the rudder of the skute. He felt a sense of freedom on the water, though the task ahead of them was no less daunting than their previous trials. He had lain awake much of the night mulling over all Liv had told him and now the cool sea air was refreshing his senses, allowing him to bring some order to his mind.

He wondered what the boy would make of him. Ari knew he appeared an imposing figure, he was aware of his qualities. He could be stern, tough and when needed dangerous; he had to be as a Jomsviking as any show of weakness would have meant trouble. Even within the fold, where only men of skill, tenacity, and perhaps the need to fight survived. It had never been a life he enjoyed, his anger had fed the urge to battle but that had gone the moment he saw her again, swept into the seas he sailed.

He felt himself becoming the man he used to be, the man who had lived on a small island with family and friends, who had a future and a purpose, a man who had dreamt of his own house with a wife by his side. It had been a simple dream. Of course he was not foolish, he regarded his mercenary past with reverence; it had served him well to learn the art of war. He had seen much of the world outside of Smols, both wondrous and terrifying, and all the more frightening for being at the hands of men. The brutality dealt against one's enemies had been severe; it had haunted him, as he knew it haunted Dag.

Ari liked to think the friendship he and Dag had formed was akin to brothers. He thought of his father Ebbe and his uncle Ove, they had a lifetime of memories as such. If his mother and father had been fortunate enough to bear more children then Dag would have made them a fine son, however, as they all knew too well, life and fate had very different plans for them all. It would seem that for the moment he and Dag were within reach of a gentler existence.

Liv sat at the prow looking out at the coastline. They had passed the fjord where the hunter's settlement sat, they had not been seen and Ari doubted the men who resided there would show much interest in a skute. They would be far more concerned in the trading ships that promised them coin for their hides. Ari gazed at his wife's profile, her small sharp features framed by her long hair of many colours blowing in the breeze; she was fine to look upon.

He knew the boy Ei had a special place in her heart, he felt sure the child would love her as much. Ari wondered if the child would ever come to think of him in such a way, or he Eileifr. He thought of how the boy might be frightened by his appearance. The scars on his jaw and neck were never far from his mind, they were an ugly reflection of his violent past, he mused for a moment that this might be how Liv felt about her runic tattoos or the branding. To him, they did not matter, he barely saw them or cared that they trailed over her body, and he knew that she did not see the scars on his body as frightening or revolting.

Suddenly Liv called out and pointed to a break in the jagged coast, peering at the spot he saw she was guiding him to a small cove. The water's surface, though unbroken by jagged rocks, offered no reassurance. What lurked beneath? Ari carefully guided the skute in as Liv lowered the sail, and their speed decreased as the skute glided into the bay with ease. There were few trees, only a small pebble shore and before them rolling hillocks of pale green grass. Jumping over the side they hauled the small boat onto the gravel, there were nothing to secure a line to and Ari did not believe the anchor would do much if the weather turned.

"Ove wouldn't be pleased to lose his skute," Ari groaned as they dragged the vessel onto the land. After catching his breath he leaned inside and pulled their packs free, "any signs?"

Liv shook her head as she swept her gaze back and forth over the land, "nei."

"Mayhap they are still inland?"

Liv nodded, "they had brought the herd down to graze on the long grass when I stumbled upon them. It's been months, I hope they've not strayed too far," she bit her lip. Taking her pack she swung it over her shoulder and led the way to where the Sami camp had last been.

They walked for some time, hours had passed and they had seen little sign of life. Ari watched with sharp keen eyes over every rise in the land, scouring the small trails and paths for signs of recent use. He stopped for a moment and took in the scenery, the grass swayed gently in the afternoon breeze under a clear blue sky. It appeared almost as if it was a sea of green tendrils moving with the breath of the Gods. Closing his eyes and breathing in the clear fresh air, he felt the sun on his skin; there was a sense of calm and peace. He felt that the Sami had chosen a beautiful place to live, though he knew in winter it would easily turn. The snow and ice would make the land harsh and cruel, unyielding and wrathful.

"Ari!" Liv called. Opening his eyes, he saw her standing looking at something moving in the distance. It appeared large and strong, shifting slowly before them on four long legs before it turned and disappeared behind a hillock.

"The herd?" Ari asked, and with a pained expression Liv turned to him, her eyes brimming with tears he could not tell were formed by hope or relief, "drop your pack... run," he said.

Obeying immediately, Liv dropped her leather bag running in the direction of the beast. Ari picked up the pack, swinging it over his shoulder, he broke into a swift pace behind her. Though the load was not heavy he felt a sweat break upon his brow. Liv was swift; she covered the ground quickly and did not appear to falter in speed.

Feeling the rush of wind on her face, Liv pushed her legs to work harder until reaching the rise in the earth, she scrambled up the side of the hillock clawing with her fingertips and pulling herself to the top. The sight before her took away what little breath was left in her lungs.

The herd was grazing in a small valley, and she could see the Sami men and women slapping the sides of the beasts guiding them towards a clearing to rest. The children ran here and there chasing one another, giggling and screaming with frenzied joy. She saw the great silver bull Silbasiidu, ambling amongst the reindeer tearing at the grass with his muzzle and chewing silently.

Her throat was so parched she struggled to call out, her eyes scanned the group for signs of Eileifr but she could not see him. A dull ache entered her chest; a painful lump grew in her throat. Behind her Ari approached and dropped the packs at his feet. He stood beside Liv looking at her, but she could not tear her eyes from the tribe guiding the herd.

"Liv?" he asked, willing her to say something. He tore his gaze from her pained expression and looked to the group.

"I don't see him," she whispered.

"Go to them," he replied.

"Ari… I don't see him," fear gripped her insides tugging and twisting in her stomach. Had she been wrong?

At that moment a cry rang out from the tribe, it was the old Sami woman. She stood with her arms raised to the sky and pointed in their direction,

"Suddjet!! Suddjet!" She cried 'protector' in her Sami tongue. "Liv!"

Then from within the herd a man turned looking towards them. It was Aslak. Liv took a breath and moved a step forward but before she could think, Aslak bent down again reappearing with a small child in his arms. Lifting the boy above his shoulders Liv stifled the sob threatening to rip from her throat with the back of her hand. The child with golden hair wriggled and shouted something she could not make out.

Turning to Ari, Liv felt the tears roll over her face and reaching for her he wiped them away, "Go," he smiled.

As Liv walked towards Aslak and the herd, Ei broke free from his hold landing on the grass on all fours, knocking the wind from his chest; unsteadily he pushed himself up onto his feet. Breaking into a run he raced towards Liv screaming her name over and over, his eyes were hot with tears, but he refused to cry, he would not let her see him weep.

Seeing the small figure running towards her, Liv picked up her pace, willing the distance between them to disappear. He called her name and it tore at her heart. She had missed the child so very much. When they were but a few feet apart Ei stopped short and stared at her with wide eyes.

"Liv," he croaked, his small round face was pink and glowing, unsure whether to smile, his chin trembled, twisting his small fingers in the twine holding his trousers about his waist.

"Ei…" Liv dropped to her knees, "I told you I would return." She tried to smile, she wanted the boy to see all was well and she desperately wanted to tell him they did not have to run any longer, but before she could utter another word the child ran into her at full pelt, knocking her onto her back. She felt his small arms tightly around her neck, his tiny chest heaving; the sound of innocent laughter erupting from his throat in her ear. She felt his wild hair that had grown much longer, against her cheek and breathed in the earthy scent of his skin.

They did not hear Ari or Aslak walking towards them. They did not see the men warily eyeing each other before exchanging a nod of acceptance.

Ari watched Liv with the boy; it was a moment of joy. He could not help but smile at the scene and at the small boy that clung to his wife with tenderness and excitement. The boy broke free and jumped up and down on the spot, yipping and laughing before suddenly stopping when he saw the tall man before him.

"This is Ari." Liv said with a reassuring smile.

Ei cocked his head in curiosity, "Ari?" a dawning of recognition washed over the boy's eyes. Ari was quite taken aback, he had not considered Liv would have ever spoken of him to the boy. He had assumed she had no reason to have mentioned him. He did not know what to think and feeling unprepared and surprised, he knelt before the boy extending his hand to the child.

"He will look after us now Ei," Liv said, urging Eileifr towards her husband.

Ei craned his neck to stare up at the man before him. With slow unsure steps he walked towards Ari, watching as the man crouched on one knee. Then grasping with a small hand he took Ari's forearm in his own and shook it.

"Ei," Ari said, he then stood and saw the child's curiosity as he squinted at Ari's face.

"I had a dream about you," Ei said.

"What did it tell you?" Ari asked firmly. Dreams were to be taken seriously and this was no ordinary child.

Ei shrugged, and then grinned with mischievous, bright sea-green eyes, "you were making something."

Shaking her head Liv stood and brushed her clothes down; some grass still clung to her hair. She moved next to Ari and slipped the carving of the reindeer into his hand. Ari then realised what Ei was speaking of, and silently praised the Gods that Liv had thought to keep the carving on her person rather than in the boat. She had not mentioned the gift to him, though he had left it for her to find that morning.

Stooping down, he opened the palm of his hand and revealed the carving; Ei marvelled it with a gaping mouth and wide clear eyes. He snatched the gift from Ari's hand and ran to show it to Aslak, the older man nodded, running his fingers over the intricate carving he patted the boy on the head and returned it to him and ushering Ei to rejoin his people, he turned to look upon his daughter.

"Manna," he said and took her hands in his own. It was the word for child, and she was his. With his rough hands he cupped her

438

face, trailing his thumbs across her brow and he smiled with the same opal eyes of his daughter. Nodding Aslak ushered Ari forward and together the three of them walked down into the small valley.

That evening they ate dried reindeer meat and plants foraged from the land. The women brewed a broth that warmed and filled their stomachs until they could eat no more. The children greedily drank the thick and sweet reindeer milk.

As the sky grew dark and the stars began to appear the children grew sleepy before being ushered into the Lavvu. All except for Ei, who lay between Liv and Ari on the Hudfat clutching his carving. Aslak encouraged one of the other men to take out his bone pipe and the women began to sing in low soothing voices.

For most of the night they lay by the fire. Ari felt the peaceful nature of the Sami soothe him, he wished they could have more time here, but he knew that soon the winter would be upon them. The Sami would move with the herd and they would have to return to Smols before the ice began to freeze the northern seas. Looking at Liv he smiled as she returned his gaze, her face reflected his love, but her eyes told him she realised their time here was short. Aslak approached and lifted Ei's sleeping form from between them, murmuring something in his own language he took the child to the Lavvu.

"I was unsure what to expect," Ari said as Aslak disappeared within the tent.

"Ei?" Liv whispered. She slid down a little further onto the Hudfat resting her shoulders on a rolled fur. Turning her head slightly, she stared at Ari and saw a vulnerability she had not expected, "of yourself?"

"He may not take to me yet," he worried.

"Nei, Ari, you have nothing to fear. You are a good man, Ei can see that," she smiled.

"He is strong, wilful I think, like…"

"Odin?" Liv suggested.

Rolling his neck Ari squeezed at the aching muscles in his shoulders, "Nei… like another," he smiled shooting a glance at her, "you've done well Liv."

"Only the future can say how well, I don't know how much Ei will remember of his past, I have tried always to shield him but his young eyes have seen much. He will have questions one day," she sighed heavily.

Resting on his elbow Ari rolled onto his side to face Liv, "Smol's will provide a good home for Ei, he will have people to care for him, the people who have cared for us. I can think of no better place. Our enemies are dead, they're gone and unable to hurt him now," he sighed. "When he becomes a man there will be difficult decisions to make, but for now I say you give him what you wish to."

"If the Gods will let me Ari… the All-Father will wait for a while, but time moves more quickly for us. I'm afraid to close my eyes for barely a moment, for when I open them it will be a grown man before me and not a boy," a frown creased her brow.

"My mother Lena used to say the same… the gift of a child is a curse and a blessing," stroking the lines on her forehead, he smoothed the worry from her face. "Sleep Liv, don't worry about what you can't change. Take heart that you're with Ei once more."

Smiling Liv took Ari's hand, placing her lips to his palm, she gently kissed his hand, "Rest, I can see the weariness in your face. Let me watch over you," without argument Ari rolled onto his back and closed his eyes. A dreamless sleep washed over him, easing the aching and strained muscles of his body.

In the morning he woke to find Liv sitting crossed legged on the Hudfat beside him. The Sami had not yet stirred. He could see Liv had collected water in the bulging skins hanging from the Lavvu tent poles and one resting beside him. Her face was still pink from the shock of the fresh stream water she had splashed upon it and her braided hair was damp upon her linen tunic, the cold morning air caused her to shiver a little. Turning to him she squeezed his arm, "we must leave today and so must the Sami," she sighed, "it grows cold so quickly, doesn't it?"

Taking a drink from the skin Ari felt the icy coolness of the water against his throat, "Ja it does." Stretching he handed her the skin, and pulled on his boots over his trouser legs before fastening the leather ties, "we will see them again."

Liv took heart that he said it with assurance, she believed him. He would never keep her from returning and she suspected he felt the same sense of peace with the Sami as she did. Standing they dressed and collected their belongings, rolling the furs and Hudfat, packing their leather sacks.

From within the Lavvu the men and women appeared. The children tottered after their parents taking instructions on the morning tasks, scratching their heads and yawning with wide, lazy mouths, they brought a smile to Liv's face.

Wandering over to the large Lavvu, Liv pushed her head through the tent flap and gazed upon her father, Aslak instructing Ei on tying knots in his own small leather sack. Ei bit his lip in concentration, a trait he had taken from her. Aslak pointed with a gnarled finger as Ei tried again and again.

Her father lifted his dark head for a moment before nodding that he understood what she had come to say and with a blink of his eyes, he turned to hide the sadness he felt. From his spot on the flooring he rose from his haunches, with his back bent he tapped Ei on his shoulder and motioned that they should go with Liv.

Ei made for Ari as soon as he spotted him by the campfire. Dropping his little sack at the feet of the warrior, he gazed up at the tall man, "have you seen Silbasiidu?" he asked.

"From a distance," Ari nodded at the small boy. Extending a hand to Ari, Ei reached up and tugged the cuff of his tunic and Liv watched as he pulled Ari in the direction of the herd. Smiling, she watched the pair of them walking with their backs to her, one large and strong, but uncertain of his role in the other's life and the other small, trusting and lacking awareness of life and where it would take him.

Aslak left her side and ambled after Ari and Ei. He knew his beasts and though he trusted their gentle nature, he would see no harm come to those Liv loved. He had watched the man Liv brought with her, he could see he was a man who could be trusted, he could see he was a man who would protect as Liv had protected. Part of him wished they might come to live with his tribe but Aslak knew though he had been reunited with his daughter, she was from another world as had been her mother. These worlds would know great joy when they met, but never would they truly be at one with the other.

As the men and Ei reached the herd, Ei dropped Ari's cuff and crept up to the great silver reindeer. Scratching its muzzle he looked for Ari's approval, the Jomsviking gave it to him by folding his arms and offered a nod. Liv heard Ari tell Ei he was very brave to stand against so big and powerful a creature and that he had never seen such a thing before. Ei grinned with pride stroking the animal's neck as it returned to grazing in the long grass at his feet.

After a moment Aslak placed a hand on Ei's shoulder and pushed him towards Liv. He stared hard at his daughter as she took the child's hand; Ari joined her and lifted the boy up onto his shoulders. Ei sat astride the man, as they made their way to the campsite, and looked back only once at Liv as she tarried by the herd.

"Ahcci..." 'Father' she whispered, her opal gaze rose to meet Aslak's.

Stepping forward Aslak rested his hands at the sides of her arms. She felt so slight, his daughter, with her strange markings and her mother's face. He pulled at her braid again remembering the woman who had been with him for a short time. They had all felt the terrible sadness at her loss; they had lost many of their people that day long ago when they were attacked.

"After the snow..." he said, finding the words in his daughter's language.

Liv nodded, "Ja, Aslak, we will come."

"Go now," he said gently before pushing her in the direction of Ari and Ei. As Liv walked back to the camp to retrieve their belongings, she turned to look at the man who had helped her save Eileifr from danger. He did not stand as tall as the men of Smols, he was dark of hair and skin, but he was as honest and unassuming as her beloved Ei. He asked for nothing but to see her again. Taking a breath Liv increased her pace to the camp. The heaviness that had threatened to bring a tear to her eyes abated and she smiled that Ei had been given the chance to know good men in his short life so far. The more men he knew that were true of spirit, the greater the chance he had at choosing a life that would honour himself and the Gods.

Chapter 32

Chapter Thirty Two

The eyes of the man grew wide with astonishment, he could not quite believe what he saw, and yet even at this distance it was clear. His throat constricted tightly, attempting to lick his dry, cracked lips, he paused at the mouth of the cave breathing with short shallow breaths.

He had dreamt of this, he had seen that it was not yet the end of his tale but the days had turned into long cold nights, the hours dragging by in tortuous slow steps. Each day he awoke from another cruel nightmare, his heaving chest and sweating brow slick with fear. He had no strength to drag himself from the cave he had sought refuge in.

The landslide from the mountain had almost killed him; his body was battered and bruised. With his fingertips he could feel his nose was broken and teeth were missing, his jaw and temples ached terribly. The hand he had wielded the long needle with had two broken fingers and his wrist was black and purple with swelling. Every breath ached in his chest and was tender to the touch but he could walk and he would do so for he now had a purpose.

Kneeling on the edge of the cave mouth he pulled his woollen cloak about his frail shoulders. The sea air had grown punishingly cold, but he thanked it for refreshing his senses and clearing his nostrils of the stench of death from deeper in the cave, where the body of Brynjar was half buried beneath rock and debris. If Harvardr had possessed the strength he would have pulled the corpse free, tossing the last of the vile man into the seas.

After surviving the fall, he had cried with pain and frustration to find Ari and Liv had managed to escape through a narrow tunnel in the fallen rock but it was not a journey he was fit or able to try. He had also lost the ring. It had been ripped from his neck in the fall and lay somewhere beneath the waters, hidden from view and his sight as a Seer. The familiar aches and pains of his advanced years had returned and reminded him of his mortality and he loathed it.

None had come to look for him; this had made him feel glad and pitiful. He had so long been consumed with his own pursuits; he had never considered what he had not achieved in the process. His manipulation and conniving had made enemies, there were none who would forgive his actions and he could not forgive himself.

He wondered what these new feelings meant, Harvardr had never allowed himself to dwell on such matters. His mind had been all consumed with the task given by the Yggdrasil Kynslod and when he had decided he wished to no longer do their bidding, his thoughts concentrated only on achieving the ring.

He had treated Liv terribly; he had attempted to kill her and failed. He should have realised then that he had created something in her he could never defeat. She had a will and desire greater than his but hers was fuelled by love, not hate or greed or lust and try as he might he had not been able to break her mind or her spirit.

When her time had come to take her revenge she had offered him one small chance at redemption and she had attempted to remind him he was more than the twisted and misguided demon he appeared to be. There had been good in him once, Harvardr reflected, but it was so battered and broken like his body there was no hope of recovery, 'so be it,' he thought.

His grey bloodshot eyes followed the line of the skute as it cut through the choppy waters, from the cave, he could see Ari Ebbesson manning the rudder, a woman, Liv, sat at the prow with a child resting in her arms. Harvardr drew a long breath.

"The ring is lost Eileifr son of the All-Father… one cannot exist without the other," Harvardr croaked, his voice ragged and catching in his dry throat.

Closing his eyes, he sighed, he knew what he would have to do. He must deliver the boy to the All-Father; it was the only way forward now. Summoning all the strength left in his old worn body, Harvardr slipped over the side of the ledge lowering himself onto the newly laid rock bed below. He would brave the thrashing of the sea and drag himself to shore because he knew they had to rest for the night, before journeying inland, for dusk was beginning to settle and the skies were clouding over.

Once again Ari and Liv jumped over the side of the skute dragging it over the shingle pulling it ashore, Ei stood at the small dragon headed prow, clinging onto its sleek carved neck.

"I would've liked to have made it all the way home," Ari frowned at Liv, wiping his hands on the sleeves of his tunic. The wind whipped about them and the temperature had dropped a little, "we should sleep in the skute, at least it will provide shelter."

"The Jarl's men are in the village, by now they will have come to their senses or imprisoned by Ove until our return. Do you think there is any danger out there?" Liv asked, sensing the stiffness in her husband's back, seeing his eyes scanning the shoreline.

"Nei, no real danger but we'll take no risks… mayhap it was wrong to sail for so long without stopping."

"Better we are here in the dark than any other place," Liv smiled and touched his arm with her hand.

Nodding Ari turned back to the skute observing the child watching them in return. Ei had taken great delight in the journey to Smol's. He had helped Ari sail the skute, asking him question upon question about his life as a Jomsviking. Each tale Ari told was received gratefully by his audience with wide eyes and a gaping mouth. Often Ei would glance at Liv to ask if Ari was telling the truth, but each time she would point at him to return his attention to Ari and no matter how fanciful the tale had become she never indicated as much to Ei.

Ari suspected Liv was allowing a bond to form between them without her forced encouragement. She knew the child, she knew her husband and she was letting them discover one another by themselves. He appreciated her thinking and marvelled how she did not fuss about the boy or covet him to herself. Liv seemed to understand what Ei needed and let it happen naturally.

Though a small child, he was robust and helped to gather the firewood when they had camped briefly allowing a few hours rest. Liv allowed him to strike the flint, blow upon the dried moss, and toss strips of wood upon the flames. He ate the dried meat and flat bread heartily, drank from the skin, they passed between them, and screwed his small nose up at the berry wine causing Liv to laugh. Ari greatly enjoyed the sound of her laughter and more so when the child chimed in. He was becoming accustomed to the idea they might form their own family, even if the time they had to enjoy it might be short.

"Ei, help Liv to fasten the sail to the boat, it will shelter us from the wind… and rain if it falls," Ari said looking to the sky.

"I can smell it in the air!" Ei sniffed the breeze before jumping down from the prow and heading to the mast of the skute.

Feeling for his axe tucked into the back of his leather belt Ari turned to Liv. She shivered as a gust whipped her loose hair about her face and taking a step closer he rubbed her arms with his palms, "I'll fetch driftwood, and scout further ahead, lay out the furs and Hudfat under the sail. You and Ei get warm in there until I return, then we'll start a small fire and prepare something to eat… by the Gods my stomach is growling like the demon wolf Fenrir!" He smiled, flashing a wide grin, "Best you get in the skute before Ei dismantles the entire boat!"

Liv glanced over to see Ei pushing the mast with all his might, however he had not pulled the iron rods free that held the post in place. His cheeks were bulging and puffing in his haste to help; shaking her head, Liv squeezed Ari's hand before climbing aboard and showing Ei his mistake. They both took hold of the rope and began unhitching the tarp. Stretching it across the two sides of the skute they fastened it with small metal hooks in the oar holes. Rolling out their bedding, they stood looking at their tent-like structure, Liv winked at Ei before ordering him to climb into the shelter.

Ari turned to face the Hornelen sea cliff and began to walk along the shore. The wind was picking up pace pulling dark clouds across the skies. He prayed that they would not suffer another storm; the memories of the last one were still fresh in his mind. Gathering fragments of driftwood along the way he kept a close eye on the land surrounding them. It was growing dark, but he decided to walk a little further before he felt satisfied they were safe enough.

Suddenly Ari came to an abrupt halt, there was something lying in the surf a few feet ahead and for a moment he thought it was a dead seal, but the dark shape reached out a hand clawing at the sand and shingle. Frowning Ari threw the wood down and carefully walked towards the body. As he grew closer he could hear raw, ragged breaths heaving from the shape, struggling in vain to pull itself from the cold sea.

Feeling dread wash over him Ari paused, as he came alongside what he assumed was a man, his sodden cloak covering his face.

Ari saw that his feet were bare, bruised and bleeding and that the hand that had clawed into the sand now lay limply at his side.

Lowering himself on a bent knee beside the body, Ari reached for the hood of the cloak and peeling back the drenched wool he took a breath and hissed the man's name, "Harvardr!" but before Ari could reach for the axe in his belt, the old man's hand shot up grabbing Ari's wrist. Trying to wrench himself free from the old man's grip Ari cursed himself aloud; how had he been so foolish, it was an old trick to appear wounded and helpless to draw in your victim. Harvardr held fast to Ari's wrist using all his strength as the Jomsviking tried to shake him off. Finally prying Harvardr's icy fingers from his arm Ari turned slightly to grasp his axe but this was all the opportunity Harvardr needed, spying the man had exposed his right side to him, he pulled his long needle from within his sleeve and with his uninjured hand he thrust it between Ari's ribs.

Ari cried out in agony, turning to face the man laying on the ground he felt pain and confusion. Staring at the Seer in disbelief, he clawed at his side trying to pull the needle free but it was useless, his lung was collapsing from the loss of air and blood made the metal rod slick. Feeling the crushing weight grow in his chest Ari fell with a thud onto his back.

Harvardr scrambled from the ground peering over the man he had taken down. Ari's face was growing pale; it was clear to see even in the fading light, however, he still fumbled with his hands, trying to pry free the needle, but to no avail.

"I am sorry Ari, but I couldn't have you stop me again! You've fought many battles and Odin will welcome you even if your death was brought forth by an old man," Harvardr tried not to sound insincere and cruel, but the words were as thick with malice as treacle. "Know that your woman will be with you soon... and the boy too if Odin denies me!"

Stooping beside the fallen Jomsviking Harvardr pulled free a dagger tucked inside Ari's boot. He glanced briefly into the man's eyes and felt ashamed that he had used trickery; Ari deserved a better death after the life he had led.

"How long will we be on Ari's island?" Ei asked. He scratched his nose turning his face up to meet Liv's as she lay back, allowing herself a moments rest.

"For as long as we are safe," she replied.

"How long will that be?" He chirped.

"I think a long time Ei... we're safe here."

She rolled her neck on the fur massaging her temples with her fingers and stretching her arms over her head, she felt a soft tickle under her arm. Laughing, she grabbed the offending finger swinging Ei over her stomach and tickled the soles of his bare feet mercilessly. The little boy screamed and giggled, tears rolled down his face before he kicked himself free and rolled down on the Hudfat, near the opening of the skute's makeshift tent.

"Are there children here?" He giggled, trying to catch his breath, his bright green eyes gleamed in the darkness of their shelter.

Liv smiled, "Ja, there is a special boy I want you to meet, he's called Thorik. Come closer Ei, the draft will chill you," Liv reached out a hand, but mischievously Ei kicked it away with a bare toe.

"Thorik? The boy with the horn?" He asked with a smile.

"And how did you know that?" Liv raised an eyebrow.

"I had a dream. Ari made me a reindeer, in my dream. Thorik and I will climb the mountain… one day."

Smiling to herself Liv turned her ear towards the sounds of feet crunching along the shore. Reaching for Ei again, she told him to put on his boots, but the child wriggled towards the opening of the tent.

"Ari!" Ei called as he disappeared from the shelter.

Before Liv could stifle her smile at the child's excitement to have Ari return, she heard a sharp yelp. Her heart stopped beating as she scrambled out from under the sail to the open space of the skute. She could not see Ari anywhere nor Ei and spinning around on the deck Liv screamed their names.

"Odin's fury no!" She gasped as her gaze fixed on a figure standing beyond the prow of the dragon-head; she could see the long white beard blowing in the breeze, the dark shape of the Seer clutching a small form to his chest, his hand covered Ei's mouth.

Raising her hands Liv slid over the side of the skute landing softly on the ground. Taking a step towards Harvardr, she paused as the old man took a step backwards. She could see he was trembling fiercely, his breath fogging in the night air.

"Please Harvardr, put Ei down," she pleaded, trying to keep her voice calm, but a tremor revealed itself nonetheless.

"It's cold Liv… light a fire so an old man might warm his bones."

His request took her by surprise; it was one he had said often when they had travelled together, "a fire?"

"Ja… then we might sit a while and talk," the words tripped from between his chattering teeth.

Nodding Liv pulled her flint and dried moss from a small pouch tucked into her boot. Lowering to her haunches to pick up scraps of bark and dried seaweed at her feet, all the time keeping her sights focused on Harvardr. Ei barely moved, his wide, frightened eyes screaming silently at Liv to save him from the man holding him and over and over in her mind, she repeated 'it will be alright Ei' focusing solely on his eyes trying to reassure him.

"You can't be certain of that Liv… it may not be alright," Harvardr said. Lowering to his knees, he held the boy fast in his grip, but relieved the strain on his legs. He knew he had to be careful, Liv could be dangerous and especially so now.

Striking the flint Liv set the moss alight, a small flame sparked and smoke began to filter up into the air. "Tis' too strong a wind… it won't last!"

"Throw more wood upon it!" Harvardr's voice broke as he barked the order at her.

"Come closer…"

"Build it up," he growled.

Reaching around her position on the shore Liv grabbed anything that looked as though it might burn. She was glad the storm from days ago had littered the shore with driftwood bark and seaweed. Tossing it onto the sorry looking flame she waited as the load caught fire.

Harvardr jerked his chin at her indicating for her to sit opposite him. She complied and took a deep breath when the sleeve of the Seer's cloak slipped and she spied the small dagger in Harvardr's other hand, it was pressed against Ei's heart.

"I don't think the child recalls me," Harvardr lowered his chin, looking at Ei's small crumpled form against his chest, "but he was only a babe… I know you Eileifr," he hissed into the boy's ear.

Liv could see Harvardr was injured. His face was bruised and grazed and his hand covering Ei's mouth was horribly swollen and misshapen. She knew he must be in pain but where was Ari, what had the Seer done with him?

"He lays some way back upon the shore," Harvardr's eyes glinted in the glow of the firelight. Her thoughts were easy to read when she was distressed. It had always been so. "I fear he will not live much longer. I confess, Liv, I cheated him from an honourable fight. His lungs and heart mayhap are punctured, with my needle. It was the only weapon I had."

Holding back the fear and rage Liv lowered her voice to a harsh whisper, "it's a vile weapon, it was never intended as such, everything you touch is turned by your wickedness." It was true, the needle had been meant for healing, a tool to deliver medicine deep within the body, but she had seen him wield it for other uses. At those times they had been running together, but her days of running were done.

"The ring is lost," he said flatly. Looking at her for a response he felt frustration that she gave him none, "one can't exist without the other."

"That's a lie," she said coldly.

"Nei Liv, we've failed. I have failed," he glanced down again at Ei and released his hand from the child's mouth. Trailing his fingers over the boy's face, he touched his ashen hair, "Eileifr, you are so small... so very small," he whispered. "I dreamt of you often. Wept for you when you wept, I've felt it all but I'm not a good man, not a man who can heal you or guide you, I'm not a man you can trust. I am sorry for that."

Swallowing Liv shifted forward onto her knees, she gently reached a hand around the side of the fire, her fingertips inches from Harvardr's cloak, "Please Harvardr, I can hear the regret in your voice... let him go."

The Seer looked up into the opal gaze of the woman he once knew. He felt anger towards her, but he wished for her forgiveness also, "Liv when I took you many years ago, I also took the life you should have had. Ari is dead, he is gone. I've done this to you. I'll take Ei now, deliver him to his father and end this legend… end the prophecy that should never have been. You were right when you said nothing good could come from aught born of grief."

"Let him go," her look grew hard. The wind had started to gust around them blowing the smoke from the fire into their faces.

Harvardr stood, dropping Ei enough to let him stagger to his feet, but still holding onto his small arm. Ei tried to pull away from Harvardr but the old man struck a blow to his face stunning the child into standing still. Liv shot up to her feet and pulled her axe from the belt about her waist.

"Nei Liv, drop it or I will deal the death blow now and you'll see his blood drain into the sea," Harvardr raised the dagger to Ei's throat, pressing it against his delicate flesh. Slowly he drew the blade enough to start a trickle of blood trail down Ei's pale tunic. The boy said nothing; his eyes fixed on Liv's, not a whimper or a tear. "Drop the axe, there!" he pointed with a jerk of his chin to a spot close to his feet.

Liv wanted to rip his heart out, she wanted to hurl the axe at his head, but she could not risk Ei. Tossing the weapon away, she cursed herself for untying her belt of daggers when they had erected the tent on the skute.

A roar of thunder erupted from the heavens, rain began to fall and the wind picked up pace. All around them the sea raged and the wind screamed. A flash of lightning tore across the heavens illuminating the beach for a fraction of a second. Harvardr stumbled back a step gazing up at the skies, the rain covering his face as a jagged smile ripped across his cracked mouth.

"You see!" He cried, "Odin is ready to claim him!" Raising his hand once more Harvardr held the dagger above Ei but before he could plunge it into the child, Liv threw herself at them.

Ei broke free and fell to the ground but before Liv could reach out for him the child ran behind her. Confused Liv turned to call for him but felt a hand wrap itself around the back of her neck. Harvardr dug his nails into her skin pulling with all his might. Liv fought hard against the assault, twisting herself to face him.

She saw all reason was gone from him, madness had consumed his soul; his eyes were lost in the frenzied anger spewing from his mouth. He cursed her with seidr magic; hit her with his fists connecting with her temple and jaw. The blow knocked her onto her back, the injury somehow still tender from months ago. Feeling the wind knocked from her body, she turned on the sand, pushing herself onto her hands and knees.

Suddenly another flash of lightning ripped across the skies, the bolt jagged and bright connected with the mountain top. In that moment the darkness lit up as if a hundred suns burned down upon them. It was then that she saw Ei was kneeling beside a man, beside Ari and that the child was pulling something from his side.

"Ari!" she screamed realising the child was pulling on Harvardr's needle.

Harvardr too saw the child and cursed aloud and standing over Liv, he kicked her viciously in her side and stamped on her back, she fell face first onto the ground. Summoning all her remaining strength Liv pushed herself up onto her feet, causing Harvardr to stagger backwards. The Seer spotted her axe on the sand and grasped it with both hands.

Hearing Liv call his name Ari pulled his axe from his belt. Ei sat beside him, staring in horror at the scene before him. His small blood stained hands had pulled he needle free from Ari's side, the crushing in his chest had ceased, but the overwhelming pain still radiated throughout his body. Following the child's line of sight he saw Liv struggling to her feet, but behind her the Seer had an axe and was lifting it above his head. With all the strength he could muster Ari threw the axe as hard as he could but it fell short of Harvardr landing by Liv's hand.

Seeing the weapon fly through the air Liv held her breath. It flew straight towards her, but lost flight landing at her fingertips. Grasping it, she turned sharply swinging it at the shadow that moved behind her. With a sickening crunch the blade connected with the side of Harvardr's temple. The axe tightly wedged in his skull the old man stood stunned until slowly his body wavered before falling to the ground and soundlessly his lips formed words that did not reach her ear.

Liv stood over the body of Harvardr and placing a boot on his collarbone, she wrenched the axe free before lifting it once more and burying it deep within his heart. Turning, she ran towards Ei and Ari, who lay some feet along the beach.

"Ari!" She breathed, the agony of her own heart threatening to destroy her completely, "don't die... don't leave me!" She grasped his face between her hands.

"Liv!" Ei started to cry quietly; with his small hands, he pulled at her tunic and seeing her turn to look at him, he buried his face against her leg.

"Ei, I'm so sorry, are you hurt?" She lifted the boy's face to meet her own, tilting his chin, she saw the cut on his throat Harvardr had made. It would scar, but he was safe from harm.

"Don't let Ari die Liv!" he cried.

"Nei! Ei, can you run to the skute? In my pack there are medicines, bring them to me," she said urging him to go, even as the small boy leapt to his feet racing for the boat. Within a moment he returned clutching small cloth pouches and two glass vials of liquid. Taking one cloth bouquet, Liv pressed it to Ari's side to staunch the bleeding and ripping a length of his tunic she formed a sling pressing his sword arm against his chest and tying the cloth around his neck and shoulder. "Ari?"

"Ja?" His voice was frighteningly weak, his face waxen and pale and his eyes were glazed with pain.

"Gytha gave me this before we left. One vial will kill your pain, the other I pray will give you strength enough to walk. I have to get you aboard the skute and sail it around the bay, it's a shorter run to the village from there than the lake and forest. Please drink this." She pulled the stopper of the vial free and tipped the contents into his mouth.

A strange warmth spread down Ari's throat seeping into every muscle of his body. The pain abated and his breathing eased somewhat. Shaking his head, he looked at her sadly, "Liv... there's no time..."

"Nei, Ari Ebbesson, you've saved me too often, I'll not have you die!" She pulled the stopper from the other vial free and lifted the glass jar to his mouth but as she attempted to make him drink the liquid, Ari fell unconscious. His head rolled back on her lap, his body still, "Nei...nei...!" Her voice cracked.

Ei bit his bottom lip; the pain radiating from Liv was terrifying; he had never known such turmoil in her. Ari lay on the ground close to death. The storm that had been so ferocious around them lost its power instantly as the small boy willed the fury of it to stop. Ei dropped to Liv's side, taking her hand, he whispered in her ear, "call his name, Liv!" He said.

Liv stared at Ei; her heart ached with a terrible pain, which bore down upon her with a weight heavier than the ring had ever been. Ei's small face streaked with tears and smears of his and Ari's blood stared at her. For a moment she saw the green of his eyes shimmer with the reflection of her own opal gaze. The blackness of the night fell, and then one by one Gimli shone its stars upon them. Together they looked upon its beauty before Liv parted her lips and screamed with all her might towards the home of the Gods.

Epilogue

ᛗᚴᛁᚱᛟᚷᚾᛗ

Thorik raced along the beach running as fast as his legs could carry him. He had run like this many times before, but this time he was desperate. The wind whipped through his thick unbound hair, his bare feet dug into the sand and skipped over pools of water left by the surf. Before him lay the sea cliff, and the great mountain of Hornelen itself.

A shout came from behind him, Thorik ground his teeth together against the burning of his muscles in his legs. The shout came again, this time it was closer. Turning his head ever so slightly he saw his pursuer approaching swiftly. The figure behind him was gaining.

"Thor's teeth!" Thorik grunted but before he could summon any more speed from his limbs, his feet were knocked from beneath him and with a thud he landed on his side. A body rolled over the top of him laughing clutching his sides and pointing.

"Hah! I told you Dagsson! You can't outrun me!" The voice rolled about slapping the wet sand.

Thorik glared at the boy before breaking into fits of laughter himself, "Ei, you cheat! How did you gain on me so swiftly?" He looked at the boy who was the same age as he had been when he first arrived in Smols. Now in his eighteenth summer Thorik was a man. He was still of a wiry slight build, but was strong and held

463

his own against the other young men of the village. He was intelligent too, having learned much from Gytha his foster mother. Dag his foster father taught him the art of fighting and Tafl, but it was the time he spent with Liv and Ei that meant the most to him.

He had been upon the cliff above Ebbe's farmyard when he had spotted the campfire far in the distance the night Ari, Liv and Ei had returned six years ago. He had sounded the horn that awoke the men. Thorik had ridden upon Grani followed by Dag, Ove, and Ebbe to the shore retrieving Ari, who had been perilously close to death. By the saving grace of Gytha's skills and quick thinking in giving Liv the vials of medicine Ari had lived.

When he had next seen Liv, she had taken him in her arms and thanked him with all her heart. It was then that she gave him three choices. The first was to stay on the island becoming the family of them all and living with Dag and Gytha. The second was to learn all that he could from both men and women and the third was the one he took the most joy in fulfilling. It was Ei.

Liv had asked Thorik to become his brother, to protect him when she could not, to always be honest and true of heart where Eileifr was concerned. She had told him of all the dangers, he knew the legend well and had lived through some of its darkest moments with her. His heart had swollen to bursting when she asked him what his decision would be but she had also promised him before he answered that there would be no penance for denying any of her requests, they were simply choices.

Ei had grown into a fine lad Thorik thought, although at this moment he wished to do nothing more than drag him into the sea for catching up with him so quickly. Something caught Ei's attention and he pointed Thorik in the direction of the cliff. Gazing up at the sun in the late morning sky, Thorik grinned at Ei. They had just enough time for the challenge before the ship would arrive and nodding to the young boy Thorik heaved himself from the sand breaking into a run with his brother at his side.

They scrambled along the sea cliff's edge, past the winding trails and paths leading to the blocked cave Brynjar had died in. Onwards they ran, slowing their pace with the steady rise of the mountain. Thorik felt his horn rocking on his back as he used his arms to haul himself over a ledge, reaching down to pull Ei up with him, he stared out to the beauty of the divide between the mainland and Smols. The water glittered today, as it did throughout the summer. Often he and Ei would sail or fish and talk of their plans for adventure. Though Thorik sometimes thought he had endured enough of that to last several lifetimes over.

Slapping Ei's back, he pressed his friend to continue up the mountainside. They had been farther than this before, but not to the point where they had been dared to venture today.

Laughing at Thorik's wild hair blowing in the breeze Ei smoothed his own hair tied in the style Ari favoured, a knot at the back of his nape. He had grown strong like his father and practised often with the men in the fields when they trained but neither Ari nor Liv allowed him to focus on one endeavour, he like Thorik, learned Gytha's arts and many a night they sat with their fathers in the hall playing Tafl.

Tearing his gaze from the sea Thorik nodded and they continued their climb. When the frost had first broken, they had made a pact together to climb the mountain before the end of the summer. It would be too treacherous to do so when the cold weather set in. Each time they made the climb they gained a little more distance on the summit than before. Each time they had been thwarted in beating their challenger to the various spots. 'Not today!' Thorik thought and grinned at Ei when they saw the ledge jutting out overhead, it was empty.

Carefully they picked their way up the trail, heaving and puffing as they climbed the mountain. The air was cooler here and the wind whipped their hair about their faces. Just as Ei hoisted himself up onto the ledge a cry of annoyance ripped from his throat.

"Thor's teeth!" He shouted.

Thorik froze and with one swift movement swung himself onto the overhang and thumping his fists onto the ground he cursed as Ei had; their opponent had done it again.

Liv grinned at the two crestfallen faces before her. She had been waiting for them for some time. They had all left the woods at the same point, but she was seasoned in running for far longer than they and she also knew Smols and the Hornelen like the back of her hand, while they were still in the age of discovery.

"Hah, I'm sorry men, but you have lost again!" Her laugh rang out as she stood from her crouched position, her eyes glinting like a wildcat. With her arms folded across her chest, she stood over them triumphant, though all she felt was pride.

Liv's long hair trailed down her back in a copper braid as thick as rope and as shining as polished bronze. Lowering herself beside them, she sat pulling the sleeves of her knee length tunic down, wiping her hands on her trousers that were snugly bound with leather into her boots.

"How is it you beat us every time?" Thorik groaned resting his back and elbows on the hard rock.

"Seidr magic!" Ei grunted flicking a shard of granite over the edge, "it's not fair!"

"There's no magic involved! You have done well though, it's a hard climb and we will try again, some other day!" She smiled at them both fondly not wanting to injure their pride as men.

"Will we ever reach the top?" Ei squinted against the sunlight tilting his head towards the top of the mountain.

"Of course... your father has done it many times," Liv smiled. She had meant Ari but the thought of Odin, and his staff commanding the aura to appear in the heavens from the top of the mountain, crept into her mind. Shaking the thought away she turned her gaze out to the sea, "Thorik... is that a ship I see?" She pointed.

Thorik turned his head sharply propping himself up on one elbow, "it is!" He pushed himself to his feet trying to contain the excitement he felt. Smiling Ei looked at Liv and then to the back of

Thorik. He knew his brother had been counting the days since the messenger had left weeks ago. It had been close to two years since they had last seen Holger. He had visited often in the first years upon his return to Srovberget with Agar and the surviving men who had accompanied Brynjar. His family had survived and were overjoyed to have their father and husband with them once more. His arm had healed and far from it becoming a hindrance to him he perfected his skills and fashioned a shield to strap to the shortened limb. He was and remained a determined man.

Jarl Inge had proven himself to be a powerful and wise leader and with Holger returned as his captain over the men they had done well together. The township had prospered, but now the men had come to talk with Ari and Dag about Bluetooth.

"Come, we'll meet them on the shore," Liv moved past the boys and started the descent down the mountainside.

She bit her lip at the thought of all they would discuss with Holger, and Jarl Inge whom he had brought with him. The Jarl was bringing his family too, his wife Solvieg had given him many sons, their hall in the village would be bursting with life. Preparations had been made for a great feast in their honour; the women had been brewing ale and mead for weeks now. It was Gytha who had told Liv to venture out with Ei and Thorik for she had worked at length making all well in the settlement.

When the messenger had come with news of what was happening on the mainland they had not been greatly surprised. Word travelled fast and the islanders of Smols travelled to the trade markets often. There were rumours that Bluetooth was becoming jealous and wary of his nephew Greycloak's growing power and prominence in Norway. That Bluetooth was building a greater allegiance with Haakon Sigurdsson whose father Greycloak's men had killed in battle six long years ago.

She thanked the Gods that Ari and Dag had not been embroiled in the wars of their rulers since then, but she feared what Inge and Holger wanted from them. Ari had managed to soothe her fears for a short time. She had long dreamt of a peaceful life and though her heart warmed at the thought of seeing the great flame haired warrior once again, she wondered what lay ahead. Part of her knew Holger's first duty would be to his family and naught else, and she was sure that he would not intentionally ask anything that would put her own loved one's in jeopardy.

As they reached the shore the great warship entered the bay. It was an impressive vessel, its long oars dipping in the water manned by at least twenty or more. The two young men beside Liv gasped at the sight of the one-armed man standing proudly at the huge carved dragon head on the prow of the ship; it was Holger.

The night had drawn to a close. The ship containing the Jarl, his family, captain and men had been well fed and their thirst slaked. The hall had been bursting with life, the villagers and the people of Srovberget enjoying one another's company. Gunliek and his band had played music for most of the evening revelling in their new audience. The Skald Inge had brought with him, told poetic tales of heroes and villains, with the champion always being a man of sound mind and brimming with courage.

Holger had been greatly received by all the islanders of the settlement. He was still a large, formidable man, but his sombre moodiness had been replaced by warmth and joy and he had brought his own son with him, a lad the age of Thorik. The young man had sat with Thorik and Ei throughout the meal talking and laughing as if they had known one another their entire lives. Holger's son was as red haired as his father and as determined of temperament. Losing many of his rounds of dice he refused to retire from the game until he had won back his losses and he managed it well enough.

Solvieg had sat with Liv and Gytha, the women spoke in hushed tones, exchanging furtive glances when it was clear they were talking about their men. Solvieg had done her best to put their worries to rest, as their journey had been one of curiosity for Inge and one of need for Holger. The warrior had greatly missed Thorik and had been impressed by the change in the young man since he had last seen him.

The men sat on the bench with Ari at the top of the hall. They had spoken for many hours. Inge had proven himself to be a man quite unlike his brother Brynjar. He had healed the wounds inflicted upon Solvieg and himself by creating their own line, and though he would never be a fierce warrior due to his leg, he was of sharp wit and intellect. Ari and Dag were pleased to find that Greycloak had been wise to declare Inge Jarl over Srovberget but bit back resentment that it had come a little late.

When the music stopped playing, the men and women began to retire to their homes and the pallets in the hall. Ari sat in his uncle's chair watching Liv as she snuffed the oil lanterns hanging from the walls. The coals from the fire pit left a soft glow in the centre of the hall illuminating her as she walked towards him, and taking her delicate hands in his own he stood up from the chair and joined her on a bench by the fire.

"The worry has gone from your eyes," he said.

"I tried to hide it, part of me thought Holger had come to ask you to battle. It would have been hard to let you go," she smiled sadly.

"I'm Chieftain now Liv, you can't be so sure I would have agreed," he gazed at the coals, "but part of me feared he might ask…"

"You couldn't have said no."

"I would have tried," he locked his fingers between her own, "Dag felt the same, we talked about it at length."

"You mean he talked and you listened?" She quipped.

"You have the right of it!" He chuckled, "what do you make of Inge?"

Pausing for a moment Liv thought briefly, "he is not Brynjar," she said.

"Nei."

"He has done well, Holger trusts him. His wife is a good woman also but he is still a Jarl, a man of power, he will be good to us but trust is earned. I think he's had to prove himself to show he is unlike his brother and so far he's succeeding," Liv looked at Ari, who bore amusement on his face, a small smile tugging at his mouth.

"Good. The island has not softened your senses then," he said slyly.

The couple laughed quietly for a moment before a pair of feet approached them from behind. It was Dag and he carried a flask of ale, two horns and his Tafl board under one arm. Taking a seat on the bench across the table from Ari and Liv, he silently set the polished soapstone pieces on the wooden squares.

"How is Gytha?" Liv asked, she had seen her friend grow increasingly tired as the night had worn on.

"She is round with child and full of ire for her husband!" Dag grinned wickedly, "apparently her man is too large for his bed and gives her no peace to sleep, so I've been sent to keep your husband from rest also."

Ari smirked at his friend who pretended to feel hard done by with his wife's pregnancy but he knew Dag was smothering Gytha with his well-meaning intentions of keeping an eye on her health. She was due to give birth any day. Ari had given them his father's house when Ebbe and Lena had died. Gytha had turned the small steading into a beautiful garden bursting with plants of every kind. His mother's smokehouse was still in use and the secret entrance to the hiding tunnels remained.

"I'll stay with her tonight Dag," Liv smiled at the man who thanked her with a nod. Turning to her husband Liv placed a hand on his shoulder as she rose from her seat but before she could turn towards the passageway to the longhouse Ari pulled her to face him and kissed her gently. The couple smiled contentedly at one another.

"My apologies for keeping your Chieftain away tonight Liv!" Dag winked, chuckling at the pink that rose in the woman's cheeks. It pleased him that his humour could still rouse a response in those who had lived a life as varied as his own.

Laughing Liv shook head before winking back at him, "I'll make do exchanging tales with Gytha!"

As she left the hall Dag lifted and eyebrow, "she jests?" He asked Ari, "what do they talk about, my wife and yours?" A look of mock horror crossed his face.

Swiping a horn from the table Ari laughed, "don't try to drag me into women's gossip, you know very well what they speak of! You're first to move."

"Ja, I won our last game," Dag slid a marker across the board, "where are our sons? And Holger's lad, come to think?"

"More than likely sleeping off the ale they pilfered in the stable and giving Grani no rest," Ari grumbled good naturedly.

"I hear Holger snoring from his reclaimed pallet."

"He didn't want a room of his own, he watches over the men," taking a drink from his horn Ari considered his counter move against Dag's piece. "What did you make of the notion Bluetooth is forming an army of Jomsviking men to raise against Greycloak?"

"The same as you, it would always have happened, Bluetooth is too power hungry to let Greycloak bask in his success for long. A fleet as large as rumoured will cause problems for the coastal kingdoms. It will draw many different men to the fold now."

"Their allegiance will be all that really matters if they are vast enough in number. Bluetooth can't be trusted and Greycloak is too good at winning his battles. We are safe enough here in the west on our island. We are also far enough north that we pose no threat," Ari swallowed another mouthful of ale. "Liv feared Inge and Holger were asking us to go to battle for Greycloak."

"She reads minds well, your wife," Dag looked up at Ari before returning his gaze to the board.

"We are Jomsvikings no longer. I needed no reminding when they asked us to think about strengthening Inge's army but I've kept that from her, our wives need not know."

"I've always been a farmer at heart," Dag smirked, taking one of Ari's markers. Placing it on his side of the board, he grabbed his horn taking a deep drink before sighing aloud, "besides Ove and Ebbe would come back from the dead if you left the island, you are Chieftain now. What's more, we both have wives who would hunt us down and flay our hides, even if our lusting for one last adventure proved to sway us!"

The men laughed heartily rousing a few from their slumber but the unrest did not last long as they returned to their game play and for a time they sat in silence, pausing briefly to refill their horns. As the night wore on the doors of the hall opened and three skulking youths crept into the darkened room; Ari caught Dag's eye pointing to the shuffling figures as they found their blankets rolled out on the floor before slumping onto them wearily.

"Ah! They've returned," Dag frowned. "Wait... hear that?"

Ari cocked his head to the open doorway of the hall. Pushing himself up from the table he strode over to the portal and stared out onto the blackness of the night. True enough Dag had heard movement. As his friend joined his side, they watched an irate father tussle with two wilful daughters from the stable across the yard. Closing the door Ari shook his head and returned to the Tafl board at the bench and table by the fire.

"Thorik is the elder, you can talk to their father in the morn," Ari said, trying to hide his glee at the thought of Dag calming an incensed man over his daughters.

"My son is honourable," Dag replied with a raised chin and slid his King into position.

"As was his father in his youth?" Ari raised his eyebrows before sliding a marker trapping Dag's piece.

"Thor's teeth perish the thought!" Dag's expression grew grim and serious, "I'll talk with the boy in the morn... best you set your own son to right, one of the girls was of an age with him. I tell you

Ari, my hair will be as grey as Gunliek's was if Gytha gives me a daughter! When I think about it, I pray Freya the Goddess grants me her to be as brave and headstrong as Gytha and Liv but they are not ordinary women!" He frowned tapping his fingers against his chin in thought, "what could turn me into an old man, but a daughter?"

"Sons!" Murmured Ari. Both men looked at one another, feeling the humour drain from them. It was true, they were fathers now, both to sons that were not their own but it mattered not. They had a duty to keep them honourable. Though the behaviour was not unusual for youths of their age, Ari and Dag knew that it would better serve them all to keep Thorik and especially Ei focused on learning above all else.

Ari thought of Liv laying beside Gytha keeping an eye on her. He wondered how she felt to watch her friend bringing a life into the world. They knew Liv had suffered at the hands of the Volur and Harvardr, their poisons and spells preventing her from ever producing a child of her own. If she had been able to there was no guarantee she would continue as protector to Ei but they did not know her and how she would love the child that in some way was formed of her own flesh and blood.

Ei never asked about his real mother, Liv's twin because he accepted only that Liv had cared for him from his earliest memory. He understood the legend attached to his name and avoided the reality of being Odin's alleged progeny. He had no interest in anything but his life with Ari and Liv and he revelled in all that they taught him, he learned quickly and had made them so very happy. It mattered not to Ari that he and Liv would have no children of their own. Fate had found a way to touch their lives with joy and for that he would be forever grateful.

As for Thorik his life as a fisherman's son had faded with the sea mist. He had asked Holger to look upon his father now and then, but if he missed the man he never said it to anyone. Liv had once told Ari she dreamt Thorik had been gifted to his mother by the sea god Aegir. Ari had learned a long time ago that anything in this life, even within the realm of Midgard, was possible.

With a final move of his King, Dag cleared the board and reset the pieces of soapstone on their squares.

"Another game," Dag said, knowing he would not be refused.

"I believe we are equal by score," and nodding Ari refilled their horns.

"Until we are old and grey Ari Ebbesson, and until our sons take our seats."

"Ja, until then," Ari agreed he toasted with his friend.

The two men played long into the night. They spoke of their lives, both new and old and when the morning sun rose and the pale blue of the summer sky shone down on the island of Smols, they walked out into the yard of the settlement. This was their home, they had made their choice.

END

Characters', Places and Terms

Liv – Ei's protector, her name means protection and life

Gorm/Ari – Jomsviking, Ari's name means eagle

Dag – Gorm/Ari's friend

Gytha – Hall maid/healer

Harvardr – The Seer, his name means guardian

Eileifr – The child Liv protects, his name means heir, also called Ei

Thorik – Fishermans son

Holger – Jarl Brynjar's captain

Jarl Brynjar – Jarl of Srovberget

Solvieg – Jarl Brynjar's wife

Inge – Jarl Brynjar's brother

Ove – Chieftain of Smols

Ebbe – Ari's father

Lena – Ari's mother

Aslak – Sami leader

Harald Greycloak – King of Norway

Rorik – Greycloak's messenger

Harald Bluetooth – King of Denmark and Greycloak's uncle

Odin – The All-Father, leader of the Norse Gods

Heimdallr – The Watcher, Odin's son, surveys the nine realms from the rainbow bridge Bifrost

Gulafjord – Township where the Thing is held

Srovberget – The Jarl Brynjar's land

Giffni – Hot spring caves on the coast near Smols

Smols – Island and homeland of Ari and Liv

Hornelen - Mountain on Smols

Lavvu – Sami tent

Hudfat – Hide and fur sleeping bag

Skald – Poet and storyteller

Seer – A person of supernatural insight and knowledge of magical arts

Seidr – Magic used by the gods and those who practice the art

Volur – Female seers

Yggdrasil Kynslod – Group sworn to oversee the line of Odin and protection to the line

Rainbow Bridge – Bridge between Midgard and Asgard, the realm of the Gods

Midgard – The world of mortal men

Asgard – The home of the Gods

Siobhan Clark

Author Bio

Siobhan Clark is a historical fiction writer based in Glasgow, Scotland, where she lives with her husband.

From a young age, she was introduced to many fictional works by family who encouraged her interest in history, not only of her Scottish and Irish roots, but that of her wider heritage stretching as far back as the Viking era.

Lightning Source UK Ltd.
Milton Keynes UK
UKHW01f0927040618
323687UK00001B/50/P